"*Beyond Passion* captures the grcharacters with such depth and intensity that you feel as if their story is taking place in your own backyard...I couldn't wait to experience the unfolding of their story, but I was crestfallen when the book ended...Tony Boyle also sets a pace and creates an undercurrent of intrigue that reminds me of John Grisham at his best."

— Mark Graham, critically acclaimed author of *The Missing Sixth*, *The Harbinger*, and *The Fire Theft*, Denver, Colorado.

"There's something about Australian writers that allows them to create a fully dimensional picture of their subjects, the wild beauty of the country, the incredible tenacity and tenderness of their characters and the subtle depth of character it takes to survive and thrive in a sometimes hostile, often unforgiving life among gum trees, deserts, savage coastlines and often-distant neighbors.

Mr. Boyle, in so aptly naming his novel, *Beyond Passion*, has this ability to place the reader squarely amongst his characters, putting them amongst the families and individuals who struggle so bravely to overcome the tests of life and pursue the pursuit of their own happiness.

Not since *The Thorn Birds* and *A Town like Alice* have I enjoyed the color, scope and emotion of an Australian novel of such insight, pace and passion. An absolute 'Must Read'."

— Leighton B Watts, Australian award winning poet, song writer and singer, Sydney, Australia.

"Tony Boyle's ability to get into the mind of the alcoholic, describing their emotions and behaviors was stunning...for the alcoholic and those closest to them who suffer the most, Mr. Boyle's compassionate narrative offers hope, and beyond the demons a love capable of the greatest sacrifice."

— Bronwen DeVore, RN, Psychiatric Drug & Alcohol Emergency Room, Denver Health and Hospitals, Denver, Colorado.

"*Beyond Passion* is a truly mesmerizing tale of culture, family pride and the everyday struggle of island life in this far corner of the world...a sweeping epic tale of two families deeply entwined in a complex web of intrigue and suspense...Tony Boyle captures the strength, beauty and charm of Kangaroo Island and her people...I couldn't put it down!"

– Diane Chado, RN, Mother, Reader, Kangaroo Island visitor, Evergreen, Colorado.

"Tony is a marvelous writer...I was captivated by the conflicts within and between the two families in *Beyond Passion*...Tony's descriptions of Kangaroo Island absolutely mesmerized me."

– Ann Camy, English Faculty (ret), Red Rocks Community College, Golden, Colorado.

"*Beyond Passion* beautifully describes the island's magic scenery and lifestyle. Great characters and an intriguing story...I can't wait for the next book."

– Carman Joseph, Islander, Vivonne Bay, Kangaroo Island.

"Tony Boyle's *Beyond Passion* is superb writing...this Australian writer captures the essence of the island where he grew up...his characters come alive in this wonderful first novel."

– Jack "Lucky" Larsen, E.D.D. English teacher (ret), Traveler and Gambler, Denver, Colorado.

BEYOND PASSION

A Novel

Tony J Boyle

STORYPOWERBOOKS LLC

Beyond Passion by Tony J Boyle

Copyright © 2007 Tony J Boyle

All rights reserved. No part of this book may be reproduced or transmitted in any form or by any means, electronic or mechanical, including photocopying, recording or by any information storage and retrieval system, without permission from the author, except for the inclusion of brief quotations in review.

ISBN Number 10: 0-9793988-0-0
ISBN Number 13: 978-0-9793988-0-3

Library of Congress Control Number: 2007901346

First Edition: May, 2007

Cover and interior design by Nick Zelinger, www.nzgraphics.com
Cover photo – Middle River, KI by Kathy Boyle
Author photo by Michael Ensminger

Published by StoryPower Books LLC

Printed in the United States of America

Visit our web sites at:
www.tonyboyle-australianwriter.com
www.beyondpassion-thebook.com

Disclaimer: While the locations in this book are real, the story is a work of fiction and any resemblance or similarities of the characters to persons living or dead is purely coincidental.

To:

Kathy–my brilliant partner, for her love, belief and support.

Uncle Les–my counsel, a real aussie, a quintessential gentleman to the end.

Michelle, Jamie, Cavell, their mother, Anne, and Andy, Carmen, Julie, Melanie, Scott, Karlee, Matthew, Lucas, Ty, Emma, Riley, Jay, Harrison and Lewis–for the blessings and purpose they bring to my life.

And to my loving God, who 20 years ago led me to the Storytellers Fellowship to make sense of it all.

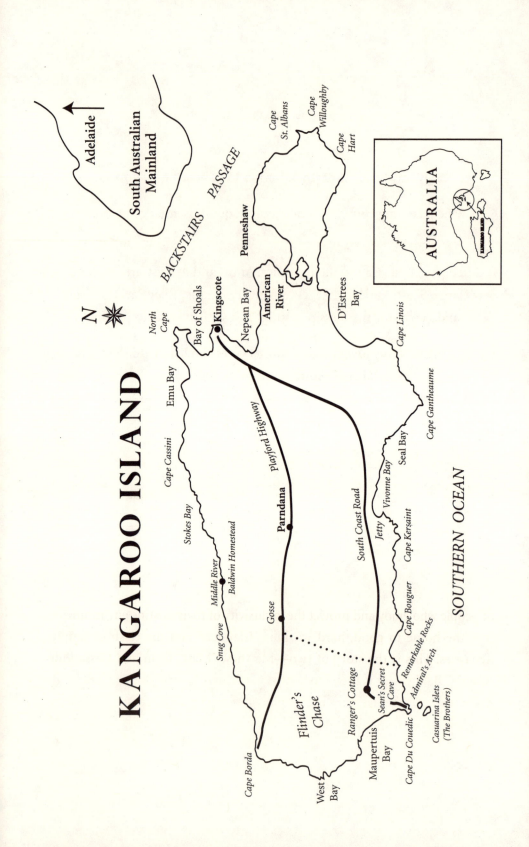

PROLOGUE

Early on March 2, 1802, the British ship HMS *Investigator* dropped anchor in the calm waters of a small island bay a few kilometers off the South Australian coast. After months at sea, the explorer sailor, Captain Matthew Flinders, took his crew ashore and slaughtered several kangaroos feeding on the coastal grasses. When the ship's stores were replenished with meat, water, and local timber; and the crew's bellies stuffed full of fresh kangaroo steaks, a thankful Flinders named this bountiful, pristine land Kangaroo Island.

Pirates, whalers, sealers, escaped convicts, and a few rugged farmers came to the island after Flinders. Then, in July 1836, the ship *Duke of York* arrived from London carrying South Australia's first settlers. These gutsy pioneers were the founders of the island's farming and fishing industries and the main town of Kingscote.

Now, nearly 200 years later, Kangaroo Island supports a large community of people who enjoy and protect the exclusivity of their pristine environment. It is the home to good, hard working 'Islanders' and the clash of family dynasties. This is the story of two—Matthew "Matt" Ryan and Cassandra "Cassie" Baldwin. It is their story of struggle and love; a love compelled by a force beyond passion, mysterious and sustaining, propelling them through—

1

On a wild August night, in the winter of 1988, the Cape du Couedic Lighthouse, rooted firmly in the natural limestone rock at its base, rises gloriously into the midst of a furious southwesterly gale lashing its thick, sandstone walls. For eighty years, the old lighthouse has stood impervious to assault, steadfastly flashing its signal to passing ships, warning them to stand well out from this dangerous, isolated, southwest corner of Kangaroo Island. From the top of the round tower, its sweeping beam pushes through the flying rain and skips along the top of massive, white-capped waves charging furiously toward the coast. At the peak of their power, the rolling giants thunder onto the rocks, exploding into plumes of spray that rush up the cape's vertical cliff walls until, losing momentum, they fall back into the sea to perpetuate the white caldron defining the island's southern coastline.

In the scrubby brush crowding the landscape, a kangaroo pushes into a thick bush to shelter from the screaming wind and the stinging rain. Lightning forks across the sky and reflects in the eyes of the trembling joey[1] peering over the lip of its mother's pouch. A clap of thunder follows, and the youngster retreats to the bottom of its furry sanctuary. With its nose twitching nervously, the anxious mother huddles under the branches for more cover, settles, and then stares out to sea.

To the west, fifteen hundred meters offshore of the cliffs of Seal Bay, a fishing cutter, its engine dead, struggles to stay afloat. For a moment, it seems lost as the huge seas bury it under a wall of water, but the plucky cutter

---

[1] Joey: Young kangaroo.

emerges as another wave lifts it precariously atop its licking tongue, like a cat teasing a mouse. A flash of lightning reveals the black letters on the bow of the timber hull—*Smokey Cloud*. In the wheelhouse, a boxy structure at the stern behind a swaying mast, a frightened young woman wrestles desperately with the ship's wheel and stares into the storm.

"I'll never give up! Never!" yells Cassie Baldwin, fighting to hold back tears—fear and exhaustion threatening to overwhelm her. As if testing her fierce resolve, an intense gust of wind hits the cutter abeam pushing her broadside into a breaking wave, rolling her dangerously close to disaster. Cassie reacts instinctively and spins the wheel to port to point the bow back into the massive waves. *This is getting worse*, she thinks. *C'mon, Matt, c'mon on, get the motor started, or*— She pushes the thought from her mind and concentrates on keeping *Smokey Cloud* pointing into the storm.

"Are you out there, mother? I am so scared. Help us, please."

Blessed with the exotic beauty of her Spanish-born mother, the feisty young woman, her body strong and athletic from years of classical dance, competitive sports, and working on her father's farming properties as hard as any man, stares ahead. *I'm not going to die. Not yet, no way.* She wipes her dripping nose on the sleeve of her sky blue sweater which had been wet ever since the wild dinghy ride to the ship from the Vivonne Bay jetty an hour earlier. The blue contrasts superbly with the olive complexion of her skin and the rich brown of her hair, pulled back into a ponytail. The wheelhouse and the wet sweater offer little warmth and her teeth begin to chatter.

More waves slam against the hull; the spokes of the wheel savagely rap her knuckles. A wall of seawater explodes against the wheelhouse window, a moment of sheer terror that sets her heart racing. Ghostly images form in the shadows and intermittent light show flashing over *Smokey Cloud* as she stares through the water-streaked window. Then—

"I knew you would come, I knew it." The wispy form floats toward her in the midst of the spray flying over the foredeck, smiling. "Mummy." She catches her breath. "Mummy, you're so beautiful."

The stunningly beautiful Spanish dancer, Kristina de Coronardo, marries Kingscote's popular young mayor, Monty Baldwin, that is what they said in the Islander.

Kristina's familiar voice resonates reassuringly in Cassie's mind. "I am with you, Cassie, always with you. Keep fighting, keep fighting, all is well." Then she is gone.

"No, no, don't leave, Mummy; please don't leave me, not again, no."

A small plane burns furiously in the hay paddock next to the Baldwin homestead. Cassie watches her father drag Kristina from the wreckage and beat furiously at the flames flaring and spitting from her mother's flesh.

She brushes the tears from her eyes. Out of the darkness, lightning snapshots the swaying mast and pitching foredeck. Is it a bird—a seagull, an albatross, her mother, soaring over the bow—*Mummy?* She slaps her cheek. *Get a grip, girl; get a grip.*

Smokey Cloud plunges into a wall of water and stalls. Cassie flies forward over the wheel, and one of the spokes cracks her under the chin, jerking her head up and sending her tumbling backward to the deck. Fighting for balance, she pulls herself upright and, ignoring the angry red welt already beginning to swell, snatches back the spinning wheel. *I can't keep this up much longer; someone has to be out there.*

She grabs the radio microphone and presses the transmission button. "Mayday! Mayday! This is *Smokey Cloud*. Does anybody read? Over."

The receiver crackles. Nothing. Again, she presses the button. "This is *Smokey Cloud*. Please, can anybody hear us? We are in grave danger: engine down, sea anchor out, not holding. We are drifting toward the coast. Over."

A wave hits again, rolling the cutter and slamming Cassie to the wooden deck. The radio crackles. "—*Cloud*. This—*Wave Dancer*—are you. We are off Point Ellen—contact—repeat. Do—copy? Over."

She struggles frantically to her feet. The spinning spokes of the wheel crack her knuckles again. "Ouch!" she cries, wringing her hand.

"*Wave Dancer*, this is *Smokey Cloud*, having trouble hearing you. You are breaking up. We are off Nobby Island. The engine is down. The sea anchor is dragging. Over."

The radio crackles. "—find you. Hang on—*crackle*—we are—*crackle*—Fire flares, repeat—*crackle, crackle*—"

"I can barely hear you! Did you say flares? Over." She listens for the voice connecting her to hope, but the scratching of static, the howling of the wind, and the waves crashing over the cutter is all she hears.

Flares, where the hell would Sam keep them? She looks about the wheelhouse. *The cabinets.* Reaching for the cabinet closest under the wheel, she slides the latch keeping its door closed, open. At that moment, *Smokey Cloud* shakes free of hundreds of kilos of seawater pushing down on her bow and charges up the face of the next wave.

The cabinet door flies open and spews out flags, ropes, tools, and a heavy metal box labeled "FLARES." A razor sharp hunting knife jams under the box as it slams into Cassie's left leg, slashes through her moleskins[2], and cuts deep into the flesh and muscle of her thigh. Blood seeps through her off-white pants. She screams in pain, falls to the floor, and then slides with the cabinet contents toward the rear of the wheelhouse. The boat reverses pitch, saving her from crashing headlong into the open hatch that drops into the engine room.

Willing the pain and fear from her mind, she grabs the flare box and, bracing between the hatch lip and the timber wall, opens it. Inside, six cartridges, each wrapped in orange cellophane, are set side by side in a shielded section, isolated from the pistol. *Good.* Quickly she snaps the lid shut and attempts to stand. The pain is excruciating. At that moment, the cutter falls off the top of another mountain of water sending Cassie crashing back to the deck and sliding to the front of the wheelhouse, the flare box flying from her hand.

The radio crackles. This time, the voice is loud and clear. "*Smokey Cloud*, Cassie, this is *Wave Dancer*. We picked up your call. Put up flares. Do you read? Please put up flares. Over."

She reacts with a burst of new energy, grasps the railing running above the forward cabinets, and hauls herself to her feet. Lurching drunkenly with

---

[2] Moleskins: Heay-duty cotton riding pants.

the violent motion of the corkscrewing cutter, she supports most of her weight on her right leg and reaches for the radio microphone.

"Understand. Will fire flares at five-minute intervals. Our situation is critical." The main cabin light, already at half its usual brightness, blinks off each time the microphone button is pressed. Realization turns into a new fear. "Oh, no!" She jabs down on the button for the last time. "Generator is down. Running on batteries—must conserve power. Out for now." She snaps the microphone back into its cradle and flicks the radio power button to "Off."

A series of loud banging from the engine room scares her. Suddenly, the wheelhouse light goes out and the ship is plunged into darkness. She freezes. *Have to calm down. Come on, Cassie, you can't panic, not now. Have to get to Matt, yes, Matt. Matt can get the flares up.*

Panting heavily from pain and fatigue, but the threatening panic under control, she remembers the flashlight hanging from a hook under the radio. A flash of lightning helps her find it. Snatching it off the hook, she quickly, painfully, drops to the pitching deck and starts to crawl toward the engine room hatch.

Smokey Cloud tips over into another vertical dive. Cassie grabs the steel ring bolted to the deck floor, saving her from sliding and slamming into the wheelhouse's front panel and open cabinet door. As the magnificent little cutter bottoms out in the trough, she drags herself over the last few centimeters to the hatch.

Sweating and gasping for air, she pauses to catch her breath. The pain from the damaged leg is suddenly overwhelming. The beam from the flashlight reveals the extent of the bloody mess. *Oh, God, I'm bleeding. My leg, I have to stop the bleeding.* Amongst the litter on the wheelhouse floor are several flags, one of which the gutsy young woman manages to snare by stretching out her good leg and dragging it in with her foot, ironically noting the skull and cross bones of the Jolly Roger. *Of course, it is Sammy!* Despite the violent pitching of the deck, she eventually gets the pirate flag around the bloodied thigh, creating a bandage and tourniquet. *Lord, I won't be able to dance. Twenty, twenty-years-old, and it's over?* She laughs hysterically. "Dance? Dance? I'll be lucky to be alive by morning." Anger replaces the laughter.

"No, no! I'm going to make it through this," she shouts.

Another flash of lightning; there, the flare box jammed between the hatch cover lip and the wall panel. *Thank, God.* She rolls onto her stomach and peers into the gloom below. "Matt!"

2

"You idiot; you bloody idiot." The angry words are quickly lost in the roar of the storm. In *Smokey Cloud's* engine room, barely lit by the single light bulb swinging wildly from the solid timber beam supporting her main deck, the smell of diesel fumes is overwhelming. A mixture of seawater and oily sludge sloshes noisily back and forth in the bottom of the open bilge. Mounted on heavy wood blocks bolted to the cutter's keel, a big Caterpillar marine engine distinguished by its traditional yellow color, crowds the space. The sound of a hammer striking metal competes with the noise of the waves battering the hull.

Matt Ryan, tall and athletic, squats between the engine and the port side of the cutter's timber shell, clasping a wrench in one hand and hanging onto the overhead beam with the other. The amber glow of the swinging light picks up the stressed features of the twenty-one-year-old face. A mop of thick, sandy-brown hair frames high cheekbones, complimenting the impish nose set between sea-blue eyes, which now register a hint of panic.

A wave slams the hull and Matt's head bangs against the overhead beam. He thumps the offending timber with his wrench. "What the hell was I thinking? Should've checked the fuel before we left." *A few more seconds and—those coppers—thank God for Dunning, but how do I get us out of this? You're a fool, Matt.*

He grows more desperate. Getting the emergency reserve of diesel from the jerry can[3] into the main fuel tank and disconnecting the fuel line to purge

---

[3] Jerry-can: A four gallon petrol container

the air blocks had taken too much time. The knuckles on his right hand are a blend of bright red blood and black oil, tearing flesh in his hurry to get fuel into the tank. He forces the fuel line connection into the injector assembly, and the brass connector thankfully grips on the first attempt.

A monster wave crashes into the cutter's port side. Matt slams into the steel fuel tank, howls with pain as two ribs splinter, and drops the wrench into the black sludge sloshing under the engine. "No!" Eyes misting from pain and exasperation, he plunges his hand into the filth. His fingers claw at the splintery bottom. Another wave hits. He cries out, pulls his hand from the sludge and clutches his chest. Desperately, he turns to Saint Anthony, the patron saint of lost belongings. "Saint Anthony, Saint Anthony, please come around, something's been lost and cannot be found." Sucking in a deep breath, he plunges his hand back into the oily water. Miraculously, it slides across the familiar object. His touch is at first timid, terrified it is not the wrench. It is.

"Thank you, thank you, Saint Anthony." He lifts the tool carefully from the filthy water and clamps it around the connector. "Don't let me drop this again. Just a couple more turns—good," he gasps. "Now, let's get you fired up."

To start the giant is an experience of torture for him. He leans over the engine to push the compression lever to the "open" position then, gritting his teeth, he stretches to reach for the switchboard and press the starter button. The single light bulb dims as the batteries struggle to provide the power to crank the shaft. It turns over, but well under the revolutions needed to start the big diesel, and the batteries are quickly running down. He pushes the lever to the "close" position. The compression builds. One chamber fires, and then another.

"C'mon, c'mon," he pleads. A third chamber in the big engine ignites, coughs a couple of times, and then dies. The switchboard explodes in a flash of arcing blue flames as the fuses disintegrate. The engine stalls, and *Smokey Cloud* plunges into darkness. The sound of the storm hammering on the ship's hull is horrifyingly close. Matt wets his pants.

Images of an earlier terror flash through his mind.

His mother, naked and bleeding, is spread-eagled across her bed. A man bends over her, fist raised. The head turns. Intense blue eyes, blurred and bloodshot from alcohol, fix on him. He pees his pants and flees, terrified and ashamed. His last memory is the bloody image of his mother throwing up her arms to protect her body from the lunging brute that is his father.

He stares into the dark, trembling. Moments pass.

A beam of light cuts through the darkness and startles him. He looks up into the glare of a flashlight. For a second, he is blinded and then the light shifts; it is Cassie, shouting to him, but her voice is lost in the noise of the storm.

She waves frantically for him to come to the wheelhouse. He stumbles to the steel ladder and begins to climb, barely able to hold onto the rungs as the pain from his broken ribs knifes through his chest. At last, as he nears the top, Cassie reaches down and, with a huge effort, heaves him into the wheelhouse.

"Aaah."

"Oh, my God, Matt, you're hurt."

"My ribs; busted," he says, gasping for breath.

Icy chills tremor through her body. "Matt. Matt, I need your help; we are getting closer to the cliffs. *Wave Dancer* is looking for us, and they want us to put up flares."

He tries to sit up, but the pain is too great.

"Please, Matt, please. You've got to help me; we have to get those flares up."

Smokey Cloud's bow lifts sharply to climb yet another wall of water, slamming the couple against the rear wall. Matt howls. The glass in the sliding door splinters and cold seawater splashes onto the floor.

"Matt, come on, please, please you've got to help." Struggling onto her good leg, she takes him under the arms and tries to lift. "Come on, you have to get up, Matt. You have to do it."

Matt's eyes stare unseeing at the shaking wheelhouse door. "I'm sorry, Cassie—my fault—I'm sorry." He attempts to get to his feet, but slumps back into her arms, unconscious.

3

Kangaroo Island: six months earlier, summer.

With a cloud of dust and gravel billowing about him, Matt Ryan slides his motor bike to a perfect stop alongside the dozen or so battered vehicles angled nose first into the dirt sidewalk in front of the Parndana Catholic Church. He slides from the seat, smacks the dust off his white moleskins, and hurries into the church.

Parndana town is located almost in the center of the island. Rusty dirt roads from every direction converge on the tiny oasis of a few shops, sport fields, a school, and a cluster of neatly kept homes. The town's prominent landmark is the praying hands design of the church roof, rising twenty meters above the surrounding flatland. Catholics from the central and west end of the island, some traveling a hundred kilometers, gather each Sunday to attend Mass, shop, and exchange yarns.

A hymn the congregation is singing, "Glory to God in the Highest," drifts through the open church doors and into the already hot morning air. The singing ends just as two black crows flap lethargically across the blue sky, cawing raucously until they disappear beyond the scrubby tree line. Silence returns for a few moments and then the altar bells ring three short bursts, signaling the change of bread and wine into the Lord's body and blood.

Inside the church, the Ryan family takes up all the space in one of the twenty-two pews made from Tasmania's finest timber, Huon pine. The pews, with their trademark golden hue adding to the holy ambience, are divided equally along each sidewall, creating a center aisle for the congregation to shuffle devotedly to the altar and Communion. Regrettably, the timber's comfort does not reflect its fine look; bums[4] get sore, and kids squirm.

Sitting in the Ryan family pew, where a small, stainless-steel plate reads *Donated by the Ryan Family*, Matt is strategically situated alongside six-year-old Sean, the younger of his two stepbrothers. Sean has a penchant for fidgeting and getting into mischief, and Matt sees to twisting the boy's ear if he misbehaves. Sean's older brother, twelve-year-old Patrick, is assisting Monsignor Byrne at the altar.

Katherine Ryan, Matt's stepmother, sits on the other side of Sean. A devout Catholic, she wears her difficult life in the lines of her face and looks more than her forty-three years. However, her faith, the Mass, Communion, family, and sacrifice give her life purpose and salvation.

Matt's father, Frank, is sitting immediately behind Katherine in the last pew at the rear of the church. A band-aid, stained and darkened by blood, covers a wound just above his right eye. Squinting through red and swollen eyes set in a lined and drawn face, Frank Ryan could easily be perceived as a man approaching his mid-sixties, rather than the fifty-two years his military service record claims.

Matt's peripheral vision catches Frank taking a nip of brandy from his silver flask. With a wipe of his mouth on the back of the sleeve of his flannel shirt and an exaggerated cough, Frank shuffles in his pew with an air of exaggerated piety. As he replaces the flask in his shirt pocket, he sees the look of disgust on the face of his eldest son. For a moment, the elder man is embarrassed, and his face flushes red with humiliation; then it turns to anger. He glares at the boy. Matt feels conflicting emotions. Shame is the big one—anger and anxiety are there, too, churning about in his gut—and the sadness, the bloody, depressing sadness, along with the powerlessness: feelings he remembers living with since the beginning of time.

The moment is broken by the shriek of the girl sitting in front of Sean. Martha is one of the Fahey family's eleven children, and big for her five years.

---

[4] Bum: Slang for backside.

The family runs a dairy farm, and the separation of delicious cream from the rich milk of the jersey cows is obviously a treat enjoyed by the family on a frequent basis; they are all big—well, "healthy" is how the locals might describe them. Rosy Fahey, the girl's mother, is not amused by her daughter's hysteria or her frenzied tap dance on the golden seat.

Matt immediately grasps the nature of the girl's distress and casts a furrowed brow in the direction of Sean, who is barely able to contain himself as he squirms and pretends innocence. As Matt looks at his brother, a small white mouse, *Snot*, pink nose twitching, sneaks along the pew toward Sean. Gently taking hold of the tiny commando, Sean places him back in the pocket of his short pants and then looks coyly, through wide, emerald eyes, at his brother and protector. He grins triumphantly.

Matt, feigning stern disapproval, cannot quite contain the crease of a warm smile spreading across his face; he puts his arm around the boy.

As suddenly as the disturbance started, it is over, leaving the church silent and the monsignor frozen in the midst of administering Communion to his altar boy. He is not amused and glares through bright blue eyes at the congregation. As he holds the silver chalice in front of his chest, the sun beaming through the skylight built into the praying hands above reflects off the sacred cup and splits into brilliant rays of golden light. The effect is stunning, an apparition. For a moment, Monsignor has descended on golden rays from heaven.

Katherine moves her rosary through her fingers one bead at a time with added intensity, her face radiant as she gives herself—body and soul—to her maker. Matt catches the look on his stepmother's face and for a second, recalls her early beauty. *She was quite the looker, once. Living with the oldman would knock anyone about. Yeah, and Mother, too; she was a looker, before he wore her down and drove her to bloody killing herself. Jesus, why did she do that—kill herself? Take your own life? How can you do that?*

After the calculated pause to signal annoyance for the disruption to his Mass, Monsignor Byrne places the wafer on Patrick's tongue and motions with a nod of his head for the congregation to come forward and receive their communion. Matt gets to his feet and follows his stepmother and stepbrother into the line leading to the altar. Frank, smelling of alcohol, steps in behind his son.

Matt approaches the altar, kneels before the priest, and takes the host on his tongue. As it melts, he prays quietly, "Dear God, I ask you to bless Cassie, my mother, Katherine, Patrick, and Sean." He blesses himself with the sign of the cross, stands, swings around, and bumps into Frank. Still shamed and angry, he stares coldly into his father's eyes. *Get out of my way, you drunken—why wasn't it you who died?*

4

The temperature is already 39°C; stinking hot, but not hot enough to deter the congregation from gathering in groups outside the church to catch up on local gossip and news, Sunday's after-Mass ritual.

"Mad" Tom Donaldson, a bachelor from the west end of the island, is one of the local characters who always attract an audience. He does not socialize much, except on Sundays after Mass, although occasionally he will attend a local barn dance. Today, he cuts a less than dashing figure in his '60s purple shirt, and bell-bottom, light-grey suit, the first and only suit he purchased brand new, fifteen years ago, for the Ryan funeral. His sense of color, or rather, lack of it, are evident in the fraying collar tips of his shirt that turn upward, as if disdaining the terrible clash of purple with the green tie he wears every week.

Tom, known for his dawn-to-dusk work ethic, lives hermit-like on his large sheep property tucked away in dense scrub between Cape Kersaint and the South Coast Road. He has no television, preferring the company of his large book collection. The only visitors who show up regularly are the local stock and station agent to do farm business, and Matt, who Tom treats like a son, honoring his writing talent and working to build the young man's battered self-esteem.

A tribe of kids, including Sean, cluster around the sixty-five-year-old eccentric. The kids love him. Considered by the locals a gifted storyteller and "a bit of a character," Tom's dark eyes glow with excitement as the kids plead with him to start on a new story. "Come on, Tom, come on; get on with it." "Jeez, Tom, we've been wait'n all week." "Hey, pull yer finger out, Tom; stop pissing around, will ya?"

Tom grins. "Now don't you be cheeky, you little bugger, or I'll have to tear your tongue out." As is often the case, Tom's story comes from one of his nightly walkabouts to Vivonne Bay and its world-class beach.

"Yeah, well anyway, last night I'm out with a couple of the dogs, taking them for a run, see, and making my way toward the fisherman's jetty. I guess it must've been around one in the morning," he says in a conspiratorial tone as he tousles young Sean's hair. "Anyhow, a truck pulls up to the jetty, see. Two blokes[5] get out and start unloading these bags onto the jetty rail-cart."

Tom's voice switches to a melodramatic pitch, appropriate for developing mystery and building tension. His eyebrows furrow. "Then, out of the gloom, a fishing boat slides alongside the far end of the pier, keeping away from the light of the jetty lamps, see, and ties up. Now, these two blokes, see, push the cart along the rails to the cutter and start throwing the bags aboard. There is a heck of a lot of shouting and cursing going on, and then one of them stumbles and falls, arse-over-head, into the boat with a death grip on the bottle." Tom's voice growls on the word "death" as he reaches out to wrap his fist around the imaginary bottle's neck.

Sean's eyes widen. Matt, who had been apologizing to the Fahey girl for Sean's prank and at the same time listening to Tom's story, joins the audience. "Did you see who the blokes were loading the cart, Tom?"

The storyteller, his face almost hidden by his mop of wild red hair and matching beard, winks at the questioner. "No, Matt," Tom lies. "The light was bad, and I was a long way off. The bloke that fell into the boat—well, he walked back down the jetty, see, nursing what looked like a hell of a whack on the head—had a bit of a limp up, too. Funny thing, though, he was still carrying and taking swigs of grog from the bottle. He'd held onto it all along; didn't spill a drop." Tom laughs. "I think he was a bit pissed."[6]

Matt knew he was lying, but he was grateful and knew he would keep his mouth shut. One thing about Tom, he had no love for the coppers. They had

---

[5] Bloke: Male person.
[6] Pissed: In this Australian context, it means drunk, but in another context it could mean angry.

come out to his property one time to question him about spying on tourists staying at the Vivonne Bay back-packers hostel. There was no proof and Tom told them to "get stuffed, he'd never do anything like that," so the island's acting sergeant of police, Reg Woodson, slammed his fist into Tom's gut and left him flat on his back, gasping for breath.

"Anyhow," continues Mad Tom. "I did make out the name on the cutter. It was the *Smokey Cloud*, Sammy Marino's boat."

5

Monsignor Byrne bursts through the church doors, a ball of energy that belies his eighty-one years. A sparkling smile replaces his earlier look of rebuke. He takes a deep breath and surveys his flock. *I'd like another fifty years here, Lord. Australia's a mighty blessing for an Irish lad who's been all over. But when ye sent me here, to Kangaroo Island, ye sent me to yer heaven on earth, to be sure.*

Monsignor joins his parishioners. "T'was a nice shot ye made to win the game yesterday, Maureen," he says, referring to the tennis match in Kingscote the previous afternoon. Sport plays a big part in the social life of the islanders. "Ye be keeping up the good work, now."

"You can count on it, Monsignor," the tall red-headed girl with emerald green eyes answers in a voice loud enough for Matt to hear; she has kept her eye on him from the time she got out of church. Maureen is pretty, tall, and athletic. She enjoys the attention of the local lads, with whom she flirts furiously, but it is the elusive Matthew Ryan, with the flashing blue eyes, she is after. "Are you coming to the parish barn-dance at Gosse Hall next Saturday night, Monsignor?"

Monsignor Byrne smiles warm confirmation in response to Maureen's inquiry, knowing of the web of seduction fashioned for the intended victim. *In all me days, I've seen no change in the generations,* the priest thinks. *The raging hormones of young, vibrant blood demanding gratification is part of God's glorious design for ensuring we survive.* The monsignor chuckles. *Ah, what a brilliant ploy is this pantomime, and it sure as hell keeps our churches full.*

He moves from group to group, exchanging greetings, shaking hands, hugging babies, all the while closing on his targets, Frank and Katherine Ryan. His concern is for the well-being of all his flock, but the Ryans cause him his greatest anxiety. Alcohol is trouble: battered wives, scarred children, and the struggle for survival. *Matilda Ryan, what a shame.*

"Hello, Katherine, Francis," says Monsignor Byrne. Frank nods and shifts uneasily as he strains to listen to Mad Tom. "'Tis good to see ye both here today."

"I miss coming when we don't make it, Monsignor, but Frank is so busy," Katherine responds.

"Yes, I noticed. Still needing the wee nip then, are we, Francis?" The priest looks right at Frank, full of care and concern, a hint of toughness in his lined face. He searches for a way to the man's soul. *God is merciful.*

Frank grimaces. "Medicinal purposes, Father. Ever since I fell off the lighthouse platform and—" Frank's sentence is cut short by a sharp interjection from Matt who, after listening to Mad Tom, crosses over to them, Sean following as closely as a shadow.

"'And blew my back out'—yeah, sure. You're a medical encyclopedia, aren't you, Dad, hey? G'day, Monsignor," says Matt, his voice on the word "dad" laced with sarcasm. Frank braces, stares at his son, threatening.

The monsignor quickly intervenes. "Ah, Matthew, I've been want'n to catch up wi' ye all week." He winks and nods his head. "I've got something for ye, so run along and wait for me in the sacristy, will ye?" he says in his heavy Irish brogue, breaking through the tension and pointing him in the direction of the sacristy. Monsignor Byrne turns back to the Ryans and Sean. "Oh, and Sean, I hope ye caught up wi' yer little friend. I don't want him scaring any more of the ladies, now. Off to the sacristy wi' yer brother; I've got something there for ye. I'll be along in a minute, but I want a few words wi' yer mother and father first." He winks at the small boy.

Sean runs after Matt, who is waiting at the sacristy door watching the priest and his parents. Shame and anxiety feed his anger, knowing that Monsignor Byrne is talking to his father about his drinking. He sees Frank kick the dirt and turn to walk back to the family truck, a beat up Landcruiser.

The monsignor continues talking with Katherine. Matt sees her attempt to smile, to make light, he guesses, of Frank's behavior. *Always making excuses for him.* The kindly old priest chats for a minute more and then blesses her. As Katherine walks to the Landcruiser, the priest turns, sees the boys, smiles, claps his hands and, with a light spring in his step, walks to the sacristy. Then with a hand on each of their backs, he gently shepherds the boys through the door.

Inside the sacristy, the air is cool. The smell of incense still lingers and catches in the boys' throats, causing Sean to cough. "Sit over there and give me jest a little minute here, Matthew," says the monsignor, pointing to a richly padded, red velvet chair.

He turns to Sean. "Now, Sean, I've got something for ye and Patrick." He opens the vestment closet and pulls out two brand new fishing rods. "Here ya go, then. I know ye boys have been trying to catch the big snapper off Admiral's Arch. Well, now ya got a good shot at get'n 'em."

"Jeez, thanks, Father," says Sean, excited.

"Holy Mary Mother of God, boy. Ye don't be using the holy Lord's name in vain, young man. Be off wi' ya and find yer brother Patrick. I want to have a few words with Matthew."

Sean is all smiles as he runs out the open door with a death grip on the fishing rods, yelling for Patrick at the top of his voice. Monsignor Byrne smiles, closes the door, and seats himself in a half-size pew opposite Matt. The old priest sits quietly for a few moments, studying the young man. *Ah, he's a good-looking boy; looks a lot like his mother—the high cheekbones, inherited her talent, too. Suicide's a bugger; the lad's done it tough, he has.*

The monsignor has watched over Matt since his baptism. He said the Mass at his mother's funeral after she drowned herself in the house-dam[7] of the sheep property the Ryans used to own. *A terrible tragedy—a wicked way to end a good woman's life*, he thinks. *Matilda Ryan was a wonderful teacher, especially for the little kids in grades one and two. The Parndana School lost a*

---

[7] Dam: On Australian farms, a reservoir of water filled by rain and used for the farm water supply.

beautiful lass there, it did, and the parents, too. Where do ye get a teacher more devoted to yer kids? Ah, that bloody grog is a killer all round those with the disease.

The monsignor reaches for Matt's hands. "Now tell me, lad, how's the writin' coming on?"

Matt is quiet, still upset. The priest waits, Matt's hands in his.

"Not real good, Monsignor. I try to find a quiet spot each night, but Dad yells and beats up on Katherine a lot and bullies my brothers. It's only when I'm there that he doesn't whack into them. He's drunk most the time these days, and I'm scared to death he'll damage the light, or even shut it down. You never know what'll set him off. Being around him is like walking on eggshells all the time."

The monsignor struggles to find meaning and inspiration. "It's hard for ye all, I know, Matthew. Who knows the ways of the Lord? I do know this— He's blessed ye' wi' a special talent, a very special talent, indeed. It carries tremendous power—power to influence, even change the course of human history for the better, and sometimes, sadly, for worse. Ye have it, Matthew, and it needs be to nurtured and put to good purpose."

The boy sits silently; the priest waits.

"You know I love to write, Monsignor. Once I start, it seems no time at all when I'm completely in the—the zone. But, something always interrupts: the oldman[8] is yelling, my typewriter jams, a fishing cutter calls on the radio for information, or the hourly weather report is due and Frank, who gets paid to do it, is bloody well flaked out."

"I hear ya, boy, but ye have to keep at it; there can't be excuses. Pray to yer God for strength." He smiles. "And there's no need to be swearing in the House of the Lord, Matthew, or at any other time, for that matter."

"Sorry, Monsignor," says Matt. He chuckles. "But I recall when you and I were building the rock wall at the church entrance a few years ago. Remember? A rock slipped after you'd spent a lot of time wiggling it into place, and you said the 'f' word. I was about twelve at the time, and you shocked the hell out of me."

---

[8] Oldman: Australian slang used to refer to a son's father.

"See what I mean? Ye remember events and details. Ye've a sharp mind, boy, and yer a bit of a wit; it's the mind of a writer ye have," says the monsignor, chuckling, building the boy's self-esteem at every opportunity. "Well, at least it did ye some good, then—shocking the hell out of ye? Now, I want ye to look at this."

Monsignor moves to a bench made from a heavy slab of redwood. Above the bench, Matt's eyes are drawn to the beautiful stained-glass window, alive with rich, vibrant reds, blues, greens, and yellows, forming the image of Jesus praying in the Garden of Gethsemane, his disciples clustered in the background.

Jesus, how often I was drawn to you while I was putting on my surplice, fascinated, sad. So beautiful and terrifying, denial and betrayal captured in the clever placement of the colored pieces. It didn't matter that were you the Son of God, they still got you.

From underneath the bench, the monsignor retrieves an oddly shaped brown case and places it on the bench top. He snaps back the two clasps and lifts out a word processor.

"Here, this is for you, Matthew. It's a tad old, but the little beast works well."

Matt's eyes brighten. "Wow, what a beauty." He runs his hand over the discolored plastic case and examines it closely. "Seems I've seen this somewhere before," he says. "I can't accept it, Monsignor." He taps a key. "Well, I could if you let me pay for it; the church always needs money, and I've got some cash coming in."

"It's a gift, boy, given to the parish wi' the express instruction that it be given to ye for yer writing. The only contract ye enter into is that ye use it for at least an hour every day, no matter what's going on in yer life." Monsignor Byrne places his hands on the boy's shoulders. "Ye see, Matthew, there are people in the parish who believe in ye, and there's a secret admirer—a non-Catholic, would ya believe—who wishes to remain anonymous."

"Bloody hell, I don't know what—tell everyone thanks, will you?" He plays with the keys. "I'll try not to let you down, Monsignor."

"Don't ye be letting yerself down, Matthew. One more thing—the

Australian National Writers' and Poets' Competition that I entered ye into—well, the 2000-word essay, along wi' yer poem is expected to be in to the judges in Sydney just two months from now, in the middle of April, or thereabouts. The details for completion of yer entry are due in two weeks. Bring them along to Mass next week, and I'll make sure they're in on time."

"Jeez, Monsignor, I haven't even finished the outline yet."

Monsignor Byrne cocks an eyebrow and waves a finger.

"Sorry, Monsignor. Look, I have a poem, but I don't think its right for the competition, too abstract. I need a new idea," he says, packing the processor into its case and moving to the door.

"Look about ye. Kangaroo Island is a wondrous place, with plenty to write about, Matthew. Trust in God, he will inspire ye if ye ask him or his angels; just begin to write. Trust yer instincts and do the work. Just write, write, write. Off wi' ye now." He pats Matt on the shoulder and opens the sacristy door. "And Matthew—"

"Yes, Monsignor?"

"One last thing, now. I had a few words wi' yer father. He wasn't too happy about it, but he won't be bothering ye about yer writing, I'll tell ye that. God bless ye, boy," says the old priest, blessing Matt before turning back into the sacristy and closing the door.

Matt begins walking toward the family truck.

"Matt, Matt," shouts Patrick as he runs up, panting. "Cassie's in town, down at the store."

"Bloody good stuff, Pat, thanks. Here, put this in the truck, will you?" He hands Patrick the case, and then runs to his bike, kicks the motor to life, and roars off in the direction of the store, a fishtail of dust spewing from the spinning back wheel.

Katherine watches Patrick place the old brown case carefully on the backseat. She smiles, satisfied.

Frank grunts, stabs out the last of his cigarette in the ashtray, and starts the truck.

6

"Nice job, nice job, Winston," says Cassie, slapping the sweaty neck of the big chestnut gelding, its flanks heaving from exertion. She swings around in the saddle and stares back at the long white beach they had just raced down at a reckless, sand-flying gallop. The air is already warm. *It is going to be a scorcher.* The sparkling seawater, blue and pristine, washes onto the sand, cool and inviting. She glances at her watch. "Darn. Sorry, Winnie, not this morning, mate. It's time to get ready for church." She turns to the rolling hills that run along the north coast of the island. The family homestead, huge and formidable, dominates the top of Constitution Hill, the highest hill overlooking Snelling Beach, or better known as Middle River by the locals. She sits quietly for a few moments, surveying a scene familiar to her since birth. Smiling, she spurs Winston lightly on his flanks and urges him toward the hill and homestead.

The homestead, built in the mid 1800s, overlooks the twenty-four-kilometer stretch of ocean separating this part of the island from the mainland. The views are spectacular, the homestead, impressive. What started out as little more than a stone cottage has grown into a massive building with walls a half-meter thick, built from the natural limestone brought by horse and cart from the pits on the family's south coast properties around Vivonne Bay and Cape Kersaint. Everything about the Baldwin homestead is expansive—the eight bedrooms, the mammoth kitchen annexed to the large dining room, where a long, solid, redwood table seats up to thirty people, but the piece-de-résistance is the huge living room with its front window, which extends the entire length of the wall. The views are breathtaking. Rolling hills form grassy spurs before dropping away to the pebbly beaches edging the sea. Slightly to the east, waves break in a white flurry of foam along Middle River's long sandy beach. At its eastern end, the river struggles to break into the sea, but a sandbar blocks its passage and prevails until the winter rains force it to give way.

Monty Baldwin is standing on the front verandah looking toward the beach, watching for Cassie while taking in the view, of which he has never tired. *Great-grandpa Harry knew what he was doing when he picked this spot to settle.* A hundred and fifty years had passed since Harry Baldwin left England with his young Welsh bride. *Shrewd old bugger worked hard and knew how to play the political game better than anyone.*

As the sun's fiery reflection dances off the surface of a flat sea, Monty shades his eyes to watch Cassie ride over the brow of the homestead paddock. He smiles as he notes her saddle posture, upright, elegant, and textbook perfect. *Her mother, ah, she taught her well.*

"Cassie," he calls. "Hurry it along; there's a good girl. It's time to get cracking. You know how the pastor hates late arrivals interrupting his service."

"I'll be there in a jiffy, Daddy. Quick shower and I'll be ready." She taps Winston with her spurs and trots toward the stockyards and the stables.

Monty watches her ride by, pensive, contemplating the coming departure of his daughter for Sydney. *It was hard enough when she was away at school in Adelaide. Having her home every two weeks kept me going after Kristina—*

He turns and looks back out at the beach.

Was it twenty years ago, fifteen, yesterday—that his young wife was alive, full of energy, in love, and happy? They made love there, on that beach many times, the brilliant white sand a vivid contrast to her body's smooth, dark skin and its perfectly sculptured contours. He knew every part of her, every minute cell and blemish, there was nothing of her he did not love passionately. She was his life.

Abruptly, the images in his mind fracture, like the interference of a rogue signal cutting across the picture of a television screen.

The picture transforms into the horror of a crashing, burning plane. Kristina's body, thrown meters from the wreck, writhes in the agony of terrible, flaming disintegration. Monty, eyes wide and wild, runs desperately through the green carpet of lush spring grass. He reaches her, breathless. "Kristina! Kristina! No! No!" The stunning brown eyes widen in a moment of recognition, and then lock into an opaque stare. His hands become small, ineffective paddles, helplessly beating, beating, beating at the flames. Her flesh bubbles, blisters, and melts into raw, red tissue. The flames burn his hands and blister his face. His urge is to tear from his body his skin, to wrap it around her and smother the flames with his love. Mercifully, in moments, she is gone. Sobbing, he turns to see Cassie, tears streaming down her cheeks, bewildered, transfixed by the horror.

Thank God for Cassie. Monty walks back to the house and into the living room, to where a cup of tea languishes on the table next to his favorite recliner. He sits and lifts the cup to his lips, sipping at the warm liquid, holding it in his mouth for a moment or two before swallowing, feeling the warmth of its journey to his stomach where it settles. *Tea,* he muses, *the Orient's gift to the British.* He raises his cup to the life size painting of Kristina, hanging on the feature wall built from river rock, floor to ceiling, to the right of the fireplace. "To our daughter's success, my love."

After a few minutes, Cassie breezes into the room, her hair still wet from the shower. She stands in front of the mirror set on the left side of the mantelpiece above the fireplace, a huge stone construction taking up a good third of the sitting room's north wall.

Monty watches her brush her hair, and as always, every time, he is reminded of Kristina. The same mannerisms, the posture, her long, arched back, shoulders held square and upright, her prominent and finely toned behind, her knee-length brown skirt falling smoothly from her narrow waist, from which her bare legs and gracefully developed calves emerge—she is Kristina. Cassie turns from the mirror, her classic dancer's line, sculptured from hours of training and dedicated schooling, capture a portrait of perfection. *She is ready.*

Honoring Kristina's wish that Cassie develop her prodigious dance talent, Monty sent her to train at the best schools in Adelaide. The recent flight to Sydney and her successful audition for a place with the Australasian Modern

Dance Company was a mix of joy and sadness for him. Just two more weeks, and then off to Sydney again, but this time to leave her there. He sighs and sips the last of his tea.

"I'll miss you."

"I'll miss you, too, and all of this," she replies, smiling and whirling around with her arms outstretched. She pirouettes to his chair and kisses him lightly on the cheek. "Where's Jordan, Daddy?"

"He's going to follow us on his motorbike," Monty replies. "He got into some trouble last night, so I don't want you to get upset when you see him. He looks a little worse for wear."

Damn you, Jordan.

She walks back to the mirror. "We're going to have to do something about his drinking. He'll finish up killing himself, or someone else."

As Cassie sweeps the brush through her hair again, she notes Monty's reflection in the mirror. *He's aging.* She considers her reflection, angry. Since the *incident*, Jordan had been a constant cause of pain and trouble to the family. His drinking had worsened to the point that Monty planned a family intervention before Cassie left for Sydney, but Grant, her older brother, was in Europe on business for his law firm. Monty wanted to wait for Grant.

"When the hell is he going to grow up? It's not fair to you; I'm going to have a few words with Jordan, Daddy. This has to stop."

As Cassie finishes speaking, Jordan limps into the room, a large cut evident above his left eye. Tall and slender, the twenty-four-year-old young man would be described as pretty rather than handsome were it not for the grotesque scar carving its way from the corner of his right eye to the right corner of his mouth—the result of the *incident*. The family still refers to the event as the *incident*, even though his near-death was the result of a stupid choice made two years earlier. The angry red crevice of the scar is made more distinct by the paleness of his skin. He had not inherited his mother's olive complexion, but the color and texture of the skin of a British aristocrat. His mouth, unfortunately, seems fixed in a permanent sneer, a feature discouraging advances from even those who might be inclined to offer him friendship. He is a self-proclaimed outcast, whose only comfort is a bottle and the fleeting solace of solicited love.

"Talking about me, I suppose. Nothing good to say, of course," he charges.

"Oh, for goodness sake, Jordan, give me a break," Cassie says, looking at him in the mirror while continuing to brush her hair. "Stop feeling sorry for yourself. It's about time you grew up and made something of your life. That stunt you pulled was two years ago. There's still a lot you can do."

Jordan ignores her scolding. "I suppose you're preening yourself for the Ryan kid. It's about time *you* woke up to the fact that the Ryan family is in no way the sort of people you ought to be getting involved with. Matthew Ryan has a reputation with the ladies, and rumor has it that he has quite an investment in some rather sordid goings-on. I told him the next time I see him with you, I'll beat the living daylights out of him."

Cassie whirls around, plants her feet, and makes fists of her hands. Her dark brown eyes flash a cold and deadly stare at Jordan as she readies for battle.

Monty cuts her short. "Enough, Cassie, enough; there's no time for this. Besides, it does no good; you know that."

Cassie looks at her father with a mix of defiance and concern. She is sadly aware that the pain and resignation in his voice reflects not only disappointment in his son, but also disapproval of her relationship with Matthew Ryan.

7

Matt slides the bike through the intersection east of the church and is almost thrown off when the back wheel grips the strip of black asphalt running the length of Parndana's short main street. A few buildings, made mostly of corrugated iron, brick and timber, front each side of the road. *Not much of a town*, a first-time visitor might think, but the locals would argue there is plenty of action behind the austere facade.

Excited, he roars toward the general store where many of the parishioners are standing on the pavement, still talking, hands brushing continuously at the small, sticky bush flies trying to settle on their sweating faces. Others are already inside the general store, shopping and sheltering from the blazing sun.

A broad grin spreads across his face as he kicks down a couple of gears with a showy display of throttle control. He slides to a stop beside the Fahey family truck, from which eleven yelling kids are scrambling over the sides of the cattle crate to head for their regular Sunday ice cream treat. Rosy Fahey is midway through the process of backing out of the truck cabin, not an easy task for her. Slowly, she lowers her generous frame through the open door and begins to probe for the road with her foot. Matt's dramatic arrival scares the hell out of her, and with a howl of alarm, she crashes to the hot asphalt. Luckily, her well padded bum cushions the fall, damaging only her dignity. Matt is shocked, but quickly recovers and then, red with embarrassment, rushes to her aid. As he struggles to lift her, she delivers a rash of invective. To his relief, members of the family crowd around, and with a mighty team effort, haul her to her feet.

Mrs. Fahey's usually jolly face, flushed red with effort and anger, rounds on Matt. "What the heck is the matter with you Ryans, Matthew? First, Sean taunts my daughter with the mouse, and then you scare the bejeez out of an old lady. You ought to know better; you'll finish up like your father. A no-hoper and a drunk—" She stops, realizing she has gone too far. "Oh, for goodness sake, I'm sorry, Matthew. I didn't mean—"

Matt is already turning away from her. Angry and humiliated, he is oblivious to a wry Monty Baldwin watching as he storms into the store. Brushing by store patrons in the newspaper and bakery section, he does not see Cassie look up from the pages of *Dance International*, a publication the local store's magazine section orders especially for her. She hurries after him.

The wine and beer racks are at the back of the store. A colorful cardboard display promises good times go with a glass of South Australia's West End Bitter. For Matt, the beer promises him relief from the sense of shame and inadequacy feeding the icy tensions churning about in his gut. *Bugger 'em all. Maybe the oldman's got it right—reckons it gets him through all the crap life dishes up. Shuts up the bloody voices, he reckons. What a screw-up he is, though. Yeah, but I'm not an alkie—can stop anytime I want. Mother said if I turned out like him, she'd—*

"Stuff 'em all," he says, reaching into the stacked beer to pick up a carton. As he straightens and turns around, he finds himself looking into the brown eyes of *his* Cassie.

"Hi, Matt." For fifteen years, they had been best mates—since first grade at the Parndana Area School. She takes the carton of beer and places it back in the display stack. "You won't need this. Sometimes, Matt, you are much too sensitive. Really, what happened out there was quite funny as it turned out, good enough for a television skit." She kisses his cheek, chuckling. "You should have seen the look on your face when Mrs. Fahey plopped on her bum."

Matt studies her for a moment, looking into her eyes, and then laughs self-consciously. "Yeah, I really made a mess of it, didn't I? I was in a bit of a rush to get here after Patrick told me he saw you. I didn't think I'd see you until this afternoon."

"Well, we weren't coming in this morning, but Daddy had some business with the pastor—something to do with Jordan. You know the story, so here I am," explains Cassie, taking his arm and guiding him back to the newspaper and cafe section.

Rosy Fahey is at the ice cream counter. "That's eleven doubles—oh, and you'd better make it two singles for Jack and me."

Matt crosses to the counter. "Mrs. Fahey, I'm sorry for scaring you out there. It was bloody stupid what I did."

The big woman smiles and wraps her arms around Matt, squeezing him tight into her large breasts. "No, Matt, it's me who needs to apologize. I was the silly one. You know, I watch the way you look after your step-mum and brothers. You're a good boy; Matilda would be proud of you." She releases him. "Hello, Cassie, dear; my goodness, the two of you together make a handsome couple."

Cassie smiles. "Thank you, Mrs. Fahey; I hope you have a wonderful day." They start toward the door. "We're still meeting this afternoon, aren't we?"

"You better believe it," says Matt, feeling much more at ease. "Hey, I'm going to bring my poem for you to look at."

She squeezes his hand. "About time; I was beginning to wonder—" The roar of a motorcycle throttling down into a lower gear rattles the shop windows.

"What the hell—" Matt looks outside to see a familiar bike sliding to a stop at the curb. The rider is dressed in black leathers, black boots, and a black racing helmet with a dark, reflective visor snapped shut over the rider's eyes. Matt tenses.

"Matt, I'll handle this," Cassie says, squeezing his arm.

Monty, who is talking to the store clerk behind the magazine section, picks up his newspapers and crosses to his daughter and Matt. "Hello, young Ryan. Saw you earlier, but you were in a heck of a hurry then," he says quietly, his voice affected with an educated correctness, but not unfriendly. "Yes, saw you get into that bit of a kerfuffle with Mrs. Fahey. Not to worry, the whole episode brightened up the day, with everyone having a good chuckle, including the victim after she calmed down." He points to the back door. "Now, I think you had better be on your way; we don't want any trouble here, do we? You can slip out through back door there."

"We are going out the front door, Daddy; you can deal with Jordan."

Too late, Jordan limps through the main entrance holding the helmet under his arm, looks about, and then crosses to intercept Matt, trouble written all over his face. "I thought I might run in to you."

"C'mon, Jordan, don't cause a scene, please; Matt and I are leaving," says Cassie.

Jordan ignores her. "I say, old boy, you have a cheek. I keep telling you not to hang around my sister. You know I do not like you or your family. Troublemakers; you would do us all a favor if you just kept to your end of the island."

Matt bristles, clenches his hands into fists, but keeps them at his side. "I'm sorry you feel that way, Jordan. I want no quarrel with you, and you can please yourself how you feel about my relationship with your sister; that's none of my business, but—" Matt's voice turns icy, "my family is my business. You'd be smart to keep your mouth shut about them; they've done you no harm." He turns his attention back to Cassie and Monty. "Better I leave now, Cassie; we'll catch up later today." He kisses her gently on the cheek, nods a farewell to Monty, "Mr. Baldwin," and steps around the smug and smiling Jordan.

"Smart move, Ryan," says Jordan. "And if I was you, I'd keep the hell out of my sight."

Matt walks through the shop door and out into the hot sun just as his father, stepmother, and two stepbrothers pull up in the Landcruiser. Sean gets out, looking uncertain and embarrassed, and walks toward the store. Matt understands exactly what is bothering the boy. Ryan Senior never goes into the store when his account is overdue; he sends in one of the boys for his tobacco and papers.

"I'll take care of it, Sean," says Matt, stepping in front of the boy.

"It's all right," mumbles a sullen Sean as he shuffles around Matt.

Within minutes, an angry Wally Wright, the storeowner, strides through the door and onto the pavement, heading towards Frank's vehicle.

"You ought to be ashamed of yourself, Ryan, sending young Sean in to get what you haven't the guts to ask for yourself. I'm tired of you being behind with your bill, so from now on you'll get nothing here unless you pay cash." He looks at Katherine sympathetically and sighs. "I'm sorry, Mrs. Ryan, I really am, but I have a business to run and a family to take care of, too."

Matt wants the earth to swallow him. *Wally must be really pissed at Frank today. He's never got up him[9] like this before.*

The people standing around outside who hear Wally are embarrassed for Katherine and the boys. Sean is upset and runs to the truck. Cassie, watching from the door of the store, tries to smile, and waves a *'don't worry about it'* message to Matt.

Frank pushes his head out of the truck window and yells at Wally, "I'll have your money to you by the end of the week, you wasp prick." He leans further out of the Landcruiser waving a fist furiously. "And as far as I'm concerned you can shove your store up where the sun don't—"

Abruptly, everybody's eyes are drawn upward. The air fills with the scream of a high-powered jet-turbine engine. The police helicopter from Adelaide lifts over the trees and banks to circle the town a little more than twenty meters above the ground. Matt looks up and sees the red face of Sergeant Reg Woodson staring through the chopper's downside door.

Frank is yelling at Sean to get in the truck. Sean runs, and as Patrick pulls him into the cab, Frank reverses to the center of the road. He grates the gears as he slams the lever into drive and accelerates along the town's main street, eventually bouncing onto the gravel road at the town limits where the truck disappears in a swirl of dust.

Matt walks quickly to Cassie. "This afternoon at three, then—usual place," he shouts into her ear. He gives her quick hug, nods respectfully to Monty, runs to his bike, kick-starts the engine, and roars off down the main street.

A smirking Jordan joins Cassie and her dad.

"At it again, are they? When are you going to learn, sis? That Ryan mob are just no damn, good."

---

[9] Got up him: Told him off.

8

Sergeant Woodson is tickled-pink with the reaction of the people on the ground, especially the Ryans speeding off in the direction of the South Coast Road. "We got right up Frank's nose," he says into the microphone, chuckling. "We'll deal with them later. That's one advantage of being on this damn island, sooner or later, people run out of road."

Constable Robert Dunning holds his earphones a little tighter against his ears. Kangaroo Island is his third posting since graduating from the police academy in Adelaide four years ago, and two weeks have passed since being transferred from South Australia's Upper North, the land of his ancestors, where the red desert and blue sky blend into an extraordinary orange ocher that goes on and on, way beyond the horizon. *Yeah, they can't go far here—sea all 'round.*

"What have you got against Ryan?" asks Dunning.

"Trouble maker; thinks because he went to Vietnam he's a hero. Alkie is what he is, and his kid's going the same way."

"Vietnam did a lot of blokes in, boss; doesn't hurt to cut them some slack."

"Bleeding hearts don't do well on my team, Constable Dunning." He turns to the pilot. "Head to Middle River, we'll catch up with the Ryans at the lighthouse later; that's where they're going, home."

As the chopper thunders over the rolling landscape, Dunning, sitting behind Woodson who is in the front seat next to the pilot, feels uneasy. The sergeant, he observes, probably reaching into his early 50s, is a short, stocky fella with an expanding paunch that pushes at the mid-section of his blue uniform shirt. The rolled-up sleeves expose thick, muscular arms extending to the largest and thickest hands Dunning has ever laid eyes on, and a neck, short and as thick as a tree trunk. Set close together in the heavy, jowly face, two beady black eyes reveal nothing remarkably intelligible except for the chilling stare, the eyes of a cobra—cold, deadly. *Dangerous bastard, that's for sure.*

A few minutes later, the helicopter is circling over Middle River and the Baldwin homestead. The enormous house is at the forefront of a complex of several other buildings. A long, narrow shed of iron and steel takes up almost the entire back area of the homestead paddock. A six-stand[10] shearing shed, stockyards, and stables stretch to the west, while on the eastern side, a cluster of silos for grain and feed storage complete the homestead cluster.

"That's where the "Island Baron" lives," says Woodson through his microphone. "He's head of one of the wealthiest grazing families in South Australia. You'd do well to stay on the right side of boss-man Monty Baldwin. He holds a lot of sway with the big boys in Adelaide."

Dunning nods. *I know the Baldwins, all right—especially Jordan.* The helicopter circles the house, and Dunning's mind flashes back to an ugly encounter with Jordan.

Dunning had gone to the same college. While Jordan exuded all the airs of the privileged class, Dunning had come from very humble beginnings. His father was a blue-collar bloke from the north of South Australia, where he worked in the Leigh Creek coalmines. He married a mixed-blood Aboriginal girl from the Port Augusta mission, despite the contrary advice of family and friends. Dunning was the finest gift their love could bring them. While he looked most like his father, he inherited some of his mother's color, giving his skin an exotic chocolate brown tone.

Harry Dunning decided the day Robert was born that his son was going to get a good education, and he worked overtime regularly to earn the money to make it happen. Happily, the talented kid responded to Harry's guidance and disciplined regime. Opportunity came through their combined efforts

---

[10] Six-stand: Capacity for six shearers working at once.

and he was awarded a scholarship to attend Kings College, a prestigious Presbyterian boarding school in Adelaide. He did well, and Harry was the proudest parent in "the Creek." Unfortunately, his hard mining life took its toll, and he developed lung disease from coal dust, forcing him into early retirement. Although traveling was hard on him, and Leigh Creek was 400 kilometers north of Adelaide, he still made it to important college events.

It was the biggest college game of the year for Kings, an Aussie Rules football match-up with their archrival, Rostrevor College, an all-male boarding school run by the Christian Brothers. Dunning was easily the best player on the King's team. He was fast, courageous, and spectacular, and for the first time in eight years, Kings had a chance to win, just one point behind the Catholic champions with a minute left to the final siren. On the run and clear of his opponent, he was in good position to receive the ball from a pass by Jordan and win the game. He was heading towards the bleachers where his father was standing with his mother, cheering wildly, when he saw Harry stiffen and fall to the ground. The ball hit Dunning on the chest and bounced into the arms of his opponent. They lost the game by the one measly point, a rare and historic opportunity, gone.

As it turned out, his father was okay; his diseased lungs were the problem. Too much excitement, not enough oxygen, and he blacked out.

When he finally made it to the dressing room, a furious Jordan was waiting. "So what the hell happened, *mate*," he said, jabbing his finger into Bob's chest. "Go walkabout[11], did we? Part of the tribe mentality, hey?"

"Let it go, Jordan," said team captain Chesty Barnes. "His dad took a turn. We'll have another go next year."

"A pox on next year," yelled Jordan. "We had it in the palm of our hand, and this darky let it all go down the gurgler."[12]

What happened next was so quick that nobody had the chance to intervene. "Darky" was a word Dunning had heard many times before, a derogatory term

---

[11] Walkabout: Generally applies to Australian Aboriginal behavior where the native leaves his or her environment on an impulse to go off into the bush for an extended period.

[12] Gurgler: Relates noise water makes when it drains from the sink.

used to insult aboriginals. Normally, he didn't react much, but this time, Dunning took the insult as a slur on his mother.

Before Jordan knew what hit him, he was on the floor nursing a bloody nose. Chesty was holding Dunning back as Jordan struggled to his feet and slammed a cowardly blow to his enemy's stomach. All hell broke loose, and by the time they were pulled apart, both boys were a bloody mess. Dunning was called before the school principal. Monty Baldwin, always politically astute, put in a good word that saved him from being expelled.

Yeah, Dunning thinks as he looks at the rolling bluffs dropping away spectacularly into the ocean. *The Baldwins—have yet to meet the daughter; they reckon she's a stunner.*

"He's got a real stunner for a daughter," says Woodson, as if picking up Dunning's last thought. "Reckon if you play your cards right, you might do good for yourself, young Bob. Nice farm to go along with plenty of fun in the cot, hey?" The more the young constable got to know the sergeant, the more he—

"Ah." The chopper drops sharply under the brow of the cliff line. Dunning's stomach lifts to his mouth and then settles as the pilot takes the aircraft a good 120 kilometers an hour a few meters above the water. As they charge west, along the north coast, Woodson watches out for unfamiliar boats or signs of suspicious activity among the many caves weathered into the cliffs. Ten minutes later, the aircraft banks and sweeps into Snug Cove, the last haven for small boats and fishing cutters before the exposed northwestern corner of the island gives way to the vastness and peril of the southern ocean. The cove is more than 500 meters across, but its narrow neck is a perfect barrier for protecting sheltering craft from rough seas. Three boats lay quietly at anchor in the calm, crystal-clear water, the shadows of their hulls prominent on the white, sandy bottom—menacing, eerily reminiscent of the great white sharks that frequent the waters around Kangaroo Island.

Woodson howls with delight as he points his finger toward one of the fishing cutters. In the same moment, Dunning recognizes it, too—the rugged hull of the sturdy boat rises to a narrow point at its bow, where a little below the gunwale, the ship's name is painted in large black letters. *Smokey Cloud.*

9

Landing a helicopter on the Snug Cove beach is difficult and dangerous, but the pilot, giving way to Woodson's direct orders, manages to settle the craft on the widest strip of sand available without burying the main rotor blades into the sand dunes just meters from the water's edge.

As the noise from the turbine fades, Dunning unclips his seat belt, opens the door and almost topples into the water lapping the helicopter's offside landing skid. Woodson exits on the sand dune side and, clutching a megaphone in one hand, hurries around the front of the aircraft and begins waving furiously at *Smokey Cloud*. Sergeant Woodson, the warrior, does not notice the water splashing over his brown shoes; he is ready for war.

"*Smokey Cloud*, stand to. This is Sergeant Reg Woodson of the South Australian police," he shouts through the megaphone. "We are to board your vessel; send your dinghy immediately."

Three men standing together at the rail of *Smokey Cloud* peer toward the beach.

"*Smokey Cloud*, I am ordering you to send us your dinghy," bellows Woodson again.

Dunning watches as the men split up. One moves to the bow and begins raising the ship's anchor, while the other two disappear into the wheelhouse.

"You know what, boss," yells Dunning. "It looks to me as if they are going to bolt."

"Get the ducky,[13] Constable," yells the sergeant, taking his mouth away

---

[13] Ducky: Slang for rubber inflatable watercraft.

from the megaphone for an instant. "Stand to, *Smokey Cloud*. I am warning you; do not run."

Dunning drags a tightly strapped rubber package from the cargo space at the rear of the helicopter. A quick turn of the tap on the compressed air cylinder screwed to the wood bottom of the package and connected to an inflation teat, in seconds, transforms the package into a rubber dinghy, big enough for two people.

Black smoke billows from *Smokey Cloud's* engine exhaust. "Come on, come on, hurry it up," yells a frantic Woodson. "They're getting away."

Dunning turns back to the chopper and snatches the small outboard motor from the cargo space. Spinning around, he drops to one knee and slams the motor onto the rear mounting plate. He pushes the dinghy into the water, slides over the stern seat, and begins pulling the starter cord. The tiny motor coughs, splutters a few times, and then starts, sending light blue puffs of smoke from its exhaust drifting across the cove. Woodson splashes through knee-deep water, throws himself into the little boat, and almost swamps his warship before it has traveled a few meters.

"Let's go," yells a pumped up Woodson, settling into a kneeling position, facing forward and grasping a rope attached to the bow. "Give it to her, Bobby boy, give it to her. Try to run from me, you bastards."

Even Dunning is beginning to feel the thrill of the challenge and the danger. A smile begins to spread across his face as the comedy of their situation, their tiny vessel almost bereft of freeboard, putt-putt-putting over the water at a mere four knots, approaching a vessel beginning to assume the proportions of a battleship, strikes him as insane.

The two policemen close to within twenty meters of *Smokey Cloud*. The man on the bow runs back to the wheelhouse. Another huge black cloud of diesel exhaust plumes into the hot afternoon air. Seawater begins to boil at the stern of the cutter as the single propeller thrashes the water, and then she begins moving slowly toward the open ocean, away from the closing ducky.

Dunning is aware of the wash rolling their way, and the propeller churning up the water at the cutter's stern. Woodson, also, is aware of the looming danger and frantically signals to Dunning to turn away, but Dunning is reluctant to swing the tiny craft broadside to the wash, fearing the craft will roll over. Woodson jerks crazily on the bow rope, trying to pull the nose around.

"For God's sake, Dunning, turn this bloody boat around before we end up fish bait."

He barely finishes the sentence when the wash hits them, swamping the dinghy and leaving the two men sitting in the flooded vessel with water up to their waists. Luckily, in part due to Dunning's quick thinking, throttling back and keeping a straight course, the inflatable did not turn over and dump them into the deep water. Their sodden clothing would have taken them straight to the bottom. Nevertheless, with their boat now 170 meters from shore, heavily waterlogged, and as Dunning quietly notes, a receding tide taking them toward the open sea, they are in serious trouble.

The thought of great white sharks, frequent visitors to the cove this time of the year, sends a shiver along his spine. *Why the hell didn't we just take the helicopter*, he thinks, looking derisively at the back of Woodson's bald head.

"We'll have to swim for it, boss," shouts Dunning as he gingerly attempts to remove his clothing, trying not to upset their distressed vessel.

Woodson stares towards the beach, where the helicopter pilot is waving frantically and pointing at something close to the shoreline. "Hell," yells Woodson pointing at the water and almost turning the dinghy over as he pushes back into its center.

"Holy mackerel," Dunning whispers to himself as he sucks in a lungful of air. His heart races as he watches a large, dark shape cruise slowly along the sandy bottom between them and the beach. "We're in a bit of strife, Sergeant."

Their eyes fixed on the shadow, both men are unaware that *Smokey Cloud* has stopped. The cutter's dinghy is being let down over the side by two of the crew who board the small boat after it hits the water. They close to within a few meters of the policemen before Woodson sees them.

"You wanna tow to the beach, Mister Woodson?" calls a heavily accented voice. He is a short, burly man with a heavy dark beard and bushy eyebrows, under which peer two black eyes twinkling with humor and a mouth creased into a beaming smile.

"You're not so smart, Sammy," snarls a very nervous Woodson. "You're going to spend a night or two in the slammer after I get my hands on you. I told you to heave to, and you disobeyed a lawful order."

"I never understanda a word you say, Mister Woodson, I thought you were giving us a friendly wave. You getta a little wet," taunts Sammy Marino, the fishing cutter's jaunty skipper. "Now, do you want I shoulda bring you in, or do you wanna to do it yourself?" he asks, nodding in the direction of the black shadow cruising along the sandy bottom.

Dunning is quick to reply, "Mr. Marino, we will be forever indebted for your kindness. Now hurry up and get us the hell out of here, will you?"

"Ah, you are a man of respect, Constable. You mussa be the new one. I have only just heard of you. Robert Dunning, eh? I am Captain Samuel Marino, the best of alla fishermen in the Southern Ocean."

"Yeah, you go fishing, all right," responds a sarcastic Woodson. "You got away with it this time, Marino, but look out. I've been on your coat tails a long time. I'll get your lousy hide eventually, and I'll nail it to the bloody jail wall."

Sammy laughs as his crewman throws a line to Dunning, who grabs onto it for dear life. Sammy heads slowly toward the beach, pulling the ducky along behind. Dunning's heart starts to beat a little faster as it becomes obvious that their route is going to take them over the path of the cruising shadow.

"Watch out for the fish," says Dunning to Sammy, his voice beginning to crack as he watches the shadow turn at the end of the beach and head back towards their crawling caravan. Sammy does not respond, and Woodson, still sitting at the front of the drowning inflatable, begins to panic as he realizes, too, that they are going to intersect the shadow before they get to the beach.

"For God's sake, Marino, do something," shouts Woodson as the shadow closes on the ducky. He tries once again to back away from the front of the boat, but this time he upsets its balance, and he and Dunning splash into the water. The shadow immediately streaks toward the open sea. Sammy and his crewman break into gales of laughter, as the sputtering policemen scramble the last few meters to the beach.

"Hey, Reggie, you just frightened a biga stingray, babee. He won't hurt you unless you stepa on him, you know," shouts Sammy through his laughter as Woodson and Dunning finally make the beach.

Sammy's demeanor changes; his face hardens as he stands in the bow of his dinghy a few meters off the beach, studying the two soaked men.

"Mr. Woodson, you are welcome to comma on my boat as a guest, but don't ever try to order me around or board me withouta an invitation or a warrant. This is bloody Australia, mate, a free country witha bloody laws for everyone—meaning you, too. Until, maybe, we meeta again, arrivederci!"

He extends a salute, which could be broadly interpreted as "giving the finger," turns and sits in the bow of his boat. His crewman opens the throttle of the outboard motor and, with a cloud of blue smoke trailing on the top of the water, heads the dinghy towards *Smokey Cloud*.

Dunning stares after the boat for a few seconds. *What a bloody character.* He had heard stories about Sammy's generosity—funding for kids programs, buildings for recreation, and he was a hell of a big donor to the Catholic Church. Despite knowing that Sammy is under investigation for alleged offenses against the crown,[14] Dunning chuckles, finding himself liking the man and puzzling over his sergeant's very personal animosity toward the Southern Ocean's self-proclaimed greatest fisherman. *I wonder if Woodson likes anyone.*

They strip to their underwear as the pilot packs and loads the inflatable back into the chopper. Woodson is brooding; Dunning's mind turns to the mundane as they climb into the helicopter. *I'll have to fill out a report on the incident and file a property loss form for the megaphone. Ah, bloody paperwork.*

Woodson mumbles to the pilot. Dunning makes out a couple of the words, West Bay, and the lighthouse. Then the roar of the turbine overtakes the whine of the starter motor.

Abruptly, in a cloud of swirling sand and flying spray, the helicopter lifts

---

[14] Crown: Australia is a part of the British Commonwealth with the queen of England as head of state.

off the beach. Climbing over the bay and sweeping above the cliffs and ocean, Dunning, watching *Smokey Cloud*, already well out to sea and moving steadily east, is disturbed by an ugly premonition about the ship and its crew.

10

The battered old Landcruiser leaves behind a hanging trail of dust as it bumps and rattles at speed along the South Coast Road. Matt, arms aching from the tension of his death grip on the handlebars, is far enough behind to avoid the worst of the dust and flying gravel. Even though he has ridden over the treacherous ironstone countless times, keeping the bike straight and level at speed is little more than a slight over correction away from disaster.

Twenty minutes later, they are clattering over the cattle grid entrance into Flinders Chase National Park. Spreading across the west end of the island, from the north coast to the south coast, Flinders Chase and its neighboring parks are home to an amazing diversity of native animals: kangaroos, wallabies, wild goats, wild pigs, cuddly koalas, spiky echidnas, cute platypus, reptiles, and the rare Cape Barren geese.

Thousands of small, colorful birds flit about the trees, filling the air with the twittering of their myriad sound. Big black cockatoos and their smaller red-breasted cousins, galahs, screech noisily as they lift from the tall gum trees, disturbed by the rushing vehicles. Crows, cunning and vulgar, their raucous squawking obnoxious, scavengers who pick the eyes from newborn lambs, search the road for new kills of reptile, wallaby, or possum.

Hundreds of wildflower species flourish throughout the rugged landscape: purples, pinks, whites, yellows, blues, and greens add spectacular texture to the thick carpet of low scrubby brush. The occasional Rosenblum poppy, survivor of the government's plant-slashing program, spot the green scrub with brilliant scarlet. Leafy crowns of soaring white gum trees growing along creek beds snake through the rolling topography, ending abruptly where the island coast holds back the Southern Ocean. Precariously, dopey koalas doze in the forks of towering gums for most of the day as their unique digestive system slowly breaks down toxic eucalyptus leaves, their staple food source.

The Ryan convoy passes the ranger's cottage, the tourist center, and its ancillary structures, and turns left, toward the southwest corner of the Chase and Cape du Couedic. As they top the plateau, Matt slows. A vista of trees and scrub drops away in front of him, where, cutting through its center, a ribbon of road winds toward a deep blue sea. Barely visible, the astonishing "Remarkable Rocks" balance precariously on their granite base, teasing spectators to ponder their permanence. To the right of the "Rocks," where the road appears to run into the ocean, stands the imposing Cape du Couedic Lighthouse.

Matt stops. He watches the Ryan truck rush ahead, gradually closing on the cluster of buildings preceding the lighthouse, their home. He sucks in the scented air and exhales with a sigh. *I'm going to miss this, my patch, my home. Ten years—not much I haven't been over.* He watches an echidna waddle, or perhaps swagger, from a yucca bush away from the road. The spiny anteater becomes aware of him and hurriedly scratches into the sandy loam, protecting his soft underbelly. Matt smiles and scans the stunning view.

He had moved with his father to the lighthouse after his mother's suicide. Frank lost his north coast farm: low commodity prices, tough seasons, the bankruptcy, and yeah, Frank's alcohol addiction. Because the farm was part of the Returned Soldier's Land Settlement Scheme, the RSL[15] made representations to the government minister in charge of the scheme for consideration of a special circumstance, a family tragedy, to allow Frank a reprieve, an opportunity to keep his land. Instead, he was offered a job by the federal government to manage the lighthouse at Cape du Couedic. It was probably for the best in the end, a government job with regular pay and retirement benefits.

---

[15] RSL: Returned Serviceman's League—Australia's war veterans' association.

He managed to get off the booze for a while and met Katherine Roden, a nurse at the local district hospital in Kingscote. She thought Frank had overcome his drinking problem for good, so she married him; after all, he was a good-looking bloke and could be quite the charmer. Patrick came along, and things seemed to be going pretty well, but it did not last. How could it? Frank had the disease; he was an alcoholic. Soon after Sean's birth, the old curse and its demons returned to haunt him, and he was into the booze again.

The prickly animal warily resumes its journey toward the scrub. *Lucky little blighter; you haven't got a worry in the world, have you, mate?* Matt re-starts the bike and turns onto a barely discernable hiking trail branching off from the gravel road, heading northwest. He pushes along as quick as he dares, dodging overhead branches of low lying brush until, a few minutes later, he stops at the top of a cliff and stares to the west over the ocean toward Wedge Island, barely visible on the horizon.

Beautiful. Glassy conditions prevail, a perfect day for diving on the wreck of the *Portland Maru*, a Japanese grain ship laying in twenty meters of water, driven onto the rocks off Cape Torrens on the North Coast during a deadly storm forty years earlier. *If it wasn't for the great whites, I'd have a go at getting some of the copper and brass still left on it; be worth a few bucks, that's for sure.* Matt turns to look to the northeast and catches a flash of light reflecting from an aircraft above the cliffs.

Bloody coppers are at West Bay. Woodson's probably taking advantage of the calm water to spot the Vennachar.[16] *He'll be there the rest of the day if he sees anything. Good stuff, gives me a bit more time.*

He pushes on along the cliff line, south, toward the lighthouse for a few meters and then turns back into the scrub. The track descends rather steeply to a creek running through the middle of a one-hectare basin. Massive gum trees, well spaced, form a leafy canopy overhead. Even on close inspection

---

[16] Loch Vennachar: Three-masted sailing vessel carrying gold bullion, which foundered with loss of all hands during a fierce storm in the late 1800s. Nothing of much value has ever been recovered because of the usually rough seas and the extremely hazardous diving conditions.

from the air, the basin floor is not easy to see. In its midst, off to the side of the creek, a small toilet-size humpy[17] is well camouflaged with bulloak bush and gum bark that blends with the natural colors of the forest floor.

Matt hurries toward the humpy. He is about to enter the front opening made of Hessian cloth when the faint thump-thump-thumping of the helicopter blades reaches his ears. *Bugger it.* He scrambles into the humpy.

---

[17] Humpy: Small, aboriginal shelter made of timber, bark, leaves, and corrugated iron, if available.

11

Looking out through the front canopy of the helicopter, Dunning can see the stark form of the Cape du Couedic Lighthouse rising from the barren southwestern corner of the island ten kilometers ahead. *If we don't get anything else out of today's grand sortie, at least I had the scenic tour of a lifetime.* As they fly quickly a few meters above the cliff line, his keen eyes continually searching each side of the aircraft, he reflects on the flight from Snug Cove.

After leaving the cove, they had flown along the north coast, tracking west. Dunning was thrilled by the aerial view of the scenery, the towering cliffs dropping sheer into an unusually calm sea, and the wild goats exposed on the steep inclines, feeding on the natural grasses of the coastal hills, scattering as the helicopter thundered overhead. They had landed at the Cape Borda Lighthouse, a neat, square, white structure built to protect all manner of seafarers passing the northwestern corner of the island, where the gracious lighthouse keeper's wife dried their clothes and served them afternoon tea. They took off again and flew west. Dunning noticed that even on the calmest of days, an occasional boomer, a monster wave—"a rogue," they were often called—would appear from nowhere, hidden among the mild swells rolling in from the southwest. *Have to look out for those,* he had mentally noted. *Lot of drownings from being washed off the rocks by a rogue.*

At West Bay, they hovered low over the water, drifting back and forth across its width. Woodson told him about the *Loch Vennachar* as he studied the rocky bottom, searching for signs of the wreck, but the incident at Snug Cove had cost them the best viewing time. "Supposed to be gold on it," he said. "None of it has ever been found." A breeze from the west had already picked up, rippling the surface and making it impossible to see the bottom clearly.

Woodson became angrier by the minute and complained that it was very rare to get a day calm enough to see the bottom at West Bay; only one or two came along in any one year. He reckoned he had an extra score to settle with Sammy Marino.

As the helicopter rushes toward the du Couedic lighthouse, Dunning continues to search the terrain for signs of human activity, but he sees only the tracks of wild animals. Woodson looks over his shoulder at the aboriginal policeman, this time grinning from ear to ear.

"We're going to have a little fun here, Constable. We'll drop under the level of the cliffs, scoot around the arch, fly into Weir Cove, and come up over the top of the cliff from behind the old storehouse ruins. Should scare the *bejeez* out of them." He laughs and turns back to look at the ground along the top of the rugged cliffs.

He stiffens, suddenly alert, excited. "Hold it. What the hell is that?" He points toward a fresh track heading into the scrub. The pilot slows the helicopter and hovers. "Follow that," the sergeant orders, pointing into the bush.

"Probably wallaby or goat trails," responds Dunning, unsure why he keeps quiet about seeing a tire track. "They are all over the place."

"Looks a bit more than that to me; I've got a hunch we might be onto something," Woodson insists. "It looks like a tire track to me, and it's heading straight into that basin."

"Well, there'd be fresh water there, boss. The wildlife has to drink somewhere."

The pilot takes the helicopter over the top of the basin.

"I can't see a thing down there It's like a jungle. You see anything, Constable?"

"Animal tracks, water hole, nothing out of the ordinary," Dunning says. In the brush on the basin floor, his sharp eyes pick up what looks like some kind of structure, one he recognizes. *I'll be damned, a humpy!* He reaches forward to tap Woodson on the shoulder, but stops. *No, stuff this bloke. I'll keep it to myself until I figure out what's going on. Scare the Ryans with a schoolboy prank? What the hell is he on about?*

"All right, we'll have to come back out here in a vehicle and check it out thoroughly. It's the perfect spot for a cultivation hide," says Woodson. He nods to the pilot and points toward Cape du Couedic. "Let's go and stir up the Ryan mob."

12

Frank's hectic drive along the rusty ironstone road through the Chase ends abruptly as he brings the Landcruiser to a skidding stop in front of one of three stone cottages lining the road 120 meters from the lighthouse. From the lighthouse, a rough limestone track cuts through low scrubby brush for another 150 meters to the famous Admiral's Arch, an incredible structure fashioned from the limestone rock over thousands of years by wind and pounding waves, eventually forming a huge arch under the rough and cratered headland. There, and on the rocks at the bottom of the surrounding cliffs, hundreds of fur seals shelter and rest, many resting from their eighty-kilometer fishing sorties out into the Southern Ocean.

To the east of the cottages, a sea mist drifts above the cliffs of Weir Cove, and further along to Kirkpatrick Point, balancing on their granite base, Remarkable Rocks hints of a Stonehenge mystique in the mist shrouding its giant, craggy boulders. Even the mild breeze stirring the air seems to suggest a lament from a Celtic pipe.

In front of the Ryan cottage, larger than the other two, and set in the southwest corner of the village, Frank slides from the truck and begins barking orders.

"Patrick, get your arse down to the lighthouse and grab the bag of poppies from under the stairs. Bring it to the stores cottage and hurry up about it; those coppers will be here soon. Sean, you come with me."

Patrick scampers off to the lighthouse. Frank and Sean hurry to the cottage in the northwest corner, the storehouse. As they reach the wire gate, Frank slides back the catch, skinning the knuckles on the back of his hand.

"Bugger." He hurries to the door and finds it padlocked. "Damn, damn."

"The truck, boy, the keys; get them and be bloody smart about it."

Sean scurries away, yelling to his mother, who is making her way to the back veranda of their cottage carrying the computer. "Dad needs the keys, Mum."

"They're still in the truck, Sean."

As he runs toward the truck, an ear-splitting scream shatters the stillness.

Rearing vertically up and over the cliff edge and the old store ruins, the police helicopter roars toward the cottages. The screaming turbine reverberates off the cliff walls of Weir Cove, scaring the life out of Katherine and Sean. She freezes. Sean's heart crowds his mouth, and he grabs at his mother's dress. Frank tenses; the sound of the chopper takes him back to Vietnam. He runs toward his family, angry and ready for war.

"Mongrels."

As he reaches Katherine and Sean, dust and small stones stirred up from the helicopter's whirling blades as it settles on the road between the cottages blast them. The pilot shuts down the power, and silence gradually returns.

Woodson climbs out, closely followed by Dunning. Sean's dog, Barney, an Australian kelpie tied to a tree in the back yard of the home cottage, starts to bark savagely and whirls madly around at the end of his chain.

"Shut that bloody dog up, will you?" shouts Woodson.

"Up yours, Woodson," says Frank, his fists clenched at his side. Barney bares his teeth and snarls.

"Well, well, well. Same old Frank, hey? It's been a while, hasn't it? Haven't changed a bit, have you?" says Woodson, striding to where the family is standing. He slowly looks them over and then acknowledges Dunning with a nod. "I don't know that you have met our new constable, so let me introduce you to Constable Robert Dunning, an expert in matters related to poppy flowers and other illicit plants. You know all about that, Frank, don't you?" He pauses, posturing. "Come on, Frank—production, procurement, and distribution—that sort of thing, hey?"

Dunning is uneasy with Woodson's threatening approach, especially with Mrs. Ryan and the young boy present. He steps forward and offers his hand to Katherine. "Pleased to meet you, Mrs. Ryan, Frank," he says. "And who is the young fella here?"

"This is Sean, Constable," replies Katherine, regaining her composure. "He's the youngest of our boys."

"Yeah, that's right; I wouldn't get too close to these kids, Constable," says the sergeant. "Like feral animals, these kids. Scratch your bloody eyes out, give 'em half a chance."

"You'd be the mongrel of the year, wouldn't ya, Woodson? Come flying in here in your fancy chopper, scaring my wife and kids half to death," says the belligerent Frank, blue eyes narrowed through hostile slits. "Don't scare me none. Flew 'em in Nam; heard you bailed your sorry arse out of contention by pleading domestic policing crap. You're a limp prick, copper; don't scare me none at all."

Woodson reddens with anger. "Why you—"

Dunning intervenes and grabs Woodson's arm, just in time. "Easy, boss, we've got nothing on Frank—no evidence that would stand up in court."

Woodson takes a breath and then smiles maliciously. "Well, Frank, things change, and I'm the only game in town for you now, which brings us to the why of our visit today. The story goes that you and your eldest kid are growing poppies around here and that you are a collection agent for Sam Marino and his mob in Victoria."

"Long bloody way from here; you think I walk on water?" replies Frank.

"Frank, we have good information about what's going on," Dunning offers in a conciliatory manner. "It's a serious matter, cultivating poppies for commercial purposes. Sure, you can have a few in your garden, and we'll even look the other way if it's a few over the limit. Look, if you come clean now, we can make it a lot easier on you. We really only want the big blokes." He pauses; Frank remains quiet. "For God's sake, man, you get yourself too far into this, and you'll end up in jail."

"Let me make it plain to you, Ryan," interrupts Woodson. "We have good information. If you're not hiding anything, you won't mind us taking a look around, will you?"

"You got a warrant?"

Woodson looks at Dunning.

"No, Frank, but the sergeant has a point. Why would you want to stop us?" says Dunning.

"I'll tell you why, Mr. Dunning," says Frank, his anger building. "I'll tell you this—I, along with a bunch of me mates, some of whom didn't make it back, and others who are so screwed in the head they're good for nothing anymore, went to Vietnam and laid it on the line for what we thought was right. We get back here, and we have the likes of you blokes interfering in our lives, trying to enforce stupid bloody laws designed to protect the special interests of a few arse-holes. That prick, your boss, is the sort of mongrel we despise, and there's no way in the world I'd lift a finger to help, period."

Frank's argument is familiar to Dunning. His people often had to bear the prejudice of a few bigot coppers enforcing white men's laws that rarely respected the traditions and laws of Aboriginal culture. He feels a surprising empathy for the troubled Frank.

Woodson's reaction is predictably the reverse of Dunning's. "You're a drunk, pure and simple, Ryan. Like many of your sodden mates, the whole war is an excuse to opt out of taking responsibility."

Frank's eyes fix a blank and terrible stare on the sergeant. He sucks in a deep breath, trying to stay under control, but his mind begins to spin, his knees weaken, and the familiar icy breath of his demons blows through the emptiness in his gut. His mind flashes back to Vietnam.

"Wombat" Hodges, his best mate, is sitting in the command position atop his armored personnel carrier. He and Wombat are roaring into battle side by side, and hostile fire from the enemy, well dug in on the ridge ahead, is flying all over the place. Frank looks across at his mate, gives him the thumbs up and a big grin, and then Wombat's upper body explodes in a cloud of crimson mist. Frank screams. With tears streaming down his cheeks, he accelerates his vehicle to full speed and charges into the enemy line in an orgy of lunacy and slaughter.

Dunning sees what is coming in time to grab Frank as he launches himself at the leering Woodson.

"Frank, Frank," shouts Dunning, wrapping his arms tight around the old soldier's arms. "For Christ's sake, calm down, or I'll have to handcuff you."

Frank begins to sag, spiraling into a seizure. Katherine hands the word processor to Sean and rushes to Frank as Dunning lowers him to the ground. She yells to Patrick who is returning from the lighthouse after hiding the bag of flowers in the scrub. "Patrick, get your dad's brandy, quick."

Patrick knows the routine and runs into the house. He knows where the liquor is kept; in fact, he knows most of the hides where his father plants booze around the lighthouse and the cottages. In trees, under bushes, in toilet basins, stashes in and around the generator shed, and even in the bedroom where there's no attempt to hide it, keeping it under the bed for when the demons come for his dad in the early morning hours.

"Here," says Katherine, grabbing the brandy from Patrick as he runs up to her. "Here, Frank, drink this," she orders.

Frank needs no arm-twisting, and he grabs the bottle in both hands. Shaking violently, he pours the dark brown miracle into his mouth; the liquid surges through him, spreading its warm glow, and then finally spills into his stomach, drowning the howling demons.

The affect on Frank is instantaneous. His body relaxes, the shakes stop, and a silly grin spreads across his face as he looks into the eyes of the young constable. "Thank you, Mr. Dunning. You, sir, are a gentleman."

"You Vietnam blokes had a hard time of it, Frank, I know a mate of—" The unmistakable high-pitched howl of a Japanese trail bike approaching from the north interrupts.

"Look, it's Matt," cries an excited Sean.

Matt slides the bike to a stop next to his mother as Frank gets to his feet.

"You all right, Dad?" he asks, taking in the situation, knowing.

"Yeah, thanks to the young copper here and your mum." Frank turns to Woodson. "You arrived just in time to wave these blokes goodbye, Matt."

Matt strives to look and keep calm. "Aw, yeah, right. Um, saw the chopper landing from up at Humpy Cliff, so I got here as quick as I could. I mean, we don't get to see a chopper landing here—err—ever, do we?"

"Where have you been, son?" asks Woodson.

"Making my way back from church, Sergeant," replies Matt politely.

"I took the scenic route, same as you."

"So, you're Matt, hey? I'm Bob Dunning. I've heard a lot about you at football training; they reckon you're pretty darn fancy." Dunning reaches out to shake Matt's hand. "Call me Bob." They shake hands.

"I've heard a lot about you. I was told that you were invited to sign with the League," says Matt.

"That's true, but I knocked it back because I like my job. Speaking of which, Matt, we're here on business today. There's information come to us that some of you folks down this end of the island are cultivating Rosenblum poppies for commercial purposes. You know anything about that?"

"Stop pussyfooting around, Constable. This young bugger is right in the middle of it all," interjects the sergeant. "He knows damn well what the drift[18] is on this deal."

"There you go again, Woodson," says Frank, "always having a go at putting the wood[19] on someone, whether they've done anything against the law or not. It's about time for you to piss off."

"Not before your kid tells us where he's been and what he's been up to," threatens Woodson. "And you keep your mouth shut, or I'll take you in for threatening a police officer."

"Calm down, boss," says Dunning. "Let me handle this." He turns to Matt. "How about you show us Humpy Cliff, Matt? We'll look around, and if there's nothing going on, we'll get on our way. Chance for a ride in the chopper, too, hey?"

"I would like to do that for you, Cons—err—Bob, but I'm already running late for a get-together with my girlfriend."

"He's going out with that nice young Baldwin girl, Mr. Dunning," Katherine offers. "You know—the family from over at Middle River?"

Dunning smiles and nods. "Yes, Mrs. Ryan, I know of them. Nice people from what I hear."

---

[18] Drift: Australian slang for story/information.
[19] Wood: In this context, Australian slang for hex.

"I can take you out there sometime next week, if you like." Matt checks his watch. "Hell, I've got to get my gear and get out of here."

"All right, Matt, I'll take you up on the offer for next week," says Dunning.

Sergeant Woodson stares at Dunning. "That's about the dumbest deal I've heard in a long time, Constable. The kid will have everything cleaned out by the time you get out here again."

Dunning ignores his boss and turns to Katherine as Matt props his bike against the fence and hurries into the cottage. "Sorry about all this, Mrs. Ryan, but we have a job to do. Will you and the boys be okay?"

Katherine nods. "Of course, Frank's really a good man, you know."

Woodson shakes his head in disgust, turns, and walks back to the helicopter.

"Frank, I've heard a few things, particularly about your fondness for the grog and how rough that is on your family. If you want some help, I've got a few mates in AA, but you have to really want to give up the grog for it to work." Frank eyes the young constable warily. The helicopter's turbine begins to whine.

"I'll be expecting to hear from you." Dunning reaches for Frank's hand, and they shake.

For the second time in the day, Dunning wrestles with a growing premonition of disaster as he watches the Ryans stare up at his departing aircraft.

13

Matt glances at his watch. It is two-thirty and another twenty minutes of hard riding before the turn onto the track into Cape Kersaint. The fierce afternoon sun has the temperature soaring toward 35 degrees Celsius, 95 degrees in the old Fahrenheit measurement, unusually hot for Kangaroo Island, but the air rushing over his body is some relief. His thoughts turn to the earlier events of the day.

How close was that? Woodson won't let up until he has us. The mongrel? Katherine and the boys don't have a bone in his war. Dunning seems like a good bloke, but as the oldman says, you never know with a copper. They'll be out to Humpy tomorrow snooping around. Damn Frank, why did he have to take on Woodson.

The bike hits a patch of bull dust,[20] and Matt's thoughts switch to survival. The dramatic cut in speed lifts his backside off the seat, almost throwing him over the handlebars. He regains control and slows to a safer speed.

Katherine is a bloody saint putting up with Frank. He's stuffed without his booze. Patrick and Sean—they deserve better. I can't just up and leave them for Sydney while the oldman is out of control. His stomach knots. *Two more weeks left before she leaves. I should be going with her like we planned. Those bloody Sydney posers, pricks in tights will be all over her. Gotta work something out, real quick.* The bike kicks sideways in a rut of gravel. "Stuff it," he yells, opens up the throttle and roars down the road, frustrated and angry.

---

[20] Bull dust: Deep, soft pocket of sand located in the road of varying length and width.

A kilometer on, he slows to turn off the South Coast Road onto the Cape Kersaint access trail and stops at the stock proof gate, closed, with a sign hanging in the middle warning, *Private Property—Keep Out*. As he opens it, he sees familiar and fresh truck tracks in the sandy loam, a sign that Cassie is ahead, probably already at the beach. There is a single track, also, and fresh. *Why the hell would he be here today?*

Matt is soon speeding along the narrow track running next to the boundary fence separating the scrub from a paddock of mustard yellow stubble, the straw debris from a harvested barley crop belonging to the Baldwins. Ahead, a shearing shed, stockyards, and a small stone cottage cluster in the corner of the next paddock. As he roars through the open gates of the stockyards, he sees Jordan's black motorcycle leaning against the wall of the cottage. *Probably drunk by now.*

The ridge ahead is covered by low dense scrub broken only by glimpses of limestone, identical to the landscape surrounding the lighthouse. The track deteriorates into a rough, barely discernable impression on the ground. He scrambles over the outcrops of crumbling limestone and the exposed black roots of the mallee trees, working the throttle furiously, trying to avoid the branches that occasionally slap his face and scratch his bare arms and legs. As he tops the ridge, a rugged carpet of rolling green scrub spreads out, split through the middle by the faint line of the track snaking all the way to the deep blue of the Southern Ocean, ten minutes ahead. Excitement mixes with apprehension as he pictures Cassie waiting at the beach. *How the hell can I match those Sydney blokes? Bugger it; I have to sort something out.*

Finally, he arrives at the top of a sand hill overlooking the Cape Kersaint Beach, fifteen meters below, and stops his bike next to Cassie's truck. Shading his eyes from the sun, he sees the lone figure lying face down on a towel near the water's edge. Before he can call out, Cassie lifts her head from the towel and waves. *Bloody psychic, I swear to God.* He grins, quickly changes into his swimming trunks, runs and rolls and slides down the sand hill, and then sprints across the beach to splash spectacularly into the surf.

Cassie watches. *You are a handsome devil, Matt Ryan. Mister blue eyes— I'll have to keep my eye on you; the Sydney ladies are going to go nuts.*

His tan body cooled, Matt splashes out of the water, jogs over to Cassie and kisses her lightly on the lips.

"Matt, you look wonderful, sooo sexy."

"I do? Huh, thanks, mate. You're looking a bit of all right yourself, hey." He drops on to the towel next to her. "Sorry I'm late. The police helicopter dropped in at the lighthouse. Dad got all bent out of shape as usual. Katherine and the boys—well, it was pretty awful. I wish she would take the boys and—" He looks out across the water, 3,500 kilometers of wild water all the way to the ice of Antarctica. "And get the hell out of there."

"Everything will work out just fine, Matt. Understandably, you worry, you saw some awful things, but Katherine is a good mother, and she'll do what's right by her boys. After all, she knows what happened to your mum when she stuck around your dad for too long. Maybe you coming to Sydney will shake him up a bit. He's not all bad."

"Yeah, but he can't do without the grog."

"You have to think about your life, too, mate. My mother used to tell me life is a precious gift that rushes by too fast, too fast, that it is up to me to take hold of it—to make the most of every moment. Mummy died in her prime, but she crowded a lot into her short life and, by God, she made most of her moments."

"Yeah, I remember your mum when she first came to the school. Mother said she was special, the best teacher she ever knew, and a wonderful dancer. Both made their mark, didn't they? Strange how they died about the same time." His voice is soft, tinged with sadness. "Bloody waste, hey?"

Cassie is quiet. Matt is aware of the sound of the surf, the warmth of the sun, the color of native wildflowers emerging from the green brush skirting the brow of the sand hills, and around the curve of the beach, the waves tumbling onto the white sand and then receding, leaving wet, shiny patches for a few seconds before vanishing. *Life.*

"Growing up here is a hell of a gift, Cassie. When I really think about it and take time to look, everyday, here is the opportunity to experience life in its purist form, what it must have been like in the very beginning. I want to write about all this some day," says Matt, his arm sweeping a wide arc over the beach.

"Yes, well, you make sure you get all the paperwork in for the competition," says Cassie, cupping her head in her hand as she delights in the sensuality of curling her toes in the warm sand. "The monsignor is going to a lot of trouble for you."

"I'm having a go, that's for sure. Hey, I brought the poem like I promised; want to hear it?"

"Yes, I want to hear it, my dear, later." She pulls him to her and nuzzles his ear. "I want you to read it to me, Mr. Ryan," she says, lightly kissing his neck, tasting the salt on his skin. "But first, I want you to kiss me."

He laughs, takes her head in his hands, and gently kisses her lips.

"I love you," she whispers, rolling onto his chest, crying out with delight as the rush of heat through her body responds to his growing ardor.

"I love you, Matt. I will always love you."

14

The lovers burst from the water and sprint across the sand to their towels where they collapse kissing, laughing, and hugging. Then Cassie, with a cry of sheer joy, leaps to her feet and launches into a routine of classical ballet movements: *arabesques, pirouettes, fouettés,* and *entrechats,* all of which are extremely erotic and provocative to a delighted Matthew Ryan. She leaps, kicks, and stretches with uninhibited abandon.

He claps enthusiastically, enthralled, aroused again. She leaps on him and crushes her lips against his, panting from her rigorous choreography. She sits up and straddles him. "Phew, I need a little more conditioning, especially for Sydney. Okay, my darling, now down to business, read me your poem."

"Right." Matt reaches into his backpack and brings out a burgundy leather journal. He leafs through the pages and stops at the one with a title at the top, "Life."

"I was going to send this in for the competition, but already I feel inspired to write a new piece. It's in here," he says, pointing to his head and then his heart, "and here."

"C'mon, Mister, read."

As he reads, she is drawn to his eyes scanning the lines, *beautiful,* watching them sparkle through changing shades of blue, reflecting the contrasting colors of the sea and sky.

"A smoldering passion, long sought,
  Is rekindled to consume its captor—"

Those lips, soft and full, mouthing the words like he is making love to every- one of them. She feels the urge to reach out and stroke them.

"But the breath of Vesta

Fans flame already raging—"

God, I love him. His handsome face perfectly framed in that wild mop of hair, and there, the hint of sadness, the vulnerability that makes me want to hold him and smother him with kisses.

"For who dares shun acceptance of Life

Finds aught but misery—Death!"

He looks up from the journal, grinning self-consciously. "So, what do you reckon?"

She launches herself at him, pushing him back onto the sand, crushing her lips against his again, kissing him until she is panting for breath. "I love you, Matt. I love you."

He squirms under her weight and then pushes both of them back into a sitting position on the towels. "Whoa. I love you, too, but the sand—it's hot."

"Oh, I'm sorry, I forgot; I had to kiss you." She reaches around to brush the sand off his back. "I think you are brilliant. "Life" might be a little too esoteric for the competition judges, though."

"Yeah, I told the monsignor I wasn't real sure about it." He winks mischievously. "After today, though, the one I have in mind should heat up some of the old stuffed shirts a bit. I'll either win the competition, or they'll toss it out for being too graphic." He laughs and tickles her under the chin. "I'll have it done before you leave for Sydney, and you can tell me what you think."

The last sentence sends a knife into his heart. *Sweet Jesus, how am I going to live without her?*

"I'll miss you; I want you with me. You know you have to get away, whatever; you have to develop your talent, and it won't happen staying here. The monsignor tells you all the time." She attempts to imitate the priest, "'Ye've been blessed, Matthew Ryan. Ye need ta get away ta learn more, ta get out into the world, and share yer gift.'"

He laughs, a happy kid's laugh—joyful. "You're funny when you do that, too British to be Irish, though."

"Hey, I'm an Aussie, mate, and proud of it." She laughs and then becomes suddenly earnest. "I want to be with you, my darling, for the rest of my life. I love you."

Matt is about to reply when he glimpses a flash of light from the top of the sand hills.

"Get dressed, Cassie, quickly. Somebody is spying on us; I'm going after them."

"No, Matt, it doesn't matter." He is already running toward the dunes. "By the time you get there, whoever or whatever will be long gone," she shouts after him.

Matt is in no mood to ignore a peeping tom. *Jordan*. He reaches the top of the first sand hill, panting furiously. Nothing! Back on the beach, Cassie is dressed and hurrying toward the sandy track leading up to the parked vehicles.

A loud roar startles him. A cloud of dust swirls around a black motorbike as it slews to a stop beside Cassie's truck, seventy meters away.

Matt's face, already flushed from the tough sprint up the sand hill, turns blood red with anger. With a wild, primordial howl, he charges toward his enemy and is about to launch his attack when Cassie tops the sand hill. Immediately, she takes in the situation—Jordan sitting astride his bike, stunned, immobilized by the maniac steaming toward him.

"Matt!" screams Cassie. "Stop, now!"

As if a brick wall had suddenly shot up in front of him, Matt props and stops. He stares at Jordan, nostrils flaring, eyes cold and hostile, sweat streaming over his heaving frame.

"What on earth has gotten into you, Matt?" yells Cassie.

"That prick brother of yours was spying on us," shouts the still war-ready warrior. "He'll go running to your dad, spilling his guts."

"What's he on about, sis, hmm?" interjects Jordan, gaining courage from his sister's power over Matt. "Have you two been at it, what?"

Cassie and Matt look at each other. Matt curses, realizing the stupidity of his behavior. *Jesus, will I ever get anything right?* "I'm sorry, Cassie." Reluctantly, he looks back to Jordan. "Sorry, Jordan, I thought?"

"Well, well, look at the two of you. You're right, Ryan; Dad's just going to love hearing about this. His prized daughter screwing on the beach like a minx with some nobody, a feral Irish kid," taunts Jordan. "Yes, somebody was spying on you. No, it wasn't me, but I'm sure Mad Tom will have another tale to tell at next week's left-legger's[21] stir. Well, don't let me keep you." He restarts his motorbike, and with a mock British salute, roars away.

Matt and Cassie watch in silence until he disappears over the scrubby ridge.

"I'm sorry; I stuffed up the best bloody day of my life."

She smiles and studies her magnificent warrior. "No, no," she says, drawing him tightly to her. "This has been the most wonderful day of my life, too, Matt."

He holds her tight. "What about your dad? He's going—"

"Shh, I'll handle him," she says, holding a finger to his lips.

He kisses her. "You are wonderful."

They watch the sun sink below the horizon. "Time to go; I want to be home before Jordan. I'll talk to him; he's not bad all the time. In fact, you and he have more in common than you realize. He's been hurt, too, and like you, he's so damn impulsive."

"I'd like to believe that, but he's got a malicious streak in him, Cassie. You watch out, and if you have any trouble, I want to know about it. By the way, there's the church barn dance coming up next Saturday at Gosse. I'll call during the week."

"Yes and just you keep at your writing, my glorious Irish bard," she says, laughing and kissing him hard one last time. "You *will* write a great novel."

"I'm an Aussie, mate," he counters, mimicking her earlier claim on the beach. She laughs and swings into the truck, starts the engine, blows him a kiss, and roars off along the bush track, heading for Middle River.

As the red taillights disappear over the ridge, Matt tries to ignore the icy breath of anxiety beginning to blow through his stomach. "Bugger 'em."

He walks to his bike. "Let's make a call on Tom, shall we?"

---

[21] Leftlegger: Slang for Irish Catholic.

15

By the time Matt's bike is bouncing over the steel cattle grid entrance to Mad Tom's property, the last of the day's light is gone. He speeds by the two massive white posts set to each side of the grid, past the white rail fences angling off for a couple of meters before they slot into the heavy strainer[22] posts, where, attached to the strainers, wire fences run into the darkness to surround the property and mark its boundary. *Nice work, Tom,* notes Matt, a common thought every time he visits the farm. Despite Tom's lack of care and attention to his personal appearance, his farm, the way he runs it, is one of the island's best, second only to the Baldwin station at Middle River.

The bike's headlight lights up the dirt track leading to Tom's homestead. Wallabies[23] scatter, disturbed from their nocturnal routine, feeding on the pastures beyond the tall Norfolk pines lining the 200-meter-long driveway. As he rounds the final curve, he shuts the motor off and lets the bike roll to a silent stop at the gate of the homestead yard. A cicada's grating shrill breaks through the silence for a few seconds and then stops abruptly. A slight breeze rustles through the leaves of the eucalyptus trees scattered about the darkened house. His eyes flick to the treetops and beyond, to the black, inky black sky, background to a million sparkling gems—the Milky Way and the Southern Cross. *Awesome,* he thinks and then turns his attention back to the house.

"Bit early for him to be in bed," he mutters as he opens the gate and

---

[22] Strainer: Big, strong posts used to take the strain of taut wire at the beginning, end, and corners of a wire fence.
[23] Wallabies: Australian marsupial; small kangaroo.

quietly walks to the veranda. A chill runs up and down his spine. *Gotta be around somewhere.* He steps onto the porch and reaches out to knock on the door when a barely audible squeak, like the sound of the wheel rounding a poorly greased section of axle, causes his heart to miss a beat.

"Looking for me?" says a gravelly voice from the darkness.

Matt squints into the gloom and just makes out Mad Tom sitting in his favorite chair, rocking slowly back and forth, his head tilted toward the treetops. A red glow grows as Tom takes a hit from his pipe.

"Why don't you pull up a chair?"

"Christ, Tom," says Matt, as he reaches and pulls a chair from where it rests against the homestead wall. He drags it alongside Tom and cautiously sits down. "Frightened the crap out of me, you did; do you have to be so bloody creepy?"

"Who's being creepy? You can hear everything for miles on a night like this. Listen for a moment; hear the surf hitting the beach out there? Nothing like sitting out here, quiet-like, and just thinking, see. A bloke spends too much time running around like a blue arse'd fly and never takes enough time to think, to maybe give a little thanks to the Big Bloke each day for all he's given him."

Tom gets up from his chair, walks behind Matt, stops and bends down to whisper in his ear. "Especially for a young bloke like yourself, who had a beaut time of it today, hey?" He straightens and moves on toward the refrigerator at the far end of the veranda, against the wall. He takes out four stubbies,[24] crosses back to Matt, and holds out two of them. "Here, get these into you, young fella. After all the energy you've given up today, you'll feel better for it, hey?"

Matt ignores the offer and continues staring out into the yard. "So it was you peeping on us today. Bit bloody sick, isn't it, spying on people like that?"

Except for the sound of his breathing, Mad Tom is quiet, unmoving. The hair on the back of Matt's neck tingles. The noise from the rustling leaves, stirred again by the gentle southerly breeze slowly taking over the warm air, is magnified a thousand times to the tense young man.

---

[24] Stubbies: Small bottles of beer.

Eventually, after a few long seconds, Tom snorts, draws up a mouthful of phlegm, swirls it about his mouth, and then spits in a well-practiced fashion into the darkness beyond the verandah. He steps to the side of Matt's chair and bends over to look him square in the eye.

"Now, there's no need to be rude, young fella. The truth is I didn't watch but a few seconds," he says, offering the stubbies again. "I knew what you was up to, see. Mate, you're like a son to me, and I like that Baldwin girl, always did; she's a fighter and a classy young lass, too. Pity she's not a Catholic, but that's not as important today as it was in my time. There's a lot of good coming your way, lad, just don't stuff it up. And as I just said, I didn't hang about perving on ya, as you put it. Besides, I could hear Jordan's bike coming, which is why I flashed you with me glasses, to warn ya, see."

Matt begins to relax, sighs with relief, takes the stubbies from Tom, pops the lid on one and takes a long swig of the cold liquid. In an instant, the amber magic hits the spot. "Thanks, Tom," he says, pausing to take another drink. "Yeah, I had a run-in with him after he showed up. I don't think he saw anything, but he threatened to tell his oldman we were at it, anyway. Cassie's gone after him. He told me he reckoned it was you, so he wasn't crapping about that. Damn it, Tom, I don't want this to get out."

"Well, you need to find a more private spot in the future. Other people besides you go down there, see, and they're usually locals. No, I won't be saying anything to anyone, but God knows who Jordan will talk to when he's on the grog. He was an uppity enough young pup before nearly killing himself, but now he's a lot worse. It's like he's on a suicide quest." Tom lifts the stubby to his lips. "What a bloody waste, if you ask me; and what's worse is that the rotten little twerp doesn't seem to give a damn what trouble he causes others who cross his path, either."

Tom takes a long draw on his pipe, and then slowly releases the smoke, watching it drift off into infinity. "Bloody awful, it is; you can see it wearing away at his oldman. It's a good thing Cassie is around, but she'll be gone soon. He will miss her, that's for sure."

"I'll second that, it's going to be bloody rough without her around the place." His stomach takes a couple of turns as he thinks of Cassie's fast approaching departure. "Tom, how come you never got married? I mean, well, don't you—don't you get lonely sometimes?"

"No. No, I'm never alone, Matt, the bloke upstairs is always around, see? Anyway, there's plenty of life going on about me all the time, so I really don't miss—" Tom's voice fades as he recalls a time when there was someone in his life. He was young then. She was a beautiful Irish Catholic girl with a full head of long, red hair and the bluest eyes, so powerful, so penetrating, that when she flashed them at him, he would have died for her there and then if she had asked him. It took him a long time to get over his hatred of God after he watched her waste away from the cancer. A few tears find their way down the weathered cheeks of the tough old bachelor. He reaches down to the verandah floor, replaces the empty stubby with a full one, takes a long swallow, regains his composure, and turns to Matt.

"Take a flower—have you ever picked one up and for a moment looked, really looked at how it's put together, taken a close gander?[25] Well, next time you pick one up, look closely for the myriad colors that make up its unique hue; it's a flaming miracle, see." Tom's enthusiasm builds. "Ever wonder about the delicacy of its composition, huh, so vulnerable? Yet, no matter what nature throws at it, see: storms, fires, whatever, it comes back to charm us year after year with subtle, seductive fragrances that tease our senses and stir our emotions, turn on our desire to love, hey, Matt?" He chuckles, obviously happy to be part of it all.

"Jeez, you could be a bloody a poet, Tom. Beautiful, mate, beautiful. I never get sick of looking at what's around us here, blessed we are; this has to be the best place in the world, hey."

They both sit silent, drawing in the extraordinary night, the young man and the old bachelor, surrendering to the soothing coolness of the evening breeze brushing lightly over exposed skin, each lost in his own thoughts, but in this most exquisite of settings, as one in their experience of God's grace.

Mad Tom suddenly chuckles. "You know, that girl of yours is a looker, hey? What I saw—the two of you together, pure art, pure bloody art, hey?

---

[25] Gander: Australian slang for "a look."

She can dance a bit, too."

Matt looks at Tom with a wry smile creeping across his face. "You saw a bit more than you let on." He laughs, "You are a perv, you old bugger, aren't you? Bit of a romantic, too. Yeah, I bet you had a few ladies charmed up in your time, Tom." He chuckles as he lifts the lid of the second stubby, the amber fluid from the first successfully killing the gut worms, replacing them with a warming 'all is well.' "Cassie's a looker all right," Matt says, beaming.

16

"Good evening, Cassandra," says Monty Baldwin as he hears Cassie enter the huge living room from the kitchen. He is sitting in his favorite armchair, looking up at the portrait of his late wife, Kristina. "How was your afternoon?" Cassie places a pitcher of iced water and two glasses on the coffee table adjacent to Monty's chair.

"Mummy loved this room," she says, looking at her father and sensing his loneliness. When Kristina was alive, this was where family and friends gathered for chats, parties, performances, games and fun. He missed that, she knew. Now, in this great room, the life-size painting of her dead mother reminding him of what once was, and about to lose another of his loves, his daughter—the child who carried him through the pain of his greatest tragedy—he looks older and terribly vulnerable.

"She did, she did, indeed, but no point dwelling on that; tell me about your day. Come on now, tell me."

She smiles warmly, and then laughs gaily and dances to the back of his chair and throws her arms around his neck, smothering him with kisses and hugs.

"Oh, it was wonderful, Daddy; I went to Cape Kersaint. It was hot, but the water was cool, and I went for a swim. Matt met me there, and we talked and danced on the sand and talked and—the sea was beautiful. The air was filled with the smell of wild flowers and salt and pure—it was all so—alive, vibrant—like dancing in the arms of God."

Monty stiffens. His head fills with chatter and the old images of the early days with Kristina. *My God, she is no longer my child. She is a woman. She's* been with the Ryan boy on the beach, just like Kristina and—*my God.*

Monty's thoughts are a stream of overlapping voices and images. He frees himself from the arms of his daughter and hurries to the open front door, desperate for fresh air.

Cassie follows, concerned and confused. "Daddy, what's wrong? Are you all right? Can I get you something?"

"Yes, um, please, some water," he replies, hardly daring to look at her.

She returns to the coffee table, pours a glass of water, and brings it to Monty. "Here, Daddy, drink this."

He drains the glass in one gulp. "Thank you, Cassandra. I'm sorry—I—it's just that sometimes you become your mother; you bring her back to the here and now."

"You scared me, Daddy. I know you have been worrying a lot, lately. I worry about leaving you here alone; perhaps this is not the best time to be going."

"That, my dear girl, is the last thing you ought to be thinking." *The last thing; I have to get you away from here, away from that Ryan boy. Hell, he's all right for a kid brought up as he has been, but he has a ton of problems that are going to grow with him. He's not right for you. And the alcohol, the curse of the Irish—look at the father and see the son. Hell, no. Not my Cassandra, not on my bloody watch.*

"Tell me, Daddy, when you—truly love someone—and you want to live with them for the rest of your life—"

"Not now, Cassandra. Not now," interjects Monty, angry about where his daughter's conversation is heading. "The important question now is how you can best develop the talent you inherited from your mother. And that, it seems to me, is to follow through with the dance company in Sydney."

"Yes, of course; I love to dance, you know that. But can't it be both?"

"It can, but later, later on. You have to develop—focus. You cannot divide your attentions. And besides, you will meet people from all walks of life who have much more to offer than—"

"Matt," she cries out. "Oh, Daddy, what are you saying? You taught me to respect people for who they are, to look into their hearts. Matt is beautiful and talented and sensitive and, yes, as deeply wounded by the loss of his mother as we are by mine. He is a good, good man. He stays here to protect his brothers." Her voice grows more strident by the word. "He is courageous, and I love him, and I will always love him."

"Enough, enough for now, Cassandra, before we say things we regret," says Monty, almost shouting, something he rarely does.

The ringing of the phone interrupts. They look at each other. "Jordan," says Monty. "What now?"

"I'll get it," says Cassie. She goes into the living room and picks up the portable phone from the small writing table next to Monty's armchair. "Hello? Yes, it is." She listens. "Is he all right, Constable?"

Monty, who followed Cassie back into the room, is worried. "Is it Jordan?"

Cassie nods. Minutes pass as she listens to Dunning. Finally, she says, "Okay, thank you, Constable. In the morning then. Okay." She returns the phone to its cradle.

"What is it? What happened?"

"That was the new constable, Daddy. Everything is under control. Jordan's not hurt, other than a few bruises." She throws her hands in the air in hopelessness.

"Well, tell me, where is he? What about the police? What did Bob Dunning say? Is he in jail?"

"Not yet, but he will be. Constable Dunning called from the Parndana Community Club. He is taking Jordan to the Kingscote jail for the night. Apparently, he reached over the bar and hit David Hill, the manager on duty tonight, after he refused to serve Jordan another whiskey. Some of the other drinkers grabbed him and tried to eject him, but he went crazy and knocked over old Rosy Fahey, who was carrying a tray of drinks to her table. Beer went flying everywhere, and her boys got mad and began to rip into Jordan. Someone called the police in Kingscote. They contacted Constable Dunning, who was already in the area heading south. Anyway, he's got Jordan handcuffed and said we can pick him up in the morning after a court hearing."

Monty seems to age another year as he shuffles to his armchair.

Damn you, Jordan, Cassie thinks. Anger and disgust mix in a perplexity of love, compassion, and deep concern for her brother and father.

"Daddy, sit there; I'll make us some tea."

Monty appears not to hear. "Last night trouble, again tonight. Why whiskey? I have told him—stick to the beer, and you won't get into trouble. I've told him that over and over," says Monty in a voice barely audible.

"It's not just the whiskey, Daddy. If it were beer, it would be the same result. Jordan is sick, mentally and emotionally sick and an alcoholic. I am afraid for him, for others around him, and for us. Look at you, sick with worry; we have to do something. I am afraid we are going to have to have him committed."

Monty looks up at Cassie, who has moved to the leather sofa next to him. "No, Cassandra, no. We are family, and family takes care of its own. I'll call his brother when he gets back from Europe next week; see if he can spend a few days here after you've gone. Tomorrow, you go to Kingscote and pick up Jordan, and I'll go down to Stumpy Flats with Harry and get on with the crutching." [26]

"Didn't you tell Harry to go out to the scrub line tomorrow to repair that hole in the fence at Jumpy Creek?"

Monty nods. "Damn it, I did."

"Don't worry, I'll call him tonight and tell him to come straight to the homestead. Well, I'd better get the smokos[27] and lunch ready; Jordan won't be here to take care of that, of course."

Monty looks across at his daughter. *So like Kristina. Not afraid of work, and a good organizer. Thank God, there is the dancing to get her out into the world and away from—*

"Come here, daughter," he commands. "Give your father a hug."

---

[26] Crutching: The removal of soiled wool from around the crotch area of sheep; usually a twice-a-year task undertaken by professional shearers.

[27] Smoko: These are two periods during the eight-hour shearing day, one in the morning and one in the afternoon, when the shearers take a half-hour break in the middle of their four-hour morning and afternoon work periods (called runs). The property owner at smoko provides tea, cakes, and sandwiches.

Cassie gently places her arms around his neck, pressing her cheek against his face. She feels the roughness of his whiskers against the smoothness of her skin, a familiar sensation that rushes her mind to the days after her mother's death, when she would settle in his lap in the evenings, arms around him, trying to lessen the pain of his loss and hers.

"Cassandra," he whispers into her ear. "I'm sorry; I want what's best for you. Go to Sydney, work hard, and let destiny guide you. If it is God's will you be with this boy, there's nothing can stop it."

Cassie runs her fingers through the old man's thinning hair and kisses his forehead. "Yes, and you just make sure you don't think you're God."

They study each other for a moment. Monty shakes his head and sees again Kristina's steely determination reflected in the steady brown eyes of his daughter.

"I am powerless," he says, struggling for a touch of levity. "I am at the mercy of a goddess."

17

Matt yawns, rolls over in his bed, opens his eyes, and squints into the early morning sun, splashing a swath of bright light across the bedroom. The alarm clock is showing 7:30. *I better get over to Humpy before Dunning shows up.*

Kicking back the blankets, he slides out of bed and crosses to the open window. Stretching away to the southeast, a panorama of color highlights the separation of land from the sea through a pattern of greens, rusty browns, and myriad blues. Remarkable Rocks, the ever-present symbol of the island's enduring character, its precarious balancing act splendidly captured in the morning sparkle, stands prominent on the balding granite cliff of distant Kilpatrick Point. Beyond, the Southern Ocean floods to the horizon, where it gives way to the powder blue pastel and orange tint of the new day sky.

Exhilarated, Matt draws in a deep breath of fresh air, stretches his arms above his head, rolls his upper body around the axis of his hips, and slowly releases the air from his lungs—his regular routine most mornings, a series of exercises for ten minutes, a shower, and then breakfast.

Katherine is already busy in the kitchen. "Morning, Matthew. I've put on some eggs and bacon for your father and the boys; I can throw a couple on for you, if you'd like."

"No, thanks, Katherine; I'll stick to my usual." He fills a bowl of favorite cereal, muesli, and then drowns it a with a princely helping of fresh, full cream milk pulled from the 'tits' of the family cow, Maria, that Katherine milks every morning.

"Your father will be in shortly. He wants to talk to you about getting Humpy sorted out."

"I bet he does," he says slicing up a banana, the pieces dropping onto his muesli. His brothers burst into the kitchen.

"Good morning," says Katherine. "It's about time you boys showed up. Your eggs are cooking, and the sandwiches are on the sideboard, over there. Pack them in your schoolbags before you forget; you have ten minutes before it's time to leave. Did you do your hair, Sean? I think not. Come here." Almost in one movement, a brush is in her hand, and she is sweeping it through the young boy's blond hair.

The boys pack the sandwiches into their schoolbags and then rush to the table, impatient for breakfast. Katherine sets three plates. "Frank, get in here; your eggs are done," she calls through the open kitchen door.

"Did you and Cassie kiss?" a cheeky and giggling Sean asks Matt.

Katherine sweeps two eggs from the frying pan with the egg slice and slips them onto the heavily buttered toast on Sean's plate. "Mind your tongue and eat this up quickly. You'll be a lucky boy one day if you can find a nice girl like Miss Baldwin."

"Do you love her?" says an undeterred Sean.

"Yeah, I do," says Matt, grinning, "but you'd better concentrate on getting that breakfast into you; we have to leave for the school bus pretty soon, so get busy."

"Yeah, well love is all well and good," says Frank Ryan as he enters the kitchen, "but you are not their kind, fella. Oldman Baldwin won't have a bar of you joining his uppity mob,[28] so as I've said before, you'd be better off forgetting about her."

"Oh sure, that's what you'd like, isn't it? Can't stand the idea of anyone being even a little bit happy, hey?" says Matt, keeping his anger under control for the sake of family peace. "Just let it go, hey? I have to get the boys to the school bus, and then back to Humpy before Dunning arrives."

---

[28] "Bar of you joining his uppity mob:" Australian slang for "won't have you as part of their privileged class/family."

"Right, I wanted to talk about that." Frank had obviously continued drinking all through Sunday after Dunning and Woodson left. *Serves him right*, Matt thinks. *Once he's on it, he never stops, until—*

"I heard it on the two-way this morning. That idiot Jordan got into some bother at the club last night, shooting his mouth off and whacking Davo from over the bar. The copper got him and locked him up in the Kingscote police cells. Yeah, young Dunning it was; I got a bit of time for him, but he'll have his hands full at this morning's court hearings, so my guess is he won't be out until this afternoon. Good thing for you, seeing as you got out of bed so bloody late this morning."

Matt holds his tongue and ignores the gibe. He is relieved that the coppers aren't coming out, but his mind is occupied with Cassie and the other problem with Jordan. *If he says anything to old Monty, I'll have his nuts.* He looks at the kitchen clock and then at the boys. "Come on, you blokes, time to get moving. Tom's driving the bus this morning, but he can't wait if we're late; you know that."

He scoffs down the last of his cereal, gets up from the table, and starts heading for the kitchen door. "See ya, Katherine, thanks for breakee. Let's go, you blokes." The two boys stuff down what is left of their breakfast and chase after him.

"Hey, what about a thank you here, Matt? I work bloody hard to put tucker on the table for you blokes," Frank calls after him. But Matt is already out the door and out of earshot.

"Ungrateful piece of work."

"Perhaps if you weren't drunk most of the time, Frank, and going off at him the way you do, he would appreciate you more," says Katherine hurrying after the boys.

From under the shade of the back verandah, she waves as they leave, calling, "Drive carefully, Matthew; and you boys, behave yourselves." They wave back, Sean distinguished by the cheeky grin spreading across his face. Katherine's eyes follow the trail of dust rising from behind the Landcruiser as it twists and turns through the green carpet all the way to the top of the distant plateau, until it disappears from view, and it is only a couple more kilometers to the ranger's cottage, the turnaround point for the Parndana school bus. "Keep my boys safe, Lord, all three of them."

"Katherine. Katherine, hurry up, luv. We've got the place to ourselves; time for a little bit of the old slap and tickle, hey?"

She sighs and walks toward the kitchen door. "Coming, Frank, coming."

18

Cassie slows the Pathfinder as she enters the outskirts of the island's main town, Kingscote. The morning had been hectic—up at five and into the kitchen to get the food ready for the day's crutching. Good old Harry arrived early and helped feed the horses. She told Monty not to worry about Jordan; she would pick him up and bring him to Stumpy Flats, where he could work off his hangover penning sheep for the crutchers. He had apologized for being unusually curt with her in what little conversation they had time for that morning. Jordan was occupying most of the space in his head.

We have to get him out of here and into treatment. She swings right at the top of the town's main access road, where the new recreation center dominates the intersection's northwest corner; the most popular building after the pubs, it is a reminder of the generosity of the principal donor, fisherman Sammy Marino. From there, the road drops down the hill and into the seaside village of Kingscote, population around 1,750 permanent residents and expanding to many times that during the tourist season. The town nestles in the top part of the western curve of Nepean Bay. The shoreline sweeps away to the east and arcs to the north, where the red bluffs and sandy beaches turn sharply toward the town of Penneshaw, and where the waters of Backstairs Passage separate the eastern end of the island from the mainland, 18 kilometers apart.

"I love this place."

At the bottom of the hill, she turns right again and drives slowly along the town's main street. The locals are already well into the business of their new day: picking up mail from the post office, lining up for coffee and newspapers at the Deli, chatting with friends, opening stores and sweeping clean the pavements. Islanders, blessed to be living in the thriving country town of Kingscote, Kangaroo Island, still, in these modern times, one of the world's best kept secrets, a consensus sentiment common to most locals and visitors alike. The smell of fresh sea air, pastry, and coffee floats through the cab of Cassie's truck. The dashboard's LCD clock flips over to 8:45, fifteen minutes before Jordan's court appearance, just enough time to meet with the constable before the hearing. *After.* She drives through the next intersection to the police station.

Bob Dunning is at his desk looking through the front window when the truck pulls into the curb in front of the police station. *Wow.* As Cassie steps out, he notes how the light blue blouse she is wearing tucks neatly into the narrow waistband of her tight fitting moleskin pants, accentuating the very feminine line of her slim body. *So, you're Cassie Baldwin. Woodson's got it right for once; you, my dear, are a honey pot. Spectacular.*

The tall, young constable holds open the front door and greets the natural beauty with a beaming smile. "You must be Jordan's sister. I'm Bob Dunning."

"That's right, Constable," she says, an edge of frustration to her voice. "I'm Cassie Baldwin. I'm a few minutes early, I know, but I was hoping I could have a few words with you before the hearing starts."

"Of course, and call me Bob. This way; it's a little more private out back." He ushers her along a narrow corridor to a small interview room at the back of the building. "The boss, Sergeant Woodson—I believe you may have met him; he certainly knows your father—would have been here, but he went to the airport to pick up the superintendent from Adelaide HQ, and then, well, they are probably already on their way south to the Chase, so I'm left here to take care of today's cases. Fortunately, there are only two, and Jordan's is the second one."

Dunning turns on the fluorescents and offers Cassie a seat on one of the three chairs set around a bare table under a small window set high in the wall.

"Interrogation room?"

Cassie might have been less caustic in her comment were it not for her thoughts about Woodson on his way to Flinders Chase. Matt told her Dunning was coming out, though all she got was his usual evasiveness when she asked why, as if she didn't know and didn't care either for that matter. She remains standing.

"Sorry," says Dunning, a little taken aback by the sudden, icy tone in Cassie's question. "This is all we have unless I use the sergeant's office, and that is rather a mess, I'm afraid."

"Why doesn't that surprise me?" *Oh, yes, I've met your sergeant—the day he came out to the property to meet with Daddy. A chill shudders along her spine. Practically undressed me when Daddy was looking the other way. Horrible little creature. Yes, I've met your sergeant, all right.*

"Now, Constable, tell me how we can get this matter cleared up. My father wants him out of here today. Jordan is sick; I think he is an addict and needs treatment. The family will take full responsibility for him."

Christ, straight to the point, thinks Dunning, still unnerved by her beauty. *I'm glad she's not a prosecutor; get on the wrong side of her, and she'd rip you to pieces.*

Dunning forces himself back to his role of policeman, already under the beauty's spell. "I booked him for disorderly conduct, not disastrous. David Hill, the club manager, did not want to press charges for assault, so that saved us from a more serious situation. I think we can get the magistrate to let him off with a warning, a fine, and damages. You should be on your way in no time. But you are right, Ms. Baldwin; he needs treatment. He'll be getting himself or someone else into very serious trouble if he goes on behaving this way."

Cassie begins to warm to the young constable. "Thank you. I am a little frustrated right now, worried about Jordan and my dad—so forgive my bad manners. And call me Cassie, please."

"No worries; I understand. I was at King's College around the time Jordan was there. We weren't in class together, but on the same football team. Maybe we can get together and talk about it sometime; I would like to help." He glances at his watch. "Oops, I'm already late for the first case, and I don't want to upset the magistrate. You can come in, if you like."

"Okay, but can I use your phone to make a quick call, first?"

Dunning grins, "Cassie, I called Frank Ryan to let him know that the sergeant was on his way out to du Couedic earlier. Katherine Ryan told me about you and Matt. So, I guess your call might be to Matt, uh? Well, not to worry, I met him yesterday, liked him right off. I'd like to help keep him out of trouble, and he might be heading that way from what the sergeant tells me."

"Your sergeant's full of bull, Bob, and I think you know it. Matt's had a tough life, but he is a good person, just ask Katherine or his stepbrothers."

"Whoa, I'm on your side. The whole family could do with a break or two; they have a lot to deal with in Frank." Dunning grins. "Still want to use the phone?"

"No thank you, Bob." She laughs. "I already like you."

19

The light blue sedan scatters ironstone gravel and sends up clouds of dust as it slides around the corner leading away from the ranger's cottage toward Cape du Couedic. The distinctive yellow school bus from the Parndana school is stopped at the front gate of the cottage where a group of the Chase kids are climbing aboard, among them the Ryan boys. Matt and the bus driver, Mad Tom, are chatting.

Good, a break, thinks Woodson, *I'm ahead of him.* His goal is to get out to the Chase early before the kid has a chance to destroy evidence, but Woodson is far from happy. In the passenger seat, his boss from Adelaide HQ, Chief Superintendent Holloway, is on the island doing the quarterly appraisal, his appraisal. Because of his probationary status, a result of disciplinary measures imposed for suspected cattle-duffing[29] activities at his previous posting in the southeast of South Australia, but for which there was not enough evidence for charges, he was demoted and sent to the island for a chance to rehabilitate his career. Holloway informs Woodson the reports about his progress are not good and warns that unless he sees major improvement in the next quarter, he will be back in Adelaide, hosing out cellblocks at the city lock up.

The sergeant is especially anxious with the superintendent along to find the suspected poppy plot before the Ryans clean it up. "That was the Ryan kid back there, boss. We get him and his oldman, Frank, it'll be a major blow to the Rosenblum cultivation and procurement operation, and, I believe, Sam

---

[29] Cattle-duffing: Term used for stealing livestock from the properties of farmers and graziers.

Marino, the fishing bloke from Victoria."

Woodson knows a big bust could get him back onside with the department. *Today is looking real good; that plot is out here somewhere, and my guess is it's in that basin we saw yesterday.* He pushes the accelerator closer to the floor. *Could not have timed it better myself with the super along for the ride.*

"Hey, slow down, Sergeant, or you'll finish up wrecking a new police car, and that'll get you in a hell've lot more trouble than you're in now, I can tell you that."

The warning is a few seconds too late. The car is already sliding on the ironstone rubble when Woodson catches sight of the fresh bike track heading into the scrub toward the area of suspected crop location. *Damn, someone's already in there—bloody Frank.* Then, Woodson makes an error no Islander raised driving on ironstone roads would ever make, he hits the brakes and swings violently toward the track.

Forces are now operating beyond the control of its driver; sliding sideways at almost a hundred kilometers per hour, the vehicle ploughs into the heavy gravel curb lining the edge of the road. The sedan lifts up and over its left front wheel, corkscrews into the air and rolls, crushing the roof and continuing to roll a second and third time, before finally coming to rest, upside down, deep in the bush.

The superintendent's last and momentary view before everything becomes a tumbling, noisy crunching of metal and breaking glass, is of the spectacular Remarkable Rocks, balancing precariously on their granite base at the edge of a very blue Southern Ocean.

A dreadful silence descends as the dust gradually settles. A few minutes pass, and then the stillness is broken by the raucous cawing of black crows arriving, one at a time, to settle in the surrounding branches of the stringy bark trees, their eager eyes checking out the wreck.

20

Frank is wary, a trifle jumpy, as he approaches the poppy cultivation site at Humpy Creek. He cuts the motorbike's engine and stops a few meters short of the canopied clearing. Sitting absolutely still astride the bike, he listens for any unusual sounds and studies the bush at the perimeter for any movement of leaves, animals, or birds that may signify a human presence. The phone call from Dunning, soon after the boys left for the school bus is a worry. *No reason for Dunning to give us a break; he seems a good bloke, but you can't be sure about coppers.*

Finally, satisfied all is clear, he picks up a half-bag of oats strapped to the back seat of the bike and carries it on his shoulder into the cleared area, checking the ground for any stray poppy material, plastic wrapping, cigarette butts—anything left behind from the last harvest that might incriminate them. A week had passed since the picking. *Good. Looks like we got it all. Bloody good thing we got 'em loaded onto Smokey Cloud Sat'dy night.* Still, the flowers he held back at the lighthouse for seed could have done them in if Woodson had come with a search warrant. *Mongrel.* The rain, the rooting of wild pigs and an assortment of animal tracks had left the ground looking like similar clearings found all over the park. Only the plastic hoses, fertilizer, and camouflage nets in the humpy could give them up. *There'll be nothing for Woodson to find after I dump that lot off the cliff.*

Frank is struggling with a small piece of the humpy's corrugated iron roof, when a loud thump echoes through the ravine. "What the hell?" He cups an ear, listening intently. *That came from the road. They can't be here already, not unless he drove like a flaming idiot,* he thinks, looking at his watch.

He waits, motionless; a couple of minutes—nothing—no noise, no vehicle. *Better get my arse into gear.*

Using the materials from the humpy, he quickly throws together a wild pig trap. *Probably wouldn't hold a piglet, but it'll fool the coppers.* He scatters oats over the rooted ground and lays a trail into the center of the trap, where he drops the bag and what is left of the oats. After a quick ride to the cliff to dump the hoses, net, and fertilizer, he returns to make sure nothing has been missed that could land them in jail.

"Good, that should fix the buggers," he says, chuckling. "See if you can get me on anything here, boys." The old, mischievous sparkle in his blue eyes, a disarming characteristic before the war, the alcohol, and the nightmares returns as he delights in the thought of putting one over on Woodson.

The moment of levity passes as quickly as it came, and his throbbing headache returns with a vengeance. He pulls a bottle of Black Label brandy from the saddlebag and takes a long, deep swallow. In seconds, the headache is gone, and the icy hole in his gut thawed.

Pushing along the scrubby track at a brisk pace and attacking the occasional cluster of bulloak with an extra twist on the throttle, his cursing echoes through the ravine when a branch whips around his face. As he nears the main road, the crows lift out of the trees *en masse*, their screeching loud enough to be heard above the noise of the motorbike. "What the hell's going on?" *Something must be dead around here.* He stops when he sees the huge gouge in the gravel that leads into the scrub. *That wasn't there when I came in. Matt, where—*

"Oh, sweet Jesus," he cries, seeing the vehicle lying upside down, fifteen meters into the scrub. He slides quickly from the bike and starts running toward the car when the roar of a vehicle coming along the road behind stops him. A speeding truck crests the hill, rounds the bend, and sends ironstone pebbles flying as the driver sees the wreck and slams on the brakes.

Frank is relieved to see Matt jump from the driver's seat of the Landcruiser.

"What's happened? I saw the skid marks, and then the car on its roof in the scrub."

"You frightened the crap out of me; I thought for a minute—I don't know; I just got here."

"A car went past the cottage a while ago. I nearly had a heart attack thinking it might be the coppers, but it wasn't their car, looked like a hire car."

"Oh hell, it must be them. Dunning called after you left to say Woodson and his boss were on their way out. That's why I'm here, I cleaned up the poppy plot. Wait here while I take a look, this might not be pretty." Frank moves quickly over the flattened scrub and then pushes through a section of undisturbed bush. "Ah, damn." He crosses to the figure laying face down, the head shockingly crushed, and checks for a pulse, nothing. "It's all over for you, Superintendent."

The snapping of dry twigs coming from behind startles him. "I told you to stay back."

"I thought you might need some—" Matt sees the crushed head of the body dressed in a police uniform and freezes, his face ashen.

"This is a dead man, son. You may as well come here for a close look; it probably won't be the last one you'll see."

Matt is close to vomiting. "Hang in there, lad."

"It was the coppers then," says Matt, fighting to stay calm.

"Woodson must be in there." Frank moves quickly to the sedan. "It's him, all right, he's jammed up in here," he calls, reaching into the interior of the vehicle just as Woodson lets out a gasp of air. "He's alive, but barely—hanging upside down in his seat belt like a rag doll. Quick, come here, Matt, I need some help with this bloke."

He runs over to join Frank, looks into the front of the sedan and vomits.

"Easy, lad, easy; you're going to have to pull yourself together. We gotta get this bloke out of here in a hurry."

"I'll be okay," he says, wiping his mouth and rubbing his hands on his moleskins. "What do you want me to do?"

"I'm going to lift him and take some of the strain off the seat belt straps. As soon as the tension eases, get that buckle undone."

Frank strains to take Woodson's weight. As the tension on the belt eases, the heavy sergeant heaves a mouthful of blood over the struggling rescuers.

Matt grapples with the belt release buckle, his hands now slippery with blood. "I can't get it."

"Stay with me, lad, you're doing great," says Frank, grunting. "I'm going to give an extra heave. Concentrate—now."

Matt's fingers grip, and then push the catch. The belt comes apart, and Frank collapses under the weight of the falling victim, barely saving him from breaking his neck. They drag him carefully from the car onto the flattened brush, where he heaves again, a bubbly red froth spraying from his mouth.

"He's going to choke on his own blood if we don't get air to him," says Frank, turning the gasping Woodson's head to the side. "Get me a knife or screwdriver from the truck, whatever you can find, but be quick about it, or we'll lose him. And get a tube, like a straw—anything narrow and hollow."

Matt scampers to the truck and rummages through the toolbox. Frank is yelling for him to hurry. Fighting to stay calm, hands trembling, he eventually finds a long, thin electrical screwdriver with pointy ends. Desperately, he claws through the contents of the glove box and digs behind the seats looking for a hollow tube. God smiles—two dirty soda straws lie on the floor under the front seat. He scurries back to Frank and the ailing policeman.

In one deft movement, Frank punches into Woodson's throat with the sharp end of the screwdriver. Woodson's eyes open wide with terror, and he flays at his rescuer with his fists.

"Grab his arms and hold him; he thinks we're trying to kill him, though don't think I haven't thought of it."

Matt holds the severely weakened sergeant easily. Frank takes one of the straws and pushes it through the bleeding throat wound. With a horrible gurgling sound, the deathly pale patient begins sucking air into his lungs.

Matt looks at his father, amazed. Frank catches the look. "Picked it up with Special Forces in 'Nam," he says grimly. "Okay, let's get him to the truck; we'll have to lay him out in the back."

Both Ryan men are panting heavily by the time they get Woodson to the Landcruiser.

"How the hell are we going to get him up there? He's a big bugger."

"Get your breath back, and then we'll lift him," says Frank.

"I'll give it a go, but I don't like our chances; it's a big lift."

"We have to get him on the truck; it's his only chance. You ready?"

Matt nods and wraps his arms under Woodson's legs. As they lift, the sergeant tries to scream through the hole in his throat, causing the straw to fly out, hit Matt, and spray his face and shirt with blood. Woodson begins to slip from Matt's grip, but with instinct born of previous crises, Frank drops to his knees, takes the policeman's full weight, and with a mighty grunt heaves him onto the flatbed.

"The straw, boy. Quick, get me the straw."

Matt is coughing and hacking, on the verge of vomiting again. He desperately searches the ground around him.

"It's stuck on the front of your shirt—in the blood."

Matt grabs the straw and hands it to Frank. Woodson begins to shake all over.

"Damn, he's going into seizure." Frank pushes the straw into the hole. The tremors intensify, and Woodson starts hitting his head, arms, legs, and feet against the steel tray. Frank slips a woolpack under his head and pushes down on his shoulders. Gradually, as the policeman sucks air into his lungs, his tremors cease.

Matt is at the side of the Landcruiser, vomiting.

"C'mon, lad, pull yourself together; you have to drive. I'll do what I can for him, but we've got to get going."

Matt, a mess with blood and vomit covering his shirt, straightens. "Sorry. I'll be all right."

"You're doing bloody good, Matt; this is tough stuff to deal with. You'd better get on the radio, let the hospital know what's happened, and tell them to send the ambulance out; we'll meet 'em along the coast road. Tell 'em to hurry, for God's sake, this bloke's ready to croak."

Matt is already crashing through the gears of the Toyota as Frank lies down over his patient, determined to do his best to keep the bugger from dying. *Although, God knows, we'd all be better off if you were dead, Reggie.*

21

Jordan's disorderly conduct charge cost the family a heavy fine and an order for reimbursement, as expected, of costs to the community club for property damage. The local magistrate warned, in a lengthy dressing down of the wayward Baldwin, that he needed to adopt a more responsible attitude in keeping with the good reputation of his family, and that if he finished up in his court again, the consequences for his antisocial behaviors would be far more serious. He would find himself in jail, and there would be no appeal about it.

"I'll be outside," says Jordan, walking toward the police station's front door.

"Keep off the grog, Jordan, or you'll be back here again, and I won't be able to do much to help you."

"Nobody asked you, Dunning. Just keep your nose—"

"Shut up, Jordan. If it weren't for Bob Dunning, you'd be in jail for the next thirty days. Now, leave, and wait in the truck."

He glares at Cassie and, protesting under his breath, leaves.

"Sorry, Bob; he needs professional help. Daddy's talking about an intervention after Grant—he's my elder brother—gets back from Europe." She passes him the check to take care of the fine and damages.

"Alcoholism is a tough one on families, Cassie. I tried talking to Jordan earlier this morning, but he's never gotten over our school days at King. Maybe you and I can get together some time and—well, I might have a few ideas that could help—some people I know."

"That's kind of you, thanks. It'll need to be soon, though; I'm leaving the island in a couple of weeks to join the Australasian Modern Dance Company in Sydney."

"Yeah, I think I saw something in the *Islander* newspaper. Congratulations, what a hell of an achievement; make the Islanders proud, for sure. Doesn't surprise me, though, you certainly have the body to—your body looks, er, you have the perfect look."

She grins, enjoying his awkwardness. "Hard work and luck, but it's tough leaving the island. I don't think there is a more beautiful place in the world, agree?"

"There aren't many places left like this with their natural beauty intact after the white blokes get hold of it, but these people here—I like them; they look after the land pretty good." He hands her a receipt. "I'll be on duty at the barn dance at Gosse next Saturday night. If you're going, maybe we can catch up." The telephone rings, and then rings again. "I'd better get that. Excuse me a sec, will you?"

He picks up the phone. "Kingscote Police, Constable Dunning." As he listens, the smile on his face fades. "He's dead? Good Lord—the air ambulance is on the way, Kingscote, right. Do you know how bad he is? I see. Right. Frank Ryan and his son are bringing him in? Just off the du Couedic road. Okay, I'll notify headquarters. Listen, no one is to disturb the scene until— Yeah, of course, you can place a blanket over him. Don't let anybody tramp all over the place—right. Good, and tell them to take it easy on that road."

Dunning looks over to Cassie, his face pale. "This is bad, real bad. That was the hospital; the police car rolled over on the du Couedic road and the superintendent was killed." He pauses to take a deep breath. "And the sergeant's in a bad way; he might not make it. How the hell do you roll a police car?"

"Oh, my God, that's shocking. What about Frank and Matt?"

"Yeah, they're okay; they're bringing in the sergeant. The ambulance just left the hospital to meet them along the South Coast Road, and the air ambulance has been alerted; it should arrive from Adelaide[30] in about an hour."

---

[30] Adelaide: Capital city of South Australia situated on the mainland 120 kilometers north of Kingscote.

"Can I help?"

He thinks a moment, and nods. "Yeah, you'd be a help just by keeping me company, but I warn you, it's going to be a tough situation out there."

"I'll get sandwiches and drinks; Jordan can take the truck out to Stumpy Flats."

"Okay, I have to phone headquarters right away. Be ready to leave in—say, fifteen minutes." He pauses for a moment, reflecting. "I liked the super; he was a good bloke. Treated me like a—he helped me out a lot."

"I'm sorry, Bob." She smiles warmly and turns toward the door.

"Cassie, thank you."

Gazing vacantly out over the hood of the police wagon, Cassie is vaguely aware of the stringy bark trees flashing by her window and the grey ribbon of road with the yellow line down the middle rushing away under the wheels. Tired from her very early start to the day, she struggles to stay alert as her head sinks slowly to her chest.

You get up in the morning to a new day, every day, life starts over and you don't really know what is going to turn up. The day Kristina died started out just great, then suddenly, horror, blood, fire, smoke—lives can change in a heartbeat, change forever.

God, how she loved her mother, her beauty, charm, the grace and style with which she moved her body through space and time, made her special. Cassie could feel her presence in the movement of her dance; Kristina's spirit, gently coaxing the muscles of her lengthening limb to stretch and combine with the perfect arching of a soaring foot, naked toes pointing, pointing, stretching to just, just reach into a cloud. "Lift, Cassie, lift and stretch and point. There it is; magnífico, my sweet little ballerina."

Hah, she was not always the perfect mother, no. She had a temper, that is for sure. She could scream and bitch the likes of which would embarrass a raging banshee to get her way or dissipate the anger of a foul bitchiness, but when the upset was over, she would laugh—a glorious, beautiful, belly laugh that would infect everyone around her. The memories sustained her, ingrained in her psyche the iron will and chutzpah to reach beyond the ordinary, to claim and use.

Cassie studies the young constable as he focuses on the road ahead. *I like you, Bob Dunning. You're different—a good heart, strong; and the color of your skin, creamy chocolate, and those handsome features hinting your ancient ancestry—a mix of modernity and instinctual mysticism there, fascinating.*

As they sweep by the turn-off to Vivonne Bay, she looks out her window to the south, beyond the low scrub, to where she can see the Southern Ocean all the way to the horizon, its blue surface choppy with white caps from small, breaking waves, signaling a stiff breeze beginning to blow in from the southwest and Antarctica. Seconds tick by as she continues watching, drawn to the wild beauty that has fascinated her since childhood.

Suddenly, the sea turns violent, the sky darkens, the waves grow huge and frightening; forked lightning scorches the water, which explodes into tiny puffs of steam. She grabs her throat, choking, drowning, gurgling—

"There's the ambulance and the Ryan truck, just ahead," says Dunning, his voice cutting through her nightmare, saving her.

What was that all about? God.

"Are you okay?" says Dunning slowing down. "You don't have to get out; I can take care of this."

"No, no, I'll be fine. I was dreaming—some kind of nightmare—too bloody weird." She sees a paramedic pulling a stretcher from the ambulance. Matt and his father are standing in the back of the truck, alongside the doctor who is working on the sergeant.

The police wagon rolls to a stop and Dunning and Cassie slide out of their seats. "How is he, Doc?" shouts Dunning, hurrying to the Landcruiser. "Hell, he looks bad. Is he going to make it?"

Woodson, who is barely conscious, recognizes Dunning's voice. "Get 'em; go and check it out. It's there, I know," he croaks, venomous. *Stone the crows, this bloke's a devil; he's like the severed head of a snake that continues to bite at anything moving.*

"He has a chance, thanks to these blokes," says the doctor. "But we need to get him to Adelaide as quickly as possible. He'll be laid up for a good bit. Another centimeter and the glass would have ruptured his jugular."

Cassie looks past Woodson to Matt. *He looks dreadful.* Blood and vomit cake the front of his shirt. Their eyes lock. He gives her the "bit of a bloody mess, hey?" look, his face grim, stressed.

"Matt, you're not hurt are you?"

"Nup, I'm all right—his blood, my chunder,"[31] he says, tapping the mess on his shirt.

"Come down here; I want to give you a hug."

He jumps from the truck, and she wraps her arms around him. The scent of his aftershave overpowers the smell of the vomit and reminds her of the day before. "Love you, love you, my darling," she whispers into his ear.

"Yep," he says quietly, "me too."

"Thank God, you're okay."

"Yeah, bit bloody rough, Cass—especially about the dead bloke. There's going to be big trouble over this; he was one of the bosses over from Adelaide."

"Thanks for what you did, today, Matt. Good job," says Dunning as he approaches and shakes Matt's hand. "I'll need to get a statement from you, but we can do that later in the week. I have to get on out to the accident scene and wait for the second ambulance. Thanks for your company, Cassie. I guess you'll get a ride with Matt."

"Yes, and thank you, again, for your help with Jordan."

"You got a good'n there, mate; take good care of her, hey?"

"Yep, I know; I'll be looking after her real good." Then, with a wink from one of his flashing blue eyes to Cassie, "I suppose, hey."

"Drop the bullshit, you blokes," interrupts Frank. "Give us a hand here before he snuffs it. We got to get him onto the stretcher, and he's a heavy prick, I can tell you that."

---

[31] Chunder: Australian for vomit.

22

The sun is barely above the horizon as Matt watches, enchanted, a group of lively fur seals race, leap, and splash in the seawater under Admiral's Arch. Another group plays on the damp rock face that slides steeply to the water from the north wall. Gleeful seal pups tumble and slip on the misty-wet surface, eventually to plunge gloriously into the narrow tongue of cold water that runs to the open sea. His soul resonates happily to the familiar smells of seawater and rotting seaweed, and to the ever-present hiss and splash of tumbling waves crashing onto the jagged rocks protecting the base of the Admiral. In his darkest moments, it is here he comes, to his Admiral, to seek refuge, renewal, and inspiration. He places a notebook and pen on the flat rock in front of him.

Already it is Saturday, and the death of the policeman the previous Monday seems a distant event. The sergeant is expected to make a full recovery, and according to island intelligence, usually amazingly accurate, although not without some degree of embellishment, he will be back on duty in six weeks. Constable Dunning did not come to inspect Humpy, but instead, took their statements over the telephone and again thanked them for their assistance at the accident scene, insisting that the sergeant would most definitely have died without the Ryans' intervention.

He caught up with Cassie on the telephone Thursday night. Her life was, as always, busy, helping with the crutching, feeding sheep, exercising Kingston, and religiously honoring her daily two-hour dance routine in the stable loft studio. *Where did she get the energy?* It was her mention of the hundred of things necessary to get ready for Sydney that he winced.

He turns from the ocean view and sits in his usual place, the comfortable writing-chair rock that overlooks the seals' playground. His attention is drawn to the movement of two adolescent pups—a male and a female swimming almost as one, their bodies entwining, coupling, rolling in unison—their large brown eyes wide with wonder, expectation, and excitement.

The pleasant sensation of hot blood rushing through his body catches him unawares as he is reminded of the graceful movements of his Cassie dancing on the sand at Cape Kersaint the previous Sunday. He smiles and laughs loudly as the female seal lifts to the top of the water, her tail beating up a flurry of foam, her front flippers slapping together in gleeful applause for the gawking admiration of her male suitor, floating on his back before her. Suddenly, a dark presence enters the space and the playful cavorting switches to a race for survival.

Seals rush from the water for the rocks. The lovers' eyes grow wide with panic as a huge dark shape moves swiftly along the tongue of water. The youngsters turn, swim desperately toward the sloping rock, and surge up onto the slippery surface, the male slightly ahead of his mate. For a moment, they appear safe, but the huge form of the great white shark, riding on its own momentum, washes up the sloping rock and takes the young female in its mouth, its exposed teeth sawing and chomping through her mid-section, cutting her almost in half. The monster loses momentum, stalls, and then slips back into the water with the bloody mammal still struggling hopelessly, caught vice-like in the killer's perfect mouth.

Matt and the surviving seals are spellbound as the shark sinks and swims slowly back to the open ocean. A red trail briefly marks the visit, but it soon dissipates, and the amphitheatre returns to its wild normalcy, except for the distraught seal and a pondering Matt. In a quick, brutal moment, nature's process was graphically demonstrated—the life of the seal for the life of the shark. *Bloody hell, did I just see what I saw? How amazing, brutal, yet beautiful, even in its savagery.*

He stares at the water, and words begin to ticker tape through his mind: passion, fire, rage, heat, alive, dark, life, lust, battle, death. He reaches for the notebook and begins scribbling more words, crossing them out, replacing them with others, rearranging their order to fit the structure of his chosen poetic form, a sestina. Feverishly, he works around a final six, each one marking the end of a line in each of six stanzas.

At last, he has the first draft of the first stanza. His mind gropes for a title, and then he writes on the top of the page, "Lust: Life's Fiery Center."

"I love to watch you write, Matthew."

"God, Katherine! You startled me. I didn't hear you coming."

"I'm sorry." She looks out to the ocean. "Here is such a wonderful place for inspiration, isn't it?" She smiles, a beautiful, warm caring smile. "I've been here for a few minutes—wanting to say something, but you were so absorbed in your work, I didn't want to interrupt. You get excited, don't you, when you are being creative? Can you tell me what you are writing?"

"Oh, I—I'm trying to put something together for the writing competition."

"Is it a poem?"

"Well, yeah, sort of."

"Can I read it?"

"Ah, I—yeah, okay, sure." He tears the page from his notebook and hands it to her.

"Thank you." As she reads, her eyes grow moist. She catches her breath, reads it a second time, and then lifts her eyes from the page to Matt.

"You have a gift, Matthew; it's beautiful, powerful. It seems that you are saying the relationship between lust and love are often considered as different or contradictory, a dichotomy, but both have primary goals—procreation, human survival. Is that where you're going with this?"

Matt takes in the view to the Brothers and delights in the ocean breeze. "Wow, you got all that from one stanza? That's great. I'm taking it further in the rest of the poem, going on to the idea of the relationship between life and lust—lust in all its manifestations, sex, food, the driven savagery of the shark eating a seal for example, and more, much more—is life's imperative. I have another six stanzas to work it out, and then I'll see if it does any good in the national competition."

Her finger taps the title at the top of the page. "Hmm, 'Lust: Life's Fiery Center'; quite a challenge you have set yourself, but I have a premonition that it will do well, Matthew." She takes a deep breath. "This is the perfect place for you to write, isn't it? This is my place, too, to replenish, to listen to God's voice in the winds and waves. Here, I feel safe, free, yet connected, a part of the big story, always."

"Yeah, I get that, and I am reminded that danger and death are a constant here, too. I watched a shark attack and kill a seal earlier, right there." He points to the tongue of water. "There were two of them, seal pups, playing together in the water, free and happy. It changed in an instant." He pauses, thinking for a moment. "Or are they so innocent? They eat fish to live, just like the shark, which was following its instinct to survive. The act, brutal as it was, carried a certain beauty and justification. Do you think we live like that, have to live like that—at times soaring, tender, loving, serene—but just as savage, brutal, and aggressive?" He shrugs. "The mix is really elemental to our evolution, don't you think?"

"Oh, how your mind asks, Matthew. I'm not one for such weighty concerns. I think God's plan is ideal for each of us, and it's simpler to leave matters to him." She looks at her watch. "You'd better run along; the boys can't be late for tennis."

He stands, ready to walk back with her to the cottage. "No, you go on ahead. I'll be along in a minute," she says, looking beyond him to the Casuarina Islets, the solitary Brothers, the du Couedic guardians who are the first to challenge the constant assaults of the southern sea. A cloud drifts across the face of the sun, turning the bright morning a sudden gray. A rush of wind blows in from the south. All at once, the air is cold.

Matt hesitates for a second. Katherine's eyes are strangely distant, focused beyond the horizon. Her lips are moving; he tilts his head to listen.

"The storm is coming," she whispers. "Lord, protect us."

23

Out in the boonies, as the outback or bush is sometimes called, farmers' are isolated, their work, hard and physically demanding. The wives often have to pitch in, and the kids, too, after the school bus drops them off in the afternoon. There are stock to feed, sheep to pen at shearing time, crops to plant, hay cutting, harvesting, grape pruning, and everyday chores, like milking the house cow before and after school, and cutting firewood for the kitchen stove. After a busy week, the weekend is a prize, an opportunity to kick back a little, catch up with neighbors and locals, pick up a snippet or two of steamy gossip, and get to the general store in Parndana, Kingscote, Penneshaw, or American River to shop for next week's supplies.

Sport plays a big part in the community's social life, too, and Saturday is sports day. The locals, including the kids, test their skills against other island districts, and the rivalry can get intense. It is not uncommon for a few wild jabs to be exchanged in the heat of a close football game, but at the end of the day, socializing over a few beers and raspberry drinks for the kids at the local watering hole is what really matters.

For the West-Enders, the small township of Gosse is the center for sports and social activity. Except for the community center building, football oval, and clubrooms, tennis and basketball courts, kangaroos and wallabies, there is not much else. Almost hidden in the scrub, Gosse is often missed by the tourist traffic speeding along the Cape Borda Road. Until the early 1950s, before the soldier settler development scheme got underway, the west end of the island was mostly an uninterrupted landscape of trees and scrub from south to north, except for two rough, pioneering tracks that snaked along two of the coasts, one southwest to Cape du Couedic, and the other northwest to

Cape Borda. Gosse sprang up around Federal Government's Returned Soldiers Land Resettlement Scheme who came to settle and farm the virgin land.

With the clock ticking past six o'clock, the bar and lounge areas of the community center are already crowded. Thirsts primed from combat in the afternoon heat, tennis and cricket players, along with spectators and kids are "dropping down" copious quantities of beer, rum and cokes, and raspberry and lemonade mixes. Three bar attendants are flat out,[32] trying to keep up with the demand. Two women calmly process orders for counter teas[33] yelled to them by cheeky voices over the kitchen counter. "Pepper steak, serve of whiting,[34] and five plates of chips for the kids," yells one mother with a kid balanced on each hip. "Hey, Meg," a young, red-haired, freckled face cricketer, still in his whites and balancing a tray of schooners,[35] shouts, "Throw a rumpy[36] on for me when you've got a sec, will ya? Medium rare would be about right."

"You'll be waiting all night if I wait 'til I'm not busy, Bluey; and where's the *please* in your vocabulary?" scolds Meg as she picks out a prime rump from an alloy dish holding twenty-plus superb cuts. "It'll be ready in a few," she yells back as she throws the steak onto the sizzling hotplate, sweat streaking her pudgy cheeks, then turns to the next customer.

A continuing flow of early arrivals for the church barn dance swells the crowd. A couple of young cricketers from the host club leap over the bar to help the swamped tenders. "Organized chaos" best describes the Saturday evening ritual as those with topped-up schooners, froth slopping over the top and sliding down frosty glasses, an image that brings tears to red-blooded Australian males when deprived of the amber fluid for too long, spill outside to make room for the growing crowd.

---

[32] Flat out: Slang for very busy.
[33] Counter tea: Refers to a meal usually ordered over the bar in an Australian pub.
[34] Whiting: Cold-water fish considered the best to eat—sweet tasting and finely textured meat.
[35] Schooners: Medium-sized glasses of beer.
[36] Rumpy: Aussie slang for a rump steak.

Matt sits with his family at a table well away from the bar, next to a window open to the southwest. A cool breeze helps to keep the temperature down in the crowded room. Frank is right at home, leaning on the bar lined with noisy drinkers, managing to get a quick one away while waiting for his order. Matt shrugs as he catches Frank's eye while he is placing the empty glass back on the bar. *Par for the course—can't help himself; better here than in the church, though. There's going to trouble before the night's over.*

Frank, in the jovial stage of his drinking day, is unperturbed, and with a beaming smile winks mischievously at Matt, like a kid caught being naughty. The barman sets the drinks on the bar: a rum and coke for Katherine, a beer for Matt, and a couple of raspberries for the boys. Frank peels a hundred dollar note from a roll as thick as his fist and passes it to the young cricketer behind the bar. He pockets the roll and change in his baggy jeans and waves Matt over to help carry the drinks back to the table.

As Katherine sips her drink, the thirsty boys gulp down their raspberry and lemonades, leaving the glasses half-full of ice.

"Can we go now?" asks an impatient Sean, gasping for breath as he bangs his glass down on the table.

Frank is sitting beside Katherine with his arm draped over her shoulder. "Yeah, all right, but before you go, take this." He reaches into his pocket, pulls out two crumpled twenty-dollar notes from the change, and hands one to each of the boys. "I want you lads to have a good time tonight. Buy your own dinner and leave your mum and me alone for a while. Now, piss off." The boys scamper off to join their mates, chuckling.

Matt is used to his father's generosity at these times. When Frank is flush, usually on payday every two weeks, or from the cash he receives from his business interest twice a year, and after he has consumed a few ales to counter his usual irritability, he slips into a philanthropic frame of mind. *It's hard to work the oldman out at times. May as well make the most of it; it won't be too long before the grog[37] turns him nasty again.*

---

[32] Grog: Slang for alcoholic beverage.

"I suppose you reckon some of this is yours, hey?" says Frank, reaching back into his pocket and drawing out the roll of hundred dollar bills.

"Yeah, right, a couple of hundred would help out right now; I'll get the rest off you next week when I pickup the Ute."[38]

"Did you get Harry to put a bull-bar on? You'll hit another 'roo[39] sooner rather than later; bastards are all over the place."

Should have taken it easy through Wallaby Lane, thinks Matt, still angry at himself for not slowing down where hundreds of kangaroos and wallabies cross the South Coast Road from the scrub on the south side to the pastures on the north where they feed every night. *Biggest bloody buck 'roo I ever laid eyes on. Three and a half thousand dollars to fix the Ute, and the bugger jumps right back up and pisses off like nothing happened.*

"Yeah, he put on an aluminum one—tough as steel, but a lot lighter. Reckons you save heaps of petrol."

"Good," says Frank, peeling off three hundred dollars and handing it to Matt. "There's a bit extra in there; buy your girl something nice."

"Jeez, you're laying it on a bit thick tonight, aren't you?" teases Matt.

"Don't use the Lord's name in vain, Matthew," says Katherine, gently scolding her stepson.

The conversation is suddenly interrupted by the roar of a motorbike skidding to a halt outside the window next to the Ryans' table. Astride the bike, a dashing figure dressed in black leathers and a black helmet, his face hidden behind the helmet's reflective visor, peers at the Ryans. Matt stares back into the visor, but sees only the reflection of his tense face. Jordan Baldwin revs the bike's motor to an unbearable scream and holds it there for a few seconds, taunting, before shutting it down and dismounting. Kids run from everywhere to crowd around their hero, Darth Vader.

Frank's congeniality is gone. "That noisy prick is asking for it; always causing a stir." He tips back his chair to get up. "I'm gonna have a few words with him."

---

[38] Ute: Pick-up-like vehicle, but made in a popular sedan style.
[39] 'Roo: Kangaroo.

"Not tonight, Dad; don't start anything here," Matt says, pushing his father back into his seat. "He's looking for trouble with us—with me, really. Let him alone; he's probably drunk already. He'll come unstuck on his own." Frank stares at his son for a moment, tosses down the rest of his drink, pushes back his chair again and stands up.

"Be sure he keeps well away from me, then, son. I won't put up with any bull from him—pommy[40] upstart. It was the likes of him and his father that threw our people into the holds of filthy ships and transported us out here—the few of us that didn't die on the way out, that is, and they still try to keep us under with their money and fancy gerrymanders, so stuff 'em." He stomps angrily to the bar.

Matt shrugs and looks at Katherine, who sighs with resignation. *She loves the oldman. God knows why; he treats her like dirt a lot of the time.*

She smiles, as if reading his thoughts. "He's really a good man, Matt; been through a lot, Vietnam and all. I pray for him; I pray everyday that he'll find his peace and be happy."

Matt shakes his head and turns back toward the bar and his father. *Yeah, but it won't happen, not with the Irish curse on him. CIA: Catholic, Irish, and alcoholic; we've got trouble coming here tonight, all right.*

---

[40] Pommy: Australian slang for a person from England.

24

Matt takes a long swig from his forth stubby and looks at his watch for the third time in thirty minutes—five after nine, and the barn dance is in full swing. The local lads, already boisterous from the effects of South Australia's favorite West End Draft beer, are crowding about the main entrance doors, snickering and gawking at the young women sitting along the sidewalls, who are themselves chatting, pointing, staring, flirting, and giggling. The band starts up again, and the older couples are quick onto the floor.

Matt, feeling pretty good about himself, pushes further into the hall, chuckling as he overhears snippets of conversation from other well-lubricated males. "Phew, she's a beauty, mate." "Jeez, Stumpy, 'ave a go at her; bloody beautiful, hey?" "She's home from college, mate; reckon the girls from there are real goers, too, hey?" "Go'n, go'n ask her."

From the elevated stage at the far end of the hall, the band's 40s and 50s-era music is stirring up the now crowded dance floor of sweating bodies swinging to a hyped-up quickstep. Kids of all ages and sizes are sliding in the sawdust, spread on the floor to make it slick and fast, skidding dangerously around the feet of the hustling couples. Sean is in heaven, slipping and sliding from one end of the hall to the other in a stylish crouch, a cheeky grin on his face as he bumps into other small kids and sends them flying off into sidewalls. Matt chuckles. *It won't be long before the little fella lets his mouse out and stirs the girls up. Bet he's waiting for Martha Fahey to show up.*

The band is going full-tilt—five local blokes who play piano, violin, drums, guitar, trumpet, and saxophone between them, while Molly Owens, a jolly, middle-aged woman with huge breasts amply displayed in the low cut of her cotton dress and a voice that can lift the roof of an amphitheatre, sings her heart out. Tradition dictates the band be kept well oiled, and the Irish Catholic church hosts are not remiss in maintaining a generous flow of the local brew within arms reach. Maxi Feldman, seventy years old, bald, cheeks ballooning as he sucks, spits, and blows through the reed of his mouthpiece, sweat pouring off his ruddy head, boogies about the stage, his notes exploding through the building, out into the warm night air, signaling "it's fun in here, folks."

Eventually, the band stops for a break. The dancers clear the floor, leaving the kids to create even greater chaos as more of them crowd onto the floor to do "broggies,"[41] and yell and squeal with gleeful malice. Martha shows up and joins in, but Sean does not even get a chance to think about getting *Snot* out of his pocket; she is quick to exact her revenge for the previous Sunday's humiliation. Picking a moment when Sean is in an out-of-control broggy and off balance, she slams into him and sends him cannoning into the women sitting along the wall. They pick him up, brush him off, and make the kind of fuss that women make over cute little boys. Martha, hands on hips and feet set apart in a defiant pose, looks at the disoriented and vanquished little warrior with a triumphant "get even" smirk.

Matt laughs and turns his eyes to wander down the line of women. When he sees her, the beautiful redhead staring at him, a tingling sensation electrifies his body, its intensity catching him off-guard. Maureen gives him an especially alluring smile and waves, indicating she wants to dance. His intuition tells him that a dance with her could lead to trouble, big trouble, so he flashes back a reluctant smile, waves, and shakes his head with a "you'll get me in trouble" look and points to his watch.

Maxi calls a fox trot for the next dance. Clasping his saxophone to his chest with one hand, he fills his empty glass from the jug of beer resting on the piano with the other, lifts it to his lips, and empties it in one swallow. Cooling and oiling his parched and rusty throat, the amber draft washes through his delighted system all the way to his gut. With a satisfying belch,

---

[41] Broggy: Slang for skidding sideways, like a car sliding on a gravel road.

he wipes his mouth with the back of his hand and burps into the microphone, juiced up and ready to boogie. He grasps the saxophone's reedy mouthpiece between his teeth with the glee of a youngster grabbing onto the nipple of its mother's breast and launches into the next number.

With the booze firing up their courage, the young blokes scoot across the hall to grab a "sheila,"[42] going after the "good lookers" first. Matt tries to quell a sudden anxiety as he sees the lovely redhead stand and begin to walk across the floor toward him. As she reaches out, a dark figure cuts in front of her, grabs her hand, and whisks her into the midst of the other dancers. *Jordan.*

Despite his gimpy leg, Jordan, with a sudden exuberance of flair and flamboyant conceit, demonstrates that he is no mug on the dance floor. Provocatively, he whirls his dazzling partner through the sawdust, swirling close by Matt, who can't take his eyes off the beauty, scanning her perfect form all the way from her red, stiletto, open-toed shoes, which support long, sexy bare legs and perfect thighs, to where those legs slip tantalizingly out of view under the hem of her short tartan skirt.

Oh, God help me, she's a bloody looker, all right. He looks at his watch, 9:15. Cassie said she would be at the hall by 9:30. *She'd have old Monty home from the airport and be well on her way here, just enough time for a leak.* He turns away from Maureen and Jordan, and pushes back through the males crowding the entrance. Maureen watches from over Jordan's shoulder, smiling—a glint of mischief in the emerald sparkle of her eyes.

He walks beyond the parking lot and into the scrub a few meters, where the bushes are thick enough to screen him from public view. Unzipping his fly, he frees his best mate from the pressure of confinement, sighs with relief and delights in the bliss of peeing unencumbered in the open air, a benefit of living in the bush easily taken for granted, but for the occasional reminder that comes from a visit to the suffocating constraints of any city. In keeping with his usual habit, he looks up at the black canopy dotted with myriad stars that form the Milky Way, a misty constellation familiar to those who live under the southern sky. As always, he is fascinated by the unfathomable

---

[42] Sheila: Australian for woman; young female.

immensity of the universe. A meteorite shoots across the sky, burning brilliantly for a few seconds before disintegrating.

A metaphor of life: what a ride, riding this rock 'round and 'round our little part of the universe, hardly more than a speck of dust in the vastness of—of—what? Infinity? Blows me mind, every bloody time.

He looks down on his best mate, the source of his pee. "What'd you reckon, mate? Is that our life? A quick flash, and then—it's all over. We need to make the most it while we're here then, hey?"

Suddenly, two arms circle his waist, "I'll go along with that, no worries. Can I help you out with your mate there?"

"Jeez, Maureen! What the hell are you doing here?"

Before he can say or do anything more, she spins him around, pulls him tight to her body, and pushes her tongue into his mouth. Her passion rushes through him like a firestorm, causing an immediate response in his exposed mate, the early beers dissolving any lingering resistance to Maureen's entrapment.

"C'mon, Matt, I've wanted to do this for a long time," she pants as she lifts her skirt.

The effect on Matt is explosive. With all control taken over by his unprincipled member, he speeds toward disaster.

"Whoa, whoa, Matt, ease up, or it'll be all over before it started."

Her breathy request is enough to cause him to stop, to think—to think long enough for images of Cassie to enter his head: Cassie dancing on the beach, Cassie unbelievably happy, Cassie, her eyes glistening, her beauty overwhelming. A horrifying and sickening sense of guilt rips through his gut, and he steps back.

"What are you doing? I don't want you to stop, just slow down a little." She moves to put her arms around him.

"No, no, back off, Maureen, please. I don't want to do this," he says pushing her away and quickly tucking his errant member into the safety of his pants.

"Well, well, well. Look at what we have here. Seems I've shown up at an inappropriate time, hmm?" says a sarcastic, slurring Jordan as he steps through the cluster of thick bulloak. "At it again, are we, Ryan?"

"Jordan!" says Matt, instantly filled with a crushing sense of dread. Maureen freezes. Jordan is smirking, triumphant.

"It's not what you think; nothing happened."

Jordan laughs. "Give me a break, Ryan; you were at it, all right, *hard* at it, *hard* being the operative word. I see it with my own eyes, and you tell me it is not what I see. I wonder what my ever-so-gullible sister will make of it."

"You rotten bastard, Jordan; get out of here," screams Maureen.

Matt waves the girl away. "Go on, Maureen, leave; I'll take care of this."

"I'm—I'm sorry. Sorry, Matt."

"I said I'll take care of it. Now get the hell out of here."

As she turns toward the hall, the heel of the stiletto on her left foot catches in the exposed roots of a young wattle tree and breaks off. She slips off the broken shoe, looks at it, screams with rage, and throws it at Jordan, missing him.

"You mongrel, Jordan, this is your fault."

"Please, please, Maureen, get the hell out of here," says Matt.

"All right, all right, I'm sorry; I'm going." She pushes through the bulloak and disappears, heading for the hall.

Despite the seriousness of his situation, Matt cannot help thinking its irony. Here, under an extraordinary canopy of stars in the scrub on tiny Kangaroo Island, riding this amazing rock called earth through an infinite universe, the very fact of its reality testing the most brilliant minds, a contemplation so complex, so deep, God seems the only explanation. Yet, juxtaposed with all of it, two males face off over something pathetically trivial in the grand scheme of things. As is usually the case, human behavior unremittingly overrides the ride with its pathetic witlessness.

"Got you cold, Ryan," says Jordan, sneering.

Matt is silent. His instinct is to walk away, but some force holds him back. The face staring at him morphs into the tragic mask of one side of the two-sided logo of the theater, the one reflecting pain, anger, fear and sadness, feelings he knows well.

He talks quickly, urgently. "You know, Jordan, I've never had anything against you. I might have resented your wealth now and again, but, hell, we've both been through some tough stuff, hey? Your mother dying in the plane crash, mine through her suicide." He pauses and takes a breath. "And you know what? I resented her for a long time over that—hated my own mother. I mean, she took herself out by her own hand. Killed herself, after telling me for years that I was her pride and joy." He shrugs his shoulders. "Drowned herself; can you believe that, walked two hundred meters in the middle of the night, in the middle of a huge bloody storm to the house dam and drowned herself?"

Matt pauses, startled by his words to a man he felt only contempt a few moments earlier. *Why the hell am I telling him all this?* Jordan, too, is confused, thrown off balance by Matt's candor and concern!

"Oh, you were never really one of us, Jordan; we all knew that. Despite giving you a bit of stick [43] from time to time, we didn't hate you. After your bloody fool stunt, you turned mean, crazy, or something, didn't you? Twenty-two years of age and you climb into an empty 44-gallon oil drum and roll down Kohinoor Hill.[44] One hundred and fifty meters before you're thrown out and—how long were you in the coma? Twelve days? The money was on you dying—nearly killed your oldman. Stuffed up your leg, ruined your sporting career, nearly took your face off, and for what? Was it somewhere down deep in your gut you just wanted to fit in, to be one of us ordinary blokes? Is that what you were thinking when those dip-shit Rankin brothers called you a gutless wonder?"

Jordan is quiet, staring at Matt, eyes glistening.

"Look at what you're doing to your family now. Cassie is worried about you, expecting one day to hear the worst, and your father's health is already taking a beating. How much more do you reckon he can handle before he goes under?"

Jordan's mind is racing, full of painful memories. The quick downing of a dozen or so beers combined with Matt's counsel is cutting through the layers

---

[43] Bit of stick: Teasing.
[44] Kohinor Hill: Steep hill approx. halfway between Kingscote and Parndana.

of protection, in place to keep him safe from being humiliated and hurt again. *Bitch.*

He was seven at the time, on vacation in Adelaide, staying with family relatives. Kristina caught him and his cousin, Tommy, in the act of exploring each other's privates. From then on, she hardly let him out of her sight—pushed him to be more male than he was, or wanted to be. Dance—he had wanted to learn to dance like Cassie, but Kristina wouldn't allow it. When she died, he was secretly pleased. *God, how I hated her then, the bitch couldn't let me be me. And, Cassie, mother's favorite and father's salvation. God damn them!*

Jordan stares blankly at Matt. For a moment, it is as if he is gone, left his body, moved to another world.

"You okay, Jordan?"

Suddenly, he snaps back to the present. "I don't know what you did, Ryan, all that clever double-talk had me going for awhile. You're a clever bugger, all right, but you can't con me. I'm telling Cassie the moment she gets here."

"For heaven's sake, Jordan, I don't give a damn about me. What's the matter with you? It's Cassie you'll hurt most."

The look on Jordan's face tells Matt all he needs to know. "You're a creep, Jordan; it's her you want to hurt, isn't it? Even more than me, you sick—"

Without warning, Jordan throws a vicious punch, but Matt is ready, sways to his side and the fist passes harmlessly by his chin. Angry and now out of control, he charges headfirst into Jordan's stomach, taking him to the ground and slamming his head into the bush and dirt. He grabs his stunned adversary around the throat with both hands and squeezes. Jordan struggles fiercely, hitting Matt in the face with a couple of light blows, but cannot break the hold; his face begins to color purple. All of a sudden, he stops fighting, his eyes roll back, and his body begins to spasm. Shocked, Matt realizes that he is killing Cassie's brother, and releases his grip.

Jordan slowly recovers, coughing, wheezing, and fighting for air. "You're crazy, Ryan," he croaks. "You nearly killed me."

Matt's face is ashen. "For God's sake, Jordan, stay away from me." Panting heavily, he stands and looks down on his enemy. "Stay away from me. Stay away, and keep your bloody mouth shut. You say anything to Cassie, you hurt her, and so help me God, Jordan, I'll come looking for you."

He steps away and walks toward the hall.

Jordan watches Matt until he is out of sight. "I'll get you, you mick bastard, I'll get you for this, one way or another."

25

Cassie is driving too fast, way too fast for the treacherous Cape Borda Road, but she is impatient to see her Matt; last Monday already seems light years away. Tired from an unusually busy day, she does not see the kangaroo standing on the side of the road until the very last second, just before it jumps out in front of the Pathfinder. She swerves violently, narrowly avoiding the animal, but the vehicle begins to slide sideways, dangerously out of control from the ball bearing-like effect of the ironstone gravel under her tires. Instinctively, she turns the front wheels against the slide, saving her from a certain rollover and, her angel working overtime, eventually sliding to a stop centimeters from a massive white gum tree growing a few meters off the side of the road. Dust swirls through the hi-beam of the headlights and then is gone; an eerie silence replaces the clatter of flying gravel hitting the body of the Pathfinder moments before.

Breathing quickly, almost panting, Cassie sits clutching the steering wheel with shaking hands, staring beyond the windscreen, struggling to regain her composure. *That was close.* She breathes deeply and shuts her eyes, concentrating on relaxing and letting the tension drain from her body. In moments, her mind is charging through the events of her day.

With her father away, it had been busier than usual: feeding the dogs, dropping hay bales into the ram paddock, feeding grain to the 2,000 ewes in the way-back paddock, taking Winston for his workout through the hills before finishing off with an easy canter along the beach and his favorite—a swim in the surf.

By skipping lunch, she was able to keep to her afternoon routine of working out in the studio. Each day at the same time, her favorite time: two hours of music, stretching, and dancing through a series of choreographed exercises until she was exhausted and exhilarated, all at once. As a child, she would watch her mother for hours dancing in the very same studio, enchanted; watch her arms, so elegant in their movements, especially when she raised them over her head in a classic *en couronne*. Be enthralled, as she swept, with her floor-foot classically *en pointe*, a gloriously sculptured leg stretching upward in a perfect *grande battement*, extending her foot in a perfectly curved arch, reaching above and beyond the level of her wild, dark hair, wet with sweat.

"Come, Cassandra, try it," Kristina would say in her Spanish-accented voice, reaching gently to take the tiny five-year-old hand and help her balance while she stood on *demi-pointe*, stretching *her* leg and arching *her* foot to almost match the perfection of her mother's *grande battement*. She would have been happy to spend all afternoon in the studio, but Monty was returning from his trip to Adelaide, and she was to pick him up.

"Sweet Jesus, thank you for watching over me." She reverses onto the road, then, in a bold display of defiance, floors the accelerator, spins the back wheels in the gravel, and fishtails fifty meters down the road in the direction of the Gosse Township. "Keep a lookout, girl," she says aloud, chuckling while snatching a look at the clock set into the dashboard, its glowing green digits showing 9:15. "It'll be little after 9:30 by the time I get there; not too bad, considering."

Her mind turns to thoughts of her father. He looked tired and pale as he stepped off the plane. *Why does he bother? It's time he gave up his Freeman Club board position.* He told her the special meeting had been particularly tough because of the Kangaroo Island discussion.

"The ultra conservatives are pushing for the liberal[45] government to enforce the state's drug laws. They want the police commissioner to target the island aggressively because of the Rosenblum poppy growing wild here and the illicit cultivation they say is starting to get out of hand. The pharmaceuticals are the ones behind it all, really—afraid they'll lose the control

---

[45] Liberal: In Australia, the Liberal Party is a conservative party.

of production and pricing of the product grown on their farms in Tasmania. They think because the island is small, it's more vulnerable to detection and quick prosecutions—just what they want."

Monty knew that many of the farmers, as well as the rest of the island economy, were suffering badly from the low wool and meat prices. Cultivating a few poppies and selling them to a mainland distribution outlet could mean the difference between keeping the farms operating and losing everything to the bankers. Islanders could legally grow three plants for personal use, but more was illegal. In Monty's view, this was not the time to harass the Islanders; they had enough to contend with, and legislation was proceeding to make Rosenblum cultivation on the island legal under license, eventually. Of course, the pharmaceutical companies know this, too. When the time comes, they want to be the only game in town by securing an overriding government license for island production, subleasing to a few, select, farmers and control the industry. The best he can do for the time being is keep his eye on the authorities, Woodson, in particular, and try to mitigate the damage.

As well, Monty also suspects that Jordan is into smoking marijuana, and probably quite a bit more than that; it would not do for the family to have a convict in its ancestral line. Grant was due back sometime in the next week, and he hoped they could convince Jordan to get help.

Cassie is aware that Monty is having a harder time with her leaving than he is letting on. Hell, she is having a tough time with it, too; he is a big part of her life. Kangaroo Island has been her life for twenty years, and she is going to miss it: the farm, the daily rides on Winston, and the freedom of living a mostly uncomplicated life on one of the earth's most pristine of environments. Ah, but how she loves to dance; it is in her blood, of course, and Monty's support and expectations for her artistic career make other choices untenable, at least for now.

Surprisingly, the separation from Matt is less of a wrench. Deep in her soul, she knew, yes, knew that they would be together—that a power greater than her, her Higher Power, was working in their lives, a Power that had been with her since her mother's death. When she got right down to it though, she did fear for Matt; no, not about losing him, but about his own sense of self-worth, or rather lack of it. The battering he had taken as a kid had left him little self-esteem, and he needed love and nurturing. Tough love, too—he had a tendency to wallow in self-pity, a characteristic she told him served no useful purpose, and that the most productive way to get over it is to do something for someone who is in real trouble. She grins; *God knows I love him, though.*

Of course, it was not one sided; he had awakened her to another part of herself—the urge to fulfill a hunger deeply rooted, but so essentially woman—to become a mother; it would be Matt who fathered her children; you could take that to the bank.

The welcome glow of diffused light above the trees surrounding the Gosse Community Center signals Cassie that she is close to the turn-off into the gravel track leading to the township. As she swings into the parking lot, her headlights sweep over the large crowd drinking and laughing in the beer garden set up alongside the hall. *I am parched, could do with a coldy myself.* She slows for a mother crossing to check on her child, asleep in one of the vehicles strategically parked in a dark area of the car park. As she looks for a parking spot, she sees Matt walk out of the scrub and merge into the crowd at the hall entrance. She smiles and swings the Pathfinder perfectly into the space between two station wagons a few meters from the main doors, hoping the light from the beer garden will discourage men from urinating near her truck, all the while aware that as the night wears on and the men get drunker, modesty becomes less of a consideration, anyway. However, Mrs. Fahey usually sorts them out. When she catches them peeing around her car, she yells loudly that if that were all they had to showcase, they would be better off to keep *it* hidden and save themselves from the mirth of the women with whom she would share their statistic. Rarely did a male ever pee near Mrs. Fahey's car unless he wanted to make a point.

Matt pushes his way through the crowded doorway, angry, angry because of his stupidity, encouraging Maureen, responding to her flirtation with his own. *Stuffed up again, just can't get it right. If Jordan tells Cassie, she'll be pissed off, that's for sure—and hurt. I'll kill him if—Ah, you're a damn fool, Matt. I'll have to tell her myself, before he gets in her ear.*

"Fair go, Matt," says one of the young drinkers, spilling his beer as Matt bumps him.

"Sorry, Bluey."

"That's one you owe me, Matt; next time you're at the bar wouldn't be too soon."

"Don't hold your breath."

Bluey is about to respond, but decides against it; Matt is looking pretty pissed off.

A quick scan of the room tells him that Cassie is still on her way. *Good, I have to think of how to tell her before she gets here. Bugger it, why did Maureen have to—*

"Yer looking deep in thought there, Matthew Ryan," says a friendly, familiar voice.

Oh, God, he'll be wanting to hear every detail at confession. What was it he asked me one night after benediction? 'How's the lovely Cassie? Have you two had sex yet?' Shocked the bloody hell out of me, and the follow-up was a real doozy. 'Be sure ya use a French letter if yer at it.' I didn't think priests even talked about it.

"Ah, not really, Monsignor," he lies, not daring to look the priest in the eye. "Big crowd; I hope the parish makes a killing tonight."

"We'll do just fine; we're gettin a share of the grog takings, so that'll push up the night's take." He places an arm around Matt's shoulders. "Come on into the supper room, and I'll buy ye a beer; ya look like ye could do with one. It'll give us a chance to chat about the coming competition. I trust yer working hard on yer projects?"

Matt grins and nods a "yes" as they walk into the supper room at the same time Maureen enters from the door leading to the female restroom. She flashes Matt an adorably innocent smile as she stops in front of them, blocking their path, and gives the monsignor a cheeky nod.

"Don't you look the catch of the night, Monsignor? Are you having a good time?"

"I am, and ya look like yer enjoying yourself, Maureen—along with everyone else, it seems."

"Yes, and I think it's going to liven up a lot more before the night's out, Monsignor." Winking provocatively at Matt, she pirouettes and sashays on into the dance hall, barefoot.

"She's a wild one there, Matthew, and she's definitely got ya in her sights, there's no mistak'n that look. Ah, the power of young hormones, and there's plenty of them dancin' about in this place tonight, I'll tell ya that. Ah, she's a good Catholic girl, I know that, and she'll settle down and make a good mother," he offers, years of ministry reflecting his understanding of the human condition.

"I wouldn't know about any of that, Father," says Matt.

As Cassie makes her way toward the door, the police wagon from Kingscote swings onto the township road and makes its way slowly toward the hall with its headlights on hi-beam, lighting up the crowd in the beer garden. Like moths attracted to light, a few of the well-lubricated lads turn to welcome the new copper with a mouthful of good-natured mockery.

"You're a bit early, mate; the footy don't start for another couple've months." "Yeah, bloke, we gotta get the snakes cleared off the oval before the first game yet, too." "On the way home, watch out for Macca's pet goanna on Hendy's corner; the bastard gets out on the road, occasionally, and you got to watch out you don't hit one of its legs; do you right in, that would. If you aim for under the belly, you'll get through all right." The locals howl with laughter as a grinning Dunning reverses the wagon into a parking place that allows him oversight of the entrance and the most active outside areas, including the beer garden. He sees Cassie.

Cassie threads her way through the crowd milling outside the hall entrance. Her beauty is not lost on a group of admiring males, many of whom she knows, having grown up with them. "Yep, g'day, Cass," says one young fellow, somewhat intimidated by the tall, elegant young woman, but finding beer-assisted courage to actually speak to her.

"Hello, Nugget," she says, smiling. "You look like you're having a good time."

She moves on, leaving a heroic Nugget swooning. "Ah, Jeez; cop[46] that, did ya, Blue? I'm in bloody love, mate."

"Yeah, you and half the mob here tonight," replies the flaming red-haired Bluey, tossing the last of his beer down his thirsty throat. "She's on with Matt, mate, lucky bugger. Here, give us ya glass, and I'll top it up."

Maxi's band is beginning a new dance bracket when she finally makes it into the hall. Pausing on the fringe of the dance floor, she looks among the dancers for Matt. Not out here. Her eyes pass over the band to the supper room door, adjacent to the stage, where she catches a glimpse of Monsignor Byrne inside talking to somebody just out of her line of sight. *That's probably him.* She starts to move off in that direction when a tap on the shoulder causes her to stop and turn.

"Now, tell me more, how's yer writing coming on?" says the priest as he pours two glasses of beer from a jug brought to him from the bar. He hands one to Matt and lifts the other to his lips. "Here's to yer writing, lad." He downs the beer in one magnificent guzzle. "A beautiful drop from the Lord hisself, that dances on the tongue of a t'ersty man, Matthew. "Tis both a curse and a blessing, but 'tis surely hit'n the right spot."

Matt empties his glass and the effect is instant; the worms retreat. He motions for a refill. "I think I'm doing all right, Monsignor. Dad was a lot quieter last week; I got the processor set up, thank you, and I'm doing better than the hour-a-day you wanted, so I've been able to make some real progress. My essay is about Kangaroo Island and, well, having lived here all my life, it gives me something I'm intimate with, at least. Bit like recording the facts and trying to make an interesting story out of it all. Then this morning, I started a poem that got me excited. A sestina, a French form of poetry that I kind of understand and like to work with—helps stimulate my thoughts. Now don't choke on me, but I'm calling it 'Lust: Life's Fiery Center.'"

---

[46] Cop: In this context, Australian for 'see that' meaning a heavy expression of admiration.

"G'day, Cassie," says a smiling Robert Dunning. "I hope I'm not intruding."

"Oh, Bob, hi, no, of course not. I saw you drive up a few minutes ago and heard the locals give you a bit of a roasting," she says, gushing slightly, unable to ignore his dark good looks and the dashing figure he cuts in his khaki uniform and light-brown Akubra[47] hat, the South Australian police badge precisely centered on its blue and white checkered hatband. The pistol holstered high on his brown police belt adds just the right touch of macho authority to his presence, and there is, again, that unmistakable hint of aboriginal ancestry in the structure of his face, suggesting that ancient wisdom deep within, from which to draw. She notices some of the young women sitting and standing around the hall staring at him. *Yeah, take your pick, Constable; you have quite the admiring audience out there.*

"I only just arrived myself, and I'm looking for Matt. I think he might be in there," she says pointing to the supper room, "talking to the monsignor."

"Ah, well, don't let me delay you, but I'd like to catch up before you leave."

"It's okay, I'm not in any hurry, and I'd rather not interrupt Matt if he's talking to the monsignor, anyhow. Want to dance?"

"I'd love to," says Dunning, "but I'm on duty, and regulations—"

"Don't allow it." She flirtatiously feigns heartfelt sorrow. "Where is the justice, but next time, no excuses. So, what do you want to talk about?"

The music stops, and Maxi reaches for the microphone. "Ah, I see our new constable out there, talking to one of our prettiest girls, Cassie Baldwin. First time out here to Gosse, I believe. Welcome, Constable Bob Dunning. We out here on this end of the island would like to wish you the best, appreciate your service, and, er, mind the goannas on the way home, hey; big as dinosaurs out in this neck of the woods." The crowd howls with laughter. "I'm told you're a pretty classy football player, too."

"Thanks," the embarrassed constable calls back. "I'm looking forward to playing, especially the Western District Football Team; I'm told you blokes are a tough crowd to beat."

---

[47] Akubra: Famous brand name for Australian outback hats.

"Just don't get too fancy when you play out here, Bob. Macca's goanna is the club mascot, and he's got a bloody foul temper, I can tell you, 'specially if the team's losing. And you can't control the bugger, neither, when he gets really pissed off," yells one of the young players from the dance floor. The crowd roars with laughter again.

Chuckling, Dunning waves to Maxi and the crowd. In seconds, the band is going all out again, Maxi's trumpet is fairly spitting out the notes, the dancers are whirling, and the kids are doing broggies all over the floor. The women left sitting along the wall during the earlier part of the evening are up and dancing with the young fellows too shy to ask earlier, before the effects of the grog kicked in to crank up their courage. Maureen, now fully recovered from her earlier encounter, is taking a more than casual interest in the two celebrities as she gets up for a dance with one of the young cricketers, barefoot.

The monsignor's blue eyes sparkle. "Like I was say'n, youthful hormones; I can't wait to be read'n it. Now, have ya got the forms filled out? Yer supposed to bring them ta Mass tomorrow, so I can get 'em off to the Institute in plenty of time."

Maxi's voice, rasping through the microphone, suddenly cuts across their conversation.

"Ah, I see our new constable out there, talking to one of our prettiest girls, Cassie Baldwin—"

Matt does not hear the rest of the sentence. Maxi's voice falls away to a dull drone in the background of his tumbling mind. *With Dunning? What is she—last Monday, they—yeah, I thought then she liked him, I could see that.*

The demons are back, gnawing into the lining of his gut. No, she wouldn't— He snatches the fresh glass of beer sitting on the table and gulps it down.

"What is it, boy? Ya look like ya swallowed a snake."

As the dancers bump and grind to Maxi and his band's wild quickstep and jive, Dunning, Cassie still at his side, is enjoying the attention. *These aren't a bad bunch at all.* "That caught me off guard. Hey, what's all this about Macca's goanna?"

"Macca's a local farmer's son who is always bragging about how big he grows things. He says that when his turkeys get out on the road, everything is okay as long as the turkey has his legs open; the cars can drive right under its belly, same as with the lizard. He's always coming up with something; the latest was his tomatoes growing so big they had to be loaded onto the truck one at a time with a forklift."

"It sounds like they've got a hell of a sense of humor out here."

"Don't let it fool you; they can take and give out a lot of bull, but there is line you don't cross. These people will give you the shirt of their backs, but you cross them, and they'd just as soon feed you to a great white. Your boss, Sergeant Woodson, doesn't get any help out of them."

"Yeah, I already experienced that."

The music is getting louder. Sweat and spit are flying off Maxi's bald head as he leans back, the saxophone angling almost horizontally from his mouth, while his seventy-year-old pelvis gyrates spectacularly.

"Cassie, the last time we spoke, I mentioned that I'd been to college with Jordan. He and I don't have much in common, except for football, but your dad did me a good turn one time, and I can see your brother is heading for big trouble, so I'd like to help. I know some professionals who are very good with people who have problems similar to Jordan's."

"That's thoughtful of you, Bob; I appreciate the offer, I really do, but my father looks at Jordan's problems as a family matter, and as far as he's concerned, the family will take care of it, and Dad can be very stubborn."

"Like his daughter, too, from what I hear." She laughs.

"Gotta go, Monsignor, gotta go. Thanks," Matt says, avoiding the priest's eyes, placing his glass on the table before moving unsteadily toward the dance hall.

"Ya look after yerself, Matt," the monsignor calls after him. *Ah, he's way to sensitive for his own good. A day at a time, lad, a day at a time; all is well. The good Lord has a plan fer ya.*

"C'mon, Monsignor, what are you doing standing there with a beer in one hand and nothing to eat in the other?" A beaming Rosy Fahey puts an arm around the priest and hustles him toward the tables overloaded with an assortment of homemade deserts. "Get something into you, Father; you're getting so skinny you'll be flat out casting a shadow before long."

As Matt passes through the door, he sees Dunning and Cassie standing close to each other, talking and laughing. Sweat breaks out on his forehead, his hands feel clammy, and anxiety claims him. *What the hell is wrong with me? Why do I get like this? I need a beer.*

Standing by the side of the stage, he sees a half-full jug of the band's beer set on a guitar case, unattended; he grabs it in both hands and pours the contents down his throat. Nothing happens—the usual affect, immediate relief from the "panic attack"—nothing.

None of the unfolding drama is lost on Maureen as she whirls about the floor. She had watched Matt come in from the supper room, stop, and quaff down the beer. Her attention up until that time had focused on Cassie the moment she entered the hall after returning from the bathroom. How delicious to see the new and stunningly handsome policeman ingratiate himself before the well-heeled princess. *She liked it, too, the bitch—flirting, wasn't she? Look at her.*

"Cassie, seriously, Jordan came out of the scrub a few minutes ago, looking very drunk and heading for the beer garden, trouble written all over his face. Maybe you could have a word with him before I have to get involved again. The magistrate will throw away the key next time."

"I'll handle it." She places her hand on Dunning's arm, "Thank you again, Bob, I'll have a few words with him now."

"Look, it can wait. Matt is—"

"I'll be back as soon as I've spoken with Jordan. I want to nip this in the bud before he does something stupid."

They move toward the entrance, pushing through the crowd of young blokes, who start up on Dunning again. "Hey, Bob, the girls have a bloody top basketball team here; they might give you a spot if you're nice to 'em." "Ground's like concrete out here, mate, not like that pansy turf you played on in Adelaide." "They're all full of piss and wind, Constable; from what I hear, we're going to have to put Matt Ryan up against you to keep you from tearing us apart."

"Well, we'll find out soon enough. Now don't you lads get too pissed and drive; it's going to take your team at its best to beat us when we get out here," says a chuckling, but serious, Bob Dunning.

Cassie and Dunning finally make it outside, unaware that Matt is watching.

26

Maureen watches Cassie and Dunning leave and then turns her attention back to Matt. *Oh, dear, that really stuck it to you, didn't it?* She unwraps from her dance partner, leaving him abandoned in the middle of the floor, wondering what the hell he had done, but drunk enough not to care too much. "Well, stuff you, then," he mumbles to no one in particular and aims unsteadily for the door and another beer.

Maureen crosses quickly to Matt, grabs his hand, pulls him onto the floor and into the midst of the dancing couples before he can protest. "Matt, I'm not up to anything. I just want to apologize for what happened outside; I didn't know Jordan was lurking."

"It's over, forget it."

"I mean it, Matt, I'm sorry," she whispers into his ear, her cheek lightly touching his, her breath warm and scented with the spicy aroma of red wine. The tempo of the music changes as Maxi ditches the saxophone and picks up his violin. Molly Owens starts singing a heartrending version of "Angel of Music" from the *Phantom of the Opera*, not the usual fare for the locals, but one they eagerly anticipate whenever Molly is on.

Maureen nuzzles Matt's ear. He pulls back. "C'mon, Maureen, cut it out. I should go."

"You can't leave me standing here; at least wait until Molly is finished singing."

"Okay, until she is finished then."

"Did you sort out Jordan? He scares me—always causing trouble."

"Oh, yeah, Jordan; we reached an understanding. I mean, I hope we did.

He was drunk, crazy; he probably had some poppy in the mix. Ah, what the hell; it really doesn't matter, anyway."

"What, what do you mean, 'it doesn't matter?' Oh, I get it, Cassie and the copper. I wouldn't worry about that; Cassie would never have anyone but you while she's here on the island." Her voice carries a touch of derision. "Of course, in Sydney—I tell you, Matt, if anything happens—I mean, if you ever split up with Cassie, I'm here for you."

"What? What are you saying?"

"Well, Sydney is a long way from here, full of good-looking blokes, and she'll be in the middle of it all—the theatre, the ballet, and boys in tights. And there's bloody old Monty, too. Do you really believe he would ever let his daughter marry any Islander, let alone one from out this end?"

"Meaning me, of course, hey?" *You can't win, she's like the oldman. A hitch-up between the blue-collar Ryans and the aristocratic Baldwins? Dream on, mate.*

"Maybe he's right," he says, almost under his breath.

"What?"

He is silent as he studies the gorgeous redhead. *You're a stunner, all right, Maureen, but a sly bitch, too.* He shrugs and breaks into a self-effacing smile. "Ah, nothing, I'm just carrying on like a mug," he laughs, snapping out of his self-absorption, gently loosening her hold on him and taking a half-step back. He kisses her lightly on the cheek. "You're a good sort, Moe. If it wasn't for Cassie, but I love her, and that's it."

"I'll have you one day," she says, a touch piqued. "You're too good a bloke, Matt. She'll be nicking off to Sydney soon, meeting all those city bull dust artists, and that'll be the end of it."

Molly stops singing and, except for the kids sliding through the sawdust, the hall is strangely quiet. Matt notices that the crowd of blokes standing around the entrance earlier is gone. Shouting and a gaggle of angry voices coming from the beer garden signals the reason why.

Sean appears at the door, sees Matt, and runs quickly toward him, sliding through the sawdust to a halt, grabbing Matt's leg at the last moment to avoid crashing into Maureen.

"There's a fight, Matt," Sean says, panting, his small, hazel eyes wide. "Dad and Jordan are into it. The copper is trying to stop them, but—you better come quick."

"Ah, here we go—" Matt is already moving to the door. He rounds the corner of the hall and sees the crowd, in their midst a brawling Frank and a manic Jordan.

Cassie is close to the two fighters, frantically shouting at them to stop. Constable Dunning is sprawled in one of the chairs, looking decidedly uncertain as to his whereabouts. Then, frustrated by her inability to stop Jordan, Cassie springs onto his back just as Frank takes a wild swing. Jordan manages to duck the blow, unfortunately leaving Cassie's lovely face fully exposed to the rounding fist. Luckily, Frank's punch, its power mitigated by his imperfect aim and lack of reach, smacks her cheek a glancing blow with just enough impact to topple her from Jordan's back and leave an angry red bruise under an instantly swelling eye.

Matt goes crazy, and launches himself at his father with a fury threatening homicide. "Damn you," he yells amid a flurry of punches to Frank's head, sending the drunk reeling back to crash heavily on the hard cement. Before Frank can recover, Matt is on top of him, punching furiously. "Can't you ever get it straight? Always in trouble, getting us into trouble, hurting people—me. You—you're a drunk, a hopeless bloody drunk, Dad."

Tears stream over his cheeks as a pair of strong arms reach around and pull him away. "Easy does it, Lad," says Mad Tom. "God knows he deserves it, but it'll bring no good to any of us if you kill him."

Matt gives Tom an angry look, breaks his grip, and turns to Cassie, who, having regained her balance, is fiercely confronting her brother. "You can't stay out of trouble, not for a minute. How can I go away and leave Daddy—"

Matt pushes between them, holding his clenched fist a centimeter from Jordan's face. "Don't give me an excuse, Jordan. You're in enough trouble already, pal. Get over there, the copper is going to want a word with you," he yells pointing to one of the beer garden chairs.

Jordan is seething, considering another attack.

"I wouldn't, mate, no."

Matt turns to Cassie, his back to Jordan, and reaches out to her bruised cheek and closing eye, touching it gently. "That looks nasty."

"It'll heal," she says, shrugging and looking at him with an expression that says, 'Life's full of surprises.' "Well, my face, that is. At least he missed my nose; a flattened nose wouldn't look good on a dancer." She smirks, winks at him with her good eye, and walks over to Dunning, who is looking a little better, but still waffling incoherently. "We're going to have to get him back to Kingscote. He'll probably want to arrest everyone if he works out what happened, so we should pray he won't remember any of it tomorrow."

Jordan retreats and sits in one of the chairs, sullen, but chastened, suddenly aware that he is in very deep trouble.

Cassie crosses to where Katherine and the monsignor are kneeling next to Frank. "Mrs. Ryan, you'd better get Frank home right away." Sean and Patrick are standing on the fringe of the crowd, upset. "Hey, Sean, Patrick, you boys okay?"

Patrick puts his arm around Sean. "We'll be fine, Cassie, thank you," says Patrick hesitantly. "Won't we, Sean?"

"Yes," says the little man bravely, his voice barely audible.

"I'll do that, Mrs. Ryan," says Mad Tom, as Katherine tries to get Frank onto his feet. "You'd better behave yourself, Frank. You're in a ton of trouble already, and you'd better hope the young policeman doesn't remember too much tomorrow." He swings Frank's arm around his shoulder and shuffles off toward the Ryans' Landcruiser. "C'mon, Sean, help me out, mate. Pat, you go on ahead and get the truck started."

"Thanks, Tom," Cassie calls after them. "Those kids make me want to cry, Matt; bloody alcohol, what you lot go through."

"Yeah, that's why I can't leave them, Cassie, not yet."

"I know." She looks at him, and wipes her good eye.

"It'll work out." He tries to smile.

"Yeah, it will. Guess you'd better get Dunning's wagon."

The crowd is already breaking up, some heading for the bar, others to the hall where Maxi and his band have launched back into a new bracket. Some are still commenting on the disruption. "The young copper is going to be pissed when he wakes up." "That Jordan needs to be put away before he kills someone." "Jeez, Matt went nuts; I thought he was going to kill Frank." "That bloody Cassie is tough; see the way she went after Jordan?"

Cassie crosses back to the dazed policeman. "I need the keys to your wagon, Bob. We are going to have to take you home."

"In the wagon, gorgeous," he replies, a clownish grin spreading across his good looks, although the swelling on his jaw and cheek are beginning to distort its usually square features.

"Huh, you won't be so jovial in the morning, I bet. Keys are in the wagon, Matt," she shouts over her shoulder. "No, sir'ee, you'll be wanting a few answers, and after a look in the mirror, a little blood, too, I think, Mr. Dunning."

Matt brings the paddy wagon to the gate of the beer garden. He gets Dunning to his feet, hooks an arm under him, and struggles toward the van. "Jordan, get off your bloody arse and help here with this bloke." Jordan does not move.

"Jordan, get over here and help," yells Cassie. Jordan reluctantly moves.

They eventually get Dunning into the passenger seat and buckle him in. Cassie walks to the rear of the wagon and opens the cage door. "Get in," she orders Jordan.

"You got to be kidding. I've got my bike, I can ride back."

"Pigs might fly," says Cassie. "You're drunk. We'll drop you at Stumpy Flats on the way to Kingscote, and you can stay there the night. Now, get in, or I'll make sure the constable files charges against you myself; it was you who hit him, remember?"

Jordan stands his ground. Matt steps up, takes hold of the front of Jordan's jacket, and in a quick move, puts his leg around behind Jordan's knees and pushes. He falls to the ground. Matt stands over him. "I've really had it with you tonight, mate. Now do what your sister tells you and get in the bloody wagon."

"Oh, I wouldn't get too high and mighty, pal. I've a few things to say I'm sure you wouldn't want my sister to hear."

"Last chance, Jordan; either get in, or I'll leave you here, and like I said, let the constable know who hit him," says Cassie. This time the message gets through and Jordan crawls into the back of the van. She shuts and bolts the door, and then walks with Matt to her car.

"Stumpy's a bit out of the way, but I don't want to leave Jordan here. I'll follow in my car while you keep Dunning amused. We'll drop Jordan off and—ah—we'll need to get Bob to the hospital—have him checked out, I suppose." She takes him in her arms and kisses him softly on the lips. "I want you to come back to Middle River tonight. I'll call Dad from Kingscote and tell him to prepare the guest room."

"Is that a good idea?"

"Leave it to me; Dad will be fine. He thinks that once I'm in Sydney, it'll be different. I'll meet lots of other people and—"

"Yeah, I heard the same thing earlier tonight."

"Who?"

"Maureen, she grabbed me for a dance after you left with Dunning."

"That vixen, the tart."

"I was in the supper room, talking to the monsignor. When I came out, I saw you with Dunning, laughing and—"

"And you thought I was chatting him up, and then she grabbed you to add fuel to the fire. Matt, I will never betray you; you must know that by now."

"I just panicked, you know me. I get scared."

"Well, you haven't been given much reason to trust anyone, have you? Your dad, your mother—" There is a shout from the police wagon. "We had better get going." She kisses him and gets into the Pathfinder. There is a hint of mischief in the sparkle of her good eye. "Oh, and by the way, you can tell me what Jordan doesn't think you'd like me to know after we get these boys taken care of. You went quite pale when he said that."

Oh, bugger. As Matt leans through the window of her truck to kiss her, he feels his face getting hot, anxiety building.

27

The seventy-minute ride to Kingscote went without incident except for one heart-thumping moment when Matt and Dunning nearly hit a kangaroo at the Seal Bay turnoff. They had already dropped Jordan at the Stumpy Flats cottage, a thirty-minute diversion off the South Coast Road. Of course, the still drunk Baldwin behaved in his usual bellicose manner as he walked unsteadily to the door, abusing Cassie for being heartless and waving his fist at Matt, promising retaliation of such severe measure that his future prospects would end abruptly at the gate of the state jail. "That is where you belong, and that is where you will stay for a very long time, you mick prick."

Bob Dunning was a completely different story. They took him to the hospital, where the head nurse decided he should be kept overnight for observation. He swore undying appreciation for their help, an open-ended declaration of eternal friendship to be called upon when either of them needed help, and the proclamation that they were the most suited couple he had ever laid eyes upon. "And God help anyone who stuffs it up."

After the nurse had scolded Dunning for swearing, she assured them he would wake in the morning with little more than a pounding headache, and so long as he took it easy for a couple days, "the constable should be fine." Then she turned her attention to Cassie's swollen eye and bruised cheek. "No serious damage," she cheerily noted after a thorough examination, "but I'd slap a bit of butter on it if I were you. Fix it up in no time. Hang on; I've got some in the kitchen."

Cassie telephoned her father from the hospital. He was furious with Jordan and concerned about her black eye. His only reaction to Matt staying overnight was that he would fix up the guest room, clearly intimating *that* was where the boy *would* sleep. She leaves a note in Dunning's vehicle, and they finally get out of Kingscote at 12:15. Forty-five minutes later, they are sitting on the sand at Middle River.

Suspended high in the midnight sky above the northern horizon, a full moon's ivory reflection shimmers along the top of a flat sea separating the north coast of Kangaroo Island from the mainland's Southern Yorke Peninsula. From the unusually calm water, tiny wavelets form along Middle River Beach and then almost at once wash onto the sand with the familiar soothing sound of splashing water, leaving luminous white lines from one end of the beach to the other.

"Beautiful. I'm going to miss all this," says Cassie, nestling into Matt's arms, sitting on a blanket spread on the sand next to the Pathfinder, a meter from the water's edge. The night is still warm, the cool southerly breeze of the South Coast yet to arrive.

"For sure," whispers Matt, brushing her bruised cheek gently with his lips. He is aware of her breathing, its rhythm, the rise and fall of her chest almost matching that of the splashing wavelets.

"Maureen is full on, hey?" Cassie, tense at first when Matt told her about the episode with Maureen and Jordan, is beginning to relax. She looks into his face, chuckles, and then shifts her gaze back to the ocean.

"Look, Matt, I'm not surprised by it. Maureen has been a hot bitch since she started to sprout tits, and I've known all along she's been bulling for you. Hell, you're a handsome devil, and she'd like nothing better than to notch you up along with the others. The harder it is for her, the more she wants. Pardon the pun." They both laugh. "No, she'll figure out a way to have another go at you, particularly now that I'm leaving."

"No, screw Maureen. I told her I love you, and that's the end of it."

"Good, but watch her. She snuck up on you tonight, and you nearly blew it. Pardon the pun, again," she says, unable to control a fit of giggling.

"You're something else," he says, laughing and kissing her forehead. "I reckon you do fancy that Dunning bloke a bit, though, hey?"

She smiles, teasing, "He'd be a good backup if you misbehave."

"You know how to cut a bloke to the quick." He holds his hands to his heart, feigning a mortal blow.

"I'm not impressed." She sits up. "Jordan. I'm so tired of his antics. It's time for Dad to give him an ultimatum. He either puts himself in a treatment center, or we have him committed."

"I can't see either of them going along with you."

"We'll see about that."

She jumps to her feet and begins unbuttoning her lovely, off-white cotton dress, which runs from her neck to her knees, small reddish flowers printed over the light fabric—light enough to allow the gorgeous contours of her body, silhouetted in the light of the moon behind her, to show. "Come on, time for a swim."

In seconds, she is out of her dress and running into the water. His face beams with delight as he strips and runs after her.

They splash, dance, and play—brushing each other, teasing, touching, and kissing until thoroughly aroused, and then they rush back to their blanket.

Twenty minutes later, after the final glorious merging of their energies, they fall away from each other, spent, but exhilarated, staring at the sky. "I love you."

"Yeah, I love you." He sighs. "Ah, I'll miss all this when you're gone." They are quiet; minutes pass, both reflecting on their coming separation.

"Cassie, I—"

She presses a finger to his lips. "Hush, hush, my sweet, not now; no more thinking. Let's enjoy the moment and relive it whenever we think of each other. Here," she says, pointing to her heart and then touching his, "is where we hold each other. I love me, and I love you. That cannot end unless we choose differently, no matter how great the distance separating us. God's greatest gift after life, my love, is that we get to choose how to live it."

"You blow me away, girl, you really do. You know, I'm fearless, almost reckless, about some things—footy, fights, driving too fast, yeah, behaving like a clown, I suppose—but deep down—and I hate this—I'm scared,

Cassie, scared, and I don't know why; I just am."

"Matt, your life has been—"

"No, I can't blame the oldman or my mother's suicide; all that stuff's over. I have to get on with my life, take responsibility for—"

"You have everything it takes, Matt. You are a good person, brilliant and talented, too. Finish your writing projects; get them into the competition. The world's out there waiting, my love; embrace and soar, my mother used to say." She begins to dress. "Matt, I'm afraid sometimes, too. At times, when I think about mummy's death, my faith in God is tested. And, dear God, if anything happened to you—or what if the world were to take you from me when you become famous?"

Matt watches as she drops her dress over her head, watches as she pulls it out and over her perfectly sculptured behind from where it caught in the sweeping arch of her lower back. *Where the bloody hell did that come from? She can read my mind, I swear to God.* He sometimes wondered whether success might change him, if then she might not be enough for him. *What a miserable worm, will the devil not leave me be?*

"I'll kill myself first."

"Ah, don't be so Shakespearean; I'll love you whatever happens," she says, laughing.

"How do you do that?"

"What?"

"Read my mind?"

"Oooh, it's my psychic powers," she gently teases, waving her hands before her like a clairvoyant behind a crystal ball. "No, you are so delightfully and beautifully transparent."

Matt shakes his head, a broad smile underscoring the blueness of his sparkling eyes. "Maybe it's what's called feminine intuition. Scary."

"Enough. Into the car, you, and take us home. I'll cook a good breakfast in the morning and then take you to Mass. I might even come in myself, if the Catholic God's Monsignor Byrne doesn't throw a fit at the terrible heathen leading his bright young writer to a perishing eternity in hell," she says, the developing fun of their conversation washing delightfully through her heart.

"Hmm, and that reminds me; he'll not be happy if you don't have the entry papers for the competition in the morning. What time is Mass?"

"Eleven; I'll call Katherine and have her bring them."

The ironstone road from the beach to the Baldwin homestead is impressive. Cut into the side of the steep Constitution Hill, spectacular beach views open up as the road winds to the top. The car rounds another bend, and the lovers see the dark outline of Althorpe Island appear on the horizon, its solitary lighthouse winking every few seconds. The sand on which they made love, brightened by the moon, continues to welcome the pearly lines of breaking wavelets. The road takes them to the edge of the universe, where the sky is crowded with countless sparkling gems.

"Stop, Matt."

"Here?"

"Yes."

They get out of the car and walk to the fence running along the edge of the road. Startled, two wallabies scatter through the pasture, then pause, cheekily observing the observers before breaking away to hide in the scrubby brush beyond.

"I love this place, Cassie."

"We'll live here eventually," she replies quietly, almost whispering, deep in thought. "Yes, we'll come back one day and raise a family. They'll have this, and the life that goes with it, I swear."

"And your dancing—"

"Won't last forever; I can teach the island kids to dance just like mother."

The moon slides under the first of the clouds arriving with the breeze from the south. The sky darkens, the air cools, and Matt shivers. He puts his arms around Cassie and pulls her tight to him.

28

"I told you to keep quiet," shouts Frank, reaching across the breakfast table and cuffing Sean's ear. "That's not what happened. And get that mouse out of here, or I'll step on it."

Sean scoops *Snot* from the table and into his pocket.

Katherine, at the kitchen sink, picks up a rolling pin and turns on Frank. "You hit that boy around the head again, Frank, so help me God, I'll wrap this around yours," she hisses. "You don't know what happened; you were too drunk, blacked out, as usual."

"I remember Matt coming at me. The piss-ant, wait'll I get my hands on the bludger. Didn't come home last night, did he? Scared to death, I bet," rages Frank.

"He give you a good hiding, Dad," says Sean, challenging him, and then scampering out of the kitchen before Frank can grab him.

"Come back here, you little bugger." He slams the table with his fist. "Why don't you bring your kids up to show some respect?"

"They are your kids, too, Frank, and you have to earn their respect. You hardly qualify for that since getting back on the drink."

Frank scowls. "That's the trouble around here; you're always having a go at me in front of the boys." He skewers a piece of sausage with his fork. As he eats, he begins to calm down. "Yeah, well, anyway, where did Matt stay last night?"

"He called from the Baldwins' this morning, asking me to bring the entry papers to the writing competition into Mass. After the fight, he took the police wagon back to Kingscote. Cassie followed in her car and they went to her place after they dropped Constable Dunning at the hospital."

"Bet her old man loved that. What the hell happened to the copper?"

"There you go; I just said you were in a blackout. Jordan hit him and knocked him out while he was trying to break up the fight. You could be in a bit of trouble, Frank."

"Why? It was the Baldwin twit who hit him. I remember now. Dunning should've stayed out of it; Baldwin was looking for a good hiding from the time he got there, and you know that. You heard him shouting we were just a mob of feral no-hopers, and that he'd fix Matt for good if he kept hanging around his sister. I still got a bit of family pride left in me, Katherine," says Frank, feeling somewhat self-righteous. "I was on the verge of giving him a good licking, too."

The phone rings. Katherine picks it up, listens briefly, and then hands it off to Frank, who is lightly touching the sore spots on his face, especially his nose, already scarred and twisted from past battles. "Sam."

"Ouch," he grunts. *Matt's getting to handle himself; packs a hell of a wallop. I'll have to watch him in future.*

"What?" says the voice of Sammy Marino.

"Nothing, Sam," answers Frank. "Matt's getting to where he can handle himself pretty damn well; kid packs a hell of a wallop."

"Thatsa one reason I'm calling you, Frank. Peter, my manager at the sportsa center in Kingscote called me justa now to say the new young copper, Dunning isa his name, I think he said—nicea young fella, met him last week—finished up in hospital and thata you had something to do with it."

"Now, hang about, Sammy. It was the Baldwin kid who hit him."

"Yes, but you were in a fight with him—"

"He dishonored my family name—" interrupts Frank.

"Momento, Frank. Listen, we hava too much at stake to create unnecessary problems with the law. They're onto us, but hava no evidence yet. I hada a close call a week ago when thata bloody Woodson showed up in his helicopter. I'm told he'sa getting well pretty bloody quick—tough fella. Anyway, we are gonna lay low for awhile."

"Righto, Sam. Sorry I stuffed up," says Frank, relieved to be out of trouble. "When will you be back? The last of the season's pick will be done in a couple of months."

"We'll be back for a load in August. Now, I know thatsa a while away, so you pick up whata they have, pay them—that'll keep everyone happy—and thena hide it under the old storehouse ruins. Tell them to hava the rest ready by August; I'll want a full load."

Katherine is busy putting away the last of the breakfast dishes, trying to ignore Frank's conversation. Patrick gives his mother a "don't worry" look.

"We'll be leaving for Mass shortly, Patrick. Find your brother and be ready to go. Frank, we've got to go to Mass."

Giving Katherine a sharp look, he covers the mouthpiece with his hand. "Will you shut up, woman, I'm discussing business here."

"Business, huh? Monkey business, if you ask me," she says and angrily rips off her apron, throws it over the towel rack, and storms through the kitchen door, shouting over her shoulder. "We'll be waiting outside."

"Thatsa no way to talk to your wife, Frank," says Sam, overhearing the exchange. "Getta yourself off to Mass, we'll talk later and—"

Frank interrupts, "Before you go, Sam, there is one more thing—money. It'll cost to pay the growers, and I don't have that kind of cash."

"I'll have $150,000 for you by the middle of the week. You cana pick it up from Peter. Get off to Mass now, Frank, and you aska the good monsignor to bless his mosta generous of fisherman, Sammy Marino, hey."

"Yeah, right, Sam." Frank drops the phone into its cradle and walks outside to where Katherine and the boys are sitting in the Landcruiser, waiting, feeling much better already—more money on the way—despite his hangover and the bruises on his face and body. *Jeez, bloody Jordan was lucky I didn't finish him off.*

Sean is sitting in the back of the cab, trying to look as small as possible. Frank looks through the driver's side door and sees him. Lifting his body up as far as the cab will allow, and with his arms reaching up and over the boy, Frank growls like an attacking bear. Sean is mortified and pushes further into his seat.

"Arrrgh," roars Frank, before breaking into laughter. "You've got some spunk, you cheeky little bugger. I'll let you off this time, but watch out in the future, hey?"

29

Matt is relaxing on the front verandah of the Baldwin homestead, enjoying the cool morning air. Lifting off the horizon, the sun's blazing rays are already bouncing off the ocean mirror and beginning to heat up the new day. *It's going to be a hot one.* Then it is dark.

"Guess," says a voice from behind. She kisses him lightly on the cheek and removes her hands from his eyes. "It's me, handsome," she chortles gaily, pirouetting to the front of the verandah, stretching with fingers fully extended, reaching for the pale blue mantle, now streaked with wispy, white clouds sweeping over her head. "Isn't this amazing?"

Does there need to be any more than this? He looks beyond her, beyond Althorpe Island to the mainland. *Maybe it's all here. Maybe this is Nirvana.*

"Perhaps we should stay here, Cassie. Maybe, there's really nothing out there that we don't already have."

"Probably, my love, but we have to go out there to know how much we have here. Wouldn't we always be wondering if we didn't find out for sure?"

"Good morning," says Monty, walking out onto the verandah.

"Morning, Mr. Baldwin."

"Good morning, Daddy," says Cassie, throwing her arms about him and kissing him lightly on the forehead. "Oh, Daddy, isn't it the most wonderful of mornings?"

"It is one of many, Cassie. How is that bruise doing? It doesn't look too wonderful."

"It'll be fine by the time I leave for Sydney. Nurse Shirley said to put butter on it, and it would clear up in no time."

"Well, good. Now run along and get us some tea, there's a good girl. Matt and I need to have a little private time for a man-to-man chat."

"Oh, I see. Just you be on your best behavior, Daddy." She rolls her eyes at Matt and then pads on bare feet toward the main doors, looking delicious in her mauve satin bathrobe. She pauses behind Matt and gives him a reassuring hug. Then she is gone.

Monty stares out to the sea, ignoring Matt for the minute. Matt studies the old man's face, noting his strong features and the firm set of his square jaw. *Whatever is going on in that head, you can bet he's got something worked out, the cunning old bugger.*

Monty clears his throat. "Matt, I overheard you and Cassie from the door, there. First of all, I want you to understand that she will not be staying here a day longer than planned; she is to go to Sydney. Her acceptance into the dance company is a wonderful opportunity, and I do not want her swayed or distracted from exploring that opportunity. Her mother would have wanted the same." He lowers himself into the single seat hammock hanging from one of the verandah joists.

Matt listens, waiting for the hammer to drop. *Here it comes.*

"Cassie told me she asked you to go with her—yes, umm, for many reasons I suppose, along with the idea that she loves you, of course. Adolescent infatuation—umm—well, I'm pleased you said no, for her sake." He pauses and looks into the younger man's eyes. "Stay here for the winter, lad; let her be for a time, and see what happens," he says, testing.

The old man and the young man hold each other's eyes. The silence is overwhelming.

Matt takes his time, carefully thinking through what he wants to say. "Look, sir, I don't want to appear rude, but the truth of the matter is that you would rather Cassie find someone more her equal and more to your liking. My father told me it would never work, but I don't accept that." Monty shifts in the hammock, a little taken aback by Matt's directness. "And I don't accept that now, just because you imply or hope it won't work out. The fact of the matter is that Cassie and I are right for each other, and I also believe it to be the will of a power far greater than yours or mine." He pauses, taking time to consider his next words. "Now, I will honor your request for the time being, but in the spring, I will be leaving the island, no matter the circumstances, and I will go to Sydney to be with Cassie."

Monty sits very still, watching the boy's face. A few long moments tick by. "Cassie told me you are a writer, Matt. Well, if you write as well as you speak, then, maybe, you will make your mark. I will hold you to the six months. After that, if the two of you still want to move your lives forward together, well, I won't stand in your way."

Yeah, right, but you'll do everything you can in the meantime to make sure it doesn't work out. "Fair enough, Mr. Baldwin," he says, a wry grin creeping across his face.

"Come and get it," calls Cassie from the kitchen.

"Well, good; that's settled. Now, let's eat; I'm sure our favorite woman has prepared her two best men a feast," *And make the most of it, lad. This little romance won't last; I'll make sure of that.*

In the middle of the kitchen, laden with fruits, cereals, milk, and cream, is a heavy wooden table built from the massive trees, ghost gums, lining the banks of Jumpy Creek. "This kitchen," says Matt, "brings back a lot of memories."

Cassie smiles. "Yes, we had some good times here. Don't hold back; help yourselves. Eggs, bacon, sausage, and toast will be ready in a few minutes. Tea, Daddy?"

Monty sits and motions for Matt to do the same.

"I remember when you used to come here as a little tacker,[48] Matt," says Monty, "when your family had the block up there on the hill. Shame you had to lose that; it's a good piece of dirt. We're in the process of buying it now."

"I heard." While Cassie pours his tea, he remembers.

It didn't seem that long ago his mother was here in this house, at this same table, alive, talking to Kristina. Lovely, kind Kristina, rattling on about the classes they taught at the Parndana School, occasionally breaking into Spanish

---

[48] Tacker: Australian slang for small child.

with her bubble-over enthusiasm. He and Cassie would sneak their tiny hands over the top of the table and reach into the biscuit tin. Kristina and his mother would smile at each other, not letting on that they could see what the two youngsters were doing. Matilda and Kristina got on well together.

Not far along the road was the farm, their farm, the Ryan farm. There, the house dam, and the police looking at the line of sleeping pills neatly arranged on the white clay below the windmill. There was the small dinghy with a neighbor and a policeman, methodically throwing a hook attached to a light chain into the murky water, pulling it back in, throwing it out and pulling it back in, until after an hour of repetition, it tightened. "I've got something," shouts one of the men in the boat.

The image blurs and is replaced with another. Matilda Rose Ryan, nee Gordon, born into the Protestant Church, but converted to Catholicism to marry Francis Ryan, nurse, venerated schoolteacher at Parndana Area School, her eyes closed, serene in her coffin in the Parndana Catholic Church, drowned, suicide, in the dam she always feared.

"Get back here and sit down, Matt." The drunken voice scratches and rips through the image of his mother, replacing it with the bloodshot eyes of the drunken Frank, sitting in the front pew behind the casket. The seven-year-old boy's eyes, defiant and vengeful, turn from his mother and cross the void to stare at his father.

"Hello, Matthew, anybody home?" says Cassie.

Matt, for an instant, is startled. "Oh, I am sorry. I drifted back to the days when my mother and I used to come here together." He remembers that Kristina died shortly after his mother. "She loved coming here, loved your mother." He pauses. "Life hardly seems fair, two good women, hey?"

"There is more than enough tragedy in life to go around," says Monty. "Life wasn't meant to be easy, seems I remember one of our prime ministers counseling." He pauses and gestures to Matt's plate. "I think Cassie wanted to know if you'd like sausage with your eggs and bacon, lad."

"Yeah, sure," he says to Cassie who immediately loads two sizzling pork sausages onto his plate.

"Welcome back, Matt," says Cassie, teasing. "We lost you there for a bit." Then she smiles warmly. "I'm glad your home, with me, here."

The delicious smell of breakfast reminds Matt he is hungry, and he attacks the food with relish, dispatching it in short order and asks for seconds. She loads his plate again.

"You had better call Katherine as soon as you finish; it's already eight o'clock." The clock with the Roman numerals set above the big wood stove is hard to miss.

"I did, early this morning; she's going to bring them. What time will you be ready to leave?"

"Quarter after ten."

"Great. Now, if I can borrow a pad and a pen from you, I can get in an hour on the sestina before we leave—in the gazebo, if that's okay?"

"Good idea." Cassie leaves the kitchen and goes into an adjoining room, her father's study, and returns with a pad and pen. "Go for it."

"Thanks." He cleans up the last piece of sausage and gravy from the plate and then gets up from the table. "Come down when you're ready, Cassie, and I'll show you what I've got. Thanks for the breaky; you're a hell of a cook." He acknowledges Monty. "Thanks for putting me up for the night, Mr. Baldwin."

"All right, then. Keep yourself out of trouble, now, young fella."

Matt nods, smiles warily and leaves.

"I'm going to the Catholic Mass today, Daddy. You are welcome to come along if you'd like."

"Humph, thought I raised you to be a good Presbyterian. Spent all that money—"

"Now, Daddy, you know my views. I prefer my God, not dogma, but I'm happy to go to any church where there's a loving God."

"Humph," growls Monty again.

Matt makes his way through the front doors and follows the grey slate path to the lip of the hill. There the path ends, and a series of limestone steps drop a steep two meters to the gazebo Monty built for Kristina for study and meditation. Solidly constructed from treated timber and lattice panels, the soft earthy colors of its paint blend perfectly with the landscape.

A light-green metal roof provides shelter from any weather.

Meticulously tended shrubs and bushes circle the gazebo. Red flowers blossom from hibiscus, white flowers from gardenias, along with the pink and purple of rhododendrons and azaleas. Pink staechelin roses snake in and out of the lattice panels and twist around the pine log supports all the way to the conical roof.

Matt sits at the round table inside, settles, and closes his eyes. As he relaxes, his mind remains active. Kristina's body lies in the grass next to the burning plane, and then he sees her laughing as she dances in front of her class. He hears a rustle, the sound a full skirt makes when the wearer moves, the sound it makes when a dancer sways her hips to—*flamenco!* He opens his eyes. An eerie chill races up his spine, his heart pounds, and then a hot flush surges through his veins. "Kristina." His mind is alive with images of her and a young Monty, playing around a small campfire on the beach. They are running, laughing, dancing, swimming, and coupling. *My God, the same spot where Cassie—we made love last night.* He hears a laugh. "Kristina?" He looks about the gazebo. No one.

Suddenly, black clouds sweep in from the southwest, chilling the air, forcing the young lovers to dress, to huddle close to the fire. Fanned by the southwesterly breeze, sparks from the flames flare into the darkness, rush across the top of the water and disappear into eternity, taking with them a floating Kristina. *It was her; I did see her.*

His heart races with excitement as he slams the writing pad onto the table and snatches at the words and images tumbling over and over in his mind, to feverishly scratch them onto the paper before they desert him. Two more stanzas begin to take shape. Cross out, reword, reconstruct, correct, spell, clarity—an intense, continuing process at once frustrating and soaring, drawing from instinct and the inspiration he knows comes from a mystical world and, in this moment, from Kristina. *Done.*

A distant voice sings through his metaphorical vision. A loving embrace from behind closes around his shoulders, and the sweet, warm breath of an angel coaxes him gently into the now.

"Matt, Matt, my darling; it's time to leave," she whispers in his ear.

He slowly turns to her, smiles, and nuzzles her arm. "She was here, Cassie. Kristina, she was here, I saw her dancing; she gave me this." He jabs the pad with his finger. "I'll have the rest of it finished before you leave next weekend."

She smiles. "I was hoping she would come. It's in this space where she created some of her best work. She tells me you are very talented."

"You've seen her?"

"She visits often."

"You never told me."

"I was waiting for the right time."

"I felt this incredible energy, and then—you look just like her," he says, still excited. "It seems I have two women looking out for me now."

"I'd like to read it."

"Next week. I'll have it ready before you leave. C'mon," he says, standing, taking her hand and laughing gleefully. "Let's conquer the world, my love."

30

Constable Bob Dunning's head is throbbing, but he convinces the local doctor to let him go home to the cabin by the water on Brownlow Beach, telling him he would rest easier there and heal quicker. The doctor gives the okay, along with a proviso that he rest and gives it a couple of days before returning to duty.

When he walks out into the bright sunlight, he doubts the wisdom of his request, but despite the fuzzy head and unsteady walk, he manages to make it across the road to the police-wagon, and sees the note.

"From Cassie, would be my best guess," he mumbles as he reaches inside to retrieve the neatly folded piece of paper from the dashboard console. As he backs out of the vehicle and straightens up, his head spins and only by grabbing the driver's side door for support saves him from toppling over. *Whoa, take it easy, Bob. Better, get some fresh air into me.* He steadies, gingerly lets go of the door and heads slowly but purposely for the edge of the bluff, ten meters away. The view out over the fisherman's jetty and the wide strip of water to the mainland, a shadowy landmass on the distant horizon, is stunning. He takes in several deep breaths and pops a couple of the pain pills the doctor gave him.

"Thought I was goner there for a minute." He opens the note. "Now, let's see what the lovely Ms. Baldwin has to tell me?"

Dear Bob,

As you read this, I hope you are feeling much better. Someone whacked you last night, could have been accidental; I don't think anyone knows, really. Anyway, you weren't quite with it, so I thought

you ought not to be driving. Matt offered to bring you into the hospital; I hope he hasn't broken any laws by driving a police vehicle. If you need to get in touch, it will have to be before next Saturday. As I told you, I'm leaving for Sydney then.
Cheers,
Cassie Baldwin.

He stuffs the note into his tunic pocket. *Nobody has a clue what happened? Yeah, right.* He quietly chuckles. *It was your brother, Cassie, and you know it—spiteful devil; I remember him looking right at me as I was hauling Frank off him. I guess it was the evener-upper*[49] *for the fight at school. Frank would've killed him, too.* He touches the bruise on his jaw. "He got me a beauty, all right, but it'll be his last. I'll be ready next time." *Yeah, you know what happened all right, Cassie, my pretty. I have a fuzzy recollection you were trying to pull Jordan off Frank when you copped one, too.*

With the pills doing their work, Dunning, decides to ignore the doctor's advice and take a quick run around town before checking into the station. Driving down the main street with the window down, the scent of coffee and pastries, drifting out of Roger's Deli is too much to resist. He noses the wagon into the pavement and steps out, nodding to the early Sunday morning coffee drinkers sitting around the outside tables, and goes inside.

"G'day, Bob," says Roger. "You're looking a bit seedy[50] this morning. Coffee?"

"Yeah, and kick in one of those cream buns, too. And no smart-arse comments, hey."

"Well, I heard early this morning. Here you go," he says, passing the coffee and bun across the counter top. "On me today, Bob."

"Appreciated."

"No worries. Ah no, here comes Scratchy. He's been looking for you all morning; you're in trouble, Constable." Roger ducks out to the back of the shop.

---

[49] Evener-upper: Getting even.
[50] Seedy: Australian slang for "under the weather."

"Scratchy" Dougherty looks decidedly pissed as he walks up the ramp and into the deli. "I waited up all night at the station door for you, Mr. Dunning. Had a rough night, and I'm bloody hungry, too."

Scratchy is one of those people found in every country town—well known, a little short of a dollar, and usually not much of a nuisance. He earned his nickname after an irate husband came home early one afternoon to find Scratchy with his wife, "at it" on the back verandah, so he filled Scratchy's backside with buckshot as he scampered for cover over the back fence. Ever since the local doctor took half a day to pluck the lead pellets from Scratchy's buttocks, he had developed a nervous reaction that manifested as a constant scratching of the pitted and itchy reminder of his indiscretion. Hence, one of the local wags called him Scratchy, and the name caught on.

He barely made a living from distilling eucalyptus oil on his small scrub block at Emu Bay, despite putting in a solid five-day workweek. On Saturdays, he would hitch a ride into Kingscote, get drunk, and then book himself into the police cells for the night on a drunk and disorderly charge. Sunday morning, tradition, along with government regulation, dictated a healthy Australian breakfast, after which the on-duty policeman would drive him out to his block.

"Give me a break, Scratchy," says Dunning. "You already know what happened to me, so cut the bull dust." He calls out to Roger, who is doing his best to remain inconspicuous. "Roger, give Scratchy a full breakfast, will you? I'll fix you up later. Now, Scratchy, I'm going up to the station to check on a few things, so you wait here until I come back, and I'll take you home. And, mate, you better eat outside; you're a bit on the nose."

Inside the police station, the red light of the answering machine is flashing. Dunning pushes the play button and listens. Most of the messages are the usual fare: cows wandering the roads, two dogs killing sheep, and a group of teenagers swimming naked in the town's seawater pool. The message from headquarters was one he could not ignore. The local hospital had notified them of his admission, and he was to report immediately on discharge.

Three calls were from Woodson, all brusque; each one, especially the last, irritated the hell out of him. Woodson said he wanted to start planning a major operation to clean up the Rosenblum cultivation problem on the island and see to it that the Ryans and Sammy Marino were put away for a long time. The message ended with the number of his bedside phone and an order to call back right away. *He's a piece of work, but I've got to hand it to him, he's a tough one. In the hospital less than a week, and already back on the phone wanting to run the show; he should be dead and would've been if it hadn't been for the Ryans.*

The affect of the painkillers he took outside the hospital is wearing off and his headache is returning with vengeance, but he manages to radio headquarters and get in the report. He calls Woodson, who answers the phone before the first ring is finished.

"About time you got back to me," he says, his voice rasping, his breathing labored. "I heard about last night. Don't ask me how; I keep my ear to the ground. Stupid young bugger; I tried to tell you to watch out for the Ryans."

"Jordan Baldwin hit me."

"Not what I heard, but never mind that now. The point is that we are going after the Ryans and Sammy Marino, big time. There was a meeting in town here, yesterday, of the state's top politicians, and they told brass to make a lesson out of what's going on over there."

"Yeah, right. Well, you know there's nothing going on here right now. A big shipment went out a week ago, and there's nothing left to go after, other than a few blokes who may have a plant or two still left around the place, but nothing incriminating." His headache is worsening by the minute. He reaches into his trouser pocket, pulls out the packet labeled "Codeine" and tries to open it with one hand, cradling the phone in the other.

"That's why I'm calling you, I want you—"

Impatiently, Dunning interrupts, "Hang on, will you?" He drops the phone, uses both hands to release two tablets, pops them, and then puts the phone back to his ear.

"Right, I'm back."

"What happened?"

"Got a headache. Look, boss, tell me later; I got to get home and put my feet up."

"Jeez, give me a break; you young blokes are bloody soft. All right, all right, here's the drum[51] in a nutshell. Do not follow up on last night, got it? We want to back off and give these blokes the feeling that the pressure is off. I figure that Marino won't be back until toward the end of winter, August, September, sometime in there. In the meantime, we poke around and see who is growing the stuff besides Ryan, find out where they're storing it, and then go for the big bust when Marino comes in to load up. There'll be a team on call from Adelaide when we're set. This is going to be big, Bobby, my boy. Good for you and me."

The codeine has yet to kick in, and Dunning's headache is starting to drive him crazy. "Yeah, well that's bloody terrific, boss," he says, barely able to disguise his sarcasm. Not wanting to let Woodson wallow in his grandiose scheme to screw the Ryans, he continues. "By the way, I'm picking up a couple of detectives from the internal investigation branch on Tuesday. They want to inspect your accident site. Seems the speed I estimated you must have been traveling at, in my report, is at a marked variance with yours."

"What the hell did you tell them?"

"I estimated eighty kilometers per hour. We both know it was faster than that, though, don't we? More like 110, 120 would be closer to the mark, hey?"

"What are you driving at?"

"You told them sixty, which was the speed you should have been traveling. No, I'm giving you a break, Sergeant; they don't take kindly to coppers killing their superintendents, especially the good ones. You owe me."

---

[51] Drum: Australian slang for information/plan.

31

Early Saturday morning, and though the sun is still low on the horizon, the day is shaping up to be another hot one. The absence of the evening's normal southerly breeze over the last five days, along with unusually high temperatures around the old century mark, meant no respite from the heat. Even the thick limestone walls of the Ryan cottage were unable to keep the inside rooms cool, making it difficult to get a good night's sleep. Last night, Matt barely slept at all. His mind kept running over the events of the week and the jarring reality that Cassie was to leave for Sydney, today.

Bob Dunning did not pursue the events of the previous Saturday night. Maybe Cassie was right when she suggested he probably would not remember much about it. The phone call to thank him for his help did not convey that impression, though. Dunning's suggestion that he stay out of trouble, and there were people who would be very happy to see him and his father go to jail, troubled him. Something was in the wind, and it did not bode well for the family. Dunning also said Woodson was recovering quickly and would be returning to duty much earlier than expected. *Should've let him die.*

The week was tough on him physically. The Hamiltons' shearing started Wednesday, and it had been months since he had used a handpiece[52]—last October, in fact, so he was not yet conditioned for the hard work, the physical and mental stress of standing and bending over sheep for a solid eight hours. Shearing is piecework; the shearer paid for the number of sheep he shears in a day. As if the work is not hard enough, they put more pressure on

---

[52] Handpiece: Shearing tool for cutting wool from the sheep.

themselves, competing with each other for eight hours a day, every day, five days a week, for the highest tally.[53] It is extra tough on a shearer out of condition, especially when the weather is unbearably hot.

He picked up his blue utility from the repair shop in Kingscote on the Tuesday. It was a relief to have it back. Harry did a nice job, and the new, aluminum 'roo bar would protect the radiator from kangaroo encounters. The insurance company had picked up most of the tab, but it still hurt when he had to pry open his cash box and drag out the $500 for the deductible.

He called into the Baldwin property at Middle River on the way home and stayed for dinner that night. Jordan was there, but, surprisingly, he behaved in a rather cordial manner, which Matt found unsettling. Jordan had agreed to check into a drug and alcohol treatment facility at the Royal Adelaide Hospital after Cassie left for Sydney. Matt did not trust Jordan's motives, but he was prepared to give him the benefit of the doubt.

He and Cassie managed to get away by themselves and make love in the gazebo. Neither of them wanted to part, so it was after four in the morning when he finally left. Of course, he would be at the airport by midday on Saturday, he promised. Yes, in plenty of time, time enough for her to read the sestina before her plane took off.

For Matt, it is the sound that goes with his place of serenity, the slap, slap, slap of the seawater lapping the rocks under the arch. From where he sits on the Admiral's cape, the smooth sloping slab of rock, the very spot where the young female seal had screamed her last breath before life's cycle took her, he studies his week's work on the sestina, three stanzas—the last of the six-liners. *Not bad.* One more left, the three-liner—the one that makes sense of it all, a summary of the whole.

Suddenly, inspiration electrifies him. "It fits; it all fits," he shouts, jumping to his feet and throwing his arms toward the roof of the craggy arch, disturbing the seals; some panic and dive from their rocky lodges.

---

[53] Tally: Number of sheep shorn in a period of time.

Snatching his pen from its granite perch, he writes feverishly, oblivious to all but the voices and images whirling around in his mind, until he is finished. He studies the work carefully, only now becoming aware of an absolute tranquility around him. The lapping of the water has stilled. Even the seals are quiet, back on their rocks, spectators, and all at once participants in his magical epiphany. He looks up from his work to look over what has become a new world, transformed for him through the practice and confirmation of his art. *This is my life—to write; to write is what frees me.*

"Are you all right, Matt?" says Patrick. He had not noticed the approach of his eldest stepbrother. "I'm sorry; I didn't mean to intrude, but I was walking on the Admiral, and I heard you yelling. Is everything okay?"

"Yes, Patrick, everything is absolutely fine," says Matt, smiling and wiping the tears from his cheeks. "Dear, sweet Patrick: my brother, the priest, hey?"

"I guess, Lord willing. You had better start heading up for breakfast, Matt. Ah, Mother said Sean and me could go to Kingscote with you; is that okay?"

"Of course; we'll be calling into the airport on the way, though. Cassie is off to Sydney for good, today, so she will be glad for the opportunity to see you. You can practice your priestly duties and console me after she leaves. What time is tennis?"

"Yes, we will all miss her. We have a bye, today, no tennis."

"Right, I forgot. Patrick, you'll make a wonderful priest. You're a handsome bloke, too. You'll have all the young shelias flocking to Mass; Rome will love you." He laughs and then waves his hand in an arc indicating the huge expanse surrounding them, eyes sparkling. "You know God, Patrick; all this is God. You can take this God to the world, and they'll know you know God." He places his arm around his stepbrother's shoulders and guides him along the rough limestone path toward the cottage. "Where is Sean?"

"He got up early this morning and said he was going to his secret cave. He still won't tell anyone its exact location."

"Yeah, over by Weir Cove, though, isn't it?" says Matt. "I don't like him going over there on his own—it is too bloody dangerous."

"I know, but it's kind of a refuge for him, especially when Mum and Dad are fighting," They continue along the path. "There he is, up on those rocks."

"I see him, good." He pauses for a moment. "Patrick, the yelling you heard? I really got a glimpse of the top Bloke this morning,"

"Yes, sounded like it."

"G'day, Matt," says Sean. He is sitting on a pile of stones set off to the side of the lighthouse's auxiliary engine shed. "Mum said we could come with you to Kingscote."

"Jesus, God." Matt tightens his grip on Patrick's arm, freezing them both to a standstill. "Don't move, Sean. Don't move a muscle."

A black tiger snake lies coiled on a large, white rock, centimeters from Sean's arm. Sean no more than flinches on hearing Matt's warning, but two meters of venomous reptile is instantly alert, threatened. The head whips back, its mouth wide, exposing it deadly fangs, glistening in the sun, and then in a lightning move, it strikes at the boy, burying its fangs deep into the flesh and muscle of his forearm. The snake draws back, leaving a red and painful swelling at the bite site and a deadly neurotoxin already spreading into the boy's bloodstream. It readies to strike again.

Sean utters a terrifying howl that sends chills up and down Matt's spine, instantly triggering his warrior instinct. He moves quickly, snatches the boy away from the snake, and spins him into Patrick's arms. Then, balancing on the balls of his feet, he moves to confront the tiger. Primordial rage feeds every cell in his body, firing an overwhelming urge to crush his brother's attacker. He deftly skirts another strike and dances behind the rearing reptile, snatches up its tail, and whirls it around his head. Then, cracking it like a whip, he drops it to the ground, and runs to Sean.

Sean is screaming and sobbing. "It bit me, Matt. It hurts," he sobs, beads of sweat forming on his little face, which is turning a ghostly white. "Help me, Matt, help me; it hurts."

Taking the small boy from Patrick and cradling him in his arms, Matt runs toward the cottage. On the verge of panic, he yells, "Run ahead and tell Katherine, Patrick. Then get the snake, put it in a bag, and throw it in the back of the Ute." He turns his attention back to Sean. "It'll be all right, little bloke. It'll be okay, I promise. Love you, mate, love ya," he says, panting from fear and exertion.

As they approach the cottage gate, Katherine is already running from the house with Patrick. Sean's dog, Barney, is barking crazily from where he is tied to the stringy bark tree in the corner of the cottage yard.

"Lay him on the couch, Matthew. Over there—on the verandah," she orders, pointing, her years of experience as a nurse kicking in. "Get some bandages from the medicine chest and find a flat piece of wood that will work as a splint." She takes the small boy's wrist as Matt lays him on the old couch. "I want you to keep as still as a rabbit hiding in a bush from a fox, Sean. You are going to be fine." The look on her face belies her knowledge of tiger snakes and their deadly venom. They have to get him to the hospital quickly; his best hope, antivenin treatment, critical within the hour.

"Patrick, go in and wake your father, quickly."

"I'm here," says Frank, hurrying from the back door with bandages in hand. "I heard the commotion. Here, the bandages. Matt, get your Ute. Katherine, take Sean, and go with Matt. I'll call the hospital; Patrick and I will throw a few things together and follow." He bends over Sean and strokes him under the chin as Katherine pressure bandages the bite and wraps the whole limb. "Chin up, mate, you're going to be okay; I promise you." Frank wipes his eyes.

Matt picks up a long, flat length of boxboard from under the verandah and breaks it slightly shorter than the length of Sean's arm. He hands it to Katherine and rushes to the shed to get the Ute. Katherine places the makeshift splint along the boy's limb and wraps another roll of bandage around it, restricting movement.

Patrick is throwing the bag holding the dead snake into the back of the Commodore Ute as Matt slides into the front seat and turns the key. The petrol needle reads half-full, plenty to make it to Kingscote, ninety kilometers to the northeast. The big V-8 motor throbs to life and in a second, Matt is spinning the rear wheels as he reverses onto the road, slams the gear into forward, and then roars up to the cottage gate.

Frank is carrying Sean. Katherine gets in, and Frank settles Sean onto her lap. The boy is quiet, tears moistening his eyes as he fights to keep from crying.

"Topped this up, you might need it," says Patrick, passing a full canvas waterbag[54] to Matt through the window. "I'll bring a change of clothes for you."

"Go like the wind, Matt," says Frank.

"She'll be right,[55] won't it, Sean?" Matt says, hoping more than believing his words as he looks at the little man's brave face. He slams the gear into drive and floors the accelerator, sending dirt and gravel behind the spinning rear wheels in a cloud of dust.

Katherine picks up the waterbag and holds the porcelain lip to Sean's mouth. He moans a little as he swallows a small amount of the fluid. The car slides around the corner where less than a week ago the police superintendent died. Katherine gives Matt a quick look. "Keep it going, Matthew; he's going into shock. We have to hurry."

Matt focuses on the road, hitting around 120 kilometers per hour by the time he bangs over the Flinders Chase cattle grid and onto the main South Coast Road. The road opens up, but its surface remains the deadly roller-bearing gravel of rusty ironstone. The speed dial climbs to 140. Dust looms from a vehicle ahead. They close quickly. Despite the absence of a clear view beyond the vehicle in front, Matt pulls to the right of the road to pass.

Suddenly, Katherine screams, "Look out!"

Matt automatically swings the wheel violently to his left, sliding in behind, almost touching the rear bumper of the car in front. Gravel flies up, battering the headlights and windscreen of the slowing Commodore. Bursting out of the dust on the right side, a roadtrain, lights flashing, horn blazing, thunders by—missing the front of the Ute by centimeters.

"Close," says Katherine, taking in a deep breath. "Keep it going, Matthew."

"The road drops into Gum Creek just ahead, I'll get a clear view from there."

The car in front dips over the lip of Gum Creek valley. Matt can see the road ahead for several hundred meters, where it scoops into the creek and

---

[54] Waterbag: Canvas container for carrying water, kept cool through condensation.
[55] She'll be right: Australian vernacular for "everything is going to be okay.".

climbs away to crest of the next hill. He moves over to the right of the road, and once again pushes the pedal to the floor, speeding quickly through 140, 155, to 160. They come alongside and within a few centimeters of the other car, Matt focusing directly on the road ahead. His speeding vehicle dances delicately on the edge of oblivion, straining to give way to its tendency to slide. Only Matt's skill saves them as he delicately corrects every movement toward disaster with minuscule adjustments of the wheel. So close are they to the right side of the road that Katherine ducks instinctively as overhanging branches of bulloak slap the windscreen with loud bangs. Matt's mind registers that the car he is passing is Max Hamilton's, the owner of the sheep he was shearing the day before. The utility bottoms out on the creek's bridge, a resounding thud shuddering through it before it flies up the other side to the crest of the hill.

Max Hamilton is white as a ghost. "That's young Matt Ryan. What the hell is he doing? He could have killed us all. I'll be having a few words with him when he shows up on Monday."

His eldest daughter Julie leans over from the back seat. "Mrs. Ryan is with him, Dad. She has Sean on her lap. They've got trouble."

Katherine holds onto Sean, worry creasing her face as she notes the boy's difficulty to breathe. Suddenly, he screams, and his face reddens. "God have mercy on us," says Katherine. "The venom is working fast; he's going into a seizure."

Sean lapses into unconsciousness, his entire body gripped by jerking muscular contractions. His back arches, the contractions of the muscles throw his body into more violent agitation, his legs kick into Matt's arm and ribs. Matt focuses on the road and ahead sees the black surface of the tarred portion of the South Coast Road coming up fast.

"I'll have to clear his airway," says Katherine. She opens the glove box and searches frantically, looking for a hollow tube, straw, anything she can use to open a passage through Sean's throat to get oxygen to his lungs. "Nothing," she cries desperately.

"The pressure gauge; use the long-stem pressure gauge," shouts Matt, reaching over, snatching the tool from the glove box and handing it to her. "The two ends come off, and the guts will shake out."

Sean ceases convulsing and lies limp in Katherine's lap. She fumbles feverishly with the gauge, manages to get the ends off, and slide out the internal parts. Trying hard not to damage the passage through his larynx or vocal chords, she pulls his head back to straighten out his throat, inserts the steel tube, and gingerly works it in as far as she is able. The little boy stirs.

The Ute bounces onto the blacktop.

"Hurry, Matthew, hurry."

The road stretches out straight ahead for several kilometers. He pushes the pedal all the way to the floor. The big V-8 engine responds with a throaty roar. Flashing lights of an emergency vehicle appear in the distance, speeding toward them. Matt begins flashing his headlights.

Constable Dunning got the call from the hospital. "Young Sean Ryan has been bitten by a tiger snake. Matt and Katherine are on their way with him; the situation is critical." Dunning was on the way out of the police station and on the road in seconds.

Ahead, Dunning spots the vehicle in the distance, flashing its lights. "Matt; hell, he's moving." Pushing down hard on the brake pedal, he slows quickly and then swings into a squealing u-turn, straightens and guns the Commodore's big V-8 engine, heading back toward Kingscote: 100, 130, 140. The image in the review mirror grows quickly larger until Matt is within three or four car lengths, both vehicles racing toward town at 175 kilometers per hour, the siren screaming, red and blue emergency lights flashing.

They thunder through the intersection where the roads from Parndana and the airport converge with the main road to Kingscote. "Just a few minutes, Katherine."

"Just keep going as fast as you can. He's fading, he needs that antivenin, now, or we'll lose him."

At last, their tires squealing, they round the bottom corner of the main road into Kingscote and speed up the frontage road to the hospital. He stops under the emergency awning where hospital staff are waiting. A nurse opens Katherine's door, takes Sean, quickly transfers him to a gurney, and whisks him toward the main entrance, the doctor already alongside, checking out the boy's vitals, Katherine running after them through the ER doors.

Bob Dunning walks back to where Matt is leaning over the hood of his Ute, exhausted, tears trickling down his cheeks. "You okay, Matt?"

"I dunno, Bob, he's looking pretty crook.[56] I don't know if he'll make it."

---

[56] Crook: Australian slang for "sick."

32

An orange hue is beginning to spread across the sky to the east as Cassie walks off the verandah of the homestead on the way to the gazebo for a few minutes of meditation before riding Winston. With her hair pulled back into a ponytail, she looks stunningly fresh and elegant country in her white riding breeches, knee-length boots, and bright lemon blouse. Arriving at the gazebo, she is surprised to see her father settled in his chair, sipping from a cup of tea, and staring off toward the sea.

"Ah, thought you might pop down here for a minute. I brought the teapot, fresh brew, and a spare cup; pour you one?" Monty asks, tapping the top of the steaming pot next to the extra cup on the table.

"I didn't expect to see you up this early. Yes, please, Daddy. Hmm, warming up already; it's going to be a stinker by the middle of the day. Adelaide will be brutal." She sips the hot liquid. "Lovely, thank you."

"I'm going to miss you."

"I will miss you, Daddy." She smiles and looks out to the Althorpes. "And I'll miss all this, too."

"It'll belong to you one day. I've made up my mind about matters affecting all three of you: you, Grant, Jordan, all of this," he lifts his head to indicate the property, "and the other interests that make up the family estate. Grant is not interested in keeping the place going and said you could handle it. I was a little piqued, though, when he said, 'Cassie can dance, but she'll get over that; two or three years in the city will drive her crazy.'"

"Mother thought Grant was the insightful one, but I will tell you this,

Daddy, I intend to be successful. My passion for dance is as great as it has ever has been."

"I'm pleased to hear that. But the estate, I don't dare leave it in Jordan's hands, God love him, and I'm not getting any younger, so I've decided to set up a trust with enough cash to pay out the boys over the next twenty years. It will be up to you to decide what you do. I would hope that you keep it going, but you won't have to make those decisions for a few years, I've still got a bit of get up and go left in me."

"No doubt about it." She looks at him steadily. "I'll keep my options open, Daddy, but I promise you this, this estate will be kept intact with the Baldwin name a part of it," she says, practical and to the point, understanding how painful the process, despite his brave face and attempt a humor. She takes a sip of tea. "If it turns out that a few years in the city is enough, if I'm good enough, of course, to last that long, I could teach the kids here to dance, just like Mummy?" Her voice trails away.

"Your mother loved watching you dance from the time you put on your first pair of ballet shoes. Ah, you are so much like her, fiery and—and somewhat prone to going off and doing things your own way, like the Ryan boy." Monty pauses, knowing he is on dangerous ground and needs to choose his words carefully. "Matt comes from an unstable background, a dysfunctional environment headed by an alcoholic father and a mother who committed suicide. He has a lot to work out, and he may never do that, Cassandra."

"Oh, Daddy, I can take care of myself. You know that, or you wouldn't have me take over the family properties. Matt is going to leave the island; he has to, and I encourage him. He'll develop his talent and find his way, and then I believe he will one day want to come back here. Anyway, what did you know of Mummy when you met her? Nothing. She came from Spain; that's all you knew, but you listened to your heart."

She's right. He picks up the teapot and tops his cup. Damn girl is way too smart for her years. "More?" He holds the pot and motions toward her cup.

"No thanks," she says, draining the last of her tea. She puts down the cup, crosses to Monty, and hugs him. "I love you, Daddy; I worry more for you than I do Matt. You know, once Jordan has settled into treatment, you should leave Harry in charge and come out to Sydney again for a long break. The crutching will be over, and Harry can manage things just fine. Besides, you have that friend in Sydney. You should look her up—er—Belinda, isn't it?" He nods. She kisses him on the cheek, rough with its graying stubble. "I have to run along. Winston deserves a good workout before I leave; it will be a while before I ride him again."

Monty pats her hand. "Actually, that's a good idea; I might do that. Yes, I'll get you settled, and then pop back again in a few weeks." He looks at his watch. "It's almost eight o'clock—off with you; we need to be leaving by eleven."

Cassie runs back up the stone steps to the slate path and stops to take a last look at the homestead, her home for twenty years—grand, rooted solidly in the earth, its thick stone walls impregnable, familiar, and comforting. She is grateful.

As she enters the stable, Winston's head looks out from the stall. She strokes the white blaze running the full length of his nose and reaches for the bridle hanging from the hook next to the stall door. Preparation for the daily ride almost always plays out the same way, but today is different, and Winston seems to sense it. Usually, when Cassie attempts to bridle him, he acts up, tossing his head about, teasing. Today, he is quiet, brooding, and she slips it on easily.

After brushing the big chestnut's back, she leads him to the saddle room, a converted stall with a well-drained cobble floor where the horses stand for a hosing down after a workout. Several saddles straddle evenly spaced pegs at the rear of the stall. A royal blue saddlecloth with an embroidered gold band running around the edge stretches over Cassie's saddle, a high pommel, Spanish riding saddle. The de Coronardo family crest of scarlet red and gold embroidery, depicting a Conquistador brandishing a sword above his head while astride a rearing horse, stands out in the left corner of the cloth.

She rubs her hand over the embroidery, relishing the rich texture and fine artisanship, and then throws it on Winston's back before turning to the saddle. A gift from her mother, she pauses to marvel at the fine, intricate carvings in the leather. With her finger, she traces the pictures formed within a complex pattern of emblems, showing a horse and rider progressing through various stages of dressage.

The sun is well up and hot. The surf is moderate, breaking with its familiar rumble before running up to soak the sand briefly, and retreat to rejoin its source. She urges Winston forward into knee-deep water, but he suddenly begins stomping and splashing with his front hooves, usually a prelude to rolling over. Cassie pulls back sharply on the reigns, trying to keep his head from dropping. Too late, he rolls, throwing her into the water, but clear of him. She surfaces, sitting with water up to her chin, laughingly chiding him, but enjoying the enforced cool-off. Winston regains his feet and stands, waiting for his rider, looking down at her with what could be best be described as a quizzical expression. She checks over the wet saddle, satisfies herself that all is well, and then remounts.

Then, like a bolt out of the blue, she is aware of where she and Winston are standing, and laughs, the wild wonderful laugh of a person happy and in love. *This is where we made love last week.* She whirls the big horse around to face the far end of the beach and kicks him into a flat out gallop yelling, "Go, Winston, go." Her excitement soars as she lays flat along his powerful frame, yelling "faster, faster" into his ear, slapping each side of his neck with the overlap of her reigns, pounding over the sand at break neck speed.

Monty is waiting on the front verandah as she rides up. "I watched you, saw you come off in the surf and then gallop the length of the beach and back, looked like you were having a wonderful time."

"Yes, fantastic." She laughs and dismounts. "Winston is quite pleased with himself, the brat. The saddle is soaked and there is sand in the carving, I'll have to brush it down and give it a good coat of saddle dressing right away."

Jordan, looking fresh and already dressed for the airport, joins Monty on the verandah. "Don't worry, Sis; I'll take care of it. Take care of your boots, too, if you like," he says, crossing to her. "Here, let me have him."

"Really?"

Jordan grins and takes the reins. "I owe you, Cassie, a lot."

"Well, thanks. I'll come with you; I have a few things to get from the studio. You're looking good this morning, Jordan. I'm impressed."

They walk into the stables together, Winston ambling along behind.

"Cassie, can I come up to the studio?"

"You haven't wanted to come up there for years. Are you sure?"

He nods. "I'd like to."

"Okay. Yes, that's a good idea. Come on up, but take Winston's saddle off first, will you?"

Jordan leads Winston to his stall while she takes the steep loft stairs to the studio. The familiar smells of the coating protecting the polished hardwood floor and the rubdown liniment spilt around the sofa waft over her as she pulls aside the multicolored silk drape hanging from the top of the door. She goes straight to the sofa and begins the usual struggle to take off her boots, made even more difficult this time because of their soaking and the suction affect created around her feet. Jordan arrives.

"Want help?"

"Thanks," she says, offering him a leg. He wrenches the boot free, takes care of the second one, and then looks about the room.

Years had passed since he was in the studio. He remembered Kristina's delight when she first danced on the floor after Monty and Harry finished building it.

"Funny, it feels alive; like it's full of a positive kind of energy. I've never felt that before."

The room is big, with floor to ceiling mirrors on the long wall. A *barre*, a rail for support when doing exercise routines, runs the length of the same wall. Reflecting in the mirrors are four life-size posters hanging next to each other along the opposite wall, each depicting a different form of dance and movement.

In the first, a male ballet dancer is mid-flight through the arc of a *grand jeté*, his movement captured in its greatest moment of perfection and exhilaration. The next poster offers a very different form of dance: Australian Aborigines raise dust from their stomping feet, dancing stories in a corroboree, the sacred rock, Uluru, a magnificent backdrop in the red Australian desert. In the third, a young lass is seen in the middle stages of an Irish jig, knee raised, toe pointed, arms and hands held rigid to each side of her body. The fourth portrays the end to a long day of rehearsal. One male and two female dancers lay on the floor exhausted, while a weary ballerina balances on her left leg as she bends, caught in the moment, removing her ballet shoe from a red and blistered foot.

Across from the sofa, a stereo system and speakers sit on top of a small bookcase. Wall shelves filled with books on dance, exercise, and biographies run off from each side of the bookcase. In the far corner, a huge glass display cabinet holding an assortment of trophies, photos, and flamenco and ballet shoes, stands alongside a rack of costumes.

Hanging on the wall beside the stereo is a life-sized photograph of Kristina, frozen in a moment of dance, jondo-style[57] flamenco. Her arms reach back in a sweeping motion above her head, her dark hair, pulled severely into a tight bun, frames the classically beautiful face and brown eyes, intense, looking out from the center of the picture, on fire, alive. Even the click, click, clicking of the castanets she holds in her hands seems to reverberate through the studio.

Cassie hears Jordan suck in a deep breath. He walks to the glass cabinet. "May I?"

"Please."

He opens the glass door, reaches in, and removes the pair of black flamenco shoes set next to Cassie's first pair of *demi-pointe* ballet shoes, a gift from Kristina shortly before she died. The flamenco shoes are scuffed and worn, but still in good shape. He turns them over where dozens of nails are imbedded in the soles and raised heels.

"These are the pair she has on in the photo?"

Cassie nods. "She wore out a lot of others."

"She, um—was quite something, hey?"

"She was the best."

---

[57] Jondo-style: Profound and serious.

Jordan's eyes glisten.

"Go ahead, let it out; it'll be good for you."

"Can't, Cassie, can't; too much water under the bridge. She, um—well, I don't want to get into that." He hands her the shoes. "These fit you?"

She nods. "Will you put them on and dance?"

Cassie looks at the clock on the wall and then back to Jordan.

"Give it five minutes, Cassie. Please."

"Okay. Put on the top album, the one of the gypsies singing with guitars." She straps on the shoes and goes to the barre to stretch and warm up. After a few minutes, she finishes, opens the cabinet, and picks out a pair of castanets. "Okay, ready. Five minutes, right?"

Jordan lowers the stereo needle onto the record. The plucking of strings, the wailing of gypsy singers, stamping feet, and slapping guitars fills the studio. Cassie, innocent and beguiling, begins to move her arms about her head and upper body, slowly clicking the castanets and stamping the heels of her shoes on the wooden floor. She increases the tempo of her dance with the building tempo of the music and gypsy wailing.

Her eyes flash across the line of posters. Always, they inspire her—fill her with thrilling bursts of raw energy translated into complex and aggressive emotions communicated through flying feet and swirling arms. She snaps her head to her right and snatches a glimpse of her mother's photo. Kristina de Coronardo stares out and locks onto her daughter's eyes, willing her presence and power into the young woman's movement. A fiery lust flares through her psyche and body, pushing her to a greater level of intensity in a wild, passionate, and creative choreography.

The click, click, clicking of her castanets picks up tempo, building until their speed matches the rapid clattering of a machine-gun. Her shoes match the tempo of the castanets, their action, stomping and stamping, become a blur of motion, beating out a blood-scorching rhythm of primitive heel and toe tap. Her hair flies untamed about her head, streaming strands whip across her face, escalating her allure. Her personae transforms into a temptress on the edge of ecstasy. The guitars and singing of the gypsies crescendo and stop.

Cassie, with a full-throated yell, "I live," stops, and then freezes, one hand flung back over her head, the other tucked into her hip. A foot anchors to the floor while the other lifts on its ball, allowing her knee to bend and point directly down stage. She is, for the moment, a statue of Venus, transfixed in the imperious pose of the aristocratic goddess and in that moment, all at once, flushed, excited, and spent.

"Bravo, bravo, magnífico, mi fantástico, Cassie," yells Jordan, standing and clapping enthusiastically, tears streaming down his cheeks. "It's amazing, Kristina, she lives within you." He hugs her.

Cassie responds. "It is wonderful to see you enjoying yourself, Jordan. It seems so long since you smiled. Staying away from the alcohol this past week seems to be working a miracle." She pauses, steps back, taking his hand in hers. "I'm glad you're going into treatment."

He turns to look up at the photo of his mother. "I hated her, you know—towards the end—before she died. She wanted me to be different."

"Come on, come on, don't be so hard on yourself, brother; life happens. She got it wrong about you, and you suffered because of it. It is not uncommon for kids to hate their parents at times. There were moments when she drove me so hard, when my feet were so blistered that it was agony to walk let alone dance, that I felt like I hated her." She places her hand on his arm. "We love you, Jordan, you're family, even though you worry us sick most of the time. Look, just get well, stay well; stay away from the alcohol."

She looks up at the clock. "Ten, time to go; we have an hour before we must leave. You go ahead, I'll catch up; I'd like a few minutes here alone."

"Yes, of course."

"Oh, come on; cheer up," she says, unbuckling the straps on her shoes. "It's not the end of the world." She laughs. "It's rather the beginning of a new one, really, isn't it?"

"I hope so," he says, trying to smile, unsure.

His footsteps fade away from the bottom of the stairs. Cassie crosses to the cabinet and returns her mother's shoes to their usual place. On the bottom shelf, her favorite pair of pearl split-sole ballet shoes catches her eye, her first pair, given to her by her mother when she was five years old; her opening to another beautiful dream—one of the many created for her by Kristina before she died.

She turns to the photo on the wall and looks up at her mother. "Thanks, Mummy." Then, smiling, she pads barefooted to the exit, stops, looks back, and gestures for her mother to follow. "Come on, Kristina, time we got on with what you started here."

33

Matt waves as Dunning drives off from the hospital to check on a report of a broken window at the Kingscote Area School. With Woodson out of the picture for the time being, Dunning is the only policeman on the island, meaning that for twenty-four hours a day, seven days a week, he is on call, and even with the island's low crime rate routine duties alone are enough to keep him very busy. *You're a good bloke, mate, even if you are a copper.* Frank and Patrick arrive in the Landcruiser and pull in behind Matt.

"How's he doing?" calls Frank, slipping out the driver's seat and hurrying to join Matt, Patrick close behind. Frank looks dreadful: pale, drawn and troubled.

"They're working on him in the ER. Katherine is with him."

"Right; I'm going in there." Frank puts his hand on Matt's shoulder. "Look, good work, Matt, the way you took care of that snake and getting in here as quick as you did— You kept your head, and Sean's in with a chance because of you."

"It was Katherine who kept him alive; did something like you did with Woodson to get air into Sean, except she used the tire gauge and went down his throat with it."

"Team effort; thanks, hey." He hurries toward the hospital entrance and disappears inside. A nurse is coming out of the ER.

"Sean in there?" asks Frank, pushing through the doors before she can answer.

Katherine is standing back from the triage table. The local doctor is pushing a needle into a vein in the crook of Sean's arm. "Nice job, Katherine;

your improvising kept him alive," says the doctor, referring to the intubation procedure she had given the boy. "He has a fighting chance."

"Frank," says Katherine, turning as he enters, reaching for his hand.

He takes it. "How is he doing?"

"We don't know yet," says the doctor, looking up at Frank. "It depends on how he responds to the antivenin."

"Jesus God," Frank says. He moves closer to the bed and reaches out to brush back the cowlick from Sean's sweating forehead, choking back a threatening flood of tears. "You gotta save him, Doc, he's just a little bloke, you know." He keeps brushing the boy's hair from his forehead.

Everyone is quiet. The doctor looks to Katherine. She stands and takes Frank by the arm. "Come on, Frank, let's go out for a bit." He resists. "Come on," she coaxes gently, "let the doctor and nurses do their jobs." She leads him from the room.

Matt is pacing about the visitors' waiting room, and Patrick is reading the local paper, the *Islander*, when Frank and Katherine enter. Seeing Frank in tears is shocking to the boys.

"Is Sean dead, Dad?" asks Patrick. Matt is horrified, unable to make a sound.

"No, no," says Katherine, wrapping her arms around Patrick. She looks at Matt. "Come here." He moves to her, and she wraps an arm around him. "Boys, he's in pretty bad shape. The truth is we don't know if he will come out of it, but he's a fighter, and he is in good hands. As long as he keeps breathing, he's in with a chance."

Patrick says softly, reverently. "He's made it this far; he's going to be fine, I know it. I know it." He starts to kneel. "Come on, let's say a rosary for him."

They kneel, all of them including Frank, using the waiting room chairs to rest their heads in their hands. Patrick leads them. "Hail Mary, full of grace, the Lord is with thee. Blessed are thou among–" Twenty-five minutes later, the doctor walks into the room.

"We have him stabilized." The Ryans stand. "He seems to be responding to the antivenin, but we won't know for sure for a few hours. I have arranged for the air ambulance to take him to the Royal Adelaide Hospital later this afternoon; they have the resources to give him the care and attention he needs. He'll be better off there."

"Can we see him?" asks Frank.

"Let's give him a couple of hours before you go in, Frank. I have arranged for the kitchen to bring you sandwiches and drinks. Katherine, I think it would be best if you went with him on the flight."

"Of course."

"I need some air," says Matt walking to the door. "I'll be outside if you need me."

With myriad images spinning through his mind, Matt crosses the road in front of the hospital, walks to the edge of the bluff, and stares out over the calm water, sick to his stomach. A white pelican, wings flapping powerfully, launches from its perch atop one of the wharf's tall light poles. Once airborne, the bird stops flapping and descends to a graceful glide along the top of the water. It lowers its feet and snatches, with a splash Matt can hear all the way on the bluff, at the seawater. The bird begins to flap again, its long, wide wings pushing rhythmically through the air with powerful, leisurely sweeps, up and down, up and down, up and down. It gradually gains height, its track taking a wide arc over the glassy water toward the narrow strip of rocky foreshore, a desperate, struggling mullet[58] trapped in the grip of its clawed feet. *A seal for the shark, a fish for the bird, a death for a life, and Sean? Why?*

"You never know, hey?" Frank says, walking up to stand beside Matt. "I mean, you know it's coming, sometime, but you just don't know when. Here today, gone tomorrow. Take this, it's one of those sandwiches from the hospital."

Matt takes the sandwich and manages a half-hearted bite. "Thanks." He looks at his father. *Man, you are so full of contradictions. You'll be a story one day, if I can ever figure out who the hell you are.*

"Seen it all, I have. Nature's creatures have it tough—brutal, hey? Hell,

---

[58] Mullet: Breed of fish.

they don't hold a patch on what the human species get up to. Should have seen 'em at work in 'Nam, bloody slaughter all over the place, it was. Bits of body, blood, and guts everywhere, hanging off trees, women, kids—bloody awful—and what'd we do it for? You know, it's ironic; we're the lot given free will and knowledge of a God."

The pelican lands on the narrow stretch of beach, drops the struggling fish onto the sand, and then scoops it into its webby mouth.

"Listen, mate, isn't yer girl leaving today?"

"Yeah, I guess she'll be wondering where the hell I am."

"What time does the plane leave?"

"Twelve-thirty."

"It's five to twelve. If you get going now, you could make it out there before she leaves." Matt looks over to the hospital. "Look, there's nothing you can do for Sean right now. He's in good hands, and we can't see him for another couple of hours, anyway. You'll be back by then."

"I'll never work you out, Dad. You're a prick most of the time."

"Get out of here, or you'll miss seeing her off."

Frank watches the boy scamper across the street to his Ute. *Yeah, Matt, you're a good kid. Thank God, you don't have to live in this bloody skin.* Frank looks at his watch, again. *One or two won't hurt.* He heads off in the direction of the town and the Ozone Hotel overlooking Nepean Bay a few minutes walk away, thirsty.

34

Kingscote's large regional all-weather airport a few kilometers southeast of the town is the only commercial airport on the island, and it gets very busy especially in the summer months, the premium tourist period. A small building, adequate most of the time and set up against the tarmac fence, houses the check-in and reception services. Several small charter planes crowd much of the space on the tarmac, waiting for the return of their tourist passengers brought to see all there is to see of the huge island in a day—impossible. A 50-seat turbo-prop, which is part of the airline fleet providing regular scheduled services to the island, a giant alongside the smaller aircraft, waits to load passengers and their luggage. A pilot walks around the bigger plane, looking into the wheel wells, kicking the tires, the required ground check before the short, twenty-five-minute hop to Adelaide.

Monty swings the big Ford sedan into the airport entrance, clatters over the white cattle grid, and drives on into the parking lot. Cassie is first out—looking gorgeous in a lightweight, blue cotton dress, which contrasts splendidly with her dark tan. As she holds onto her broad-brim straw hat, which wants to lift off in the light breeze, she looks among the people milling about the airport building.

"Looking for Matt, hey?" says Jordan. "He's not here; can't see his Ute."

Monty is pulling luggage bags from the trunk. "Don't worry, he'll show up. Jordan, give a hand, will you?"

Cassie takes a bag, a small carry-on, and heads for the airport building, worried. A vehicle rattles over the cattle grid; she swings back to look, another tourist bus. *Something must be wrong.*

Monty and Jordan join her at the check-in counter with the rest of the luggage.

"Morning, Mr. Baldwin," says the clerk, nodding his head in greeting. "Cassie, Jordan; all three of you off to Adelaide today then, hey?"

"Yes, Jim," says Cassie. "You have a customer phone I can use, please?"

Jimmy points to a phone on the corner of the counter. "It's the company phone, but please, feel free."

"Thanks." She dials the Lighthouse number. No answer. "He should be here by now."

"We will be boarding in five minutes, Mr. Baldwin."

"Thank you, Jim," replies Monty taking the boarding passes Jim hands to him.

"Daddy, I'm scared. Something has happened; I'm sure of it."

"Yes, your right, he should have been here by now. I'll give the police station a call, if you like."

"Please, Daddy."

After three rings, an answering machine responds. "This is the officer in charge, Constable Bob Dunning. The station is temporarily unattended. Leave a message, or if the matter is an emergency, please call 000."

"Bob, Monty Baldwin here, we are at the airport, and young Matt Ryan was to meet us, but he has not turned up. Just checking to make sure everything is okay. If there is a problem, call us and let us know, will you? We are staying at the Adelaide Hilton tonight."

"Mr. Baldwin, I'm sorry, but I have to ask you to board the aircraft now, sir," says Jimmy interrupting.

"Yes, of course." Monty puts his arm around Cassie's waist, and shepherds her toward the door. "Sorry, dear, he must have had a blow-out or some kind of breakdown. It can happen anytime on these roads."

"I know something awful has happened."

"There's nothing we can do now, Cassandra. We have to get on the plane. I told Bob Dunning where to get in touch. But, my bet is he has a flat tire, or something minor like that."

"I hope you're right, Daddy," say Cassie, her voice uncertain.

Cassie keeps looking over her shoulder. Then she is on the plane, buckling into her seat next to the window. The aircraft propellers begin to rotate slowly; the engines ignite and quickly build to their familiar, high-pitched scream. The pilot lets off the brakes, and the plane begins to move across the tarmac. Cassie stares out the window toward the entrance to the airport.

Matt roars away from the hospital, *that plane better be late leaving*. By the time he flashes through the town's outskirts, he is already doing ninety-kilometers-per-hour, breaking the speed limit, set at sixty, unaware of the police vehicle approaching from the school road that intersects with the main highway.

The red and blue flashing lights of the pursuit car quickly catch up to him. "Bloody hell, what now," he shouts, thumping the steering wheel as he pulls to the left shoulder of the road and then jumps out. Dunning stops close behind him and gets out of the car looking angry.

"What the hell are you doing, Matt, speeding through town like that. That's a busy intersection back there; you could kill someone."

"I'm trying to get to the airport before Cassie leaves."

"That's no bloody excuse, mate. You got young Sean in hospital already, haven't you? That's enough, isn't it? It is for me. I don't want to be dragging you from a wreck, dead, or someone else from the town for that matter."

"I'm sorry, Bob. I'm not thinking straight."

Dunning shakes his head, "Look, I'll let you off with a warning this time, but if I catch you at it again, I'll book you hard. Now on your way, and stay within the bloody speed limit, will you?" He looks at his watch. "You can still make it. They rarely leave on time." He begins to walk back to his car, pauses, and turns back to Matt. "Don't take my friendship for granted, Matt. I am a policeman. Just don't cross the line, all right, I've got a job to do."

"Yeah, right, sorry, Bob." Matt hurries back to his car, jumps into the driver's seat and roars off, screeching the rear tires as he leaves. Dunning shakes his head, returns to the car, and turns around to head back to Kingscote.

Creeping over the speed limit, Matt curses himself for running foul of

Dunning. The encounter set him back five minutes; he pushes the pedal a little harder. As he approaches the airport turnoff, the car clock is already showing 12:30. Two minutes later, he bangs over the cattle grid, his heart sinking as he sees the plane beginning to taxi from the tarmac. *On time—today of all days, bugger you, Jimmy.*

"There he is," says Monty as the blue Ute bounces over the airport cattle grid and rushes to a sliding stop at the tarmac fence. Cassie stares through the small aircraft window, murmuring a sigh of relief as her bloke gets out of his vehicle, stands by its open driver's side door and waves. She pushes her face against the window; tears trickle down her cheeks as she brings her right hand close to her face. As if she were caressing his cheeks, she touches the plastic window and slowly waves her hand back and forth.

Matt slides to a stop at the fence, jumps from the Ute and looks along the line of windows for Cassie. *Could easily be on the other side—no, is that her? Yes, yes, it is.* He can barely distinguish her features, the angle of the aircraft causing the window to impede any clear view, but her perky nose, the slow wave of her hand across the plastic—it can only be her. He waves and waves, willing her his love.

Then she is gone. He rails briefly, slams his fists against the hood of the Ute and kicks the front tire, and then curses as pain shoots through his foot. "Bloody hell, bloody hell," he shouts hopping about on his good leg and shaking the hurt out in the other.

The aircraft turns to line up on the runway, and he slips from her view. She does not see him bang the hood of his Ute with his fists or kick the front tire and hurt his foot.

He watches the plane line up for takeoff, suddenly weary, sad and lonely. The high-pitched scream of the turbo-props build to full power. The pilot eases off the brakes, the plane lunges forward and quickly gathers speed as it races toward the end of the airstrip, and then, deliberately, it lifts into the air over the bush boundary, climbs, arcing north to eventually track to Adelaide. His eyes follow until the plane becomes a speck in the sky and disappears into a bank of dark clouds, carrying his love and best mate. Anxiety begins its deadly creep.

He remembers the copy of the sestina lying on the seat, retrieves it and begins reading—

> *Oh, just this moment do I long for my river where the waters surge*
> *In tumultuous victory over the earth's impede—and where the heat*
> *Of conquest so stirs the heart to beat and keep this warrior alive*
> *To vanquish mortal fear, and destroy the eternal dark.*

35

Patrick is watching the cricket on a black and white television when Matt walks into the hospital waiting room. "How's he doing, Pat?"

"Mother is with him now. You can go in, if you like."

"You doing okay?"

"I've been watching the test match, but if you asked me the score, I wouldn't be able to tell you."

"Yeah, I've been feeling crook in the guts all day. Hang in there, Pat. I'll be back." He leaves for the ER and is about to push through the swing doors when a nurse calls to him from the end of the corridor.

"Oh, Matt, hi. We moved Sean, he is in here, the ICU."

"How's he doing, Linda?" Linda is from a farming family on the east end of the island and has two brothers who play football in the Island League competition.

"He's doing a little better. The antivenin is taking hold."

"Good. Is it okay to go in?"

"Gosh, yes, of course. We're all praying for him here, Matt."

"Thanks, Linda."

Katherine is sitting alongside Sean's bed, dozing. Sean is breathing from a ventilator through a tube inserted in his trachea. An IV line runs from a clear plastic bag of saline solution hanging beside the bed to the Catheter needle in his wrist. A number of thin electrical wires attach to small adhesive patches stuck to parts of his chest and feed into an EKG machine. A green line registers his heartbeat on a monitor screen, a sharp ping accompanying each beat, a printer running continuously, recording the vital signs on a chart. He is deathly pale.

"How's he doing, Katherine?"

Katherine wakes, instantly alert, and reaches for his hand. "He's doing much better. The doctor sedated him; we didn't want him waking up and fighting the treatments."

"Is he going to be okay?" asks Matt, barely able to get the words out for fear of the response.

"He's getting the best of care. Doctor Wilson is confident, but we have to monitor him closely. One of the dangers is that antivenin can cause a heart attack, but he is responding. We'll be going out to the airport in about an hour."

He nods, releases her hand, and moves closer to the bedside. "Hey, you're going to be good as new, mate," he says, picking up Sean's hand. The boy shifts a little and grimaces. "Hey, did you see that, Katherine? I reckon he heard me. You little, bloody beauty, hey."

"I told you I reckon he'll come through," says Patrick, who picks up the last of Matt's words. "He's tough, and God is looking out for him." He pauses and clears his throat. "Er—do you know where Dad is?"

"You haven't seen him?" asks Matt.

"He said he was going outside to speak to you the last I saw him."

"Yeah, well he did, about two hours ago." He shakes his head. "Ah, no, don't tell me he's down at the pub." He looks at Katherine.

For a second, her eyes flash with anger, but then she shrugs and sighs. "It's his way of dealing with things. You'd better get him, if you don't mind, Matthew."

Matt heads for the door. "I'll be back." He signals for Patrick to follow.

"Make sure your mother has her bag with her when she goes to the airport," he says quietly as they walk along the passage to the hospital exit. "You can come out with me when we leave to follow the ambulance. The oldman isn't going to be worth a damn, but I'll try to get him back up here."

"What's the use, Matt?"

"That's his kid in there, and he ought to be here."

The Ozone Hotel is one of two watering holes in Kingscote. Both are popular, and the patrons often move back and forth between them several times over the course of the day. Matt goes into the main bar and looks around; Frank is not there. "Yeah, he left fifteen minutes ago; said he was going over to the Queenscliffe," says a local fisherman over the top of his beer.

Minutes later, Matt pushes through the swing doors of the front bar of the Queenscliffe Hotel. A few thirsty blokes, it is early afternoon still, are bellying up to the bar, chatting and downing schooners of cold beer. Frank is sitting at the far end of the bar on his own, placing an empty glass back on the bar top, gesturing to Sparky Johnson, part-time electrician and barman, to "fill 'er up."

Matt walks purposely over to Frank. "Bloody hell, what the—this is just great, isn't it? Sean is up in the hospital fighting to stay alive from a snake bite, and here you are in the pub getting pissed. What sort of a mongrel would you be, hey?"

Frank's mood is ugly. "Yeah, well I was just coming, wasn't I? Only had a couple, and if you think you want to do something about it, have a go."

The bar crowd goes quiet.

"Who'd you say got bit, Matt?" says Sparky.

"Sean, my brother. The Doc reckons he'll make it, but he's not out of the woods yet—flying him to the Royal Adelaide this 'arvo."[59]

"What the hell are you doing in here, Frank?" shouts a voice from among the drinkers. "You ought to be up there at the hospital with your kid and your wife."

"Why don't you shut ya mouth, ya bloody drongo,[60] and if you want to make something of it, I'll be outside." Frank slides unsteadily from the stool and pushes his way past Matt and through the pub's patrons. Matt follows, angry, disgusted and embarrassed.

"Give our best to Sean and Katherine, Matt," says Sparky. "We'll all be pulling for him."

The noise in the bar resumes as the drinkers begin discussing the latest Ryan disaster. "Tough little bloke—Ryans' is been through it all—Frank's

---

[59] 'Arvo: Slang for afternoon.
[60] Drongo: Australian slang for 'fool.'

an alky, mad as a cut snake since he got back from Vietnam—first wife committed suicide—"

Matt follows Frank through the pub's[61] swing doors. "You lying bastard; you were setting up in there for rest of the day. What the hell is going on in that head of yours?"

Frank avoids the question. "Look, calm down, I needed a couple beers to settle me nerves, that's all, and now here we are on the way back again, no harm done, right? There was nothing could be done anyway, but wait."

"You could've stayed with Katherine; she's Sean's mother, for God's sake. Don't you think she needs a little support from her husband? Bloody hell, like I said earlier, I can't work you out." They come to the Ute, parked along the curb in front of the Ozone. "Get in," says Matt, pointing to the passenger side door.

Monsignor Byrne's car pulls in behind them as they stop in front of the hospital. The agile old priest is over to the Ute's driver's side door before Matt finishes unbuckling his seatbelt. "I got Katherine's message when I got in from Cape Torrens a few minutes ago."

The monsignor, an avid naturalist, spends days at a time each month camping out along the north and west coasts, looking for fossils, rocks, and animal skeletons for his third book about Kangaroo Island, *Kangaroo Island's Fascinating Historical Relevance.*

"Where is Sean, Matthew? How's he doing?" Frank is now standing next to the priest.

Patrick calls from the hospital entrance. "In here, Monsignor, Mother said for you to come right on in, please, right away."

"I'm *cooming*, Patrick"

The monsignor studies Frank for a moment. He catches a hint of shame in the man's bloodshot eyes. *Good, there it tis; he's feeling it.* "Frank," he says, putting his arm about his shoulders and guiding him toward the door, "let's go inside to the boy and Katherine, shall we? I'm *tink'n* it's a good time for a rosary. C'mon, Matthew."

---

[61] Pub: Hotel.

36

A cool breeze has finally arrived, blowing in from the southwest, relieving the stifling heat of a very unusual week of weather for Kangaroo Island. The sun has set, leaving behind the familiar pink hue, now spreading across the fading pastel blues of a sky moving slowly toward darkness. Matt and Patrick are sitting on the front verandah of the cottage, watching the wind ruffle the face of the Southern Ocean swells as they line up to attack the cliffs of Cape du Couedic.

Frank is in the lighthouse, giving the local weather report to the bureau over the radio. *Probably knocking a few back, too,* thinks Matt.

"What a day. I'm glad he's in the Children's Hospital tonight. Mother sounded a lot better, too. Praise be to God, he's going to be okay," says Patrick.

"Yeah, close one, hey? Poor little bugger's going to be pretty crook for a while. I can do without another Saturday like today, we all can."

"Mother said he would be in hospital for a week, if everything goes all right."

"Yeah, but we're going to have to watch him over the next six months, though; the symptoms can recur at anytime, the doc said, especially in a little bloke. Barney's having a hard time of it." Barney, sitting at Matt's feet, looks up at the mention of his name.

"When I let him off the chain, he ran straight to Sean's bed and started whining."

The phone rings, interrupting the boys' conversation. Patrick leaves to answer it and is back a couple of minutes later. "It's Cassie."

Matt hustles into the kitchen and picks up the phone. "G'day, Cassie, sorry I missed you at the airport?"

"Thank goodness I caught you, Matt. I'm so sorry about Sean. I was horrified when I found out. Bob Dunning called Dad. I was worried sick about *you* until I saw you arrive at the airport. I still didn't feel right, though; I knew something bad had happened."

"Yeah, bit of a roughie that's for sure, but the main thing is he's going to be all right. Miss you already, bloke."

"Thank God, he's going to be okay, poor little chap. Miss you, too; I'd love to give you a big hug right now." She pauses. "We checked Jordan into the alcohol rehabilitation clinic this afternoon. I hope it works out; he has been behaving so much better not drinking all this week. Anyway, Daddy and I are about ready to leave to visit Sean and Katherine. Is there anything he would especially like?"

"He likes chocolate a lot; get him a Cadbury's Dairymilk, and he'll be your friend for life. And give him a big hug from all of us, will you? What time do you get into Sydney tomorrow?"

"About lunchtime; I have to be at the dance studio early Monday morning, ready to go." Matt hears Monty's voice in the background. "That's Daddy; the cab is here. I'll call again before we leave in the morning." She is silent for a moment. "Matt, I love you."

"Yep, love you, too." They both wait, listening to each other's breathing, not wanting to let go.

"Tell Patrick I'd like to talk to him longer next time, and say hello to your dad for me. Tell him you're all in our prayers." He hears the click of her phone cutting them off.

Back on the verandah, Matt settles into the old sofa. "Cassie says she'll talk to you longer next time. They are going over to the hospital to see Sean and Katherine, said we are all in their prayers."

"Oh, that's nice; yes, she said she had to hurry. I really like her, she's kind."

"Yeah. Look, I'm going for a wander over to the Admiral. Barney can come along, too; he's really having a hard time about Sean." He motions to Barney, who is lying flat out on the concrete. He raises an eyebrow and looks at Matt. "Come on, you, before it gets too dark; a walk will do you good. Sean's going to be all right, but you're going to have to take good care of him when he gets back, hey?" Barney stretches, gets to his feet, and runs after Matt, switching his tail in anticipation of new scents and chases.

He takes the long way to the Arch, skirting the lighthouse deliberately to avoid running into Frank. On the cliff above Weir Cove, he looks over at a fishing cutter swinging on its anchor below. Barney tears about the bushes and limestone outcrops, sniffing for signs of animals that may have trespassed on his territory. Every now and again, he lifts his hind leg and fires a squirt of pee onto a bush or rock to mark and reaffirm his claim. At the bottom of the cliff are the remnants of the old jetty, once used to land supplies for the lighthouse keeper, his assistant, and their families. In the early days, ketches transported people and cargo before the land route from Kingscote was established. The boats would carefully tie up to the jetty, load the basket and winch it to the top of the cliff. The supplies then transferred to the stone storehouse—now a crumbling ruin—behind the winch housing. Sometimes conditions were too rough for getting in alongside the jetty, and the supply drop could be delayed for days or even weeks. *They had it tough then.*

In the distance, across the cove, Remarkable Rocks balances, as always, precariously on its granite base. *Wonder if they'll ever tumble?* His eyes pan to the south, to where the islets, the sentinels, surrounded by white foam, stand out spectacularly from beyond Cape du Couedic's rugged thrust into the Southern Ocean.

Matt grins at Barney still busy staking out his territory. *That's right; Sean has his hideaway here somewhere. Little bloke's done a great job of keeping the location secret.* Barney peers over the edge of the cliff and begins to whine. *Yeah, he always takes Barney along with him, doesn't he? I bet he knows where it is.*

"Go on, Barney, seek. Find Sean. Show me." Barney's whine grows more intense as he paws at the edge of the cliff, throwing sand and small rocks back along his flanks. "No, Barney, not down there, I want you to show me Sean's secret place." Barney stops, but keeps looking over the cliff and barking loudly. "Ah, c'mon you silly bugger, he can't have it down there, too steep, no way to get down." The breeze coming off the ocean stiffens. He shivers, feels uneasy and spooked, sensing a presence, an energy trying to tell him something. *What the hell?* Then, it is gone. "Bugger this," he says quietly. "We're out of here." Barney is still barking and looking at the jetty. "Come on, Barney, we're off."

There is little light left when they reach the Arch, but Matt settles down in his favorite spot. Barney races around the rocks, disturbing seals and causing them to seek refuge in the water. After demonstrating his dominance, wet from his splashing about, he returns to where Matt is sitting and shakes the water from his hairy coat, dousing Matt, and then stretches out on the flat rock beside him.

"You better watch out, swimming in that water down there. Great whites like dog tucker," he says, remembering the seal taken the week before. He ruffles Barney's head and returns to his pondering; the water and the seals, unable to get the imagery out of his mind; the foreplay, the young seals, stunningly exotic, teasing, moving inevitably toward copulation, and then, without warning, the shark stuffs it up, brutal. *The colors, lots of red, blood swirling, crimson mixing with blue. The red goes, and the blue and white bursts aflame with the sun's fire—yellows, reds, and orange.*

That's it. Inspiration and excitement sweep over Matt, and his mind explodes with images of dancers in vigorous, sensual movement: red, blue, and orange colors mix in fiery ribbons of light, casting dramatic and changing portraits of life as they dance its story. *Yes, for Cassie, a story for her to dance. Yes, yes—Fire, Fire in the Center.*

37

Sydney is big, brash, and magnificent, an international city, crowding around the waters of one of the finest harbors in the world. A bustling cosmopolitan city, home to over three million friendly people, offering the very best of what the world has to offer, and for those who strive to excel, opportunity.

Looking out from the large scenic window of her Lavender Bay terrace house, Cassie can hardly contain her excitement. "Sensational—what a view, Daddy."

Monty smiles as he follows her through the open double doors that lead to the patio. The warm, humid weather, typical for a Sydney summer, is comfortable enough for the two islanders to be outside to enjoy the fresh air. Lavender Bay is on the north side of the harbor, across from Sydney Cove, and today, for Cassie, the scenic wonder before her is even more beautiful and alluring than her Middle River.

In the sweep of the bay, dozens of small and medium-sized yachts swing around their moorings, rocking back and forth in the wash of vessels that throng the harbor on any given Sunday. The wire halyards of the rigging clack against the boats' metal masts, sending a constant mix of discordant sound over the harbor, but as Cassie is soon to discover, lending an individual and identifiable character to each of the boats.

Looking across the water to the south side, she marvels at the grandeur of the Sydney Opera House, set like a fortress on the sandstone rock of Bennelong Point on the eastern flank of Circular Quay. Bennelong Point, named for an Aborigine befriended by Captain Arthur Phillip, Sydney's first governor. He had a hut built for the "highly intelligent" native on the point. In March 1791, in a gesture of gratitude, Bennelong arranged a concert for the governor, who, along with his party of twenty-four men, women, and children, danced to the accompaniment of beating sticks and stomping feet.

Now, over two hundred years later, Bennelong's spirit carries on in the thousands of concerts performed in the Opera House built on the very site of the native's old hut. Adjacent to the signature white sails, the Sydney Harbor Bridge soars above the water to link the north and south sides of the city.

"There, Daddy, there to the right of the bridge pylons," says Cassie, pointing to a line of renovated warehouses on the south side. "The third one is the company's theatre and studios."

"Yes, of course; it is one of the reasons I bought this place for you. A few minutes by ferry from Blue's Point wharf to Circular Quay, a brisk walk to warm you up, and there you are, ready to dance. Of course, the views from here are spectacular, too."

"What a lovely way to go to work." She hugs him, peeping over his shoulder to watch yachts and cruisers compete for space under the bridge and around the opera house. "How fun. Thank you, ever so much, Daddy."

He steps back and looks at her, smiling. "You look splendid. Now, I expect you'll want some time to settle in, maybe put your feet up and relax for awhile, so I've arranged to spend the afternoon with an old friend of Kristina's whom I hadn't seen for a long time—until recently. Belinda Cohen, the friend you mentioned yesterday—a lady you also met here in Sydney with your mother, shortly before she died. She still lives in Rose Bay, on the north side." He glances at his watch. "It is 12:30—umm, how about I get back around 6:00 and take you to dinner? There's a charming little restaurant, 'Sails,' on the water below us." He leans over the deck rail and points to a roof partly hidden by two large fig trees, some of their branches extending out over the water. "That's it, where the ferry berths at Blue's Point; it specializes in fish dishes. I've tried their whiting, not quite the King George whiting of the island, but pretty darn good."

"That would be lovely. Yes, just lovely." She looks at him happily. "Can I order you a cab, Daddy?"

"Oh, I almost forgot, follow me."

He leads the way down the stairs to a lower level, where another set of stairs leads off from the kitchen and descends into a two-car garage. At the bottom of the stairs, he ushers Cassie into the garage ahead of him. The first thing she sees is a bright red Mazda RX7. Monty reaches for a set of keys hanging from a hook next to the door. "Ah, here we are." He hands them to her and nods toward the Mazda. "Yours. It's not new; 35,000 kilometers on the clock, nothing really—get you around beautifully. Belinda found it for you," says Monty, beaming.

"Oh, my gosh; I love it," she says, opening the front door of the two-seater and sliding behind the wheel. "Stick-shift, too; perfect, Daddy, perfect, you spoiler, you." She gets out of the car and hugs him again.

"God knows you've earned it, girl. Besides, I don't want you to have to think about anything other than your career."

She laughs. "Sometimes, Daddy, your motives are quite transparent."

"I'm not quite sure I understand."

"Oh, yes, you do, but the deal is six months, right?"

"Cassandra, you are your mother's daughter, that is the truth. Now, do you think I might borrow the keys?"

Cassie slides the door of her wardrobe cabinet shut, the last of her suitcases empty. On the bedside table, she places her favorite photo of Matt, a close-up of his handsome features and blazing, blue eyes looking out over a cheeky grin. She smiles, responding to the warmth of his energy radiating from the photo. *Well, my dear, you are going to like this place.*

Her new home is a smart, Sydney, three-level, three-bedroom, remodeled terrace house, tastefully furnished throughout all of its rooms with rich textured Persian rugs spread over polished hardwood floors. *Probably Belinda; her taste is impeccable.* She goes to the refrigerator, and finds it full of food and drink. *The woman is incorrigible.*

She pours herself a grapefruit juice, prepares a plate of cheeses, dry cookies, and fruits, and makes her way to the deck. There, she relaxes into a layback chair and begins nibbling at the snacks, soaking up the sun and allowing the tensions of the last twenty-four hours to ease from her body.

Strange. It was just yesterday she left Kangaroo Island, now it seems light years away, all a dream. Matt called before she left Adelaide and asked how the visit with Sean had been. "Oh, he's so brave, such a little fighter," she told him. *So scary; thank God, he is going to be all right. Daddy was so kind, especially to Katherine.* Fire in the Center *sounds exciting the way Matt described it. I hope he soon comes to realize how talented he is.*"

As she relaxes, she drifts toward sleep. Images of bodies, silhouettes against myriad colors, stretching, extending, and leaping to the music of guitars and drums, stirs her body. The sun, hot on her bare legs. *Ooh, Matt,* Fire in the Center, *all right—bloody raunchy, mate.* Then, she is asleep to the voice of her mother whispering through her subconscious. "I'm with you, my darling. Here, we begin the dance; always, I am with you."

Cassie wakes to the voice of her father. "Cassandra, Cassandra, wake up; I have someone I want you to meet." Monty is standing next a woman in her mid-fifties. She is tall, her posture, carriage, and physique are obvious—a classical dancer.

"Cassie, Belinda; you met her once when you were just a tot—probably don't remember, hmm?"

"Oh, Monty, of course the poor dear doesn't remember. My goodness; the image of her mother, isn't she?" She bends down and kisses Cassie on the cheek. "Hello, dear, it is so nice to meet you again. Your father has told me all about you. Lovely." She smiles. "I danced with your mother when she first came to Australia. She could have gone on to become a celebrated artist, but your father took her from us." She looks back at Monty. "Oh, Gawd, they are just going to love her, my dear man. This one will be the toast of Sydney in no time." She turns back to Cassie. "You'll soon forget all about that island of yours, I'll promise you that, dear."

Cassie is a little overwhelmed and immediately on the defensive. *The woman hardly takes time to breathe, patronizing old bitch.* She gets up from the deck chair and gives Belinda a cursory handshake. "Actually, I do remember something of our first meeting, Belinda. If I recall correctly, you whisked me from the waterfront wall of your mansion, on which I was balancing rather unsteadily, to save me, I believe, from toppling into the harbor. I suppose I owe you a debt of gratitude, but it was the whack on my bum from your hand I remember most vividly." She looks at her father. "Daddy, I am a little surprised that you would be discussing my life on the island with Belinda, and, that is really all about who Matt is in my life, isn't it?"

Monty flushes with embarrassment. He shrugs, disconcerted, and clears his throat. "You don't have to be rude, Cassandra."

Cassie turns back to Belinda. "Yes, well, you started off beautifully," she says and points to the house. "Thank you. Yes, and for the car, too, perfect. Now, we will get on wonderfully, if you understand that my personal life is not up for any meddling; I will be on the lookout for any scheme you or Daddy may concoct to undermine my relationship with Matt. Now, I'm going to slip into something appropriate for dinner, so please excuse me; I'll be ready in a few minutes." She leaves.

Monty is beside himself. "I do apologize, Belinda. I can't remember her ever being so rude. Forgive her, she's probably worn out."

"Oh, don't be silly, Montgomery. What a spirit; she is wonderful, her mother's daughter, no question, wonderful." Belinda is smiling and animated. "Yes, she is going to take this city by storm." She holds Monty's hand and pats it. "Now, don't you worry about a thing, this is all going to work out just how it should. She and I will get on famously, believe me. Yes, and I must have that word with Timothy Barton."

38

The Monday evening ride on the ferry back to the Blue's Point landing is as glorious and fascinating for Cassie as her ride in the morning. A sea breeze works slowly up the harbor from the Pacific, replacing the stale city air. As the Hagerty ferry's wooden hull slaps through the wash of busy ferries taking home city workers, the spray of seawater occasionally lifts over the bow, splashing and cooling a happy Cassie's face. A train roars overhead as they cruise near the Harbor Bridge, prompting her to look up to the spidery web of steel girders forming the arch that curves away to the left and right to eventually punch through the granite towers supporting them on the north and south sides.

"The locals call it the 'ol Coat Hanger," says a deck hand as he leans over the gunwale, taking a last drag on a burned-down cigarette. "You're not from here, are ye?"

"What a vulgar name for such an elegant structure," she replies, looking across to the rough, thirty-year-old decky. "I am now. I'll be traveling on this most days."

"Ah, good, get to know ya a bit then. Know a few good pubs around here—take you along some time?" he says, a cautious upward inflection judiciously accompanying the tone of his question.

She laughs. "I don't think so. My boyfriend is the jealous type, and he's young and big."

The decky's response is a sarcastic grunt of disbelief. "Yeah, right." He moves on to prepare for the next landing.

She is beginning to feel the effects of her long day—weary and sore from two lengthy sessions of class and rehearsal, one in the morning and one in the afternoon, each of three hours' duration. The rocking of the boat and the fresh salt air gradually lulls her into a drowsy contentment, and she reflects on her first day at the studio.

It had been interesting. She was amazed at how much she could learn in one day; the nuance of movement, how the tiniest adjustments in posture and technique could improve balance and make a huge impact on a performance. She had not realized how many dedicated people it took to run a professional dance company.

At dinner the previous night, she also learned Belinda Cohen was the company's biggest and most influential patron, the founding member. How, after a successful career as an international artist, she had to retire because of an injury. She married a wealthy Jewish financier and started the company, convincing a still performing and talented ex-partner, Timothy Barton, to join her as the artistic director and principle choreographer. The company became hugely successful and internationally renowned. Aaron, her husband, died, and Belinda withdrew from managing the company, reducing her shareholding substantially, selling the greater part of it to Timothy.

The harsh bump of the boat against the Kirribilli wharf startles her. A number of the passengers, many carrying briefcases, disembark. *This has to be the best commute in the world.* Her eyes take in the line of apartment buildings set on the edge of the water. *Bet it costs an arm and a leg to live here.* The ferry moves on, and she returns to her day in the studio.

Timothy—what an unbelievable ball of energy. Like Belinda, the man does not take a breath. He was showing her around the building, "For orientation," he had said. "Yes, I saw your audition from behind there." He pointed to a wall mirror at the head of the rehearsal studio. "My office and lounge are behind the two-way—that's how we keep an eye on things. Sometimes we can pick up an injury a dancer is trying to cover up and have it treated before any real damage is done." He waved his hands about as if directing traffic, pointing out various aspects of the room. "Toilets and changing rooms run off the far door. The cafeteria is further along the corridor, located on the end of the building, where you are literally suspended over the harbor. Our patrons and public also eat there, so we ask that you be discreet in your conversations and behavior."

She had been distracted by the view of the harbor, which took up the entire wall of one side of the studio; he noticed immediately. "Beautiful, inspiring, yes, but you'll soon get used to it. Your focus will be on that wall." He points to the *barre* running the full length of the opposite wall with mirrors floor to ceiling. He rattled on. "We liked your audition. Of course, we did, or you wouldn't be here, humph? You certainly have the talent, flair, and presence, but do you have the dedication, the stamina, the heart, for the hard work it takes to be great? Well, we shall see, shan't we?"

He smiled warmly and energetically rubbed his hands together. "You have six weeks, and then we will meet again and review your work. We will watch your progress with great expectation." He took her hand and patted it warmly. "Belinda called me last night. I want you to know that she and I are here for you, any time. Now, come," he said and led her out of the studio by the hand.

He turned back along the corridor toward the land end of the building. "I want you to meet the company. They're in here," he said, turning into an open door. In the room, sitting on the floor, stretching, relaxing, and talking, were nineteen dancers. Timothy clapped his hands. "Everybody, this is the new girl I was telling you about—Cassandra Baldwin, known as Cassie, who did that stunning audition here late last year. Get to know her and make her feel welcome."

She had felt nervous and even a little sick. *They look so fit, so confident.* "These are your peers," Timothy said, waving the back of his hand in a gesture indicating the whole group. "They form the core of the company, and they will help you settle in. Our principal dancers are among them, but we do not mollycoddle anybody here. There are no prima donnas, myself excepted, of course." He smiles. "We are family; our goal is to excel as artists, and as a great international dance company."

He gestured to a male dancer. "Please, Shamus, come." A handsome young man, twenty-two years of age, sprang athletically to his feet from his cross-legged sitting position in front of the *barre*. "Cassie, I want you to meet Shamus O'Brien. Shamus will be your male partner for the next few weeks; he is very experienced and—oh, how do I say this without launching his highly charged ego into the stratosphere—he is *very* good."

Cassie was slightly taken aback when the young Shamus stretched to his full height and flashed an ingratiating smile, his white teeth showing off the glint of ivory highly valued for toothpaste commercials. His long, dark hair, resembling the mane of a wild animal, fell about his muscular shoulders and ran down to the middle of his back. *Probably a big cat. Panther—yes, he moves just like one.*

"G'day, Cass," he said in a broad Australian accent. "Welcome aboard, we're going to get along just great."

Good God, spare me. Timothy, you rotten little queer, this is a set-up. You and Belinda, I bet. She had given Shamus her best cold stare and flashed him a smile of deference, she hoped.

He had just stood grinning, understanding, assuming a pose that had his tight pants straining about his perfectly proportioned body, a pose she was unable to ignore. *Oh, is that the extent of your talent?* No, it was not, she had to admit, later.

In the afternoon, they moved into rehearsal mode, where the dancers were responsible for self-motivation and no longer prodded to excel by the class instructor. They had to build from their own creative resources, choreography, working from a number of musical pieces Timothy had selected from modern dance favorites. Shamus awed her with his extensive range of movement, and his aggressive style of performance. Once working, he was thoroughly professional, very generous and helpful in offering the benefit of his experience for subtle refinements in her technique, placement, and style. He was intolerant and impatient when she failed to match his effort and intensity. Still, she had sensed a thrilling and powerful surge of excitement in the marriage of their talent, performance chemistry, and perfectionist expectations.

She is again jolted back into the present by the grinding of metal on metal as the deck hand slides back the safety rails of the ferry gate. The boat slows and slips in gently alongside the Blue's Point wharf.

"Ah, hope I didn't offend ya earlier. You know, you're about the best looker I've seen around here in a long time. Me name's Jerry." He smiles, revealing a dirty line of tobacco stained teeth as he expertly flicks another spent cigarette into the water.

She gives him a gratuitous smile. "I'm sure you say that to all the girls."

The boat stops, and Jerry tosses a rope over the mooring post to hold the vessel steady for the passengers to go ashore. He watches intently as she steps ashore and walks off along the wharf, "You're one of those dancers, aren't ya?" he calls after her, drooling as the sun shining through her light cotton dress bares the outline of her body, panties and bra.

"Yes, I am," she says airily, looking back over her shoulder on the way along the foreshore path to her terrace house.

"Uppity bitch," says Jerry under his breath. "They all get sorted, eventually." He coughs up a mouthful of phlegm, swirls it noisily in his mouth, and spits a gray-brown mass of gunk into the water and watches it drift away, fascinated.

Monty is peering over the deck railing, expecting her. "I thought you'd be home about now, heard the ferry. Fully intended to walk down to meet you, but I fell asleep."

"You must have needed it. I'll be right up," she says, pushing her key into the front gate. Minutes later, she is on the patio, sipping a cold beer. "Hm, nice drop, what is it?"

"Tooheys New, a New South Wales beer. The bottle shop fellow told me it was popular here. I'm glad you like it." Monty takes a sip of his scotch. "So, how was your first day?"

"Tough, but wonderfully exciting." She drops into a deck chair, places her bare feet on the footrest, and draws her dress up over her knees. "I'm worn out and devilishly hungry."

"How about you take a rest, and when you are ready to eat, we scoot up to the Blue's Point Café, a three minute drive from here in your car?"

"Sounds good," she says, studying the bubbles rising through the amber fluid to join the creamy froth on top. *Funny how something so refreshing can level a family,* remembering the struggles and tragedy of Matt's family.

"Daddy, we don't usually keep things from each other, do we?" She waits; a pregnant pause ensues. "Is there something you ought to be telling me?"

Monty coughs and takes another mouthful of his scotch. "I'm a little at a loss to know what you are driving at."

"You sound like the politicians you dislike so much, Daddy." She takes another sip of beer, stands, walks to the deck rail, and looks out over the harbor toward the Sydney Opera House. "One day, I'll dance there." She smiles at Monty. "Well, Daddy, first of all, Belinda indicates that I'll soon forget the island, meaning Matt, of course. And then today, I get teamed up with a bloke who could only be described as simply gorgeous; Belinda wouldn't be behind that either, would she?"

"Belinda has only your best interests at heart, Cassandra. From what she told me, young Shamus is an extraordinary talent and your art can only benefit enormously from his involvement. She believes that you are the perfect partner for him, and when the right work comes along, the two of you will be sensational—a big draw, using the marketing terminology. Now, I would consider that a hell of a compliment—wouldn't you?"

"Ah, you're ducking and weaving, a dead giveaway. So unlike you, Daddy, but he will make a sensational partner." She smiles coyly. "He's another Catholic, you know, and Irish."

Monty coughs again. He swallows the rest of his scotch. A moment passes. "Cassandra, I—I do have something else to tell you," he says hesitantly. "Belinda will be joining me for a brief stay on Kangaroo Island; she is leaving with me tomorrow night."

She laughs affectionately. "Wonderful." She crosses to Monty and hugs him. "I thought you two might have something going; you look stunning together."

"I, umm, she is a very wealthy woman, and the family arrangements I have made—you, the boys, the farm—will not be affected in any way if anything should come of this."

She tickles her father under the chin. "You are a little further along than I guessed, you sly devil. No, it's wonderful; you deserve all the happiness there is to be had, Montgomery Baldwin." She chuckles merrily. "Let's have dinner and celebrate; quick shower and we're off." Energized, she dances through the double doors with a series of swirling *pirouettes*, heading happily for the shower.

Monty watches her disappear into the terrace's lounge. He turns to stare over the water, and his face reddens with shame as he experiences his first feelings of guilt.

39

Matt is at the word processor typing furiously to get his thoughts onto the paper before losing them. The monsignor's idea to write an essay about the island was perfect. As he researched the history and spoke to descendants of early settlers, the more he came to appreciate the uniqueness of his numinous home. He pauses. *Let's see; maybe I can sum this up with a question mark or two about the, umm, yeah, the numinous, perhaps mystical aspect.*

He resumes typing.

So, where are we? Oh, yes, Kangaroo Island—mysterious, transcendent, center of enlightenment, the final destination of the seeker? Yes or no. What answer is appropriate? I do not dare offer mine, for I am too close to it all, but among those who posture that part of the question are some who say the answer may lie within the Rosenblum poppy. The Rosenblum poppy? Yes, now there is a tale.

The Rosenblum poppy is an herbaceous flowering plant variety, a cousin of the opium poppy, Papaver somniferum. *A native, it thrives spectacularly in the wet, well-drained, ironstone soils of the island. The Islanders claim it for its extraordinary benefits, ranging from healing all manner of body and mental ailments, to aphrodisiac properties, to spiritual awakenings.*

There is nothing mystical about the poppy, though, is there? No, it seems straightforward enough. The plants are picked before ripening and stored in plastic bags, where the milky sap, rich in alkaloids containing morphine and codeine, mix with the materials of the stem and petals as they break down, kind of an "out-of-this-world narcotic," really. The stem contains another alkaloid that stimulates blood flow—an aphrodisiac some claim. The two color pigments in the petals act as antioxidants, stimulating the immune system—the healing.

The older locals, aware of the "poppee" benefits ("poppee" the popular name given the plant), some of whom pick and suck on those growing wild, claim a vitality and youthfulness that defies their years. It did not take long for the odd cultivated plot to show up in backyards and isolated scrubby hides. Given the same status by the Australian government as the opium poppy, cultivation and marketing was legislated illegal, unless a license for growing was granted, and then, only for legitimate pharmaceutical procurement. This was an impossible situation for Kangaroo Island producers. The legal market was limited to a drug manufacturer in Melbourne supplied from licensed farms in Tasmania, which provides twenty-five per cent of the world's supply of morphine. With the public on the mainland becoming aware of Kangaroo Island's Rosenblum poppy, demand exploded, pushing up the price, and "illegal" cultivation really took off.

Matt pushes his hand through his hair and stares at the words on the black and white screen. *Hmm, it's getting there.* The essay, "Kangaroo Island, South Australia's Mystical Secret?" had to be in the mail by Monday with the day's date stamped on the envelope and on its way to Sydney. After putting in five nights a week, for the six weeks since Cassie left, he is almost finished. *How do I wrap this up?*

His thoughts turn to Cassie. Anxiety begins to stir in his gut as he stares into the screen. The letters of the essay begin to transform into dancers. They blur and swirl into a spiral of mixing metaphors, laughing and teasing his mind. A toy plane whirls above the dancers. *He attempts to put his foot on the first step to board the plane, but he keeps missing it. The plane is the shape of a boomerang. It starts out heading for Sydney, but flies in an arc and keeps returning to Kangaroo Island. His hand reaches out, snatching for Cassie as she whirls by, circling with a hysterically laughing Shamus. The letters form and balloon, like dialogue in a comic book, from the male dancer's laughing lips, "Can't catch me, can't catch me, can't leave the Kangaroos, ha, ha, ha, ha."*

Matt slams the desk with his fist, and they are gone.

Damn, one letter in six weeks and a phone call. Every time I call her, she's never in. She could get an answer machine if she really wanted to hear from me, bloody hell. No letters for weeks in the delivery that comes to the ranger's house twice a week, nothing. The letter that told him about Shamus did it; he felt threatened, jealous and angry.

Yes, she called once to tell him how Shamus loved his *Fire in the Center* concept, how he would like to dance it with her. Timothy Barton thought they might be able to fit it into an opening for a four-week season in July, the Newcomer Series, which plays the same three selected works, every night at the Sydney Opera House. And yes, he was going to submit *Fire in the Center*. "You'll be credited with the concept. Timothy can't wait to meet you, and he thinks you are brilliant. It is all here for you, my darling," she'd said. *Yeah, right!*

"Matthew," interrupts Katherine, calling from the kitchen, "dinner is on the table."

"Thanks, be there in a minute."

Cassie had picked up the tension in his voice. She told him she loved him, to trust the process, and not to worry about the outcome. Precise outcomes could not be forecast because they were likely to change, anyway. Participation and experience in the process, moment to moment, is what really counts. "That's how we get our answers," she said. *What happened to knowing that we would live all our life together?*

Angry, he looks back at his essay. Suddenly, he is flooded with new energy and the thrill of inspiration lifts him. *Thank you, my God.* "It's in her last line, the wrap to my essay—my readers must come to Kangaroo Island. In their experience, they'll discover for themselves the island's secret. Come to the island and experience the mystique. Yes, there it is, the answer is in her last line."

Matt taps the beginning of the next sentence into the word processor, saves the file, closes down the machine, and makes his way to the kitchen.

Sean is sitting at the table when Matt walks up behind him, gives him a hug, and tousles his hair. "G'day, mate, love ya a lot. How'd you do today?"

Sean's progress after the snakebite had been spasmodic. A couple of times, Katherine had to place him on the ventilator when his muscles constricted around his throat, a symptom of the snake venom that would continue to affect him for six months or more.

"I had a beaut time today, Matt. Dad, Barney, and me went for a walk along the beach in Weir Cove; the tide was out." Sean's upward inflection at the end of the sentence infers the timing of their visit to the beach was special because it was rarely exposed. "Got some big abalone shells and Barney went for a swim. Lots of seals in the water, there were."

"Got the silly bugger out of there, quick smart, didn't we, Sean?" says Frank. "He'll finish up shark bait if he keeps swimming with the seals."

"Yeah," says the little fellow, happy his dad is looking out for him. Frank had been spending a lot of time with Sean since the boy got out of hospital. He had been drunk only once in the last six weeks.

"Good on you, mate," says Matt, sitting down to his favorite meal. Katherine had roasted a leg of lamb in the oven of the wood-fired stove. The delicious aroma had percolated through the cottage all afternoon, whipping up the Ryan family's hunger. "Thanks, Katherine," he says as he plucks a half-dozen crispy baked potatoes from a bowl in the center of the table. He pours a generous amount of rich, dark-brown gravy over the meal and begins eating. "Aw, bloody beautiful; you're a hell of a cook, Katherine."

She smiles and wipes her hands on the front of her apron. "I know you love roasts, Matthew." She sits. "You hear from Cassie today?"

"No. Ah, she's pretty busy; reckons they might do *Fire in the Center*, though, in the opera house."

"Oh, my gosh, that's wonderful. Frank, we may have a famous son sitting here at the table."

"That'll be the day. *Fire in the Center?* Humph. You'd be better off concentrating on your football, there's where you've got a bit of talent; take after your oldman, yeah?"

"Yeah, I heard you were pretty good, reckon you could have played league if Vietnam hadn't buggered you."

"Your mother was very talented; you take after her a lot, you know," Katherine offers.

"Whatever; it'll work out," says Matt, a fleeting moment of remembrance of his mother's death showing in the sudden edge to his voice. He looks at Sean. "We have a trial game at the Gosse oval tomorrow afternoon, and a barby after that, mate. You want to come with me and Pat in the Ute?"

"Can I, Mum?" says Sean. Katherine looks at Frank.

"Yeah, 'course you can. We're going, too, aren't we?" Frank looks at Katherine, who nods. "We'd better take the ventilator to be on the safe side, hey, Sean?" says Frank, reaching out to the boy and giving him a gentle pat on the head.

"Sammy Marino called last night, Dad," says Pat, emerging from a meditative silence. "He said he wanted to talk to you. Something about next week." He looks up at Katherine. "Meal's wonderful, Mother, thank you." She smiles, pleased.

"Right. I, er, need to get together with you, Matt. I'm going to need a hand; Peter Ferrano is leaving the island for a few days."

40

"That's it, you blokes, good job; you battled through and showed some guts. Finish it up with a couple of laps," shouts Jamie Walls, the Saints' football coach, striding onto the oval after the final pre-season match. "We'll talk about next week's opener after the team's picked Thursday night."

Matt is gasping for air as he pounds out the last few meters of his laps. Despite the sweat streaming down his cheeks, the air carries the distinct chill of the coming winter. He cools quickly under the roof outside the changing rooms, panting, the consequences of Australian football's violent, body-contact nature, bruises and fatigue suddenly felt in his stiffening body. Drizzling rain falling throughout the afternoon made the conditions miserable; the match became a test of endurance. There is only relief that the game is over, and every player is more than ready for the steaming shower, the barbecue, and a beer or three, beauty.

"Any sore spots in need of a rub, Matt?" asks Jordan, wearing the white track-suit of the club trainer.

"Nope." Matt can hardly believe the improvement in Jordan since coming back from treatment. *Bloody night and day.* He is wary, though. The old saying 'a leopard does not change his spots' flashes through his mind. Nevertheless, he works at giving Jordan the benefit of the doubt.

"Been busy?" says Jordan.

"It's slowing down with winter coming on, but there is always something to do. You heard anything from Cassie?"

"She's working hard on that dance you wrote, her and that Shamus stud—I know that," says Jordan, unable to stop himself from slipping in the dig he knew would get at Matt.

"Right," Matt says, wanting him to tell Cassie to write and get a bloody answering machine, but loath to give Jordan any inkling that he has not heard from her. He strips, heads for the showers, and joins the other naked bodies under the steaming water. Jordan watches, conflicted.

Frank, Katherine, Pat, and Sean are sitting around their usual table in the bar area of the Gosse Hall when Matt joins them.

"Bit of a limp up there, lad," says Frank. "You young fellows wouldn't get a game in my day, too bloody soft." Frank is sipping on a coke. "My buy—what do you want?"

"I could do with a beer; I'm as dry as a bone."

"Good as done." Frank gets up and crosses to the bar.

"We're going to have something to eat, then head home early; want to get Sean home and into bed," says Katherine. He is sitting on her lap, looking pale and exhausted.

"You played real good today, you did, Matt. That Maureen lady thought so, too, she was yelling out to you all day. I reckon she really likes you. She come over and told me and mum, too, didn't she, mum?" Katherine nods. The little fella's cheeky grin goes straight to Matt's heart.

"Ah, she likes all the blokes, especially good looking one's like you," teases Matt.

Frank returns with a round of drinks and hands Matt a stubby; he drains the bottle in one swallow. "Beautiful."

"Hell, you got a thirst up, all right."

"Yeah, hit the spot, that's for sure," he says, getting up from his seat, again tousling the youngster's hair as he passes. "Another one would be right on the money. I'll load a plate of chops and sausages from the barby while I'm up; want to help, Pat?"

The two go out to the beer garden where "Plunk" Plummer is sweating over the open barbecue. Several players and supporters are standing around the hot fire, stubbies in hand, trying to keep warm in the cold drizzle. Matt grabs one from the bar.

"G'day, Matt, Pat," says a giggling Maureen, looking stunningly chic in her black tracksuit. Wet strands of hair tease her forehead and stray over her cheeks. "I watched the game after we finished basketball." She moves closer to him. He is aware of her wet and exposed cleavage. She touches his arm. "You looked terrific out there, no doubt about it."

An unexpected surge of excitement and anticipation delights Matt, along with the tingling sensation tantalizing his body. *God in heaven, save me from myself.*

Patrick is at the barbecue, picking chops and sausages from the hot grill. "Thanks, Maureen, thanks." Surreptitiously, he looks about to see if anyone is watching. A few of his grinning teammates give him a wink. "Look—" He pauses; her effect on him overwhelming. "Um, I—you're looking bloody gorgeous tonight, mate." He pauses again, the effect of the beer beginning to mitigate his caution. "I—" Jordan walks onto the garden patio. *Bloody hell.*

Matt shrugs, his ardor cooling instantly. "Yeah, well, thanks, Maureen, nice of you to say so." He turns to join Patrick, but Maureen grips his arm, stops him and whispers into his ear.

"I told you, Matt; I'm going have you. Cassie is going to forget all about you, if she hasn't already." She nods in Jordan's direction. "He was telling me that she can't get enough of some dance stud over there. I think he said his name is Shamus; seems even the bloke's name is a bit of a pun, hey?"

41

Dunning swings the police car over the white cattle grid and drives toward the airport building. The turbo-prop plane is already unloaded, and Reg Woodson is waiting by the luggage trolley, talking to Jim.

"About time you showed up, Dunning," says Woodson. The brusque tone of voice leaves no doubt in Dunning's mind the eight weeks of the sergeant's recovery have in no way induced a kinder, gentler Woodson. "This is Ronnie Perkins, brand spanking new, right out of the police college."

Dunning shakes the huge, outstretched paw of the young policeman. *Hell, he's a big bugger.* "Bob Dunning," he says, pulling his hand back from the crushing grip of the probationary copper. "Got you fixed up at the Queenscliffe for the time being until you find somewhere you like."

"Let's get this young bloke settled in," commands Woodson. "What did they call you in college, Perkins? The Enforcer, wasn't it?" Woodson tries to laugh, but it sounds more like the cackle of a rooster, a result of the damage to his throat, affecting his voice with a discordant pitch wags like to joke about in the safety of their own group, of course. Woodson swings his suitcase from the cart to the trunk of the car. "There'll be plenty of that to do here, lad."

"Yes, Sergeant," says Perkins. "But that was on the football field, sir." The young policeman looks uneasy. *Must be about six-four in the old measure, thinks Dunning. Reckon he weighs in at a hundred kilos, and not a scrap of fat on him.*

"Missus is coming in tomorrow, being Sunday, so I'll have the day off; we'll get into it on Monday," says Woodson.

With all his hair shaved off, he looks more of a gorilla than before. Looking on with a wry grin, he watches his sergeant vigorously attacking an obviously irritating hemorrhoid.

"By the way, Dunning, your promotion to first-class constable has been published in the gazette. Maybe we can call it even, yeah?"

Dunning knows that Woodson is referring to the accident inquiry. "We'll see, boss; the promotion was routine, anyway."

"Not without my recommendation," says Woodson, his annoyance apparent in the cadence of his voice. They load into the car. "Nine-thirty, Monday morning, we meet at the station. We'll have an interesting guest there, a bloke keeping an eye on the comings and goings of our poppee producers." His voice is smug. "I haven't been sitting on my arse, letting the grass grow under it while I've been away, First-class Constable."

Dunning guns the car over the cattle grid, swings toward Kingscote, and pushes quickly toward the 100 kilometers-per-hour mark.

"Take it easy," says a nervous Woodson. "You could kill someone."

"Yeah, right, Sergeant," says Dunning, easing the throttle for the turn at the intersection, and then flooring the pedal again to roar along a straight stretch of road before the Cygnet River Bridge. He looks at Woodson. "You'd sure as hell know all about that, wouldn't you?"

Monday morning at 9:30, Dunning watches the rookie copper enter the front door of the police station. "How'd our enforcer sleep in his new digs?"[62]

"The sea breeze blowing in from the bay knocked me out right off as soon as my head hit the pillow, Mr. Dunning," says Perkins as he dumps a parcel of fruit and nuts on the desk.

"I told you to call me Bob, Ron, unless we have an official matter going on in public." The front door opens. Dunning is at first a little taken aback, and then wary. *I think we have a little conspiracy building here.* "Well, well, don't tell me you're our surprise guest this morning?"

---

[62] Digs: Place of temporary residence.

"C'mon, Bob, let's bury the hatchet for the time being, shall we?" says an unusually fit and alert Jordan Baldwin as he reaches over the station desk for Dunning's hand. "After all, we are going to be working with each other for the next few months."

"Is that right? Nobody bloody told me," says Dunning, ignoring the offered hand.

"Yeah, well I'm telling you all now," says a surly Sergeant Woodson as he wrenches open his office door and walks into the station's front desk area. "Thanks for coming, Jordan." He points to Perkins. "Meet our new lad, Ronnie Perkins, er, the Enforcer." Woodson cackles and waves them toward the interview room. "Follow me."

The four men file into the room, where a large map of Kangaroo Island is pinned on the wall alongside a whiteboard. The map is spotted here and there with different colored adhesive dots. To Dunning's surprise, a box of doughnuts and four paper cups of coffee are set on one of the tables.

"Help yourselves. From the deli, and damn good," says Woodson, gesturing toward the refreshments as he rustles through documents on another table.

"Okay, let's cut to the quick. This whole poppee business has been getting out of hand over here, and the brass and politicians want to come down hard on it." He looks over his troops and smiles. "That suits me just fine, because I was going to end it, anyway." He walks to the other table, sugars a coffee, slurps, and goes over to the map.

"Okay, different colored dots—why?" he says, pointing. "The four red ones are priority. The half-dozen blue, I'm not too concerned about; they don't grow a lot, and they're, well, they're friends of the family, so to speak."

More like they are padding your wallet, Dunning thinks, noting that the four red dots are stuck on Cape du Couedic, Kersaint, Vivonne Bay, and Kingscote. *The Ryans, Mad Tom, and Sammy Marino.*

"The green dots represent small-time growers; they are scattered all over the island. They are slap-on-the-wrist targets; we upset too many of them, and we'll have the public coming down on the politicians, and they will not like that. We'll throw an occasional eye over them and see who is picking up and paying them off—that'll be the Ryans, of course, and maybe we'll even bust one or two to give the case a perceived balance."

You blokes are after the Ryans; that's what this deal is all about. Dunning looks at Jordan. And, you are the stool pigeon. Dunning is disgusted. *Is the oldman part of it? No, he couldn't be; he's not a bad bloke, saved my neck once. Why would—hold on. Oh, yeah, this is about Matt and Cassie, his daughter—that must be it. The oldman wants to kill the relationship.* He stares at Woodson. *These white boys are bloody treacherous the way they go after their own.*

"And I have good information Marino's not coming back until August for his next load. So, here's what we are going to do. For the time being, we keep an eye on things, bust the odd green one here and there and, more important, we find out where the Ryans are holding the stuff." He takes a long, noisy slurp of coffee. "I asked Jordan along this morning so we could all be on the same page. He's hanging out on the west end of the island, getting acquainted and keeping his ear to the ground. Got yourself into the football club, haven't you?" Woodson says, directing his attention to Jordan.

"Trainer,"[63] says Jordan. "They tend to loosen up when I rub them down before the game; learn a lot then."

"Jordan keeps me up to scratch with what's going on. Now and again, we get some useful information. Even getting friendly with Matt Ryan, aren't you, mate?"

"He thinks he's pretty smart," says Jordan, a measure of arrogance causing even Woodson to wince. "I wouldn't say he's smart, as much as he's been lucky. Yes, very lucky. He's a bit of a sap, really." A touch of mirth mixes easily with his chuckling.

Woodson continues, "I want to catch them when they're loading the stuff onto the *Smokey Cloud*. That way we get them all, especially the two Ryans." He smiles grimly. "We'll put them away for a long time over this."

"Don't get too carried away, Sergeant," says Dunning. "They've outsmarted you before."

---

[63] Trainer: Usually a volunteer who massages players' leg muscles and wraps support bandages on suspect joints.

"We'll have help from Adelaide," says Woodson, deflecting Dunning's sarcasm with a little of his own. "Besides, you're here to help us now, aren't you?"

"I have some good information, Sergeant," says Jordan, interrupting. "Last night, I got a tip from Flecky Martin that he had two bags of dried poppy being picked up Wednesday night. He said Frank Ryan's coming over."

"Flecky, hey?" Woodson points to a dot on the map towards the southwestern end of the island. "Here he is, here, a green. Why would he be turning snitch?"

"He follows the local football team out there. I got friendly with him, found out he was a grower, let him know you were onto him and that there was a big push coming on to find and prosecute offenders; frightened the hell out of him. I told him if he helped us, he would be looked after. He was reluctant at first, but at the end of the day he was on board." Jordan throws a hand out in a gesture of triumph. "He rang last night."

"Bloody good work, Jordan." Woodson traces his finger along the South Coast Road. "All right, there is the entrance to Martin's, up along Gum Hill Lane about a kilometer," Woodson says, thinking, and jabbing his finger back to the road junction. "Right off here runs an old gum cutter's track, overgrown with scrub, but passable in a four-wheel, so the Toyota wagon will do the job. Now, here," he says, pointing, "it leads to a ridge overlooking the Martin place. We'll set up there." He turns to the three men. "Frank will have to come back to the junction, so we can see which direction he takes from the ridge. My bet is that it's back to du Couedic. The hide is there, I'm sure of it. Any questions?"

"If he spots us, are we going to arrest him?" asks Dunning.

"No way, not yet; we let him go. I already told you, I want them all— Frank, the kid, Marino—all of them." He looks at Jordan. "Good work, Jordan. We'll take it from here; I don't want you anywhere near Martin's Wednesday night."

The men begin filing from the room. "I want to talk to you in my office, Perkins," says Woodson. "Jordan, give my best to your father for me, will you?"

"Righto."

Dunning walks onto the street with Jordan, who reaches out to shake hands. "It'll be nice working with you blokes, Bob."

Dunning ignores the offered hand and looks hard into the grinning traitor's face. "Envy is the worst of the seven deadly sins, Jordan; it's malicious. You'd be better off picking up the booze again, fella; that way we can lock you up and keep you off the street, safe from yourself."

At that moment, a blue Ute passes the police station. Dunning looks up and catches Matt Ryan looking at him. The Ute takes a left onto the frontage road and disappears.

"Matt Ryan just rode by, Jordan. I'd keep to the other side of the street if I were you; he might guess at what you're on about." He smiles. "I think he's pretty smart, actually, and didn't he already give you a hiding recently?"

Dunning does not wait for a response, but strides off toward the post office, leaving an uneasy Jordan staring after him.

42

Matt taps the large brown package lying on the passenger side seat and winks at himself in the rearview mirror. *Good work, Matt, you finished what you started.* The urgent honking from a car horn jerks his attention back to his driving as he cuts in front of a car about to turn into the Kingscote Area School access road. He waves an apology. *Oops, "Donk" Dobson. Don't want to upset the big bloke; he could hurt me again.* "Donk" is already out of sight. *When did I see him last? Yeah, the second before he hit me; would've been a goal for sure. I was crook for a week after that. Nice bloke, though, really, bought me a beer after the game and said sorry.* He smiles with the memory, content and pleased with himself as he raps his fingers on the package.

The mid-morning sky is clear and cool, and for a Monday, traffic is light. His back route to the post office takes him near the police station, and as he drives by, two familiar figures are standing on the pavement, talking. Dunning looks up and sees Matt.

What the hell? Bob Dunning and Jordan? Bloody weird for Jordan to be in town this early, unless he was locked up again, back on the booze—No, Woodson's back. Hang about, he must be in with the coppers.

The sea sweeps away to his right as he rounds the esplanade corner, takes another left turn to circle the block and stops in front of the post office. As he steps out of the Ute with the brown envelope, Dunning is walking down from the police station. "What now?"

"Matt, can I have a word with you?"

Matt notices the new stripe on his uniform. "Get a pay raise, Bob?" he says as the tall, dark first-class constable joins him.

Dunning grins. "Just shows even a darky can make some headway with the white man's mob." They shake hands. "I heard young Sean is coming on. Good."

"Yep, thanks. What's up with Jordan? Not back on the booze, is he?"

Dunning eyes Matt. *He's no mug, sharp as a tack.* "We might be better off if he was. Look, I saw you go by and I—well, I like you; you know that. I don't want to see you get into trouble. Just look out for yourself with that bloke, hey?"

"Working for you blokes, is he?"

"I didn't say that." Dunning scratches his head. "He, er, look—Woodson's back, and he's on a mission. You and your oldman—" He turns and looks toward the police station. Woodson and Perkins are standing on the front step, watching. He turns back to Matt. "Look, take my advice and stay right away from the poppee, okay? It's going to heat up over here. Woodson is on a mission, and a few people in high places are pushing him right along."

High places, right. He nods to Dunning, understanding. "High places—locally?"

Dunning shrugs. "Both here and in the city; like I said, keep away from the flowers."

"Thanks for the tip off, Bob, I owe you." He taps the large envelope and grins. "I have to get this posted today; it's my essay for a writing competition—about the island. Has a lot to say about the flowers; I'll send you a copy."

"I'd like to read that, Matt, I really would. I mean for the writing, too; I've heard you're pretty good."

"We'll see." Matt walks up the steps and into the post office. *So, oldman Baldwin's in on it, too?*

43

Monty relaxes, enjoying the view he never tires of, and the myriad smells from the sea mixing with the morning air that give him the delicious sensation of health and well-being. From the gazebo, he can easily see all the way to Althorpe Island on the horizon. A single-mast fishing cutter is working slowly across the water heading west. Monty turns to the woman on his right, who is watching the same boat through binoculars.

"How profound," says Belinda, handing the glasses to Monty, returning to her chair at the table and cup of tea. "There, as we watch, people are at work, hard work, harvesting fish to feed us for another day." She sips the hot fluid and sighs with contentment. "It's good to be reminded of that; we city folk take for granted the food on our table. You know, just go off to the supermarket, and there we are, everything we need, no more hunter-gathering for us."

"I think of our effort here, Belinda, as being part of a hard working community, employing people, producing meat, fish, cereal, and wool. I like being among these people, being one of them; there's something to said about having to scratch a living, literally, from the dirt, that helps keep our feet firmly planted on the ground."

"Yes, of course." She pauses, thinking. "And there is art, which I think is hugely important—stimulates curiosity, entertains, informs, questions—and religion, without art, what? The Bible, the scrolls, the poetry, the paintings—Michelangelo's great works on the walls and ceiling of the Sistine Chapel in Rome, magnificent; art, whether the ancient Corroboree of Aboriginal dance, or today's movie, all of it informs and enlivens our story." She takes another sip of tea.

"I must say, I enjoy your musings, Belinda; I am reminded so much of Kristina. She touched on such insights frequently, displaying them in bursts of exuberant choreography, right here in the gazebo." He takes Belinda's hand. "I am glad you came back again."

"I am happy to be with you, my dear Montgomery." She pauses, reflecting. "The same exuberance is demonstrated in your daughter's work. She is doing magnificently with Shamus, and I must tell you," she says, her speech quickening with excitement, losing its unusual affectation, a quality cultivated to blend with the affluent of Sydney's eastern suburbs, "when Timothy and I agreed to submit *Fire in the Center* for the Newcomer Series, we could not predict the astonishing passion of their coupling." Belinda turns to Monty and squeezes his hand. "She is a very talented young woman who is going to cause a sensation when the show opens."

"I live for it. I owe it to the memory of Kristina."

"Yes, well, it is only a matter of time. The two of them are bonding, and her dance is quickly becoming an all-consuming passion. Her work ethic, Monty, is extraordinary; her quest for perfection, obsessive."

"Her mother again; I am so pleased she is away from the island, that boy, and his family."

Belinda looks fondly at Monty and says with a touch of concern and caution edging her tone, "Oh, my dear man, that boy, as you so harshly put it, is the writer of *Fire in the Center*. He is obviously very gifted and a deep thinker. She still talks a lot about him, and she believes he will win one of the National Writing Awards to be announced in Sydney next month."

"Oh, damn, he's going to Sydney? First I heard of it."

"If he wins, of course, and our company will have to fly him to the opening of *Fire in the Center*, anyway. He will be high on the list of credits."

"Please don't do that, Belinda, for my sake. I would like the boy to succeed in his work, but not at the expense of Cassie's future."

"What does Cassie want? That is the question, Monty. Have you really sat down with her and asked?"

"She has yet to fully understand the consequences of youthful passion," he says, his voice short, abrupt. "It is a silly infatuation, and a distraction from what is truly important."

"Oh! And what of Kristina? *You* took a great talent from all of us to satisfy *your* passion."

"We loved each other."

"Precisely; there is a force far greater than any of us that must have its way; if not, the consequences we bring upon ourselves are intolerable—miserable lives, insanity, or even suicide." Her voice becomes that of a counselor advising a client. "Let me tell you something, Montgomery, you are jeopardizing the future of your relationship with Cassie; that is what you are doing." She gathers her thoughts and continues speaking as a woman who understands betrayal. "Don't you see? If you destroy her relationship with Matt, she will feel terribly violated; she is, after all, the daughter of Kristina de Coronardo. Imagine Kristina's ire if you had been unfaithful to her. Cassie's revenge will be equally as devastating; cut you off in a second, psychologically, and leave you feeling mortally wounded and completely alone. Do you want to risk that?"

"I will risk all for my daughter's future," he says, his earlier, relaxed posture stiffening. "If you are unwilling to help, Belinda, so be it." The hard edge to his voice surprises her.

An uncomfortable silence disturbs the earlier ease Monty and Belinda were enjoying. The light breeze of mid-morning begins to pick up speed. Layers of cloud wisp across the sky, heralding the approach of a bank of black clouds lifting off the horizon in the southwest.

"Then the risk is yours, Montgomery. I do not mind intervening to test the waters, but I will not be party to malicious mischief threatening terrible harm to both the girl and the boy. That is not right, and I'm sure your late wife is turning in her grave right this moment."

They sit, silent. The bright light from the sun gradually fades as the clouds grow thicker. "The air has chilled, Montgomery; I'm going inside," she says, wrapping her shawl around her bare shoulders as she rises from the table.

She squeezes Monty's arm as she moves past him and walks briskly up the steps to the house, disappointed, but exuding the energy of a mature, confident and independent woman.

Monty continues staring out to sea, shaken and uncertain. *All my women are bloody Kristinas.*

44

"Stop here, Perkins," orders Woodson. The police van rocks to a stop. "Not bad for a city kid fresh out of police college, hey First-class Constable?"

"He's learning," says Dunning, tired of Woodson's deliberate use of his new title, but glad to get out of the vehicle after enduring the bruising journey along the old gum cutter's track.

"There's the Martin place." Woodson points to the buildings, easily picked out by scanning along the big tree gum creek that runs to within a hundred meters of the shearing shed. "Too bad we're not knocking them off tonight—easy target here." He lifts a pair of binoculars to his eyes. "It's too dark to see much. Look out for a light from Flecky or the Ryans' truck."

"Frank's smart enough not to use his lights," says Dunning.

"Doesn't matter, Jordan set Flecky up to flash his outside floodlights as soon as Frank loads up and heads out of there. They should be along soon." Woodson turns to look behind him. "Where are you, Perkins?"

"Over here, Sergeant, untangling these spotlight leads."

Five minutes later, Dunning rises from his crouched position and cocks his ear to the south. "Vehicle," he says.

"I can't hear anything except Perkins shuffling about the wagon," says Woodson. Perkins freezes.

"There, see? A little dust on Gum Hill Lane." Dunning stares into the dark. "Ah, he just turned into the scrub."

"Can't see a thing," says Woodson, looking through the binoculars.

"Have you got them turned the right way 'round?" asks Dunning, chuckling. "Just having you on, boss; I'm using a bit of old black fella magic to see them."

Woodson scowls and the two coppers resume their crouching positions, waiting.

"I've got a real bad feeling about this." The night is cold. The two figures scramble up the bank of the creek they have been stumbling along and pause, straining to see through the thick bush. They can barely make out the outline of a shearing shed and sheep yards a hundred meters ahead of them. A quarter-moon emerges briefly from behind a scattering of thickening clouds. They get a clearer view of their target. A man is sitting on the shed loading dock, smoking a cigarette.

"There's Flecky," says Frank whispering. "Everything looks clear; you go back and get the truck."

Matt remains still, his eyes scanning the ridge rising up from a large, flat paddock, nearly a kilometer away. "Look, I told you, Woodson got back last Saturday, and he's setting up to come after us, big time. Are you sure nobody but us and Flecky Martin knows about this?"

"Do you think I'd be out tonight if I wasn't sure?" A sudden breeze rattles the leaves of the tall gum trees; a thump, like the fall of a heavy foot on hard soil, startles them both. "What the hell?" says Frank. They spin around, expecting the worst. A koala looks up at them, for a moment bemused, and then scampers through the bush to find another tree. "Phew, little creep frightened the crap out of me for a minute."

"Bit edgy for someone who's got it all covered, hey?" says a relieved Matt, mild sarcasm in his voice. "You see anything on that ridge?"

"Too far away for anyone to see anything from there; get the truck, will you?"

"They'd be looking for lights."

"Leave the lights off. Besides, I told you; only Flecky and you know."

"I said I don't feel right about this. Something's off. Let's give it a miss and get out of here," says Matt, becoming agitated.

"All right, you stay here; *I'll* get the truck. Stone the bloody crows—you young blokes don't have it in you any more, do you?"

Frank moves into the creek bed to head back to the Landcruiser hidden in the scrub two hundred meters from the track into Flecky's property. *Shouldn't have brought the kid along; he's not up for this caper.*

Matt hears the Landcruiser coming slowly along the Martin's track into the shed area. He watches Flecky stub out his cigarette, walk into the shed, and reemerge a few minutes later, dragging two bulging woolpacks onto the loading dock. Frank arrives and reverses up to the platform. Flecky hauls the two bags onto the tray top and then jumps to the ground to greet Frank, who then offers Flecky a cigarette.

Matt watches as the two men light up. "Come on, come on," he says quietly, under his breath. Frank pulls a roll of notes from his pocket and passes them to Flecky. Suddenly, a bright light sweeps in a brief arcing flash across the ridge. Matt, instantly alert, springs to his feet and sprints in his father's direction.

"Get the hell out of here, Dad," he screams. "They're on top of the ridge."

"What the hell?" yells a startled Woodson, spinning around to see Perkins tearing the leads of the spotlight from the wagon's battery terminals.

"Didn't know it was turned on, Sergeant," says Perkins. "Sorry."

"Your brain scrambled?" says Woodson. "The whole damn world will know we're here now."

Frank tosses his cigarette to the ground and jumps into the truck. "You rotten little turd, Flecky," he shouts as he floors the vehicle in the direction of the running Matt. "I'll be back for you and the money later." He leans over to push open the passenger side door. "Here, boy, jump in." He stomps on the brake, allowing his son time to leap into the cab.

Frank is blinded for a second as the whole area suddenly lights up. "What the hell? Flecky, the mongrel, he's turned on the bloody floodlights."

"What the hell, now?" shouts Woodson. The area around the Martin buildings lights up in a blaze of brilliant white light. "Damn idiot, he was only supposed to flick the lights on and off after Frank left."

"There's a vehicle heading out of there now," says Dunning.

"Course there is; what a screw up, Frank's onto us now. Let's follow him," orders Woodson. "Bob, you drive. And remind me to leave you behind to do the filing next time, Perkins; I can't believe you are so damn stupid."

Frank bounces down the Martin driveway. "What the hell got into him?" he shouts.

"I don't know, but he's got a tribe of kids to feed, and wool prices are in the sewer. He needs the money, I suppose. Somebody got in his ear," yells Matt over the screaming engine. "Jordan, I bet. I saw them having a yarn Saturday night at the barbecue."

The truck slides out of the Martin homestead driveway and speeds toward the South Coast Road. "That's probably it, then. Jordan. Matt, I'm going drop you off; no sense you getting caught if that's what they are after. My guess is that they were going to follow us, see where we store the stuff. It'll take the coppers a few minutes to get off the ridge, that old gum-cutter's track is pretty rough. You can walk across Ritchie Meadows and head for Tom's place." He brakes abruptly and slides to a stop. "Right, get out; stay at Tom's until you hear from me."

Matt jumps from the vehicle. Pushing the accelerator to the floor, with the rear wheels spinning in the ironstone gravel, Frank fishtails into the night, his lights turned off.

He walks through the roadside scrub to the wire fence bordering the Ritchie Meadows pasture and then squeezes between the strands of wire to begin the three-kilometer walk to Tom's place. A couple kangaroos feeding on the pasture lift onto their hind legs to stare at the intruder, nervous, and then they scatter, two dark boulders bounding into the darkness. He hears the old Landcruiser slow for the intersection and roar off in the direction of Vivonne Bay. *Cunning old bugger is leading them away from home. He grins. I bet Woodson is livid.*

As they bounce down the old track, Dunning sees Frank turn at the intersection. "Seems you were wrong, boss. He just turned to the east."

Trees flash by on both sides of the road as Frank looks for kangaroos. *Can't believe it; he turned us in. Jordan is in with the coppers, all right. Always knew he was no good.*

He slows down, letting the dust behind ease to little more than a transparent veil. He switches the lights on and keeps checking the rear view mirror. Within a few minutes, the lights of the police wagon show up in the mirror. They back off.

"Ah, thought so. They're looking for where we stash the stuff, all right. Well, Sergeant bloody Woodson, have I got a surprise for you."

The reflectors on the mail box at the entrance to Stumpy Flats sparkle red in the distance. Frank turns into the driveway, opens the gate, and heads for the Baldwin shearing shed, leaving the gate wide open, an invitation.

Dunning swings into the Stumpy Flats entrance and stops at the open gate. The red taillights of Frank's truck, moving along the track toward the Baldwin buildings, are in clear view. Dunning slaps the steering wheel with his hand and bursts out laughing.

Everything is quiet as Frank runs the Landcruiser to a stop alongside the Baldwin shearing shed. He pulls the two sacks of flowers from the tray top and drags them underneath the elevated shed into the carpet of dark, pebbly, sheep droppings.

"Oh, he's got your number, all right, boss," says Dunning. "He's dumping what he's got at the Baldwins. He knows we know Jordan has dabbled with drugs in the past. He knows if you go after him here, you're going to be opening a whole new can of worms." He looks at Woodson. "And we know this is not where Frank stores it; your call, Acting Sergeant."

45

Sydney's early afternoon sun is having little impact on warming the unusually chilly winter day, but the mansions sprawled along the harbor shoreline still show up spectacularly in its unaffected radiance. Belinda's mansion fronts the harbor waters of Rose Bay, a locality in the affluent eastern suburbs. The view, of course, is wonderful, although for a Sunday, few sailing boats are plying the usually busy waterway. The two-story building uses one-third of the half-hectare [64] property, while a flourishing collection of flowers and shrubs adorn a manicured lawn running to the edge of a stone wall, which drops vertically into deep water.

"It is such a beautiful place, Cassandra," says Belinda, looking out of the window of the sunroom. "There is nothing like the sea to give one perspective and serenity."

"I like it, especially my view of the opera house from my terrace. It inspires me," Cassie says.

"Yes, dear, of course, but I was thinking of your place on Kangaroo Island. The view from the house and gazebo are out of this world."

A generously endowed, matronly woman with a jolly demeanor lighting her round face walks into the room carrying a tray laden with a pot of tea, scones, strawberry jam, and a bowl of rich, thick, dairy cream.

"Put them on the table, Molly," says Belinda, indicating the coffee table set on a large Persian rug in front of the sofa where she and Cassie sit.

"Oh, how delightful," says Cassie. "They look delicious; thank you, Molly."

---

[64] Hectare: Equals two-point-two acres in the old measuring standard.

"You're welcome," says Molly. "Tuck into them now, Miss; you could do with a little more meat on that beautiful young body of yours."

"That will do, Molly," gently chides Belinda. "The girl is perfect for her role in *Fire in the Center*."

Molly pours two cups of tea. "I shall eat them all, Molly," promises Cassie. She smiles and returns to the kitchen.

"She has been with me for twenty years now; don't know how I would get on without her. She was a tower of strength when I discovered Aaron was having an affair with the girl who replaced me after my injury; the lead ballerina, would you believe? Somehow, with Molly's help, I stumbled through it all and we reconciled before he died, thank God. He really was a good man, only a silly one at times, something most men can lay claim." She pauses, thinking. "Life can be awfully cruel, dear." She remembers Kristina's death. "But, of course, you know that already, don't you?" She pats Cassie's knee. "Do help yourself," she says, indicating the refreshments on the coffee table.

Cassie spreads her scone with generous helpings of the strawberry jam and cream. "Scrumptious," she says, biting into the pastry. "I'm sorry, I didn't know about—about your husband." She demolishes the rest of the scone and begins spreading another. "I am starving." She sips her tea. "How did you and Daddy get on at home?"

"We had a nice time, except—" Belinda considers whether she should go on. "Except, well, we had some disagreement about a matter involving you."

"Oh," says Cassie, feigning surprise. "I hope it wasn't anything to do with my personal life."

"Yes, it was, I am rather afraid to say. You see, Cassie—despite what you might believe about me interfering in your personal life, I happen to be on your side. I am not at all happy with your father's interference. We had words about that, and I left him in rather a disappointed frame of mind, I am sorry to say."

"Yes, Matt," says Cassie, reluctant to think too much about it. "He'll come around. I think deep down he really likes him, but, well, it's the Catholic thing, as well as Matt's dad being an alcoholic that upsets him. Anyway, we have a six-month agreement."

"I hope that is all it is, dear." Belinda picks away at a plain scone, and then takes a sip from her tea. "Now, tell me, how do you find working with Shamus?"

Cassie looks out the sunroom window. A large, red, container ship carrying a full load of different colored containers on its deck fills the window as it passes up the harbor to unload. *I wonder what part of the world it's come from.*

"You know what you said about men being silly? I find the same thing with Shamus; he is so professional when we rehearse, but the moment we are finished, he collapses into an irritating smart aleck. His focus seems to be to add me to his list of conquests."

"You are a very attractive girl, Cassie, and you will probably drive all men crazy. Timothy and I teamed you with Shamus because you are both incredibly attractive and talented. The two of you together will mean good publicity and a very profitable season for the company." She smiles, acknowledging with a nod of her head the importance she attaches to the business aspect of the dance company.

The container ship moves on to reveal a harbor maritime ferry packed with passengers, passing grandly on its way to the suburb of Manly. *Not many people on the outside deck today; too cold,* she observes.

"That's good," says Cassie. "If I can keep injury free, it'll be wonderful. We open in just six weeks. I'm so excited."

"Is there anything we should be worrying about?"

"I have had trouble with shin splints in my right leg, but I am taking good care—ice packs and bandages. The stone bruise has healed, although Shamus was less than sympathetic about my two days off."

"You have worked very hard. I was at the rehearsals yesterday, watching from Timothy's office. Your work is coming along famously. Timothy is ecstatic about what you are doing with *Fire in the Center*. You will be a sensation on opening night; he is expecting rave reviews."

"He is so clever. The way he choreographed Matt's concept is outstanding."

"Ah, some news for you. Timothy and I have agreed Matt should be officially invited to opening night. We will pay for his expenses, of course, but we thought we should mention it to you first."

Cassie leans across to Belinda and hugs her tightly. "How wonderful, Belinda. Yes, of course. You are going to be thoroughly smitten when you meet him. He is handsome and brave and extremely talented."

"I shall look forward to it. Monty will be here, so I am hoping he will put his misgivings behind him and celebrate your debut. Besides, I am rather attached to him, you know."

"Thought so," says Cassie, a mischievous sparkle in her eyes as she sits back in the sofa. "He is with you, too." Cassie looks at her watch. "Oh, look at the time; I said I would meet Shamus for coffee in Double Bay at four o'clock." She finishes her tea and stands. "Have to go. It has been such a lovely afternoon, Belinda, thank you so much."

Belinda rises and walks the girl to the entrance door. "It has been a delight for me, also, young lady—given me a chance to get to know you better. Remember, I am always here for you." She kisses Cassie lightly on the cheek. "One last thing, Cassandra, fame has a way of distorting our grasp on life; think of Kangaroo Island when you feel life running away with you."

Cassie nods and starts climbing the stairs to the property entrance.

"And watch out for that Shamus; he is a rascally devil," Belinda calls after her.

46

The wild weather pounding the Gosse football oval has many of the islanders attending the Kingscote versus Western Districts football match at the Gosse oval sitting in their cars with the windows up and the motors running to keep warm and dry. Except for Matt, who is out on the field playing for the home team, the Ryans stayed back at the lighthouse. Frank had to be on station for weather reporting and any distress calls that might come in due to dangerous seas whipped up by the gale force winds. Sean was having a struggle with shortness of breath from the protracted effects of the tiger snake venom, so Katherine put him on the ventilator and Patrick decided to stay with Sean.

The rain is hammering blue and red tattoos onto the exposed skin of the freezing players. Parts of the muddy oval are sheets of water; the conditions are miserable; the final siren to end the game, at last only seconds away.

"I'll be glad when this is all over," says a mud-splattered Bob Dunning, grinning at an almost unrecognizable Matt Ryan, who is lining up to kick for goal from a penalty awarded by the umpire.

"After this kick, Bob, it's all over; we win."

"Just kick the thing, so we can get in for a hot shower."

Matt slams his boot into the heavy, wet ball, but to the chagrin of his teammates, it wobbles off the side of his boot and splashes into a lake of water in front of the goal posts. As players rush to cover the ball, thankfully, the siren sounds an end to the game and a draw.

"Good kick for us, Matt; crappy one for you."

Matt grins and they shake hands. "I can see why they wanted you in the league; great game, Bob."

"I was told you were pretty good; they weren't wrong. We could qualify for water polo after this. You on for a beer after the shower?"

"Yeah, no worries. What about hanging around for the barby later?"

"No, have to be back in Kingscote for the Lodge Ball tonight. Woodson's the guest of honor; welcome back and all that bull, and he wants me and Perkins there in full dress uniform. Bit uppity, hey?" The two gladiators split and walk to their respective rooms to shower and change. The storm continues to grow worse.

The roaring fire in the clubhouse lounge is popular with all the players as they push up close to warm their frozen bodies. "Ron Perkins, the new copper, Matt Ryan," says Dunning, introducing the two men to each other as they warm their hands over the fire. "What'll it be? Schooners all 'round?"

"You play it hard," says Matt to Perkins, nodding a yes to Dunning. "I bloody near drowned when you flattened me."

The manager of the bar is already heading to the group with a tray full of beers. "Saw you come in. On the house, Constable," he says as he hands over three schooners. "Owe you that for the hit you took breaking up the fight last time you were out here, hey."

"I'll have to come out more often," says Dunning.

"Couldn't get near you, mate, too bloody fast and slippery, you are. Like the night a few weeks ago at Flecky's, hey?" says Perkins, downing his schooner in one go.

"Ah, was that the night you made a bit of a goose of yourself, mate?" says Matt. "I heard the spotlight mentioned by someone, might've been Flecky. He finds it hard to keep his mouth shut, doesn't he?"

Dunning finishes his beer. "Enough of that, Perkins; we don't mix business with pleasure here," says Dunning. Perkins grimaces self-consciously, a little peeved at the chiding. "Well, here's to no more days like today, for footy,[65] anyway." They raise their glasses and toast. "How long is this blow[66] on for?"

---

[65] Footy: Slang for football..
[66] Blow: Storm.

"Supposed to back off by Monday," says Matt. "Still, we've got to expect more of them from now on."

The three men continue to talk about the weather and its affect on their football. Dunning is having a hard time adjusting to island conditions because many of his games were played in the dry outback regions. Perkins played in the city where the ovals were perfectly groomed, the ground perfectly flat and much easier to play on.

"It evens it out for everyone," says Matt, draining the last of his beer. "That is, if you're any bloody good at all, hey, Constable?"

Perkins gives Matt a hard look as he gathers the glasses and heads to the bar to buy another round.

"Ease up on Perkins, Matt. You already have Woodson gunning for you; you do not need to turn Perkins into a zealot. By the way, it was you out there the other night, you and your old man, wasn't it?"

"You know as much as I do, Bob. You also know the Rosenblum poppy is going to be legal soon." Matt leans closer into Dunning. "Woodson's onto it now because he wants to do us before that happens. You know he's wrong, and it gets me you back the bastard up."

"Hang about, mate. Right now, it is the law. I am a police officer, and I have to uphold the law as it stands. I'm trying to give you blokes a break, but I can't keep on doing it. I told you before; stay in the clear. You've got some influential interests wanting to get control of the stuff for themselves."

"You can't hold it back, Bob; it helps people. Hell, the bloody stuff grows wild here." He pauses and looks about the room. Perkins is pushing his way back through the crowd, clutching three schooners of beer and doing his best not to spill them.

"No good is going to come from what Woodson is on about, Bob. Mark my words; we're all going to be sorry if he doesn't lay off," Matt says keeping his voice low.

"Sorry about what?" says Perkins, offering a schooner each to the two men.

"Don't worry about it, Ron." They all take a beer.

The conversation returns to the football game, and the glasses are soon empty.

"Another round, you blokes?"

"All right, one for the road," replies Dunning. "Then we have to get out of here, or the boss will start calling. Besides, it doesn't look good for a copper with a DUI on his record."

"What are you going to do, arrest each other?" says a chuckling Matt as he begins to push his way toward the bar.

"Cheeky blighter," says Perkins. "I reckon the boss is right about him." The young copper, with a habit acquired during police training, braces himself by drawing to his full height, squaring his shoulders and tightening his buttocks. "You think we should be drinking with him?"

Dunning grins and looks wryly at Perkins. "Do yourself a favor, lad; you'd be smart to take some time to get to know and like the locals. They're good people, particularly down this end, and tough, too. They have to be. But if you ride them too hard, they can make your life miserable."

Dunning looks towards the bar. Matt is ordering their drinks when Maureen O'Flaherty pushes through the crowd to his side. She cups her hand about her mouth and whispers into his ear. *Oh, oh,* Dunning thinks. Matt nods in the direction of the two policemen. Dunning turns back to Perkins. "Ryan's a good kid, trying to make the best of a tough life. A break or two will do more good than harm. Woodson thinks they're easy pickings, thinks he can salvage his career on their backs without causing as much as a ripple."

Matt struggles through the crowd, leaving Maureen at the bar. "Here you go," he says as he hands over the beer. "It's a bloody tight squeeze through there. Thirsty work." He tosses down half his beer.

"Have you heard from Cassie recently?"

"To be honest with you, Bob, not for a while—seems she's busy rehearsing for a show that is going to open in the opera house, or else the mail is not getting here," he says, unable to hide the uncertainty written all over his face.

"I'm sure she is as busy as hell, that's all," says Dunning. He drains his glass and turns his attention to Perkins. "Drink up, Ronnie, me boy, time for us to go." He flips him the keys. "Warm up the wagon, hey?" Perkins leaves and Dunning turns back to Matt. "I enjoyed the game Matt, and the opportunity to have a few beers with you. Like I've said before, I like you, but watch out for Woodson; the push is on. Say hello to Cassie for me, hey?" He shakes hands and leaves.

Cassie? Don't know about that anymore, mate, I think she and that Shamus bloke are at it. He turns to go back to the bar and finds himself looking into the flashing green eyes of the Irish redhead.

"Here; for you," Maureen says, handing him a schooner of beer.

He takes the drink, and smiles. "Bewdy, Maureen, thanks."

She raises her rum and coke. "Here's to a good time tonight, Matt. Yeah, to you and me, hey?" They clink glasses, the earlier drinks already bringing a warm, mellow glow to the quickly thawing Ryan.

47

"Bless me, Father, for I have sinned. It is a week since my last confession, and—" says a remorseful Matthew Ryan as he begins his confession of a list of venial[67] infractions in the confessional box located inside and close to the main entrance of the Parndana church. Inside the 'praying hands church,' the rat-a-tat-tat of wind-driven rain hammering against the tin roof precludes any attempt at conversation among the waiting congregation. Matt is thankful for the noise as he comes to his most reluctant admission. "And also, Father, I, um, had sex last night."

"Mm—yes, me boy, and *that* would be Maureen, now, wouldn't it?" The monsignor pauses for a moment. He sighs. "Well, it figures. Tell me, were ye wearing a French letter?"[68]

Matt can hardly believe his ears. He is aware the monsignor has a reputation for not pussy-footing around sexual matters in discussions with his flock, believing he serves a more useful purpose when dealing with the subject in the language of his audience, particularly adolescent males, but—

"No, Monsignor."

"Well, then, we'll be finding out what the good Lord has in mind for ye before too long then, won't we, Matthew?" says the monsignor, a touch of impish humor in his voice. "'Tis as well she's a good young Catholic girl, although with, maybe, a *tooch* too much excitement running through her hormones—but the good Lord is in charge, hey, Matthew?"

---

[67] Venial: Easily forgiven.
[68] French letter: Condom.

"Yes, Monsignor," says Matt, ridden with guilt from his betrayal of Cassie.

"For yer penance, say a decade of the rosary and ask the Holy Mother if she'd be so kind as ta be quelling yer passions for the time being." He gives the boy absolution.

"Thank you, Father." He leaves the confessional and joins Katherine and Sean. Patrick is waiting in the vestry for the priest. Frank is sitting in his usual place, the smell of alcohol once again on his breath. He winces, but his father's picking up of the booze again had almost come as a relief. The longer Frank remained sober, the more intolerable he became as the demons of his dry-drunk agitated.

The spring-loaded door of the confessional slams shut, and Monsignor Byrne hustles up the middle of the church to the vestry to dress for Mass. The O'Flahertys file into family pew, two rows ahead of the Ryans. Maureen is glowing, nodding to Matt as she passes, a smile lighting her pretty face. He ignores her and stares ahead at the altar, pretending to be deep in prayer, but sick to the stomach, full of guilt and self-loathing from the events of the previous night. The hangover from the alcohol along with a throbbing headache is becoming unbearable, the need to vomit overpowering. Suddenly, he pushes past Sean and Katherine, uttering a barely audible apology, and dashes outside to vomit behind the church. In seconds, he is soaked to the skin.

Then, dry retching, he runs for the Ute, yanks open the door and slides into the seat, cold, wet and shaking uncontrollably. Maureen is watching from the church entrance. She waves as if signaling 'wait for me,' but he ignores her, starts the motor, and speeds away, leaving the concerned redhead staring after him. What she does not see is the Ute stopping after the first turn in the road and Matt stepping out into the pouring rain to get a six-pack of Westend Bitter,[69] stored under the rear canvas cover, and bring it back into the cab with him. She does not see him snatch a stubby of beer from the plastic wrapping, twist off the cap and, with shaking hands, drain the amber contents in one gulp. She does not see him reach urgently for another as,

---

[69] Westend Bitter: Popular brand South Australian beer.

laughing manically, he wrenches the gear stick into 'forward' and roars off toward the South Coast Road, the bottle already at his lips.

When the Ryan family finally arrives home late in the afternoon, the gale is approaching its worst, and what light of day is left is fast retreating under heavy clouds and furious rain. Matt is sitting on the back porch, a dozen empty stubby bottles scattered around the old sofa.

They run through the rain from the Landcruiser to the verandah, Katherine carrying Sean in her arms. "Ha, the Ryan family, headed by the celebrated and chief drunk Francis O'Malley Ryan, does approach. Hail, oh, great Exemplar." Matt laughs hysterically. "It is I, your son—drunk. A chip off the old block, so to speak," his speech slurred. "The perfect fit, hey, Frank? I am the son of the father, make no mistake."

Katherine and the boys are frightened. Sensing a violent confrontation looming between the two men, they scurry past, Sean wheezing heavily.

Frank is still primed, having maintained a manageable level of alcohol with small nips from his brandy flask at regular intervals during the day. "Oh, you're a real charmer, lad," he says, experience telling him to be wary of the boy. "I don't know what's gotten into you, but it might be a good idea for you to sleep it off." Matt's eyes glaze over for a moment. He slaps his face a couple of times to stop from passing out. Frank shakes his head, somewhat amused by the boy's suffering, and walks into the kitchen. Matt rises unsteadily to his feet and follows.

Frank is already reaching into the liquor cabinet for the half-full bottle of brandy and pony glass he keeps ready. He fills the glass, tosses down the contents in one shot and then pours another before sitting at the table.

"I'd offer you one, but you've had about all you can handle," Frank says, a sarcastic edge to the tone of his voice.

Matt tries to focus. Patrick and Sean move into the lounge room adjoining the kitchen.

Katherine senses the menace in Matt's demeanor. "Matthew, there are two letters here for you; they were at the post office in Parndana," she says, handing them over in an effort to deflect his attention from Frank.

"Thank you, my lady." He looks at the first the envelope. "Hah, what about this, everybody—from the National Academy of the Australian Literary Society." Matt looks melodramatically about him as he rips open the envelope, takes out the letter and begins to read aloud.

"Dear Mr. Ryan,

Congratulations. We are pleased to inform you that you are to be awarded a Meritorious Newcomer Scholarship to the University of New South Wales for your poem, 'Lust: Life's Fiery Center.' Details are to follow, but the presentation ceremony will be in Sydney on the afternoon of Friday, July 5. We hope you can be there—"

Matt looks up, eyes peeping surreptitiously over the top of his arm, held up in front of his face as if a cape lays over it. He laughs madly and stares at Frank. "Well, well, do you think, perhaps, I, son of Frank, just might have inherited a fragment of talent from my teacher mother?" His voice rises on the last five words of the sentence.

"Seems you just might've," says Frank, aware of how tenuous the situation is becoming.

"What wonderful news, Matthew. Congratulations," says Katherine, breaking in. She puts on her apron. "This calls for a celebration; I'll bake some nice fresh scones to have with strawberry jam and cream." She busies herself about the cooking area, pulling oven trays from the stove and bowls from the cupboards. "Who's the other letter from?"

"Ah, the other letter," he says as if making an announcement of an important discovery. He looks at the writing on the envelope. "I'll be damned; it's from Cassie—about time, too," he says, in a voice beginning to settle. He pulls out two pages and a small cream envelope. Inside the envelope is a card with gold lettering on it. "Well, well, well, an invitation from Cassie's dance company to attend the opening of *Fire in the Center* on July 5. July fifth, that's the same date as the scholarship award, unreal." He throws the invitation on the kitchen table in the same moment that a deluge of rain driven by the force of the gale hammers the roof, making further conversation almost impossible.

Matt glares at Frank and then turns away to walk unsteadily into the lounge, where a log fire set by Patrick is already warming the room, and settles onto a sofa to read Cassie's letter.

Dear Matthew,

It seems such a long time since I heard from you. I miss you terribly, particularly when I think about you holding me. Everything is going well with my dancing, although minor injuries sometimes slow progress, but it is to be expected as a dancer. The opening to Fire in the Center is fast approaching, as you will see from the enclosed invitation. I am so excited about seeing you. Timothy, Belinda, and Shamus think you are brilliant and can't wait to meet you.

As he runs a finger over the familiar writing, the earlier feelings of shame and guilt begin to break through the anesthetizing effect of the alcohol. He stares into the fire, remembering the warmth of their couplings, a vastly different experience from his mad sexual escapade with Maureen. He takes a deep breath, slowly exhales, and returns to reading the letter. Cassie describes her life in Sydney, the demanding schedule that leaves her exhausted, and the way she covets her Sundays to do nothing other than rest and recover her energy, or write letters, or journal her week's experiences.

Finally, my darling, in reply to the last letter you sent me, which seems such a long time ago, I want to say I cannot understand why you have not received my letters—there should have been at least three—or why you did not return my phone calls, two in the last couple of weeks. I spoke to your father each time, who I must say was rather short with me; surely he passed them on to you.

Matt does not finish the rest of the letter, but stares into the fire, a dawning realization racing through his mind. Incredulity turns to rage. The pain of violation and betrayal is so powerful it seems his heart is being torn from his chest.

Frank is sitting at the table with the two boys when Matt slams Cassie's letter against his chest so hard he almost knocks him off the chair. "Got the rest of my letters have you, hey? Have you?" he shouts. Katherine and the boys are shocked and scared. The violence in Matt's voice is murderous. "And the phone messages—didn't pass them on, hey? Why not?" He is screaming now, shaking Frank violently by the front of his shirt. Patrick moves from the table. Katherine clutches her apron. No one notices Sean get up from his seat and slink through the kitchen door and out onto the back verandah.

"Come on, Frank, why did you do it?" Matt shouts, tightening his grip on the front of his drunken father's shirt. "Why did you do it?" he screams again. The young man, on the verge of tears, starts pounding Frank's chest with his fists.

Frank pushes up from his chair, grabs Matt's arms, and swings him across the kitchen and into the cupboards, almost knocking Katherine down as she tries to catch him.

"I'll tell you why," says Frank. "Those Baldwins will bring you no good, boy. They are rich swine and have no room for the likes of you in their family. Oh, they may say one thing, but believe me that old man is already working at getting you out of his daughter's life."

"Cassie loves me, Dad, don't you see that?" pleads Matt, dumbfounded, beginning to hyperventilate. His rage returns. "C'mon, come outside and have a go if you've got the guts."

Katherine holds him. "That'll settle nothing, Matthew. I'll take care of this." She turns on Frank. "The girl loves Matt, Frank," yells Katherine. "What on earth is the matter with you, taking the boy's letters? Do you have no shame? You had no business—"

"Shut up, woman," yells Frank. "You don't understand these people. They are the scum who sent my mates to their deaths in Vietnam and stayed home and made money from the war. Do you think we mean anything to them? We are a commodity, cannon fodder, labor to them."

"The Baldwins had no more to do with the war than you or I. I know a lot happened to you in Vietnam, Frank, that has left you hating, but I tell you I am tired of it affecting our family. You have no right using Matt to get at them. You'd better get some help, or I'm taking the boys and leaving you."

For a moment, both Frank and Matt are quiet. Neither had heard such deadly intention in Katherine's voice before. Frank knows she is offering an ultimatum, no ifs, ands, or buts about it. Matt's mind is suddenly full of the many terrible ordeals his mother endured with Frank's neuroses and drinking, the precursors to her suicide.

"I was doing it for you, lad," he says. "I'll be in the lighthouse, if you want to take this further." He steps around Matt and walks to the door. "Where's Sean?"

"He must have gone to his room; he usually does when things get like this. He hates arguments, and it scares the life out of him when you are drunk, Dad," says Patrick quietly. "He'll be down when he knows you've gone."

Frank turns to Matt. "You'll find those letters in the top right drawer of the office desk—unopened. I'm sorry, son. Katherine is right, I had no business—" He shrugs and walks out of the kitchen.

Sean is scared. Matt's fury and violent confrontation with his father is more than he can handle, and his main thought is to get out, to escape. He slinks through the kitchen door, takes a raincoat and hat from the clothing pegs on the laundry porch wall, walks out onto the verandah and puts on the hat and coat. The rain is coming down in buckets, the wind furious. Barney is out of his kennel, straining at the end of his fully extended chain, wet and barking furiously. Sean crosses to him and releases the catch on the chain.

"C'mon, Barney, we're going to the cave; c'mon, boy." He starts out for the south side of the cottage fence, head-on into the driving rain stinging his face and blurring his vision. "We're going to our secret place."

The last of the light is almost gone, but the small winding track to Weir Cove is so familiar to Sean that he could walk it blindfolded. *Always fighting and yelling when Dad's drunk and now even Matt's drunk. I can hide in my secret place. Nobody can find me there; then they'll be sorry.* He trips over a piece of protruding limestone, falls forward and skids over the sharp rock, scraping skin off his arms and hands. Tears form in the little bloke's eyes and run down his wet cheeks. Hardly able to breathe, the wheezing worsening, he struggles to his feet and pushes on doggedly toward his destination.

He finally makes it to the lip of the cliff where it drops away to the old supply jetty 65 meters below. Looking down at the water, he watches the huge swells rolling toward his cliff, building into lines of arching peaks before crashing over the rocks and thundering up the steep walls toward *his* fortress.

Sean crosses to a large clump of scrubby bush to the right of the path, reaches in amongst its prickly branches and pulls out a rope about twenty-five meters long. On one end is a snap catch, which he attaches to a rusty metal clamp anchored into the side of an old concrete block a few paces from the cliff. He throws the other end over the edge and then, clasping his hands around the rope, turns his back to the sea and works his body down the almost vertical wall. Barney barks crazily, as if pleading with the boy not to go down tonight. The rain is incessant.

"Go to the cave, Barney, that's a good boy, go on; I'll meet you there," he yells. Barney has his own special way of reaching the cave. A track made by wild goats, too narrow for a human to traverse safely, zigzags across the face of the cliff to the rocks at the bottom, passing the cave entrance 15 meters below the cliff top. Barney scampers off as Sean works cautiously down the wet and slippery rope. His wheezing grows louder; he gasps desperately for more of the cold air. With a meter to go to the cave entrance, disaster, he slips, burning his already battered hands as he tries to clamp them back tight around the wet rope. For a moment, God intervenes, and his feet hit the edge of the cave floor where it protrudes slightly from the cliff wall, stopping his slide. He clings to the rope, panting, desperately trying to suck more air through his tightening larynx. He reaches with his foot, trying to find more of the floor. Barney arrives, sizes up the small boy's plight, and grabs for the bottom of Sean's pants with his mouth.

Sean's mind starts to wander. Already weak from the snakebite, his strength is quickly failing. Barney manages to snare the bottom of the boy's pants between his teeth and tries to pull him into the cave. Slowly, very slowly, the gallant kelpie makes progress and drags the lower part of the boy's body, centimeter by centimeter, toward safety. Rainy squalls continue to lash at Sean. Hypothermia threatens. His fierce grip loosens, and he slips farther down the rope, past the safety of the cave entrance. Barney hangs on tenaciously, and Sean manages to tighten his grip again and stop the slipping; the faithful dog's grip holds. Sean is now hanging upside down. Barney clings to the fabric, pulling frantically, trying to drag Sean's feet back into the cave.

An enormous, white flash of lightning fills the sky; the wind howls around Sean, swinging him out from the cave. He begins to drift into delirium and what is left of his strength quickly erodes. He lets go of the rope and tumbles head over heels down the steep face of the cliff wall to the rocks, fifty meters below, taking a frantic Barney with him, still latched, vice-like, onto the tearing fabric of his pants.

Matt fights his way to the lighthouse. The heavy rain, driven by the fury of the *sou'westly*, is almost impossible to penetrate. The wind screams around the unyielding limestone and granite walls of the tower; its brilliant light, never failing, continuously pushing its sweeping signal of warning out across the Southern Ocean.

He slams through the door. Frank is at his desk, holding a cigarette almost burned down to the filter between two fingers of his left hand. The printout of a weather map of the storm shows a low-pressure area, the isobars wound tightly together, centered over the southwestern end of the island. An almost empty glass of brandy sits next to an ashtray full of cigarette butts.

"We can't find Sean," yells Matt.

Frank looks up and cups his hand to his ear. "What did you say?" he shouts back.

Matt leans closer to his father. "We can't find Sean. We've searched the house. Pat and I looked all through the sheds and other cottages."

"Did you look under his bed?" He picks up his glass and drains the last of the brandy. Matt slaps the empty glass from his father's hand.

"Did you hear me? We can't find him. He may have gone to his secret place, but none of us knows where it is other than over by Weir Cove somewhere."

The seriousness of Matt's message begins to penetrate Frank's consciousness. His past military experience takes over, and he snaps into action. "Bloody hell, if he's out in this weather, in his condition, he won't last long." He looks at Matt. "Get the Landcruiser, ropes, spotlights, radios, blankets, and flasks of hot tea—now," he orders. "We may need help. I'll call Tom; he can round up some people." Matt is transfixed for a moment, panic and fear threatening to crush him. Frank grabs his shoulders and shakes. "Come on, lad, brace up, we don't have much time. I'll be along as soon as I've spoken to Tom." He pushes him toward the door.

Matt pulls the Landcruiser up by the cottage gate as Frank runs up from the lighthouse. He has one of the spotlights set up and turned on. Patrick is running from the verandah with flasks of hot tea. Frank and Patrick leap into the truck. "Go," yells Frank, "to the cove."

"Wait," cries Pat, "Mother's coming."

Katherine is running from the verandah, carrying a flashlight and pulling a raincoat over her shoulders. She runs to the truck and throws herself into the back. Frank leaps out of his seat in the front cabin.

"Katherine, it would be better if you stayed here," he yells.

"That's my boy out there," she screams. "Now, let's get going." Frank nods, leaps onto the steel tray, puts an arm around her shoulders and bangs on the cab roof, signaling Matt to get moving.

"Tom is getting a search party together, just in case," he yells into Katherine's ear.

The truck bounces over the rough limestone towards the lip of the cliffs. Patrick sweeps the bush with the spotlight as they go, its beam reflecting off the shiny, wind-torn leaves, forming scary, demonic images from myriad shadows.

They reach the edge of the jetty drop-off and sweep the area with the spotlight—nothing.

"Matt," yells Frank, leaning into cab-side driver's door. "Head for the Admiral."

They drive along the narrow track until it ends. All of them get out and search along the cliff and under the arch, both spotlights on, beams bouncing off rocks and rough water, nothing.

"Katherine, take Patrick and your flashlight, keep looking here. Matt and I will head farther around the cove. If you find him, send Patrick after us."

The two men return to the truck, searching the terrain back to the old storehouse, nothing.

Matt stops the truck. "Keep going," yells Frank above the shrieking wind.

"He might have gone down the path into the cove, where we went the other day. A few rocky outcrops of limestone offer some shelter along there."

"No, I'm going to look about here," Matt yells back, getting out and taking the second spotlight. "You look there."

Frank does not stay to argue. "Righto, take a radio; and be careful." He hands over a handset and slides across into the driver's seat. Matt watches the truck's red tail lights bounce crazily as it moves over the rough track and into the darkness.

He's around here; I can feel him, he thinks, trusting the insistent urgency of his intuition. A blinding flash of lightning followed by a sharp crack of thunder startles him. He looks at his watch. An hour has gone by since they started searching. "Hurry up, Tom, hurry up; you should be here by now," he screams into the storm, panicking. He again sweeps the beam slowly along the edge of the lip. As it cuts through the wet darkness, the light picks up a narrow black shadow stretching along the ground from the old concrete block. His first thought is that it looks like a snake. Then, his heart skips a beat as he realizes—

A rope! Picking it up, he follows it to the cliff edge. *His secret place is down there.* He peers over the lip, following the rope down with the spotlight to where it ends, well shy of the bottom. The beam of light stretches to its limit, barely illuminating the jagged rocks, white with turbulent water. His eyes strain to make out what appears to be something moving in the foam of the crashing waves. "Barney! That's Barney. Oh, Jesus God, no!" he screams as he makes out the form of his stepbrother lying limp on the rocks. Barney is tugging at Sean's jacket, trying to keep his head above the water and away from the breaking waves threatening to drag them both into the sea.

Matt, half-crazy with anguish, pushes the transmitter button of his radio and shouts into it. "He's here, at the bottom of Weir Cove jetty. It looks bad; I'm going after him. Hurry, Dad, please hurry." Breathless, he grabs the rope and prepares to lower himself over the lip. Suddenly, a wall of light from a bank of spotlights attached to the bull bar of a truck blinds him. "Where do you think you're going? Stop right there." The commanding voice of Mad Tom stops Matt cold.

"Tom! Thank God, you're here. Sean's down there," he shouts, pointing.

"Others are on their way." Tom looks over into the deep drop, his more powerful spotlight, hooked to the truck's power system, clearly illuminating Sean's horrifying situation.

"I've got two long ropes in the back of my truck; get them," he orders.

"But—"

"Get the bloody ropes, tie them together, and give me that radio." Matt hesitates. "Now!" shouts Tom, brutal. Matt lets go of the rope, gives Tom his radio, and runs to get the ropes from the truck. Tom grabs Sean's rope and positions himself to go over the lip. Matt runs back to Tom dragging the two ropes.

"No, Tom, let me go." He drops the ropes on the ground.

Tom looks menacingly at Matt. "I said, tie them together, and then feed them down to me." He disappears over the edge.

As Tom reaches the end of the first rope, Matt feeds him the other. He quickly knots them together and then rappels the rest of the way to the bottom. Matt lights Tom's path with the spotlight. The rocks are jagged and slippery. Barney barks excitedly as Tom makes his way to Sean and scans the boy's broken body.

Sean's face is deathly white; a trickle of blood comes from the corner of his mouth and washes away in the rain and seawater. One of his legs twists at a horrible angle from his thigh, obviously broken. Tom feels his wrist for a pulse. It is weak, very weak; the boy is unconscious and close to death.

More light from the top floods the area. The radio crackles. "Tom, can you hear me?"

He reaches for the radio slung over his shoulder. "I can hear you, Frank. It's bad down here; I don't want to move him, but these waves are getting closer. I have to."

Matt and Frank peer over the lip and watch as Tom lifts Sean into his arms. Katherine and Patrick arrive, along with a large group of rescuers, who have been listening to the radio transmissions. Katherine is frantic and rushes to Frank, crying.

Frank holds her briefly and then gives her the spotlight. "Here, keep this on Tom and Sean. I'm going down." He tosses the radio to Matt and grabs the rope. In the same moment, Matt glimpses a large wave rolling in from the southwest, already beginning to curl into the bay. It is the one in a thousand, the one twice as large as any other—a rogue wave.

He screams at Frank and into the radio. "Watch out, it's a rogue—coming into the cove now." Frank looks toward the open sea and sees the big wave arching above the rest, fast closing on the jetty. He leaps from the edge, rappelling head first down the rope as he had been trained to do in special forces. Without gloves, the rope tears into the flesh of his hands as he plummets, barely under control, to the bottom.

Tom, cradling Sean in his arms, hears Matt's frantic voice screaming over the radio. Barney begins barking furiously again. "Watch out, it's a rogue—coming into the cove now." He glances over his shoulder to see it arching above the others, still fifty meters off. He runs, jumps, and slips across the rocks, cracking his shins but still clutching the unconscious Sean, Barney leading the way. He hears the roar of the breaking rogue racing up behind them.

Then he sees Frank, swinging off the rope, his arm reaching toward them, ready to grab for the boy. As the wave hits, Tom almost throws Sean to Frank, who snatches the boy in a vice-like grip to his chest. He manages to scale a meter of the cliff before the overwhelming force of the water threatens to tear them from the rope. In a few seconds, it is over; the water withdraws in a swirling torrent back to the sea. Frank holds on to the rope, clutching his son as Tom sweeps by, caught up in the receding turbulence, flailing desperately, bouncing off jagged rocks and then disappearing into the open sea.

More ropes slap against the cliff floor next to Frank. Rescuers quickly arrive. They gently take Sean from Frank and wrap them both in blankets. Barney, wet and bloody, sits next to Sean, licking his little master's face and whimpering.

A ranger from the Chase tending Sean looks up at Frank, tears rolling down his cheeks. "I'm sorry, Frank; he's gone."

48

The storm has passed, and a full moon is high in the now clear sky. The police, the ambulance, and the monsignor arrive within minutes of each other. Already, a huge and growing crowd of neighbors, friends, parishioners and emergency service volunteers are quietly gathering about the Ryan cottage. Parties of rescuers continue to search the cliff bases for Tom, hoping for a miracle.

The wailing of the distraught Katherine cared for by the local women inside the cottage, drifts through the eerie calm settled around the cape. A murmur of greeting rises from the crowd as the monsignor hurries into the house. Katherine's wailing fades to a quiet sobbing as the priest hugs her and then kneels next to the small boy laid out on the sofa, to anoint the body with holy oil and administer the last rites. Gently, he strokes Sean's face, his eyes teary. Reaching out to Katherine, who is clasping her rosary beads and standing at the head of her son, he brings her to kneel next to him and begins the rosary.

Woodson and Perkins are conversing in the back yard while Dunning talks to the locals. Perkins splits from the sergeant and heads toward the lighthouse. Woodson motions for Dunning to join him and they walk to the cottage door.

Matt, Frank, and Patrick are sitting at the kitchen table. As he looks into the faces of the Ryan men, Dunning's heart wrenches painfully. He attempts to offer his condolences, but chokes on the words as he struggles to hold back tears. Woodson nods to the Ryans and mumbles his condolences, adding that an inquiry into the two deaths will have to be conducted and they "might as well get started."

Matt offers the two policemen a cup of hot tea. Woodson nods a "yes," Dunning a silent decline. Matt starts to fill one of the cups set out on the table. As Woodson sits, he pulls a notebook from his tunic pocket. "All right, let's start at the beginning. Frank?"

Matt stops pouring, slams the pot down on the table and fixes Woodson a terrible look. "You mongrel, Woodson, we should have left you to rot in the scrub." Before Woodson can react, Matt storms out of the kitchen.

Dunning stiffens and follows. He squeezes through the crowd outside and hurries after him striding angrily toward the Admiral.

"Matt, hang on," calls Dunning. Matt slows and Dunning catches up. "I'm so sorry for what just happened in there. I swear to God, I'll drag that mongrel into the scrub myself one day and do him." He pauses and then places his hand on Matt's shoulder. "I hardly know what to say, what words to use to tell you how I feel for you and your family."

"It's my bloody fault, Bob, pure and simple," says Matt, tears tumbling from his eyes, their distinct blue vividly surreal, despite their bloodshot backdrop. "I'm no bloody good; I as good as killed the two of them myself."

"Hey, hey, lad; take it easy, take it easy."

"You don't understand. I got drunk today and went after the oldman. Sean got scared and took off for his secret place at Weir Cove. If I hadn't been such a dickhead, he would still be alive. I really am a piece of work, Bob. Last night I went out with someone else, and I—I really stuffed up."

"Cut it out. Go easy on yourself, for God's sake. Life's not black and white; life happens, things happen for reasons we don't understand. There is a power—God, Nature, call it what you like, and it runs through our lives, taking us with it."

"No, Bob, no excuses. Life gives us choices, and I've made too damn many wrong ones." He rubs his eyes and takes a deep breath. "I loved that little bloke. Lord God Almighty, why, why, why?" He glances up at the sky, and then back to Dunning. "I need some time to myself," he says reaching out and shaking Dunning's hand. "You're a hell of a bloke, a straight copper, and good to us out here. Thanks." He leaves, but after a few paces, turns. "I left a message for Cassie. If she calls, tell Patrick I'm down at Admiral, will you?" Head down, he shuffles off in the direction of the Admiral.

"Of course," Dunning calls after him. He watches the solitary figure, silhouetted against the full moon, gradually fade and blend in with the dark, rocky terrain of the Admiral and the silver ocean beyond. As he turns for the cottage, he spots Perkins coming out of the machinery shed.

"What are you up to, Constable?"

"Taking a bit of a bo peep,[70] Bob," says Perkins. "The boss told me to do a little snooping while we had the opportunity."

"Did he now?" Dunning sighs. "Why don't you get the car started, Mr. Perkins? Get it warmed up, hey? Bring it to the lighthouse; we'll meet you there. It's about time we let these people alone. We can come back and tidy up the paperwork some other time."

Perkins hesitates for a second. "Get on with it, Probationary Constable Perkins; I'll find Mr. Woodson." The two men split; Perkins walks in the direction of the police car, and Dunning to the cottage.

"And you can get the hell out of here now, Woodson," says Frank. Dunning walks into the kitchen and a very angry Frank.

"I want you to answer the question, Ryan," says Woodson, angry and agitated, the recent injury to his throat edging his voice with the strangely eunuch-like pitch. "You'd been drinking, right? You didn't see the kid walk out into the storm, right?"

Dunning places his hand on his sergeant's shoulder. "Can I see you outside, boss? Something you need to know," says the first-class constable, his voice tightening. Woodson glares at Dunning, annoyed by the interruption. Dunning squeezes Woodson's shoulder until it hurts and stares coldly into his eyes, signaling a very serious matter needs his attention, now.

"I'll be back, Ryan, and I'll want answers."

"Don't make it anytime soon," says a defiant Frank.

---

[70] Bo peep: Look.

Dunning leads the sergeant through the swelling crowd of neighbors and rescuers, a growing murmur of disquiet and resentment following the policemen. A couple of older men aggressively jostle Woodson. A few insults follow: "Keep going, copper; we don't need your kind around here." "Let's feed the bastard to the whites, plenty of 'em off the Admiral." "They'd spit him out." "Not a shred of decency in the man." Dunning hustles Woodson through the gate and turns toward the lighthouse.

Perkins has the car waiting in the parking area, idling. "You wait there; we'll be back in a few," says Dunning. They reach the tower and he opens the door. "Here we go, sergeant," he says, closing the door behind them.

"This had better be good, Dunning."

Dunning, his back to the door, braces himself, and fixes his sergeant with a deadly stare full of contempt. "For crying out loud, have you no decency, no compassion, Reg?" he says, his voice icy. "This family has just lost a child, and you're behaving like you're conducting an inquisition. You even sent Perkins to snoop about tonight."

"Who the hell do you think you are?" responds an angry, but wary, red-faced Woodson. "I'm running this game, and it's in your best interest to do as I tell you, you darky prick."

Dunning's temper detonates. Memories of insults hurled at his Aboriginal mother, his hopeless attempts to defend her, the stinging sense of shame he felt each time he thought of his inability to end the bigotry, to stop them from hurting her.

Woodson never saw it coming, or knew what hit him. The whip-like snap of Dunning's right hand, slaps the sergeant's face and ear so violently that the man tumbles over Frank's paper-covered desk. "That's for my mother." Woodson staggers upright, his ear ringing. As quick as the first, Dunning slaps the man on the other side of his face. "That's for Sean." Woodson slowly straightens, bewilderment glazing his eyes. Dunning's hand snakes out again—a final slap, with all his power behind it, and Woodson collapses into Frank's chair. "And that's for the Ryans."

Bob Dunning sits on the edge of the desk. "We're even now, Sergeant. From now on, you can come after me as hard as you like, but a word of warning. If you ever call me a darky again, I will personally feed you to the great whites." He bends over to within a few centimeters of Woodson's face. "And that, mister, is a promise."

"I'll have you drummed out for this, Dunning," snarls a cowering Woodson, his ears hot and ringing. "Assaulting a superior—they'll probably send you away for quite a while."

"Oh, I don't think you'll try that just yet, *Reggie*. You've got too much to lose. They would reopen the inquiry into the superintendent's death if they had new information. Racial bigotry would not sit well with your future aspirations, either, *Reggie*, especially with the dicey resume you have already built up in that area. Nope, you will just sit tight for the time being, biding your time. Later, if you're still around, you'll come after me." He chuckles. "But I'll be ready for you, *Reggie-boy*."

Dunning opens the door. "We'll be in the car waiting; we're going back to Kingscote. Don't take your time." He walks to the police car's driver-side door and opens it. "Slide over, Ron; I'm driving. The boss will be out in a minute." He smiles at Perkins. "He'll want to ride in the back."

49

The tall, square block of apartments, rising twelve floors above the harbor, sits on a prime parcel of land at the end of Blue's Point Road. Isolated by its position on the jutting point, the plain, boxy design, a relic of the 60s, is a bone-of-contention among many of the local residents. The views of the harbor, however, from inside the building, are extraordinary. High on the ninth floor, his balcony looking east toward the harbor entrance, is the two-bedroom apartment of Shamus O'Brien.

"What a delightful meal; you're quite a cook, Shamus," says Cassie, drinking the last of her red wine. She places the empty glass on the table and dabs her mouth with a napkin, careful not to smudge her red lipstick. Flames from the gas fire reflect in the large dining room window overlooking the harbor, giving the impression that flames are dancing on top of the water. Beethoven's "Moonlight Sonata, adagio sostenuto," playing in the background, fits perfectly with the evening ambiance.

"Wonderful red," says Shamus, emptying his glass.

"A Shiraz from Penfolds McLaren Vale vineyards; their wines are popular all over the world. I thought you'd like it."

"We have some spectacular whites grown in the Mudgee and Hunter Valley regions, too." He opens the refrigerator door and pulls out a bottle of chilled white. "I found this at a relatively new winery on my run up through Mudgee today. I tasted it—superb—so I bought a case of it. Rather fruity for a Semillon; I hope you like it. Oddly enough, the winery is called the Farmer's Daughter. I thought it an apt kudos to my talented partner and a worthy complement to Chef O'Brien's dinner this evening."

He places two clean wine glasses on the coffee table, in front of the sofa positioned to take advantage of the view. "Come, sit over here, I have a tasty desert prepared for later."

Cassie shifts to the sofa. Shamus pours a small amount of Semillon into a fresh stem glass and offers it to her. She swirls the straw-colored wine around, tastes it, and swallows the rest. "Hmm, nice," she says, holding out the glass for a refill. "Fill 'er up please, sir." The effect of the red wine over dinner is already causing her to feel a little light-headed.

"Glad you like it." A very suave Shamus grins and fills her glass to the brim. As he passes it back to her, he kisses her lightly on the lips. Cassie is caught, surprised, not by the kiss, but by the rush of erotic energy tingling through her body. For a moment, she holds his kiss, and then pushes him back.

"Whoa, boy, I'm not up for any hanky panky here." She puts the wine on the coffee table. Shamus lowers himself into the sofa somewhat pleased with himself and nonchalantly fills his glass. Cassie straightens and pushes her dress down over her knees.

"Ah, come on, Cassie, you got a bit of a buzz out of that, didn't you? Hell, we've been dancing together for over four months. We can't ignore the attraction we have to each other." He edges closer to her. "We have a lot going for us that's not just professional."

"Oh, yes it is professional, Shamus." She pauses for a moment, considering. "Look, you're very attractive and talented, but that's it for me." She reaches for the glass and takes another sip. "This white is good." The next track begins—"Barber's Adagio."

Shamus rests his arm on the sofa, behind her shoulders. As she sips her drink, he edges even closer. "No, it is much more than that." He brushes aside the hair from her ear and lightly bites at it before she can move away. The tingling sensation returns, and with her head swirling from the effects of the wine, her resolve begins to weaken. The hypnotic magic of the harbor view, the Opera House, magnificent, calling her, mixes with the seductive strings and clarinet arrangement of the "Adagio" sweeping her toward the realm of fantasy. Shamus's warm breath gently caresses the nape of her neck.

The red light of Cassie's new answering machine is blinking urgently on her bedside table. She is angry. *The bugger wouldn't take no for an answer.* "Groped me, touched me," she yells at the wall, flinging her bag on the bed—angry, also, because of the part of her that enjoyed it. "And it was my own fault. Well, he bloody knows now. Professional—or it'll be another kick in the nuts for him." She jabs at the play button on the machine.

"Cassie, this is Matt. I must talk to you; I have some terrible news. Please call me when you get in, no matter the time; I love you." Click, the machine shuts off. Her heart skips a beat. *Oh, no, it's Sean.* She snatches up the phone and dials.

The phone at the other end is picked up almost immediately. "Hello, this is Frank." The passive tone of his voice sends a chill through Cassie.

"Mr. Ryan, this is Cassie Baldwin. I'm sorry to bother you, it being so late, but I had a message from Matt telling me something terrible has happened. Is it Sean, the snakebite? Is he all right?"

There is a long silence; her heart is racing. "Ah, Cassie, love, thanks for calling. Yes, it is Sean, I'm afraid. A nasty accident; he fell off the cliff at Weir Cove. He's dead."

Cassie's heart freezes. She stares at the photo of Matt.

"Cassie, are you there? Are you all right, luv?"

She hears Frank telling Patrick to find Matt quickly.

"Mr. Ryan, I'm so sorry, so sorry—" She begins to cry.

"I hear you, lass. He really liked you." She hears Frank's voice beginning to break. "I've sent Patrick to find Matt. I think I hear him coming—yes."

"Mr. Ryan, tell Mrs. Ryan and Patrick I love you all."

Frank begins to cry.

"Cassie, Cassie, thank God you called," says Matt. "Just a minute, my love." She hears Matt tell Patrick to help his dad back to his chair. "Dad told you, hey?"

"Oh, my God, Matt, I don't know what to say. I'm so sorry." She sobs uncontrollably.

Matt is crying. "I know, my love, everyone is devastated. And Tom Donaldson is missing, swept out to sea trying to save him. He saved my bloody life, too, Cassie—stopped me from going down after Sean. Little bloke, he was beating the snakebite—I don't understand what the hell—it's my fault, Cassie. I got drunk and started a fight with Dad, and Sean took off in the storm for his secret place and fell. All because of me."

"Don't say that, Matt. You loved him and he loved you; he idolized you. Carry that as your memory of him. We have been together for a long time, Matt. Your family is as dear to me as my own, and I love you absolutely."

"Cassie, I have something else to tell—" He sighs. *Get a grip, not now.* "I love you, too. No matter what happens or what you may—my heart is yours forever." Still sobbing, he pauses. She hears people moving about in the background. "Cassie, they're about to take Sean out to the ambulance. The monsignor is going to say a prayer first, so I have to go now. Will you be okay?"

"Yes, Matt; I'll call Belinda. I want to be with you when Sean is buried. I'll say a prayer for Tom. I love you. Bye, for now."

"Bye."

She places the phone in the cradle and rolls face down on the bed. The bedding mutes the terrible cry that she draws up from her soul. "Ahhhhhh, no, no, no, no, no!" she wails, beating the bed violently with her fists. Eventually, she rolls over and faces the ceiling, sobbing, sobbing. Time crawls. The ticking of her bedside clock, thunderous in the silence of her room, brings with each tick a new image. Sean's cheeky smile as he walks with Matt, his tiny hand in Matt's; Matt running from the water at Kersaint; Matt waving from the side of his Ute at the airport; and Shamus groping her body— *While Sean was dying.* She gags.

"Jesus Lord, forgive me," she cries, pounding the bed with her fists. She rushes to the bathroom, undressing as she goes, and turns on the cold-water tap to the shower. In a trance-like state, her mind and body numb, she steps into the icy stream, and without so much as a shiver, begins to vigorously soap and scrub, soap and scrub, every part of her body.

50

Later on in the same week after Sean and Tom's deaths, Thursday, Tom's body is still missing despite thorough searches out to sea and along the south-coast coves and cliff bases.

On a hill overlooking the Kingscote Township and the blue waters of Nepean Bay, the air is crisp and cool. The winter's mid-morning sun brightens the sky over the gathering crowd of mourners forming around the gravesite. Cars in the procession from the Kingscote Catholic Church where the mass was said for Sean, nearly a kilometer away, are still arriving. Most of the Islanders are here; schoolchildren from the Kingscote and Parndana schools line the entire route from the church to the cemetery. Sean's classmates—boys and girls—all dressed in white, form an honor guard from the cemetery gates to his grave. The local Member of Parliament, the mayor, the district councilors, and clergy from the other churches stand a respectful distance from the Ryans. All three policemen are in full dress uniform; Bob Dunning is standing behind Matt.

The Ryan family waits by the side of the hearse for the last of the mourners to arrive. Sean's flower-covered casket is visible through the open back door of the coach. Monsignor Byrne stands between Frank and Katherine, who are both dressed in black. Matt and Patrick, also dressed in black suits, stand next their parents, Patrick holding his mother's hand and Matt, an arm around his father. Cassie, dressed in a black dress and wearing a black hat, has her arm around Matt's waist and is dabbing at her eyes. A black veil attached to Katherine's hatband covers her face; Frank's head is bowed. The boys do their best to control their emotions, nodding occasionally to Islanders whispering their condolences as they pass. The six-year-old Hamilton twins from Sean's class, Charles and Rebecca, stand in front of the monsignor, holding baskets of white rose petals. The last of the schoolchildren lining the route from the church file silently into the cemetery and form up at one end of the grave.

The funeral director calls the pallbearers forward. Frank, Matt, and Patrick line up on one side of the casket; Sammy Marino, Bob Dunning, and John Walls, the football coach who also coached the juniors, line up on the other. Slowly, they draw the small casket from the hearse, and turn to follow the monsignor and the twins, who sprinkle the ground in front of the casket with the white rose petals. Katherine and Patrick, close relatives and friends supporting them, follow. The cortège moves slowly through the center of the honor-guard to the graveside. Classmates cry, men wipe away tears, women weep.

The six men rest the casket on the cradle set across the top of the open grave. Matt releases the casket handle and motions to Cassie, who is standing with Monty and Jordan among the front group of mourning Islanders, to join him. She crosses, and he takes her hand, gently squeezing it, and pulling her close to his side.

Monsignor Byrne walks around the casket, sprinkling holy water. Then he addresses the mourners. "We cannot know the reason the good Lord has chosen ta draw his little lamb Sean ta his bosom at this time. Any reason cannot, nor should it, pacify the terrible pain inflicted on Katherine, Francis, Matthew, Patrick, and all of ye here who love him. In this moment, 'tis good ta remember the joy he brought ta us all, and the lesson he leaves through his early departure. He reminds us that in our love for each other, it is wise always ta be kind, patient, and caring, fer we cannot know when the final call will beckon us from this life's cycle. 'Tis good to remember also the great love of Thomas Donaldson; a more humble, kindly and unassuming man one could not hope to meet, yet when he was called, 'twas to demonstrate once again 'that no greater love has a man than he lay down his own life for another.'"

The monsignor walks to Katherine and her family. He takes her hand and nods to the funeral director. The pallbearers pick up the canvas straps looped under the casket. Then, on a signal from the director, the men ease the casket into the grave.

Katherine cries out, sobbing, "My boy, my little boy." Cassie moves to comfort her.

The men step back from the graveside, and Frank turns to Katherine and Cassie. He puts his arms around the two women; Matt joins them, and then Patrick. They stand as a group, crying, hugging, and comforting each other. Then Frank takes Katherine's hand and leads her to the side of the grave. With a trembling hand holding the red rose, she drops it onto the casket. Patrick hands Frank a rose, and he drops it onto the casket. They bless themselves, and then follow the monsignor back to the family car. Matt, Patrick, and Cassie, tears rolling down their cheeks, pray silently together and drop their roses. Then the rest of the mourners begin filing by the graveside, each dropping a single red rose onto Sean's casket.

It was said by the groundsmen, later, that when the last mourner dropped her rose, a red hue could be seen rising above the grave, lifting to God's place.

51

The members of the Country Women's Association of Kangaroo Island organized a magnificent after-burial supper in the Kingscote Sports and Recreation Center. The community pitched in to help, tables were loaded with meats, salads, breads, fresh baked cakes, cookies, scones, tea, coffee and cordial for the youngsters. Locals who lived on one end of the island caught up with those who lived on the other. The Ryans were inundated with offers of help, money to defray expenses, the use of vacation shacks on the island and the mainland to get away for a few days, and small things like taking care of mundane chores around the home cottage. Late in the afternoon Katherine, a sober Frank—he had not touched a drink since Sean's death—and Patrick left for Cape du Couedic. Frank took really good care of Katherine throughout the day, and when Monty and Jordan approached to offer their condolences, he politely accepted. Matt and Cassie did not leave until after the last of the mourners had gone.

Matt is sitting on the sofa in the big room of the Baldwin homestead sipping a cup of tea, keeping warm in front of the log fire crackling away under Kristina's portrait. Monty and Jordan have long since gone to bed.

Cassie pours herself a cup and then sits next to Matt, her eyes still red from crying. "Belinda and Timothy were very kind, making the bookings and getting me to the airport. I had to be here, Matt. I couldn't sleep; I couldn't get Sean out of my mind. I kept seeing you and him together, God, how he loved you, idolized you, even tried to walk like you sometimes, and when he smiled, it was your smile." She dabs her eyes. "I think today was the worst day of my life since the day I watched Mummy die."

"Yeah; you were about Sean's age then." He takes another sip of tea and stares into the fire. "I want to hate God for this, but it's myself I really hate sometimes, Cassie." He chokes back threatening tears. "I was so full of it, not thinking about anyone else but me, me, always me, bloody pathetic. I knew the little bloke hated arguments, hated them myself when I was his age—still do." He looks at Cassie. "I can't drink, Cassie, I just have to stay away from the stuff. If I don't, I'll finish up like the oldman."

"I'd forget about blaming yourself; it's not going to help, and I think Sean would be really ticked off to put it bluntly. He'd want you doing something positive like leaving the island and getting on with your writing, so you can write a story about him." She grins, puts down her cup, and snuggles into him. "Remember how mischievous he could be? Especially with that white mouse of his, what did he call him, Snot, wasn't it?"

"Yeah," he says with a grin beginning to crease his face. "Patrick had him at the funeral today."

"Patrick is a lovely boy. He was telling me he is going to study be a priest, that the monsignor was organizing to get him into Rostrevor College[71] next year, and the Knights of the Southern Cross[72] are helping to pay for it. I think it is okay for you to come to Sydney now, Matt, don't you?"

"After Christmas; the next few months are going to be really tough, particularly on Katherine. Dad's broken, horsewhipped; I don't know he'll pull through. Strange, it occurred to me watching him over the last few days, I think he really loves us; it's just he can't live without the booze—too many demons living in his head. I think I understand a little bit about that."

"Yes, booze can take you places you don't want to go, I know that for sure." She strokes his cheek. "Christmas, then, and I am soooo ready. Hey, you'll be in Sydney in two weeks for your award and the opening of *Fire in the Center*. Ah, you are going to be blown away when you see what Timothy has done with your work."

---

[71] Rostrevor College: Christian Brothers boarding school for boys in Adelaide.
[72] Knights of the Southern Cross: An order of Catholic men committed to promoting the Catholic way of life throughout Australia.

"Yeah, I'm already crapping myself."

"They'll love you."

They hold each other, silent, exhausted, thinking, until they fall asleep, her head resting on his chest.

Later, Monty comes into the room and puts more logs on the fire. He looks on the sleeping couple, his mind tormented with conflicting thoughts. Reaching down, he gently brushes a lick of hair from his daughter's forehead, and then, picking up the knitted afghan from the back of the sofa spreads it over the sleeping couple.

52

"And so it is with great pleasure I present this award, the Australian Meritorious Newcomer Scholarship, to Matthew Ryan for his work, the sestina, 'Lust: Life's Fiery Center.'"

Matt gets up from his chair next to Cassie and Belinda and walks to the dais. The annual event is being held on the lawns surrounding the imposing white stone building of the Sydney Conservatorium of Music. Originally built on this prominent city hill during the governorship (1810-1821) of Colonel Lachlan Macquarie, it was once the stables of the then government house. Now, the conservatorium looks over the imposing white sails of the opera house, a perfect backdrop for today's occasion. Academics, producers, literary agents, city politicians, and society members are in the crowd of over five hundred. Television cameras and journalists cluster in a roped off area designated "Media."

As Matt steps onto the dais, the chairperson of the judging panel shakes his hand and presents him with the award certificate. "Congratulations, Matthew." There is a round of enthusiastic applause. "Now, Matthew doesn't know about this, so it is a surprise, but I have here a Special Recognition Certificate from the board of the Society for his essay 'Kangaroo Island: South Australia's Mystical Secret?' For those of you who do not know, Kangaroo Island is where he was born and raised, a place that is rapidly becoming an international and local tourist destination for that dream vacation; lucky Matthew, hey?" He hands him the award certificate and the microphone. "Well done, Matthew."

Matt grabs the microphone as if it were a lifeline. "Thanks," he says his heart racing his legs turning to jelly. *Could do with a cold beer right now.* He wipes his forehead with the back of his hand as beads sweat start to run down his cheeks. *What the hell am I doing here?*

"This is such an honor—I—hardly know what to say. Um, look, first of all, I want to dedicate this award to my little brother, Sean Ryan, who—" Matt stops, struggles to go on. "Who died a couple of weeks ago back on Kangaroo Island—he was a terrific little bloke, and I miss him like hell." He stops and wipes his eyes; the crowd are absolutely silent, absorbed by the sudden sharing of a new intimacy with the young man on the dais. "I want to thank the Society for giving me this award—there are special people who encouraged me to write, who saw something and believed in me when I was starting out. Katherine, Cassie, and Monsignor Byrne, who set deadlines for me and made sure I kept them. You know, mentoring—" His mind goes blank for a second—a panic attack threatens— "I think mentoring—well, it means a lot to me, and I'd be bloody useless without it." *Have to get out of here.* "Thanks. All right." He almost runs from the dais and back to his seat next to a smiling Cassie.

"That was beautiful, Matt, lovely. Sean is looking down on you now, and he is so proud of his big brother," she says, hugging him. "I am so proud of you, too."

As the applause subsides, the chairperson takes up the microphone again. "Thank you, Matthew and God bless, Sean. I think I can say from all of us here, that our hearts and prays go out to you and your family. Ladies and gentlemen, tonight, the Australasian Modern Dance Company will open," he says pointing over his shoulder, "as part of the Opera House's Newcomer Series Season, with the debut of *Fire in the Center*. Cassandra Baldwin, also from Kangaroo Island, will dance the concept written by Matthew Ryan and choreographed by the renowned Timothy Barton. Please, Cassandra, let us see you." A smiling Cassie stands and waves. The crowd responds with a round of enthusiastic cheering and clapping.

The jaunty Hagherty ferry pushes out from Blue's Point pier and begins to nose through the wash of busy boats, a course set to take it under the bridge and onto Circular Quay. Despite the chilly breeze of the July winter, Matt sits up in the bow, the combination of spray, bright colors, rattling trains, and soaring buildings delighting his keen senses. A fully loaded cruiser cuts across their bow. The ferry skipper sounds the siren and at the same time turns sharply to port to avoid a collision. Alcohol-plied diners hoot and shake fists with good-natured derision.

As the ferry turns under the harbor bridge, across from the opera house, its towering white sails a familiar landmark around the world, Matt is a mix of excitement, anxiety, and eager anticipation. Minutes later, the ferry bumps against its Circular Quay berth. The quay is colorful and lively, a hub for people arriving on ferries, trains, and buses from all over Sydney. Buskers, street people, and regulars mingle, some heading to concert halls and theaters, others joining luxury boats for harbor cruises. Pier-side food vendors offer tasty delicacies from around the world.

He lingers, savoring the rich blend of aromas, sights, and sounds. *Wonderful!* A large station clock with roman numerals, hanging from a beam at the end of a wharf, catches his eye. *Seven-thirty already; c'mon, boyo, shake a leg.*

The tension inside the playhouse is electric. The chatter of the crowd grows louder as the moment for the opening performance of *Fire in the Center* approaches. The pace over the last week had been insane: the stars coping with the added pressures of intense promotional activities and rehearsals, pictures and interviews of Cassie and Shamus, newspapers and television screens showing a public excited and hungry for the debut of a new talent. Already, the season is a sell-out.

Matt is ushered to the front row, where Monty and Belinda are already seated.

"Lovely to see you again, Matt. You were wonderful today and looked so handsome receiving your scholarship," she says, smiling and patting his leg. "We'll be seeing a lot of you next year." She turns her attention back to the stage. "Oh, I'm so nervous, I can't stand it."

"Hello, Matt, sorry I couldn't be there this afternoon," says Monty, reaching across Belinda to shake his hand. "Congratulations. The scholarship is quite an achievement."

"Sure, right," says Matt, uncertain. "Bit of a surprise, really; I have a lot ground to cover, though, before I can start at the university here next year."

"Right," says Monty. "You can never be sure; a lot can happen."

The lights fade to black. The crowd noise settles to a restless silence: the annoying odd cough, the blowing of a nose, and the rustling of programs. Then the primitive drone of a didgeridoo begins to drift out into the auditorium. Blue light fades up through the blackness, backlighting the stage to reveal the silhouettes of seven figures sitting in a wide circle, facing their center. The raucous cry of a crow and the sharp sounds of Australian native birds precede the slow clack, clack, clack of beating sticks. The silhouettes begin to sway and bend in a worshipping motion toward the center of the circle. Then, emerging from the stage floor, confined within a meter-wide circle, a cluster of multi-colored shafts of laser light—reds, oranges, blues, and yellows—pulse upward. Theatre smoke wafts through the light of the lasers, creating the illusion of fire. Drums begin to beat.

A female dancer bursts onto the stage and whirls around the lasers in sweeping pirouettes, flinging her arms wide, stretching her body from the balls of her bare feet up into the blue hue of the stage lighting. She appears nude; a flesh-colored body liner hugs her, a short, light blue cotton skirt swirls provocatively from her narrow waist.

Matt is sweating. Belinda grabs his leg again; her fingernails dig into his flesh. *My God, she is beautiful, shocking, glorious,* he thinks.

"I told you," Belinda whispers, first into Monty's ear, and then into Matt's. "She is her mother, a goddess."

Cassie continues to circle the fire, probing the fringe, fascinating her, jumping back, reacting to the heat. As the stage lighting turns to burnt orange, the silhouettes transform into full-bodied dancers who rise on their bare feet and begin to mimic Cassie's probing movements. Their bodies are almost bare. The four females, two Aboriginal, wear only mauve body liners. The others, males, wear loincloths. Cassie becomes more adventurous. She reaches further into the outer shafts of the fire. Suddenly, a loud clap of thunder accompanied by a blinding white flash of lightning illuminates the scene, frightens her, and sends her scurrying into the wings.

The drumming intensifies and Shamus springs, with a sensational *grand jeté*, onto the stage, his black mane flying until it falls about his shoulders spectacularly when he lands, his body already glistening with sweat from his warm-up. He launches into a series of leaping, sweeping turns about the fire. The chamois cloth about his loins is little more than a thong. The crowd goes crazy. The women move restlessly about their seats. The seven dancers react, increasing the range and tempo of their movement, teasing the fire, moving to it, away from it, circling, parting, goading the inquisitive Shamus to probe further the flames. The sound of the didgeridoo grows louder; the dancers start clacking the wooden sticks louder and begin chanting to the rhythm. Cassie returns to advance, hesitantly, toward the fire and Shamus; the ritual of fascination and discovery envelopes the two principal dancers.

Matt is spellbound, caught up in a mixture of emotions: awe, fear, worship, and jealousy. Time seems to disappear as he watches their bodies move in a blue haze of slow motion frenzy, carnal desire, the core impetus of their movement, pushing toward climax, all too real.

The seven silhouettes open their circle to the fringe of the stage, still clacking their sticks. They stretch upward, spin, bend, weave, and high step to the rhythm of the raw, native sounds of beating drums and the high-pitching drone of the didgeridoo. Their chanting increases, words form a repetitive mantra: "We are the fire. We are the fire. We are the fire. We—"

Cassie and Shamus grow bolder, testing the flames from opposite sides of the circle, springing in, springing out, gradually edging further into the dancing flames, discovering more of each other. Shamus, raging with desire, leaps towards her, a lion leaping for its prey. Cassie dances deftly around him, a young lioness, teasing, seductive, and sleek, mocking his passion. They circle, their movements growing more intense, deliberate, fighting to close on each other, but constrained, as if held at the end of imaginary elastic cords. Their bodies glisten with sweat. Shamus' black mane, wet, whips about his head, as his leaping grows more urgent. He circles her. The drumming grows louder. Cassie, now in the center of the flame, lifts *demi-pointe* on her left foot and slowly raises her right leg above her head, stretching her right foot to pointe toward heaven, a perfect execution of *grand battement*. The audience goes crazy. Cassie's mind flashes to her dance on the beach at Cape Kersaint after making love with Matt. She feels the warmth of the sand on her body; the all-consuming fire of that moment of union engulfs her. Her body trembles as Shamus finally catches her around the waist and slowly turns her full circle, gradually taking her to the floor as she lowers her right leg until she lies on her back, for an instant, still.

Shamus leaps over her. The music builds toward crescendo. Cassie arches her back and raises her knees, tucking her feet tight against her buttocks. Shamus stretches over her, his hands either side on the floor taking his weight. He lowers his body to within centimeters of hers. Their noses almost touch. She cries out.

The chanting, "We are the fire. We are the fire…" grows louder, more intense. Matt watches, his eyes wild and savage. Blood surges through his body, arousing him. The final stanza of "Lust: Life's Fiery Center," courses through his mind:

This dark battle is, maybe, a metaphor for lust's rage
When it transpires among the heat of coupling bodies, passion
Intensifies the fire of orgasm, and lovers scream, "We're alive!"

Suddenly, it is over, and the curtain drops. For a moment, there is stunned silence. The audience erupts with wild applause. "Bravo, bravo, bravo," they shout. Matt finds himself clapping hysterically. Belinda is slapping him and Monty on their thighs. Monty, too, is clapping madly, a triumphant gleam in his eyes.

The curtain rises, and the dancers run onto the stage and bow. Then Cassie and Shamus appear down stage center. The audience goes crazy. Timothy hurries onto the stage a few moments later, carrying a huge bouquet of roses, and hands them to Cassie. The crowd's applause bounces from the walls and roof of the theatre into one thunderous roar.

Cassie shades her eyes from the glare coming off the lighting grid and looks into the front row of seats. Her smile widens as she sees her father, Belinda and Matt. Taking a rose from the bouquet, she motions to Matt to come to her. He hesitates, but Belinda urges him forward. As he reaches the lip of the stage, Cassie bends to hand him the rose. A beaming Shamus winks cheekily.

Cassie pours a little more of the red wine into her glass. Matt takes a sip of his. "Not a bad drop."

She raises her glass. "Here's to a fantastic day, my darling, your awards, my debut, the magnificent banquet on the promenade; not bad for a couple of island kids, hey?"

"Yeah, I couldn't take to that Shamus bloke, though; cheeky bugger winked at me. In love with himself a bit, isn't he?" He sips the wine and then puts the still half-full glass on the coffee table. "He's got the hots for you, that's for sure; bloody tough to keep my thinking straight watching you two dance like that."

She chuckles. "A touch of jealousy there, hey? Good, keep you on your toes," she teases. "Besides, I can handle him. He liked you, though; thought you were way too handsome."

"That's right," says Matt, pushing his hand through his hair and looking at his reflection in the window. He becomes serious. "How long before you'll be home again?"

"Belinda told me earlier tonight, at the banquet, that the director from the National Dance Company of New Zealand was at the show and loved it. She wants to book us for a four-week tour over the Christmas season as the opener to their perennial ballet, the *Nutcracker Suite*. The topper is I can come home for all of August." She laughs gleefully. "I have to keep fit and be back in time for rehearsals in September. Isn't that wonderful?"

Matt laughs heartily and hugs her. They kiss. "Bloody oath, it is. I'm not surprised, though; you were awesome. I must tell you, I got turned on."

She puts her drink down. "What about now?" They laugh and fall back on the sofa. "I love you, Matt."

53

August, the month when the wildest storms hit the island, is living up to its reputation. Six o'clock, Sunday evening, and it is dark. The streetlamp in front of the Kingscote police station throws a single orb of light onto a flooded pavement as driving rain smashes against the glass of the yellow-lit windows.

"I don't think Marino is so stupid that he'd risk sailing in this storm, Dunning," says Sergeant Woodson as he places the weather map on top of the inquiry desk and points to the center of a tight circle of isobars twenty kilometers southwest of Cape du Couedic. "It would be lunacy; he'd run slap-bang into the worst part of this before he got to Vivonne Bay." He nods toward the front door. "Listen to that wind. It's going to be full-on by midnight."

"We haven't heard from your snitch in Port Hacking for two days," says Dunning, his voice thick and rasping. "Sam Marino is the best boat skipper there is around these parts. If he gave it a shot and left two days ago, he'd be here and loaded by now."

"Yeah, well, Jordan has been keeping an eye on things at Vivonne. If Sammy was there, he'd let us know."

"I wouldn't count on it; he's back on the booze." Dunning walks to the front door and looks out into the rain. "It's getting worse." He sneezes. "This bloody flu—can't get rid of it."

Woodson grins at Dunning's discomfort. "What's got into you, anyway?" he says, picking up the map and pinning it back on the notice board. "It's sort of out of character for you to be concerned about those who are breaking the law, well, growing Rosenblum poppies, anyway."

"I'm still a policeman," says Dunning. "I haven't changed my view on the law being wrong, though. The flower grows wild and produces a drug that helps a lot of people." He takes a handkerchief from his pocket and blows his nose. "You know as well as I do that this is just an effort by the pharmaceutical boys to keep the lid on this so-called island secret until they can figure out a way to control production and distribution." He coughs, spitting a mouthful of phlegm into his handkerchief. "All you want to do is crucify the Ryans." He coughs again. "I want to be around to make sure you don't get way out of line."

"You and I are never going to get on, Dunning. When this is done, you'll be on your way. I've requested that you be transferred." The phone rings. Woodson picks it up. "Yes, Jordan? What? Do you know if they loaded the—okay—tonight? No, you stay out of it." He slams down the phone. "That was Jordan." Woodson shakes his head. "He's calling from Middle River. Flecky Martin phoned him from Vivonne; Marino's boat is in the bay, can you believe that? He says he didn't see them loading anything, though." He looks at his watch. "Get Perkins up here, fast. We'll have to do this on our own; the boys from Adelaide won't fly choppers in this weather."

"Can't it wait until morning? Marino's not going anywhere in this tonight."

"He's here, isn't he?" Woodson shakes his head. "No, I want us at Vivonne tonight; we'll stake it out for as long as it takes. They'd be flat out loading the boat in this weather, so we'll be in place to nab them when they do."

54

Monty pulls the front door from the homestead verandah shut and takes off his wet raincoat. "The gazebo is still intact," he says walking through the big room to the kitchen and the back porch to hang up his wet gear. "If this storm gets any worse, it could on the mainland by morning."

Jordan, his back to the fire, is holding a large glass of port. "A toast to you, my dear sister; it seems that you went, conquered, and now, have returned." He raises his glass. "Well done."

Cassie is sitting on the sofa adjacent to the fire, looking extraordinarily sophisticated and beautiful. The blue sweater she wears compliments her complexion and dark hair, pulled back into a neat ponytail. She smiles politely, barely able to cover her deep disappointment over Jordan's relapse; his drinking had become worse than she imagined.

Monty, pulling on a light, tweed jacket, enters the big room. "Ah, that's better." Picking up his glass of port from the mantelpiece, he stands next to his afflicted son. "Jordan is right, Cassie, it is *good* to have you home. The place is not the same without you." He raises his glass. "Here's to you, Daughter, and your extraordinary performances. Hmm—fruity, great drop. Yes, from Hardy's Chateau Reynella, one of South Australia's finest, my favorite."

Cassie raises her glass. "Thank you, Daddy, it is nice to be home," she says and drains the last of her red wine. "Oh, this is lovely, too," and then picks up the bottle and looks at the label. "No wonder, another McLaren Vale red, Tintara, Cabernet Sauvignon." She nods approval to Monty. "These South Australian wines keep getting better and better, Daddy; maybe we should start growing grapes here."

"I have been thinking about it, talking actually, to a few farmers who have approached the Research Center chaps in Parndana to work up a pilot project."

"Trust you to be right onto it. Thanks for picking me up; it was a horrible day to have to come out. Matt would have come, but his father wanted him around the lighthouse in case of any trouble. They are having a really hard time missing Sean, especially Katherine."

"Tragic," says Monty. "Burying your child is not what we sign up for when raising children."

They sip their wine, listening to the howling wind and driving rain getting worse. Jordan drinks the last of his port and goes to the liquor cabinet.

"Don't you think you've had enough, Jordan?" asks Cassie.

"No I haven't, and I'll drink as much as I like, thank you, very much," he replies, irritated, filling the glass to the brim.

"How long has Jordan been back to drinking, Daddy?" She looks at her father, noting the deeper worry lines. *He was looking so much better in Sydney; and Jordan, my God—he looks twenty years older.*

Monty shrugs. Cassie gets up from the sofa and turns to glare at Jordan. "You're killing Daddy, Jordan."

Jordan glares back. "That comment is a little far fetched of you, isn't it?"

"I've never been more serious. I'm going to be here for the rest of the month, and I won't put up with what Daddy does from you. Either you stop drinking, or you get out of here."

"Who the hell do you think you are, little sister?" snarls Jordan, the deep scar running from the corner of his mouth contorting his face into a tragic mask, made more grotesque by the tiny red veins beginning to show in the skin on his cheeks, spotting his pale complexion. He steps toward her, swaying unsteadily. "You think you can dance back in here and throw your weight around like you own the place, huh?"

"I do."

"Cut it out, both of you," barks Monty. Cassie and Jordan stop, surprised. "Enough, enough, please; we'll sort it out tomorrow."

"Oh, Daddy, forgive me; I'm overtired. The flight from Sydney took forever and it was bumpy, especially in the small plane from Adelaide to Kingscote. I'm going to make a cup of hot chocolate, and then go to bed. Would either of you like one?" The two men decline.

"Come and say good night before you go to bed, Cassie," says Monty.

"Of course." The phone rings, and Jordan picks it up.

"Yes? Flecky."

Cassie fills the kettle with water, puts it on the stove and goes to the kitchen cabinet to find the chocolate powder. As she pulls the can from the shelf, an envelope drops to the floor. She bends down to pick it up and sees it is open and addressed to Monty with Belinda's return address on the back. *Oh, goodo.* She smiles and reaches up to place it back in the cabinet, but the letter falls out of the envelope and it drops to the floor, partly unfolding. As she stoops down to pick it up, an underlined paragraph in the middle of the first page catches her eye. Curious, feeling guilty at the same time, she reads it.

I urge you, Monty, do not go ahead with this; you will ruin the boy's life, and cause Cassandra to turn from you forever. Don't do it.

For a moment, the letter's words do not register. She reads the piece again, and this time, the meaning becomes clear. Her heart races, her mind reels, her breathing becomes short and rapid. She crosses to the kitchen door that leads back into the big room and stops. Monty and Jordan are arguing, shouting loud enough for her to hear over the noise of the storm.

"It's a mistake; I made a mistake. I want you to phone them back and tell Woodson to call it off," says Monty.

"Look," says Jordan, "they're already on their way; you can't stop it now. Those bloody Ryans have got it coming, anyway, and that smart-arse Matt—" He stops, mid-sentence. Cassie is standing at the kitchen door; Monty sees her in the same instant. His eyes drop to the letter in her hand.

She walks deliberately toward her father, holding up the letter, shaking it and staring at him. "What the hell is going on?" Monty is speechless. "What have you done?" He looks away. "What the hell have you done?"

Monty's face is ashen. The noise from the rain beating against the corrugated iron roof seems louder. For a moment, he thinks of lying. "I don't know what to say," he says weakly.

"You—you have betrayed me. I can't believe it; you damn well bloody betrayed me. How could you, you—"

"Jeez, calm down, Cassie, for God's sake, calm down. He did it for you, you know," says Jordan.

She ignores him and stares into her father's eyes, pleading, willing him to tell her it is all a nightmare. Moments pass. Then, her voice, colder than ice, rends his heart. "If anything happens to Matt, I will never forgive you—*never* forgive you, Daddy." Her eyes are cold and clear. "You are going to tell me what is going to happen."

Monty hesitates. She screams. "Tell me!"

He looks at her and grimaces, defeated. "The police believe the Ryans are involved in poppee growing, and they are staking out the jetty at Vivonne tonight. Marino's boat is there; he transports the stuff, but they don't think it has been loaded yet—too rough," Monty says, resignation and sadness in his barely audible voice, his shoulders slumping. "They don't know where the Rosenblum is being held, but suspect it's at the lighthouse, or somewhere close to the boat." He bows his head. "They are going to arrest them when they start loading the *Smokey Cloud*."

Cassie stares at Monty, shaking her head, and then reaches for the phone.

"Who are you calling, Cassie?"

"Matt—not that it's any of your business any longer." She dials; it rings twice. "Yes, hello, Mrs. Ryan—it's me, Cassie. Could I speak to Matt? It's urgent." She waits. "Yes, Matt—I love you, too. Yes, it's bad here. Listen, the police are staking out Vivonne Bay; they know Sam Marino's boat is there. They think you and your dad are involved; you have to stay away from— What? So that's what you were doing today. No, you don't have to be sorry; I don't care, I love you. I suspected it anyway. No, it's a ridiculous law. Yes, but stay away— No, don't do that, it's too dangerous— All right, then, but I'm coming, too. No, I'm coming. You wait for me, you hear? You wait for me. I'll meet you at the shack. Right, we can use the Harriet River to go around them. I'll leave now."

Cassie drops the phone back in its cradle, hurries to the kitchen and then into the back sunroom. She is putting on her oilskin coat and elastic side boots when Monty appears. "Where do you think you are going, Cassandra?"

"I'm going to meet Matt. I'm going to make sure that he and his family don't get into any more trouble." She looks at him as she takes her keys to the Pathfinder from the key rack. "You are so unlike what I thought I knew of you, Daddy." She shakes her head and leaves through the back door, disappearing into the storm.

Monty goes back to the kitchen door. "Jordan, get out here; we are going to Vivonne. I want to see Woodson; I'm putting a stop to this, tonight."

55

At Cape du Couedic, the southwesterly gale is gusting to 55knots and getting worse. The light from the top of the lighthouse continues to sweep through the storm, despite the relentless assault on its tower's thick walls. From a window at the base of the granite structure, a light shines out into the storm. Inside, three men sit around Frank's office desk, drinking beer.

"I'm ahappy to be off the boat tonight, Frank. This astorm was the worst I've been in," says Sammy Marino. "Peter, here, says he's only agunna fly to Kingscote in future." Sammy laughs. "But I told him he's agunna come back with me; I needa his help."

"Should have had his regular crew in this weather," says Peter Ferrano, still looking deathly pale from an earlier bout of seasickness.

"No, it would have beena too obvious if the crew wasn't at the pub lasta night," says Sam. "Thisa way, the snitches would've missed us. Thisa morning, was already so big a bloody storm, no one woulda been able to see if any boats were out." Sammy points to the latest weather map on Frank's desk. "By the morning the storm, she willa have eased off enough for us to get outa here."

"I'd love to see Woodson's face when he finds out he's missed the boat. This storm works in our favor," says Frank, draining his glass and howling with laughter. "That boy of mine has got some guts; see the way he went over the side of the dinghy to save that bag of flowers?"

The radio crackles, interrupting Frank. "Lighthouse Cape du Couedic, this is the grain carrier Holbrook, Port Lincoln. We are fifty kilometers south of you en route to Port Melbourne from Esperance, Western Australia. We are encountering ten-meter seas with the occasional rogue at twenty meters. Wind to seventy knots. Advise all shipping caution. Do not leave harbor, over."

Frank picks up the receiver. "Thank you, Holbrook. Advisory's are out. Safe passage, over."

"Thank you, out."

"I'm glad we're not out there tonight," says Peter.

The door opens and Patrick steps inside, his raincoat and hat dripping water. "Mother said to tell you dinner's on the table and to come right away before it gets cold."

"You tella your mother we are coming, Patrick. Right away, thanka you very much." Patrick leaves, and the three men throw on their oilskins.

Even before they enter the kitchen, the men smell the rich aroma of roast lamb and potatoes. The table is loaded with plates of meat, vegetables, gravy, and bread.

Sam crosses to Katherine and swings her into his arms. "Katherine, you—you are a saint." He lowers her back to the floor and holds up a thumb and middle finger joined at the tips to form a circle. "Mom-a-mi; itsa look a beautiful."

They all sit. Frank looks up to Katherine. "Where's Matt?"

"He left about an hour ago. Cassie called; she got back from Sydney today. He's meeting her at Vivonne."

"Vivonne, tonight? That's bloody odd."

"He left this. I read it earlier," she says, her eyes teary as she hands him the letter.

"Patrick, get us all a beer, will you?" Frank opens the letter; tears begin to trickle down his cheeks as he reads down the page.

Dear Mum and Dad,

I thought I'd write this to let you know that I've arrived here in heaven. Things are pretty good; I have lots of friends and plenty of pets to play with. I know it is hard for you with what happened and all, but I can still keep my eye on you from here. Tom comes by from the big people's heaven every now and again. He likes it there, and he sees God every day. God put him in charge of the sheep and the lambs. He says to say g'day, and that he's sorry he couldn't save me. I tell him he gave it a bloody good go.

Thanks for taking good care of me, Mum. I love you. You can have that sheep rug Tom gave me, Pat. Tom said God reckons you'll make a good priest. Dad, thanks for having a go at saving me, you were terrific. I hope your hands are better now. Look out for Matt; he loves you, too.

Lots of love,

Sean

PS. Give Barney a hug for me, will ya?

Frank places the letter on the table and wipes his eyes with the napkin. "Did he say why they were going to Vivonne?"

"No, but he did say that Flecky Martin had told the police Sam's boat was in the bay and to tell you not to go near there."

"Good God in heaven, Katherine, the coppers are onto us. Why didn't you tell me sooner? God forgive me, he's going to get aboard that boat and sail her out of the bay; I'll bet my life on it. He's going to dump the load."

"Not in thisa weather, Frank, no," says Sammy. He thinks for a moment. "I didn't fuel up. The tanks, they are almosta empty."

"Come on," says Frank, jumping up from the table. "We gotta move fast."

56

Matt swings the Ute onto the ironstone road that runs from the South Coast Road to the Vivonne Bay jetty. After traveling a few hundred meters, he turns left into the large parking area that borders the Harriet River and Sam's shack, 100 meters in. Cassie's Pathfinder is already there. Driving with his headlights off, the pouring rain adding to the difficulty of finding his way for the last two kilometers, had cost time. A single globe lights the back door of the shack; he lets himself in.

Cassie, busy lighting the stove fire in the kitchen, looks around, yells gleefully, and throws herself into his arms. "Oh, Matt, you're here at last," she shrieks, kissing him hard on the mouth and taking a step back to look him over. "You've lost weight, but, oh, you look wonderful." She hugs him. "I have missed you terribly."

"Me, too," says Matt, beaming, crushing her with his hug. The fire is roaring, competing with the rain hitting the roof and winning.

"Let me put the kettle on, I'll make us some tea."

"So, Jordan's still at it, hey?"

"It's not just Jordan; Daddy is in on it, too."

"I thought he was up to something all along, but I didn't want to believe it," he says his voice edged with anger and disappointment. "It must have been bloody awful for you when you found out."

"Shocking, I'd say," a gritty firmness set in the line of her jaw. "I'll deal with it after we get tonight sorted."

"Cassie, I have to get that boat out of here and dump the load. Come morning, those coppers are going to be all over it. Dad and Sammy will go down for sure, and Woodson won't be satisfied unless he's got me, too."

"I know." She puts more wood on the fire. The kettle begins to whistle. "So, let's figure the best way to get on the boat without them spotting us."

"Hang about, Cassie; this is going to be very dangerous. That storm is the worst we've had in a long time. The flowers will have to be dumped well out to sea, out of the bay, or they'll wash back up on the beach."

"So? Sam's boat is one of the best; I'm ready." She takes the kettle and pours the boiling water into two huge mugs, each with a tea bag. "Drink this. Oh, and by the way, I've already scouted the jetty area."

"What? How?"

"Don't worry, they didn't spot me. I took the old bush track that goes along behind shack row. Bit of a feat with the headlights off and the rain and all, but I know most of this area pretty well." She warms her hands, wrapping them around her hot tea mug. "One of the police cars is in front of the shacks, set up to look out over the bay. I got close enough to see Woodson—easy to pick—the gorilla head and all, and the new bloke I saw at Sean's funeral. The other vehicle was hidden just off the road, in the bushes on the crest of the hill overlooking the bay and the jetty."

"Probably Bob Dunning." Matt takes a drink and lets out a howl, spilling some of the steaming hot liquid onto the floor. "Yowee, that's hot."

"Try sipping it. I think if we use the Harriet River to get to the beach, we can walk to the jetty under the lip of the sand hills and avoid being seen."

"Ross Dennis keeps his tinny at the bottom of the boat ramp; we can use that," says Matt. "Sam usually keeps an outboard in the garage."

"It's there; I checked earlier, checked it for petrol; it's good to go." She watches him sip a little more of his tea. *I love him.* "Finish that, and then we'd better go, Galahad."

The Harriet River cuts through the sand hills alongside Jetty Road for a few hundred meters before it empties into Vivonne Bay. During the summer and autumn months, a sandbar closes across its mouth at the beach, forming a large lake of still water behind it and a favorite place for the locals to bring their kids swimming, canoeing, and barbecuing. Matt and Cassie spent many summer holidays there, taking swim lessons in the state-sponsored "learn to swim" classes. Both of them knew their way about the area intimately.

As he carries, sometimes drags, the outboard through the heavy, wet sand, Matt has to stop frequently to wipe the rain from his eyes and rest. Their progress is painstaking. Cassie leads, alert for any sign of discovery or danger. They eventually make it to the mouth of the river, where the sandbar is breached, and the river water, swollen by the rain, is rushing out into Vivonne Bay. The high tide leaves only a narrow strip of sand between the sand hills and the seawater for the 500-meter walk around the bay to Ross Dennis' tinny.

"It's not very wide, and it will be tough going through that heavy sand, but the police won't see us," yells Cassie.

"Yeah, it's the best way, all right."

"Ready?"

Matt nods.

Ross's tinny is turned upside down, tucked close under the lee of the limestone cliff face that drops off sharply a few meters away from Jetty Road, where they expected it to be. Getting it to the water's edge is the hardest part. "This is some workout," says Cassie, breathing heavily as she stands next to the boat while Matt attaches the outboard to the stern. "At least we're keeping warm—wet, but warm."

"We'll stay close by the shore and keep under the lee of Point Ellen for as long as we can. That way, we will avoid the big waves, but we'll have to make a run for it from inside the point to *Smokey Cloud* as soon as there's a flat spot."

They push the boat into the water. Cassie moves up to the bow and Matt leaps in over the stern. The motor starts on the first pull of the rope, which is just as well because a wave is rushing at the beach—a small wave, but big enough to swamp them if they were to be caught sideways under it. Just in time, he guns the motor and the tinny smacks through the top of the wave as it starts to break, and then he turns to run close along the shoreline, heading for Point Ellen. A series of sheet lightning flashes lights up the sky as they approach the jetty.

"Nothing we can do about it, but pray they don't see us," yells Matt through the noise of the wind and rain. They slip carefully under the jetty and keep going close in along the now rocky shoreline until they are under the lee of Point Ellen. They circle slowly and wait for a flat spot in the waves.

"Keep a lookout for a break in the pattern, should be able to pick one up in the lightning." Cassie nods. "Take off that oilskin, your sweater, and boots. If we go over, the weight will take you straight to the bottom."

She gets the oilskin off when, suddenly, a searchlight beam sweeps across the water in front of them. "It's coming from where Dunning is," she shouts. "I swear to God, those Aboriginal blokes can see in the dark."

"Natural instinct; they never lose it," yells Matt. "No, I don't think he's seen us yet, but he knows someone is out here." The bigger waves on the ocean side of the Point are breaking right over the narrowest part in the neck of land that juts out for a couple of hundred meters into the western end of the bay, sending up huge plumes of spray to mix with the rain, some of it dumping into the couple's boat.

"We can't stay here or we'll swamp; we have to make a run for it now," yells Matt. "Hang on." He twists the throttle lever around as far as it will go. The tinny leaps forward, bucking, bouncing and crashing over and through the waves, heading in the direction of *Smokey Cloud's* mooring. The searchlight sweeps across their bow, comes back, and holds for a moment, then swings away to fix on the white hull of the fishing cutter, pitching and tossing in the rough water, dead ahead of them.

"He's lighting up *Smokey Cloud* for us," shouts Cassie.

Matt runs the tinny past the stern of the cutter, turns sharply along its lee side and cuts the motor. Cassie, rope in hand, leaps for the safety rail, grabs it, and hangs on grimly. She dangles in space for a couple of seconds before the cutter rolls away into the trough of a passing swell, and then manages to scramble over the gunwale. Still holding fiercely onto the rope attached to the tinny, she wraps a few loops around a capstan bolted to the deck in front of the wheelhouse and ties off.

The tinny is almost full of water as Matt grabs for the rail, but it is out of reach. Cassie throws him the overlap of her rope. Just in time, he grabs it as the tinny sinks from under his feet. The rolling motion of *Smokey Cloud* suddenly lifts him high into the air and then slams him against its hull as it rolls back into another trough. Cassie, clinging to the rope, is able to get a couple more loops around the capstan. Matt gets a grip on the steeply angled hull with his bare feet and half-walks, half-drags himself up the side of the cutter until Cassie grabs him by the sweater and hauls him over the rail and onto the deck

"Cassie—the wheelhouse, quick; start the engine and move the ship ahead slowly up on the mooring. I'll go forward and let the chain off. The moment we are free of the mooring, head straight out of the bay for the open sea."

She stumbles along the rolling deck to the wheelhouse. It is dark inside. The boat pitches forward, throwing her off-balance, sending her crashing into the ship's wheel and bruising her chest. "Ow, that hurt," she cries, rubbing herself with one hand and searching the instrument panel with her other for the key to the ignition. She finds it, turns it and the big engine begins turning over right away—the revs build, but the piston chambers won't fire. A flash of lightning shows a tag under a red knob reading, 'compression switch.'

"Of course; it's diesel." She slams the big red knob hard against the panel. Right away, one after the other, the engine's twelve cylinders fire and a thrilling, powerful roar throbs above the sound of the shrieking wind. She engages the gears and pushes the throttle forward.

The pitching, rolling *Smokey Cloud* moves slowly up on her mooring chain. Matt slips the shackle holding the cutter captive; as it comes free, the wind blows the heavy cutter broadside into the waves. Cassie reacts, applies more throttle and spins the wheel to starboard, swinging the bow back to point into the oncoming waves.

Matt bursts into the wheelhouse and slams the door shut behind him. "Okay, good work; let's go."

She pushes the throttle to full ahead. *Smokey Cloud* shudders as its propellers thrash the black water at its stern into an expanding flurry of white foam. The heavy boat moves ahead and gradually picks up speed, the spray flaring over the bow glowing with an eerie candescence.

57

A continuous flow of engine gases from the police pursuit vehicle's exhaust discharges as steam into the wind and rain. Inside the car, Bob Dunning has the heater fan on high, trying to keep warm. His coughing and runny nose is not much better even after taking the antihistamines he picked up from the pharmacy shop on the way out of Kingscote. He takes out a thermos flask half-full of hot chocolate from the canvas bag on the passenger side seat, pops open the lid and pours the steaming liquid into the paper cup balancing precariously between his knees. Then he takes out a roast lamb sandwich and bites into it.

Dunning's eyes continually scan the darkness. His stakeout position in the bush off to the side of Jetty Road, where it crests before dropping down to the jetty, offers a potentially good view of the bay. When the sky lights up with lightning, he can also see the other police vehicle 500 meters ahead, to his right, sitting at a higher elevation in front of the shacks on Shack Row. There is no let up in the wind and rain beating against the windscreen of his car, forcing him to keep the wipers going at full speed. *Nobody would be stupid enough to come down here tonight. I could be in bed right now.* He wipes his nose, looks towards Woodson's car and shakes his head. *I got a bad feeling about this.* He coughs up a mouthful of phlegm, winds down the window, and spits into the rain. It blows back into his face. "Damn."

Before he can wipe the glob away, a series of lightning flashes light up the bay, and for a few moments, it is as bright as midday. "What the hell?" he mutters. Snatching up the binoculars, he leans through the open window and peers through them, straining to see beyond the rain. *Nothing.* He wipes away the phlegm and takes another bite of the sandwich.

He chews mechanically, not really tasting, wrestling with his thoughts, subconsciously aware of the searchlight plugged into the car's power system. "Something's going on out there," he mumbles, snatching up the searchlight and stepping out into the storm. The wind threatens to tear the Akubra hat off his head, so he jams it tight over his ears and lifts up the collar of the oilskin coat. Shivering from the cold, he flicks on the searchlight and stares along its beam, sweeping the shoreline from the jetty to Point Ellen. Nothing. Another series of sheet lightning lights up the bay.

"Yeah, something—someone's—out there, all right!" The searchlight picks up the tiny boat charging out from Point Ellen. Gotcha, a tinny with two people—have to be heading for *Smokey Cloud*. "They'll never make it." He swings the light to the cutter and trains it on the white hull. "There you go boys, good luck," he mutters.

As Dunning keeps the light on the fishing cutter, he reaches into the car and picks up the microphone. "Boss, do you copy? Over."

Perkins' voice crackles back. "Read you loud and clear. Over."

Dunning is about to speak when a car roars by.

The radio crackles. "Car just went by you; did you see who it was?" It is Woodson's voice.

"No, going too fast, but there is a small boat with, I think, two people trying to reach the *Smokey Cloud*," says Dunning into the microphone.

"What?" says Woodson, his voice crackling over the radio. "We've bloody well got 'em. Set up a road block right there, Dunning; we'll go after the incoming vehicle." He laughs. "We got the bastards jammed in at last."

Dunning watches the lights of Woodson's vehicle cut through the darkness as he dashes from Shack Row to the jetty. He looks back in the direction the cutter, but is unable to find her again with the searchlight. Another series of lightning flashes and, for a split second, he catches a glimpse of *Smokey Cloud* again. "What! My, God, they're heading out to sea," he says, hardly believing his eyes. "In this? They have to be crazy."

Stuff the roadblock; we've got trouble, now, real trouble. He steps back into the police car, slams the gear lever into reverse, guns the motor and roars backwards out of the bush hideout onto the road. As he speeds down to the jetty, he sees Monty Baldwin standing in the rain talking to Woodson. Skidding to a stop behind the Baldwin car, he joins the sergeant, Perkins and Monty, noticing that Jordan is sitting in his father's car.

"I'm not going to call anything off, Mr. Baldwin. I have these blokes as good as caught. They've been breaking the law, and now they are going to pay," says Woodson.

"Enough harm's been done, Sergeant. I am warning you, if you don't call this off, I'll see to it that you spend the rest—"

"It's all academic, now, Mr. Baldwin," says Dunning, interrupting Monty. "The *Smokey Cloud* just left for the open sea with at least two people on it."

"What? Who?" shouts Woodson. "Bloody Marino—he wouldn't leave in this weather."

"Looks like he has," says Dunning.

Suddenly, headlights from another vehicle drop over the crest of the hill and rush down the road to the jetty. All at once, Frank Ryan and Sammy Marino skid to a stop and jump from the Landcruiser, Ferrano following.

"You blokes seen Matt?" yells Frank.

Woodson can't believe his eyes, but Dunning realizes what is happening. "Oh, hell no, *Smokey Cloud* sailed out of the bay about five minutes ago, Frank."

"It's sailed? It can't have bloody sailed already." Frank runs to the jetty and peers into the darkness.

"Looks like we got you at last, Ryan," screams Woodson through the rain and wind. "Where's the poppy? In the back of the truck, are they, hey? Check their truck out, Perkins."

Monty is under no illusion about the identity of the second person on the fishing cutter. He steps alongside Woodson, grabs his shoulder, and whirls him around so that he can look him directly in the face. "My daughter is on that boat, Sergeant. Stuff the drugs. We have to mount a rescue effort, now," shouts Monty, pointing out to the sea. "*Wave Dancer* is here in the bay." He yells to Jordan. "Jordan, get your backside off that seat and get the chain off the dinghy. The keys to the padlock and *Wave Dancer* are on the key ring in the car, and hurry—your sister and Matt are on *Smokey Cloud*." Jordan grabs the keys and scampers off to get the Baldwin's tinny, chained and padlocked to the light pole, halfway along the jetty.

Perkins returns from the Landcruiser. "Nothing, boss."

"What?" shouts Woodson. "They're on the boat. The flowers are on the boat; you bastards loaded it today, didn't you?" He looks out to sea. "We've got to get that boat."

"Yeah, that's right, Sergeant," says Frank sarcastically. "If you want us, you have to have the flowers, which means you have to get the boat, right?"

Woodson snarls. "I've got you, Ryan."

The men hurry down the jetty to the light pole where Jordan is freeing the dinghy. "Mr. Baldwin, our besta chance to make it to *Wave Dancer* is for only one-a us to be in the tinny. It'sa less likely to swamp." says Sam. "Here, Jordan, give-a me that key to *Wave Dancer*. I bring her back and picka you all up."

Jordan looks at Monty, who nods. "Get on with it, Sam," he says, "and be as quick as you can."

The men turn the tinny over, free the leg of the outboard, already clamped onto the stern, and slide it down the jetty ramp into the water. Sam jumps into the rocking boat with professional dexterity, starts the motor, and pushes off into the waves, quickly disappearing into the gloom, steering in the direction of *Wave Dancer*.

The men on the jetty wait anxiously. The wind is howling and getting stronger, driving the rain almost horizontally across the bay. The minutes tick by, and then a glow appears through the darkness, moving rapidly towards them. *Wave Dancer*, a thirty-meter, steel-hulled fast boat with two 360-horsepower Caterpillar Marine diesel engines, throbbing powerfully, all working lights blazing, bursts into view rolling and bucking through the rough water. Sam guides the vessel expertly in a tight circle to bump broadside on against the heavy timber jetty.

Frank, Dunning, Monty, and Jordan leap aboard. Woodson yells to Perkins to stay back and monitor the police radio. Ferrano has already returned to the Landcruiser, seasickness claiming him from the few minutes on the jetty. The moment Woodson's feet hit the deck, Sam pushes the throttles forward full speed. The twin propellers whip the water at the stern of the fast boat into a cauldron of white foam. *Wave Dancer* surges forward and quickly gains speed, smashing through the rolling swell and sending mountains of white spray flaring off each side of her bow. Sam sets course for the open sea.

Dunning, Monty, and the others join Sam in the half cabin. He flicks on the switches to the radio and the radar. The radar's luminous screen casts an eerie green glow on the swaying men who stare at the white dial sweeping around it. "It'll be hard to make-a out *Smokey Cloud* with all the bounca come back off the whitecaps, but we might getta lucky," shouts Sam.

Dunning stares through the glass. Frank has moved up to the bow, sweeping the ship's main searchlight through the wild night. *Whatever else Frank may be, he's all warrior when the chips are down. I bet he was a hell of a soldier.* He catches Monty looking across at him. As if reading Dunning's mind, Monty nods. *You're a tough old bugger, too, white man.*

They push ahead. Twenty minutes later, the crackling of the radio breaks through the anxious thoughts of each of the men. "Mayday! Mayday! This is *Smokey Cloud*. Does anybody read? Over."

The men look at each other. "Cassie," Monty yells.

58

"Matt! Matt! We have to get the flares up," shouts Cassie, shaking him. "They're looking for us; we have to get the flares up, now."

Matt's eyes flicker, open, and fix on Cassie. Her voice echoes through his spinning head as he gradually becomes aware of the noise and the pitching and rolling of the boat. Scattered images of *Smokey Cloud* in the storm, of the engine running out of fuel, of how she had dragged him over the lip of the engine room hatch, tumble through his mind. He sees the bloodstained bandage wrapped around the leg of her moleskin pants.

"Cassie, your leg; you're hurt."

"No time to worry about that," she says, pointing to the flare box caught near the hatch. "We've got to get a flare up."

"But your leg—"

"It won't matter a damn if you don't get those flares up. We've a chance, not much of one, but *Wave Dancer* is out there, looking for us," she yells holding her leg, grimacing. "Get them; get the flares, for God's sake."

Oh, God, what have I done? He stares at her, full of despair and shame, unable to move. "Cassie, I'm sorry, I'm sorry, I got you into this, I'm sorry."

Angry, she turns from him and reaches for the flares. "There comes a time when you have to fight, to never give up," she shouts, managing to grasp the box with her fingers. After a couple of attempts, she gets the pistol loaded, and then, as a violent wave pitches *Smokey Cloud* into a thirty-degree roll, she slides across the deck and smashes into the wheelhouse door. He slams into the cabinets under the wheel, crying out as his ribs crunch on impact.

She pushes herself upright, howling with pain as she straightens her leg and lunges for the latch of the door, and then struggles to slide it open.

"For God's sake, Matt, don't you see? Everything comes down to right now. This is it. God will help, but we have to do our part," she yells, angry, struggling for breath and fighting the pain. "He wants us to live, and I'm not giving up." The door comes free.

At that moment, another wave slams broadside into *Smokey Cloud*, into Cassie, and rushes into the wheelhouse. She screams, drops the flare gun, clasps a hand around her wounded leg, and hangs onto the door with the other. The cold water washes over Matt. Cassie's scream is like a slap in the face. Suddenly, the fear is gone. He scrambles across the water-covered deck, snatching for the sliding flare pistol, wrapping a hand around it, pushing to his feet, and shutting the pain of his broken ribs from his mind. Swaying with the motion of the boat, he reaches Cassie and wraps an arm around her.

"Can you hang on to the door?" he shouts.

She nods, panting with the effort. "Get the flare up, Matt, get the bloody flare up."

The shrill howling of the wind and the stinging spray hits him full on as he steps outside the wheelhouse. *Smokey Cloud* pushes to the top of a foaming wave. A new sound alerts him, the thunder of water crashing over rocks. Lightning flashes, and there, soaring above the boat, are the cliffs of the Haystack, not more than four hundred meters away.

Matt reacts with hysterical laughter. The pain from his ribs is gone, swallowed up in a heady euphoria, as if the storm itself is empowering him. An enormous exhilaration fills him; every muscle in his body tightens, the primitive instinct to survive fully alert, and he yells provocatively into the storm, "Come on, come on, I can take it. I can take your best. I'm not done yet."

He raises the flare pistol and pulls the trigger. The flare streaks ahead of a fiery trail shooting through the blackness and eventually bursts into a brilliant sun at a thousand feet, turning the night into a surreal daylight, textured metallic blue.

Unbelievably, only three hundred meters away, *Wave Dancer*, lights blazing, is balancing on top of a mountainous wall of seawater, about to slide away into the next trough.

"We must be close if thata image on the radar is them," shouts Sam from the wheel of the *Wave Dancer*. "Thosa bloody cliffs are close."

The night explodes into daylight. "There! There she is," yells Dunning, holding tightly to the safety rail that runs around *Wave Dancer's* deck. The five men wipe their eyes, dazzled by the sudden brilliance of the bursting flare. He points. "There, by the wheelhouse; it's them." They lose sight of *Smokey Cloud* as they drop into another trough.

Matt waves frantically. *Wave Dancer* falls off the wave, but moments later, she reappears one hundred and fifty meters abeam. Several figures are holding onto the side railing looking at *Smokey Cloud*. Because of the rain and spray, he cannot tell who they are, except that one looks familiar. *Must be Monty.* The flare dies, plunging them again into darkness.

He turns to Cassie and hugs her, laughing, and then steps back into the wheelhouse to get another flare. Luckily, the box is caught tight between the hatch cover and the wheelhouse wall, the same place it had been before. *The Big Bloke is helping us, like Cassie said.* He shoves another flare into the pistol, but before he can get a shot off, the night once more turns to daylight from a flare off *Wave Dancer*, which is now within a hundred meters of *Smokey Cloud*.

Smokey Cloud's flare falls into the water and the black curtain drops again. "Geta flare off, Jordan," orders Sam. Jordan, holding the loaded pistol, points it into the sky and pulls the trigger. Daylight returns as Frank, Monty, Woodson, and Dunning look over the rail toward *Smokey Cloud*.

"We'll never make it," yells Woodson. The looming cliffs are close. "We've got to get out of here."

Woodson rushes toward the wheelhouse. Frank steps in front of him, drops his shoulder into Woodson's chest and sends him tumbling to the deck. A wave hits the boat at a forty-five-degree angle, washing Woodson across the deck and slams him headfirst into the gunwale. Frank and Dunning, wash along with him. Dunning is able to grab Woodson's leg, saving him from going overboard. The boat pitches forward and they pull Woodson into the shelter of the half-cabin. Blood is running from a deep cut in the unconscious sergeant's forehead.

Sam is wrestling with the wheel and engine throttles. "Jordan," he yells. "Puta bloody Woodson in the crew quarters up forward." He twists his head skyward. "Anda hurry up about it; we'll needa another flare in a minute."

Another of the figures becomes clear to Matt. A feeling of elation soars through him as he recognizes his father, standing on the stern deck of *Wave Dancer*, its nose now pointing into the heavy sea, reversing gingerly back to *Smokey Cloud*, whose bow, thank God, still points into the storm, her sea anchor holding her—a temporary respite. As the gap between the two boats narrows, Frank holds up a rope and signals that he is going to throw it. He whirls the weighted end above his head a few times and then tosses it, sending it flying over the top of the wheelhouse.

Matt stretches his left hand upward and grabs the dangling rope. Frank waves for him to haul it in. Cassie, lying on the deck behind him, grabs his belt to help keep him from falling overboard. Attached to the lead rope is a stronger, heavy-duty towrope. Frank and Monty feed it over *Wave Dancer's* stern.

Matt works his way to the bow, at the same time pulling the towrope across the gap until he reaches the forward capstan. The rope is wet and heavy, and as he struggles to loop it around, a breaking wave slams the two boats. Cassie sees Frank tumble over the side of *Wave Dancer* and surface clear of the threshing propellers. Suddenly, it is dark.

Another flare fires from *Wave Dancer*; its searchlight sweeps over the water, looking for Frank.

Struggling to keep *Wave Dancer* from crushing the hull of *Smokey Cloud*, Sam Marino watches as Frank whirls the lead rope about his head. Monty holds the hitch-knot to the towrope, ready to feed it over the stern. Frank tosses the rope, watches it sail over *Smokey Cloud's* wheelhouse and then turns to Monty. "He's got it." They start feeding out the heavier rope over the stern rail. "Keep it clear of the props, or we'll all be done," shouts Frank.

Dunning is on his way back to help when a huge wave hits the two boats. Water cascades over the deck of *Wave Dancer*. Frank loses his grip on the rope, and the swirling water carries him to the ship's side. Dunning lunges for him, but it is too late, and he disappears over the rail. "Frank, no!"

Shaken and soaked, Dunning stares at the turbulent water. Frank surfaces and is swept toward *Smokey Cloud*.

"Can't do anything for him now," shouts Monty. "I need your help; we've got to keep this rope free of the props." Then, the flare goes out. A second later, Jordan fires another and then swings the searchlight over the water, looking for Frank. He finds him.

Frank's life jacket helps keep him afloat, but the turbulence threatens to pull him under. Matt struggles to haul in the towrope, and Cassie drags herself along the deck with the lead line, ties one end around the bottom of the mast, and throws the weighted end to Frank. On the third try, he is able to catch it and hang on. She looks around for help from Matt, who is struggling to wrap the huge towrope around the capstan. Clasping a hand around her injured leg, she crawls along the deck, and working together, they manage to get the rope looped twice and locked.

Matt signals to Monty and screams, "Go! Go! Go!" Almost immediately, the rope snaps taut as *Wave Dancer* takes up the slack, her propellers thrashing up a storm of foam slowly pushing her forward, Sam expertly working the throttles.

The thunder from the waves crashing on rocks is louder. Another flare soars into the sky from *Wave Dancer*. Their hearts race as they look behind and see the looming cliffs and the boiling mass of whitewater around their base, but *Wave Dancer* seems to be edging forward, pulling *Smokey Cloud* with her.

"Your dad—he's in the water, holding onto the rope—there," she says, pointing, trying to catch her breath.

"What?"

"He fell overboard; hurry." Matt starts for the rope, and sees seawater pouring through the wheelhouse door.

"The hatch cover is open," he yells. "It will flood the engine room; we'll swamp."

"I'll get it," she shouts, pulling herself along the deck, one hand holding tight the bandage around her wounded leg. "Get to your dad."

A wall of water slams the cutter; Matt saves himself from going over the side by grabbing the handrail and holding tight until the rushing water is gone. Gasping for air, his arms aching from fatigue, he finds the lead line, taut; Frank still has a grip on the rope.

"God give me strength," he cries. In that moment, he experiences a *presence*; a surge of energy fills him. He heaves on the rope and sees Frank's head surface alongside the cutter. Their eyes meet, and for the first time, Matt knows he knows he loves his father. He reaches for his dad's outstretched hand; they touch, but a breaker rolls down the side of the boat and pulls Frank with it, burying him under a mass of water. Matt is distraught and screams to God a second time, and in the next minute, a wave of backwash literally hangs Frank over the handrail. Matt grabs him, and they collapse in a heap on the deck.

Frank rolls over, his face close to Matt, coughing up seawater. "You're a hell of a bloke, Matt. Thanks." He hugs Matt as they roll to and fro on the deck.

Cassie appears at the wheelhouse door. "The hatch cover is broken," she yells. "It won't close."

"C'mon, Matt, there's no time to waste, let's get you two out of here." Frank, bleeding from cuts all over his body, staggers to his feet, moves to Cassie, and sees she is hurt. He pulls the two-way radio from the webbing pouch secured to his belt. "*Wave Dancer*, Frank here, do you read, Sam? Over."

"Loud and clear, Frank. I thoughta you were a goner," says Sam, his voice crackling over the radio. "We have a serious problem; we are not amaking any headway anymore. In fact, we are alosing ground. What'sa your condition? Over."

Frank looks at the two kids. "Critical. Cassie has a bad leg injury, and the boat is taking water fast. We have to get off here quickly, Sam. *Smokey Cloud* is done, and she'll drag *Wave Dancer* down with her if we don't move fast."

He looks about, thinking. "Get in tight, as tight as you can with the winch, and throw a couple of pots over the stern onto the foredeck."

As Frank finishes speaking, *Wave Dancer* is already reversing and closing fast. On the stern deck, Monty picks up the slack on the towrope with the winch. Dunning and Jordan untie two crayfish pots and hold them over the stern. Sam pushes the gear lever forward and the towrope tightens and holds, *Wave Dancer's* stern a meter from the cutter's bow. The men throw the pots onto *Smokey Cloud's* foredeck.

Frank lifts Cassie into his arms and staggers forward. Matt follows, holding onto Frank's belt to keep him from falling. When they reach the pots, Frank puts Cassie feet-first through the opening in the top of one, takes off his life jacket, and puts it on her. As he tightens the straps, he kisses her lightly on the cheek. "Good luck, Cassie; you're one hell of a gutsy woman, luv. Now, hold onto that rope tight."

Cassie grabs Frank's hand and yells through the noise of the breaking waves and howling wind, "Thank you, Mr. Ryan; thank you for coming."

Frank squeezes her hand, and then signals Matt to help him lift the pot. They take a position at each side, and with loud grunts, they lift it up above their heads. Dunning, Monty, and Jordan take up the slack on the rope and haul the young woman quickly over the stern of *Wave Dancer*.

Monty reaches for his daughter as they lower the pot to *Wave Dancer's* deck. "Thank God, thank God, we have you," he shouts, lifting her from the pot and hugging her.

She hugs him. "You got to hurry, Daddy. Get Matt and Frank; there's not much time." She pushes away from her father and falls to the deck. He moves to her. She waves him away. "Get them, get them," she screams, almost hysterical. Another wave crashes into *Wave Dancer*. Seawater washes over her, pushing her into the stern gunwale. The water recedes, and she pulls herself upright to peer over the stern. Frank is lifting Matt into the other pot, as the flowers wash out of a hole in *Smokey Cloud's* bow.

A bigger wave smacks violently into both boats and *Wave Dancer's* steel hull smashes into *Smokey Cloud*, splintering her foredeck and opening a hole into the crew's quarters. A large number of bags are crammed into the small space; two split open. Seawater pours through the broken bow, washing hundreds of Rosenblum flowers into the sea.

Frank motions for Matt to get into the other pot. "Get in, get in," he shouts. "There's not much time." Matt is suddenly aware of the terrible pain returning to his broken ribs. He cries out and collapses to the deck. Frank drops to his knees, picks up his son and puts him feet-first into the second pot. Gasping for breath, he hands Matt the pot rope. "Hang on tight a bit longer, son; you're almost home."

"What about you, Dad, how are you going to get off?" Matt shouts, tears streaming down his face.

"No worries, mate, I'll be along." Frank winks and grins. "I love you all, Matt; tell them so for me." He hugs and kisses his boy on the cheek, signals for the men on *Wave Dancer* to pull, and then lifts the pot and his son with one final burst of energy.

As Matt clears the stern of *Wave Dancer*, Frank sees *Smokey Cloud* is quickly sinking back into the whitewater at the cliff base. He pulls the radio from the web pouch on his belt.

"Sam, Sam, gun it—quick, for God's sake—get the hell out of here, or it's going to take you, too." He drops the radio, kicks the ratchet locking the towrope free, and watches as *Wave Dancer* suddenly surges forward and away from the stricken *Smokey Cloud*.

EPILOGUE

Matt, his hands in the pockets of his white moleskins, ambles across the road from the hospital to the park and sits on the bench overlooking the water to the mainland. A small fishing boat chugs across the bay, its wake spreading for hundreds of meters on the gray, glassy water. Seagulls hover around its stern, some drop onto the wake fighting over bits of fish gut thrown out as the fisherman cleans his catch. The Monday morning air is chilly. He pulls his leather jacket a little tighter around his shoulders and neck. Behind him, way to the southwest, a dark sky signals approaching squalls.

A car rumbles up the hill from the town, does a U-turn, and pulls into the curb. The door slams, and Matt twists around to see Bob Dunning walking over the grass.

"G'day, Matt," he says, holding up his hand. "Don't get up." He shakes Matt's hand, sits next to him and stares out at the fishing boat. "I often come up to the bluff and sit, sometimes for hours, staring out over the water when I want to think through a problem or try to make sense of this crazy world. It talks to me, the sea—you know, gives me perspective, meaning, peace. You know what I mean?"

"Yeah, I do that at Admiral's Arch; that's where I get a lot of ideas for my writing." He pauses, grunts as he reaches inside his shirt to adjust the bandage around his chest.

"Sore, hey?"

"It's nothing; I'm alive. I'm trying to make sense of the last six months. Dad, Sean, Tom—Cassie's career finished." He stares at the sea. "And yet, despite it was me who stuffed-up, I'm still here. Dad gave his life, you blokes risked yours, and Cassie and I get to live. There has to a lesson there somewhere."

"To me, the simple lesson is that we learn the value of life and use it to better ourselves and others. Which, reminds me—your scholarship—you earned it; use it. Your talent is a gift to be developed, and you can always come back here to live later; Cassie loves you, she'll be around," says Dunning. He pauses and places his hand on Matt's shoulder. "By the way, some good news—Sergeant Woodson has been recalled to Adelaide. They are replacing him, and I know the new bloke; he's all right. The whole Rosenblum matter has been dropped. The politicians are going to introduce legislation in the next session of parliament for the provision of licenses for growing it here."

"If they'd done it earlier, none of this would have happened."

"Hold on, Matt; we are all responsible to some extent. As you said, there's a lesson or two in this for all of us."

They are both silent for a moment. "You're right," Matt sighs, "a bloke could go nuts trying to figure it all out. I guess it just is, hey?"

Dunning stands up to leave. "I've gotta get going. One of my more pleasant duties—I have to take poor old Reggie out to the airport. He is pissed, I can tell you, but he had it coming. Reggie is a prime example of someone never learning a lesson. Oh, I almost forgot; Monty Baldwin is recommending to the Royal Humane Society that your dad receive the bronze medallion for bravery. We're verifying the recommendation."

Matt's eyes are misty as he shakes Dunning's hand. "Bloody hell, makes the oldman a hero for real, hey?"

Dunning grins. "Your dad was always a hero, Matt; the demons got him for awhile, that's what happened, but he beat them in the end. I'll be at his memorial Mass tomorrow—Parndana Church, right?"

"Yeah; thanks, Bob. Thanks for being a mate—for all your help."

"No worries. Get those ribs healed; the footy finals will be here before you know it."

"Yeah, we'll have you blokes," Matt calls after him.

Dunning drives off, and Matt turns back to his view of the sea. The fishing boat is gone, but its wake still lingers, and on it, a few seagulls remain to squabble over the odd piece of missed offal. He takes a deep breath. *I'm going to make the best of the chance you left me, Dad,* he thinks, bunching his hands into fists and lightly thumping his thighs.

"I saw you and Bob Dunning together," says Cassie, arriving quietly at the rear of the bench, on crutches. The tartan-pleated skirt she is wearing balloons over the plaster wrapped around her left leg from thigh to ankle. "I didn't want to interrupt."

Matt, startled, jumps to his feet and squeals with pain. "Ahh, forgot," he says, grinning stupidly and clutching his chest.

She drops the crutches, and, using the back of the bench for support, hops around to Matt and hugs him gently, laughing. "We're great pair."

They both sit. "Bob's a good bloke; one of a kind. So, what did the doc say?"

"Nothing's changed; he checked to make sure the blood is circulating properly and told me the Adelaide surgeon's report arrived last Friday. It confirmed what they told me before; my professional dancing career is over."

He nuzzles her neck, taking care not to hurt his ribs. "We won't give up, Cassie. There are breakthroughs for treatment occurring all the time. Belinda is checking out a doctor she heard was doing good work at some sports medicine clinic in Vail; I think she said was in America—Colorado or somewhere. No, we won't give up."

"We'll talk about it down the road, but for right now, I'm happy to be alive and with you. It has always been a dilemma for me, anyway—should I stay? Should I dance? Besides, I want to have time for Dad and me to heal our relationship. He is a mess and needs all the help I can give him. Belinda will be here next week, and that will be good for him. Jordan is going back into rehab, thank God, and I don't what to see him back here until he is well."

Ripples begin to ruffle the surface of the water and a light breeze lifts over the lip of the cliff. Cassie shivers, zips up the front of her leather jacket, and lays her head on his shoulder.

"I talked to Patrick about Tom's farm, and he agreed it's a perfect place for the church to use as a holiday camp for orphan kids and kids from families having a rough go of it." Matt smiles. "Monsignor likes the idea, and Katherine says she would live there, be the nurse, and cook for the kids. Patrick will be off to the seminary eventually, but we all want to keep the farm running, so we reckon that between the three of us, we can make it work. We want to dedicate the camp to Tom."

"He loved you boys. What a brave, wonderful man; I could help Katherine out when you are at university next year."

"I might have to put that off, Cassie."

"No, no, no, you are going, you must go. There is our place in North Sydney for you to use, and I could come and stay some of the time."

"You would—that would be fantastic. What about Monty?"

"He thinks we will do very well together."

"Does he? Well, that's good," says Matt. He gently hugs her and looks into her eyes. "I love you, Cassie; I will always love you."

"Hmm, love you, too, Matthew Ryan." They kiss. "Oh, there is one other thing, I want to take communion at the memorial tomorrow to honor your dad; do you think that would be okay?"

"No worries. Dad will probably round up Sean and Tom to watch," says Matt, smiling.

"And Kristina and Matilda, too. There's a lot of love up there looking out for us."

A moment later, the clouds scatter and the sun emerges to brush the sea with a sparkling, golden hue.

"I reckon they just gave us the nod, Cass."

ACKNOWLEDGMENTS

Bob Woodworth, from Sydney, Australia, for his wisdom, belief and encouragement; Ann Camy for her editing and feedback over a cuppa or two and many hours at Starbucks; Len Marino, a constant advocate whose New York enthusiasm is infectious; Joni Cuquet, Los Angeles, for her editing, commitment and care that kept me going when I needed a lift. Kathy, my wife, whose creative talent, editing, professional acumen and support made it possible to complete this work.

There are many others too numerous to mention, but you know who you are, and my heart is full of gratitude for your support.

About The Author

Tony Boyle grew up on a sheep and cattle farm on Kangaroo Island, South Australia. He received the greater part of his education from the Christian Brothers' schools in Adelaide, Christian Brothers College and Rostrevor College. He came back to the island for his final year and attended the Parndana Area School where his mother was a primary school teacher.

After several years of working the farm, he sold out and moved to Sydney to pursue a career in the entertainment industry as a writer and actor. He had small roles in Australian television series, appeared in many commercials and free-lanced as a writer of promotional, training and industrial scripts for various clients.

In 1986, Tony opened his own production house on Blue's Point Road, North Sydney, produced videos for corporate clients and spent time in Africa and Central Asia filming documentaries for a refugee NGO.

He moved to the United States in 1990 where he worked in theater, television drama, commercials and numerous corporate productions as a producer, writer and actor. He has written several movie scripts including the recently finished *Death in Time*, a science fiction, psychological thriller set in Chicago and Cancun, and *Chrysalis*, a family drama with a spiritual theme set in South Boston.

Beyond Passion is his first novel. He is presently working on the screenplay adaptation and the book sequel, *Under the Southern Cross*. He lives in Golden, Colorado and travels frequently with his wife, Kathy, to Kangaroo Island where they will soon begin construction on their island home.